Singularity

To Viv
Thanks for coming!

Singularity

By

NJ Matthews

[signature]

Manufactured in Canada.

Library and Archives Canada Cataloguing in Publication

Matthews, N. J., 1932-
        Singularity / N.J. Matthews.

Also available in electronic format.
ISBN 1-897098-39-1

        I. Title.

PS8626.A88S55 2004   C813'.6   C2004-903672-6

TreeSide Press
2610 Selwyn Road
Victoria, B.C., Canada V9B 3L5
http://www.treesidepress.ca

Acknowledgments

As anyone who has tried it knows, writing is a solitary activity. It not only requires perseverance on the part of the writer, but the support and encouragement of others around that person.

I count myself fortunate to have had that support in great abundance, from Wanda, my wife of many years, who has put up with my prolonged absences hiding out in front of my computer. And from my three daughters, Colleen, Karen and Shelley.

I single out my daughter Karen for special mention. First, because of her enduring interest in what I was doing and for believing I could do it. Secondly, for her courage in the face of her own adversity. In spite of which she has helped immensely in the outcome of this book.

To my sister Eileen Mucci, a best pal as well as someone I can bounce ideas off of without fear of ridicule (well, not much anyway!).

A special thanks to my good friend Reg Skene, who knows more about writing and books than anyone else I know, for all of his valued suggestions.

And I thank Miriam Toews for her interest in my work and her encouragement to go forward.

Chapter 1

Dr. Arnold Soper poured two fingers, more or less, of Glenfiddich into the leaded crystal low-ball glass. As he stoppered the whiskey, the telephone rang. It was his wife Ashley, his second wife to be more exact.

"Arnie? So you are back. I wasn't sure when you were arriving, how was the trip."

He paused before answering her and took a comforting sip of the liquor; "Yes I'm back, where are you?"

"I'm at the club of course, where did you think I'd be?"

He could tell from her voice that she had been into the Manhattans. This was not going to be pleasant, he was glad of the distance between them.

Before she could continue the conversation, he said "Ashley, I've done some thinking while I was in Nairobi, I am going to call it quits."

"What do you mean, your going to call it quits?"

"I mean us, we're done, I am moving out of the Condo, you can stay if you like. I'll send for my things tomorrow.

I can make it part of the settlement".

There was a sharp intake of breath on the other end of the line.

"You son-of-a-bitch! I had an idea something like this was going on, who is she?"

He smiled to himself, he knew this would be her reaction, blame it on somebody else.

"There isn't anybody, I am simply tired of you, tired of the bullshit games you play, I want my freedom. I'll start the process tomorrow, you'll be hearing from Ted Franklin."

"You bastard!"

He replaced the telephone on the hook and took a long pull at his drink. It was done. He would see that she and their son Ellis were looked after in the settlement. Better to make this arrangement now as opposed to after the news breaks. He knew he could not control the media much longer, once he had to go public all hell would break loose and it would obviously effect the settlement and not in his favour.

He refilled his glass and moved out onto the balcony, spring in Toronto, a nice evening breeze off the lake, pleasant, after the heat and humidity of Nairobi. Why the hell they had to have a Pharmaceutical Conference in Nairobi was beyond him, but it had been a worthwhile trip. He'd been able to hire a replacement for Peter Mytryk his research director.

He felt he could not trust Mytryk completely ever since the episode of the security leak. An American Company had been able to obtain patents on a significant new product that Soper Research had been just about to file.

They missed filing by only a matter of days, and the similarity in the product was striking, but different enough that Soper was unable to challenge the patent.

Although Mytryk had been exonerated in the ensuing investigation, his gut told him he could never trust the man again.

He smiled as he looked out over the city skyline from his balcony, the sun was setting. He liked this city however with impending developments at Soper Research, it may not continue to be head office for his company. His legal and accounting people were preparing recommendations for his consideration regarding the best tax haven location.

His absence from the office bothered him; he needed to get there now. He didn't need any snags or problems that might complicate the biggest deal of his life.

He downed his drink, picked up his car keys and a small overnight bag and headed for the parking garage. He gave a quick glance back as he pulled the door shut, he knew he would never be back.

His Mercedes SL55 AMG was parked exactly where he had left it, he had insisted on securing the two adjacent stalls as a condition of the condo purchase, there was some wrangling with the developer but he prevailed. At $195,000, he didn't want anybody doing damage with car doors or fender scrapes. He stopped and admired the sleek lines of the coupe. He chuckled as he remembered the look on the face of the dealer when he insisted on "British Racing Green" as his colour of choice, but he knew that the square head would not let that be a "deal breaker."

Turning the key and pressing the start button, the SL55 roared to life, it didn't matter how many times he got behind the wheel, he could feel his juices begin to flow and there was always a thrill.

He drove out of the underground parking garage and headed west on Lakeshore Drive to the Queen Elizabeth Way, his office and research lab were located in Sheridan Park about 30 kilometres west of the city.

Reaching over he caressed the soft kid leather of passenger seat, smiling as he remembered the car salesman's comment, "As soft as the thighs of a beautiful woman," he was right, but he loved this car more than any woman. Soper always equated possessions with his achievements, and the SL55 was just the most recent.

He maintained the same speed as the majority of the other cars, some 20 kilometres over the posted limit, it was just about 7:30 on a pleasant May evening. He settled back to enjoy the 30-minute trip, inserting a Diana Krall CD into the player and just letting the smooth sounds of the piano and her voice flow over him.

The sun was just beginning to set and he was driving into it, the light began to bother him. In spite of the fact that he was wearing sunglasses, the glare was considerable. He began to feel the onset of a slight headache, probably as much from the lack of sleep over the last 48 hours as anything else. He would pop a couple of Tylenol's when he got to his office.

He began to notice a fuzziness affecting his peripheral vision, and a sense of almost overwhelming tiredness seemed to overtake him. "I'll just do a quick check at the office to see how things are going and then I'll check in to the Hamden Suites," he thought.

Soper Research maintained a permanent suite in the hotel located in the Park, it was useful for visiting dignitaries as well as for the many times he worked late and chose not to return home.

As he continued his trip, it became increasingly difficult for him to keep the SL55 in his lane, he kept drifting to the right and tended to over correct when he tried to keep the car in his own lane. He slowed his speed to the legal limit.

Although he had the top down, he was beginning to feel very warm, he cranked up the air conditioning and that seemed to help. The spell passed, and taking a deep breath, he began to feel somewhat better.

He arrived at Soper Research at about 8:00 PM, it is a modernistic 3 story building of stainless steel and green tinted glass which made it impossible to see inside. He pulled into his parking spot, again with permanently reserved stalls on either side.

The building had "state of the art" biometrics security system. Unauthorized visitors were allowed in the building. There was a telephone kiosk outside the main door were prospective visitors could contact their "minders" and if they had an appointment, they would be escorted into the building.

For the people that worked at Soper Research, the first level of security to gain access to at least the front door was a fingerprint scanner. Which would identify the employee, open the front door, log them into the computer system, and even greet them by name.

This procedure applied to Soper as well, he placed his finger on the scanner pad. After a few seconds he heard "Good Evening Dr. Soper," and the heavy glass door swung open onto an atrium, in the centre of which sat a security guard. There was an array of video screens linked to security cameras at strategic locations throughout the building and grounds. In addition to providing "real time" monitoring, each camera input was being taped for posterity.

"Evenin' Dr. Soper, glad to see you're back, good trip?" "Travel is a pain in the ass Ben, but yes and I am glad to be back. Have you been looking after things while I was gone?

"You betcha Dr. Soper! Will you be in long sir?"

"No, just got to check my mail and messages, shouldn't be more than an hour or so."

Soper's office was located in the high security wing of the building and as such required a retinal scan in order to access the area. He put his chin in the rest and looked into the lens with his right eye, at the same time he pressed the push button activating the device. He peered into the blue light and after a short time the door to the high security area swung open and he was again greeted by a disembodied voice.

As he passed down the hallway to his office, he was aware of a dull ache originating from behind his right eyeball; his headache seemed to be coming back.

"Hi Arnie, welcome home." It was Peter Mytryk; he followed Soper into his office.

"Thanks Pete, it's good to be back, I still can't figure out why in Hell they have to go all the way to Nairobi to hold a conference. Seems like I have been awake for a week straight, my biological clock is still screwed up."

Soper did not intend to share the news of his recruiting coup to Mytryk, even if it had no impact on him, Mytryk would be sure to see a conspiracy against him "Bloody suspicious Europeans!" The fact that the new recruit was ultimately going to be Mytryk's replacement didn't bother Soper, he would deal with that when the time came.

"Pete, give me an update on the FDA situation, we can't leave anything to chance, this is the biggest thing we have ever done!"

"I know that Arnie, I have been on top of our contact at the FDA and he assures me that we will have approval to release the vaccine for public use by June 15th, no question about it!"

"It had better happen, that son-of-a-bitch has been sucked a lot of cash out of me so far, it's time we had the opportunity to make some money on this thing."

"Look, our contact has done everything we asked of him, we have had inside information all the way through the process. We have been able to amend our submission as needed, we have even been able to adjust some of our test data and he approved it."

"Yeah, Yeah, and he has $250.000 of my money in his pocket, we have been putting out now it's time pull some profits in."

"Arnie, have you decided when to take the company public? I think I deserve to be in on the IPO, I have put a lot into this company, call it sweat equity if you like, I want an opportunity to cash in too."

"You Asshole! You have put a lot into this company! This is MY Company! I built it from nothing! I have taken all the risk, you; you're nothing but an employee and a highly paid one too, maybe too highly paid! What I may or may not decide to do is none of your business! Might I remind you that you are under a personal service contract to me! You observe the confidentiality clause of that contract to the letter or you will never work again! Just make sure you keep your mouth shut regarding anything you think you know"

"Arnie, Arnie calm down. I know it is your company, I know how hard you have worked to build it, it's just that I would like to be acknowledged for my part albeit a small part in the success of this company."

Soper hit his fist on his desk, his right eye was twitching violently and he began to shake, Mytryk stood with his mouth open and watched what appeared to be the disintegration of this normally cool and composed individual.

Soper struggled to talk, grasping his throat when he was unable to utter a sound other than a strangled rasp. His body began to convulse and he collapsed to the floor, after a brief period, he became motionless, Mytryk was sure he was dead.

He felt at his neck, there was an irregular pulse, and he was extremely warm to the touch. He got security on the telephone and directed them to get an ambulance immediately, "Dr. Soper has been taken ill, this is urgent Ben, get on it right away and then notify the hospital immediately." Yessir Dr. Mytryk, right away."

Mytryk went to Soper's desk and checked the Rolodex. In spite of all his high technology gadgets, Soper preferred it. He found the direct number to Soper's physician, Jim Nelson, and placed the call. Nelson was not just Soper's personal physician, but was as close as the man had to a friend.

Surprisingly, Nelson answered on the third ring, "Jim Nelson here."

Dr., Nelson, this is Peter Mytryk at Soper Research, we have an emergency!"

Sensing the anxiety in his voice, he responded, "Calm down Dr., Mytryk, what is it."

"It's Arnie, he's had some kind of attack, a seizure I think."

Mytryk repeated the facts of the episode, omitting of course the argument, but included Soper's current comatose state and the fact that an ambulance was en route.

"You will direct them to the University Hospital!"

"Yes of course."

"Good, I will meet them there, please be there as well."

"Of course."

Just as he hung up the telephone, the paramedics arrived, escorted by Ben. They checked his vital signs, got him on a gurney. His colour was beginning to return to his face and his breathing seemed less laboured.

"University Hospital Emergency, right?"

"Yes, and hurry. This is a very important man."

The female paramedic muttered, barely under her breath, to no one in particular, "Ain't they all."

Jim Nelson arrived at University Hospital just shortly after Soper was placed in the Emergency Room Ward; the duty nurse was preparing the paper work as Nelson walked in.

The duty nurse was not a particular favourite of his; in fact, he had been heard referring to her as "That pigeon breasted bitch!" "What have you got so far?"

She gave an insolent shrug and responded "Considering he just got here, not much."

"Do you have any idea of who this man is?"

"Should I?"

"This is Dr. Arnold Soper and for your information he is a major benefactor of this hospital, he donated the MRI machine on the third floor as well as funding several research projects within the hospital. So a little special attention is deserved, don't you think?"

The nurse was a little flustered "Yes Dr. Nelson, of course."

"Get the on duty doctor in here. Stat!"

"Yes Sir." No hint of sarcasm this time."

The doctor in charge of the Emergency Room came up behind Nelson, "Hi Jim, what have we got here?"

Nelson couldn't remember his name "I think you know Arnold Soper, CEO of Soper Research, he seems to have some kind of attack or seizure at his office, sometime in the last 45 minutes. I'm his family physician, his office notified me just after the occurrence, so I have just arrived."

"Hmm, any history of seizures in the past? Do any family members suffer from epilepsy?"

"Not to my knowledge, and I have been treating him for the last 10 years, generally I could say he has been as strong as an ox."

"OK, I'll order a complete work up, blood tests, X-rays, EEG, EKG, the whole schmeer, we'll see what we can find."

"Pull out all the stops. This man has been good to this hospital, as you likely know."

"You got it!"

Soper's breathing had become much more regular, his blood pressure, while elevated still, was dropping. He seemed to be in a rather deep sleep.

Nelson held open Soper's right eyelid as be aimed his flashlight at the eyeball noting the fact that the pupil was constricted to a tiny point. As he checked the other eye, the two orderlies arrived to move Soper down to the X-ray Lab.

He caught up with the Emergency Doctor in the hall, "I'm going down to the cafeteria for a cup of coffee, please have me paged as soon as you get anything. And thanks for the prompt action."

"Not a problem."

He sat at an unoccupied table in the corner of the cafeteria, close to the pay phones; he took his coffee to the phone with him.

Nelson was not only Arnold Soper's physician, but he was on the Board of Directors of the company and was in fact an important member of the Executive Committee. He was fully aware of the significance of the impending new product development and the impact that Soper's collapse might have on the future.

He placed a call to Declan Mahoney at Mahoney Associates; they handled Public Relations and Security issues for Soper Research. He gave Mahoney a "heads up" on what had happened with respect to Soper's attack. Nelson told him that he would keep him posted on any developments so those appropriate press releases could be prepared should Arnie's condition worsen.

Declan also advised him that he would be in contact with hospital security. To make sure that if any members of the press got wind of the situation, they would block access to any staff treating Arnie and to Arnie's room as well.

His coffee had gotten cold during the conversation; he went to the urn and refreshed it and ran into Peter Mytryk. "How is he doing? I can't seem to get any information. He isn't in Emergency and it doesn't look like he has been admitted."

"No, he hasn't been admitted, he is undergoing a battery of tests. It will be some time yet before he comes back down. As nearly as I can establish, there has been little change from what you saw when the paramedics arrived. His breathing is improved but he was still comatose when I last saw him."

"Jim, I am not sure that it means anything, but I think that you should know" he paused before continuing as if he was weighing what Nelson's reaction might be to his next statement. "Arnie injected himself with the vaccine."

"What! What in God's name for, when did he do this?"

"Just before he left for Nairobi."

"What the hell would have possessed him to take such a risk, this is like something out of a "B" movie!"

"He didn't believe there was any risk, certainly any of the clinical trials we conducted did not evidence anything like the reaction I witnessed today. As to why? Call it macho I suppose, this is the most significant development project in the history of the company, I think he just got carried away."

Nelson thought better of any spontaneous reply. "You are probably right, this is likely not related to the vaccine, but it is important that you not discuss this with anyone else, if it gets out it would be blown out of all proportion."

"We'll see what the tests reveal, I will inform anyone that needs to know of this, if and when it becomes necessary. Thanks for letting me know about it Peter, it could be important."

The two men proceeded to the Emergency Ward and found that Soper had been returned to the area. He was still not conscious, but seemed to be resting comfortably, breathing was regular, and the fever had receded. As much from habit as anything else, Nelson reached down and took his pulse, it was normal as well.

Leaving Mytryk in the room, he went to the nurses' station and spoke to the same duty nurse, "Would you get the doctor for me."

She went to a curtained patient area and advised the doctor. It took a few minutes but the young man joined him. "You saw that the patient is back?"

"Yes, any idea when we will see any results? I'd really rather not be here all night."

"Shouldn't be more than 20 minutes longer, we got the best guy on it, it just happened that our Chief of Neurology just happened to be in the hospital tonight. I asked him, as a special favour to look at the traces and x-rays. When he heard who the patient was, he promised to get right on it."

It was just at that point that a studious looking little man with a gray goatee approached the two men. He was carrying a docket and x-ray Folder with him.

"Hi Cyril, that was quick, sure appreciate it, you know Jim Nelson of course?"

He looked quizzically through his rather thick lenses, and then his eyes widened "Of course, of course, it's been some time, Dr. Nelson".

Jim Nelson knew Cyril Pickard very well, he knew him to be not just a brilliant neurologist but a crafty manipulator of people, to his own advantage. This craftiness had paid off for him and made him a wealthy man outside of his medical practice. In fact, Nelson considered just how similar Cyril and Arnie were in this regard.

"What do you have for us Cyril?"

"Well, I am afraid not too much, all of the tests came back pretty much normal. What is the patient's current condition Doctor?"

"Still not awake, but appears to be breathing normally, temperature is OK, colour is good, I just checked his pulse and that is normal as well."

The little man nodded, "Let's go see him."

Peter Mytryk was standing at Soper's bedside when the three men arrived. Nelson touched his arm and whispered "Peter, would you mind, we want to examine him further."

"No, No of course not."

Cyril stroked his goatee and muttered to himself, he raised an eyelid and peered into the pupil, moved his light horizontally from right to left and back, he did the same thing to the other eye. There was no sign of responsiveness to the light.

"He is unresponsive and even though the tests produced normal results they are really inconclusive, I would recommend that you admit the patient and place him under observation. Perhaps it would be worthwhile to schedule an MRI, that could be more definitive"

Nelson responded "I would agree Cyril, we can't afford to take any chances, will you make the necessary arrangements Doctor? It's Ben isn't it?"

"No problem Jim, I'll look after it right away."

Jim touched Cyril's arm as Ben went to the nurses' station, "Cyril, might I have a word with you?"

"Certainly, come to the on duty office it's just down the hall a bit."

When the two men were seated in the rather spare office, Nelson provided the Neurologist with additional background regarding the patient. He told him of his recent visit to Africa and then paused for a moment before proceeding.

"Cyril, you know something of the activities of Arnold Soper and his company Soper Research, I am sure."

"Yes of course, in fact I have been personally involved in several research projects here at the hospital that were in funded by Soper Research and funded quite generously I might add."

"Good, Good, Cyril I am going to tell you something in the utmost confidence. And I am telling you because there is a possibility that the information I am about to give you may help you in your diagnosis of Arnie's problem."

"Whatever you tell me will remain strictly between us." The little man's eyes seemed to sparkle at the promise of anticipated intrigue.

Nelson continued "Soper Research is on the brink of a breakthrough that could be considered of very great significance to much of the world population." He paused, wondering just how far was safe enough to go.

"Go, on, Go on."

"Soper Research has developed a vaccine that will revolutionize the treatment of a disease that has affected millions of people for decades."

"What vaccine, for what disease."

Nelson hesitated, he had been sworn to secrecy by Arnie but this information could be of significant value in any recovery. Conversely, Arnie could awake at any time and be normal, in which case he could expect to get his "ass fried" nine ways to Sunday.

"He swallowed hard and said "A vaccine for Alzheimer's!"

"What?"

"I said, a vaccine for Alzheimer's"

"Do you mean to tell me that Soper has found and identified a virus responsible for Alzheimer's, that's not possible! All the papers I have ever read on the subject, which believe me is many, never has it even been discussed that it could be a virus."

"Nevertheless, Soper Research has discovered it and developed a vaccine and in fact it is on the verge of being released for human trials by the FDA!"

"Astounding! If this is true, this could be worth millions!"

"Exactly, which is why it must be treated with the utmost confidence."

"Of course, of course, but frankly it surprises me that you are telling me this at all, why have you?"

"Because Arnold Soper injected himself with the vaccine before he left for Africa two weeks ago."

"What? But that is stupid and he never appeared to me to be a stupid man, why would he do such a thing?"

"I can't answer that question, but if in fact his current condition is related to the vaccine and he does not fully recover, the trials could be over before they begin. The potential of huge earnings would evaporate. It is even conceivable that the company could fail"

"I understand."

"Arnold Soper must recover fully! Cyril, if he doesn't, then whatever happens to him, must not be related to the vaccine, we must buy enough time to make whatever modifications are necessary to the vaccine."

"I am not sure what you are asking of me."

"I think you do, just remember, how you deal with this case could make you a very wealthy man."

"I see."

Chapter 2

Ashley had spent the night in a downtown hotel, she awoke with a monstrous headache, too many Manhattans, she staggered through to the bathroom, she had a thirst that needed to be quenched.

As she ran the water, she looked up into the mirror, "Shit, I've got to cut back, I look like one of the three witches from MacBeth."

She tossed back two Tylenols and downed the water, filled the glass again and headed back to the bed, sprawling out waiting for her pills to kick in.

"Damn Arnie, the Asshole, he never even gave her the opportunity to vent her rage, he never did, he either hung up the phone or just turned his back on her and left her presence.

While she had accused him of having another woman, she didn't really believe that herself; it might have been easier if it was true. She was sure that this was business. It's all that consumed him, business and possessions. At one time she had been one of his possessions and she felt, a prized one at that, but that was a long time ago, now she was of no value, apparently.

She remembered how they had met; he was Chief of Psychiatry at Mount Sinai, just divorced, as was she. He was considered a great "catch" so she set out to make him hers.

But on reflection, she was not so sure that it wasn't him doing the stalking. She was the daughter of a major real estate developer in the city, went to all the best schools and travelled in the upper echelons of Toronto society.

She was well connected to families of the power brokers, the movers and shakers in business, through her father and her school friends.

They married after a short courtship and not long after he moved into private psychiatric practice catering to her powerful friends and acquaintances. His practice prospered, she was happy with her life, tennis, yachting, and other social activities but she decided after four years of marriage, that she wanted a child.

She knew that Arnie had a son from his first marriage and had not been involved in his son's life since the divorce and not likely even before that. Therefore, she did not consult with Soper with respect to her interest, but conspired to get pregnant without his knowledge, by skipping her birth control pills.

She managed to conceal the pregnancy well into her second trimester, until it was too late for an abortion before she told him. Predictably, he was furious.

After she made her announcement, he became noticeably distant in his relationship with her often working late, serving on community boards, and attending various meetings and functions just to avoid her.

However, Ashley was thoroughly enjoying her impending motherhood, she immersed herself in decorating the room she had designated as the nursery. She hired a professional interior designer and ran up major expenses in her pursuit of the ideal environment for her child.

The rancour increased as a result of her preoccupation and the amount of money she was spending, the distance continued to grow between them.

Finally, on April 6 1999, their son Ellis was born, he had his mother's blonde hair and, she said, her good looks as well. Soper was indifferent to the birth, Ashley had hoped the child would bring them back together, but that didn't happen.

Ellis did not seem to progress normally in his first two years of life; he seemed withdrawn, uncommunicative and could throw violent tantrums. Even Arnie noticed and suggested Ashley take him to a psychiatrist, since he could not treat his own child.

The child was diagnosed as autistic, the doctor had told Ashley that the case was severe and that she should get professional help on a full time basis. She resisted and attempted to handle the child herself, however, the violent outbursts became even more aggressive and frequent, and there was no support forthcoming from Arnie.

After two years of attempting to cope with the situation, there was little option but to place Ellis in a care home that specialized in helping Autistic children. This effectively ended any semblance of a family relationship that she had craved, she and Soper grew even further apart, her only solace was the two weekends a month she was able to bring Ellis home with her.

About that time, Arnie decided to found Soper Research Inc. Although Ashley was unaware that this was happening, there was a sudden warming in the relationship between the two of them.

In reality, the motivation was the fact that he was in need of some private investment capital to get this venture off the ground and the way to that capital was through Ashley's family connections.

Ashley was blinded by the attention that Arnie began to shower on her and even upon Ellis on the weekends all three were together.

Ashley's father was oblivious to any problems that existed between his daughter and her husband, Ashley had always kept that part of her life private. All her father saw was a hard working and talented husband looking out for his daughter and his unfortunate only grandson.

Consequently, when he and Soper sat down and reviewed the prospectus for Soper Research Inc. he was quick to ante up 25 million dollars for preferred stock and a small equity interest in the Company. In addition, he convinced two of his poker cronies to do likewise.

In a few weeks, including his own investment of less than 3 million dollars, Soper had managed to raise approximately one hundred million dollars and still held effective control of the share equity.

He threw himself into the project, hired top-notch researchers, built a world class research lab for them and began the climb to the stage the company is at today.

With his investment capital secured and his dreams about to be realized, he felt no need to lavish his time on his wife and child. Therefore, with the excuse of hard work, long hours, and commitment to the investors, including her father, their relationship reverted to the distance and acrimony that prevailed earlier.

Ashley began the downward spiral of parties, alcohol and other men that brought her to her current situation. Likely, the only reason she woke up alone in the hotel was directly related to the number of Manhattans she had consumed the night before. She had no idea how she had ended up in this hotel, but she was glad she had not attempted to drive home.

The Tylenol was beginning to work, her headache was receding and she was able to think, "So, he's leaving, no big loss, I am just pissed off that's all" she thought.

"But I will make life difficult for him, his money and his possessions, the only things he thinks about and of course his precious company. I'm going to get my share and for Ellis too!"

She found the telephone book, looked up Ted Franklin's number, and dialled it, "Franklin and Sergeant Attorneys at Law."

"Ted Franklin please."

"Ted Franklin here."

"Hello Ted, its Ashley Soper."

"Well hello Ashley, what can I do for you?"

The rather cheery greeting confused Ashley; it was not at all, what she was expecting.

"I think you know why I am calling Ted."

"No Ashley, I don't." He was guarded in his response; one never knew what was going on from one day to the next with the Soper's. The company was his major client and he did some family work for them as well.

"You mean Arnold hasn't told you he is divorcing me?"

"No he hasn't been in touch with me since he got back from Africa, at least I assume he is back?"

"Oh yes the son-of-a-bitch is back all right! He said I would be hearing from you with respect to a settlement!"

"Ashley. Seriously, I have heard nothing. In any event, I couldn't discuss it with you anyway. I would be in a conflict of interest because I represent Arnold. I can recommend a good lawyer for you if you like."

"Piss Off! I can find my own lawyer!" He slammed the receiver back onto the cradle.

"That's interesting, she doesn't know anything, something curious going on here."

Just after Ted hung up his phone it rang again it was Jim Nelson.

"Hi Jim, what's up?"

"Arnold Soper is in the hospital."

"What! I just got of the phone with his wife Ashley, she didn't say anything about it."

"What did she want?"

"Jim, I don't think I can discuss my clients with you."

"Don't screw me around Ted, Arnie is in the hospital. The last I saw of him he was in a coma. You know what's going down so tell me, what did Ashley want?"

"She said that Arnie was divorcing her, apparently he told her I would be in touch with her. However, he never talked to me about it; it's not a great surprise though. I told her I couldn't help her and suggested she get her own lawyer."

"What did she say to that?"

"Told me to Piss Off!"

"Sounds like Ashley. Tell me, does Arnie have a will?"

Ted was beginning to feel very uncomfortable with the direction the conversation was taking; he was getting into deeper ethical waters.

"Jim I can't..."

"The hell you can't, you know exactly what's at stake here and what it means to you personally and to your whole firm."

"OK, OK, no he never got around to it, as a matter of fact I have him on my calendar for this week, we were to get it done on his return from Kenya."

"Shit, for a smart guy, he sometimes does dumb things, you're going to fly to Africa and make a will when you come back. If you come back, what kind of crap is that."

"Look, I've been after him for months, but he's always too busy."

"Ted, we need to meet somewhere and lay out a strategy, I am going to the hospital to check on things. Meet me at Mama Rosa's on Avenue Road. Get your secretary to call, get a reservation for 2:00 PM in the rear booth."

"OK, if there is any change, I've got your cell number I'll call you."

"You can't, I am at the hospital, remember, no cell phones. Just be there!

Ted was irritated at being ordered around by Jim Nelson, but there was no option, Nelson was right, there was a lot hanging in the balance, he punched the button for his secretary.

*

Soper had been sent directly to a private room in Intensive Care. Arrangements had been made to provide a private nurse around the clock. When Nelson arrived, the duty nurses had just changed shifts; unfortunately he missed the verbal exchange between them so he was forced to interrogate the oncoming nurse.

"How is he?"

"Not much change Doctor" she had recognized him when he came in.

"His blood pressure is normal, oxygen levels are at 95, heart rate at 72." She punched a couple of buttons on the EKG machine; "His brain traces look normal, at least as far as I can tell."

"He is going up for an MRI at 11:00 AM, we should know more by then."

"Thanks, Nurse."

Nelson moved to the bedside, and as if by force of habit, he reached out to take his pulse and then realized, all he had to do was read the display. As he withdrew his hand, he thought he saw Soper's eyelids flutter slightly.

"Arnie, Arnie it's me, Jim Nelson, can you hear me?"

He thought he saw another flicker of the eyelids. Nelson started when Soper's eyes popped wide open, "Where am I? He stared at Nelson, "Jim what are you doing here, wherever here is."

"Arnie, you are in University Hospital, you collapsed at your office last night, you have been unconscious ever since."

"I need a drink, I'm thirsty, can I have some water?"

Nelson poured water from the carafe into a Styrofoam cup and passed to Soper. He tried to grip it with his fingers only to have it slip from his grasp, dumping the water onto his chest as the cup tumbled almost silently to the floor.

"Shit, I've got no feeling in my hand, I couldn't feel the cup when you handed it to me."

"Easy Arnie, easy!"

Nelson could see he was getting agitated, he could also see his vital signs jumping around wildly, he didn't know precisely what was happening but he continued to attempt to calm Soper.

"Don't you understand? I can't feel anything, in either hand! I can't feel anything in my hands or legs!"

Suddenly, Soper's body stiffened, his eyes rolled back in his head so that only the whites were showing and violent tremors began to seize his body.

The nurse had already called for assistance and was beginning to administer a massive dose of Valium through the intravenous connection.

"Doctor Pickard left instructions to administer the Valium, in the event something like this should happen."

"Yes, yes, I understand."

Cyril Pickard came through the door; "I heard the code, what's happening!"

Nelson responded "He came to, seemed lucid for a few moments and then began to convulse."

"Did he say anything?"

"I tried to give him some water, he couldn't hold the cup. He said he had no feeling in his hands or legs. Then he began to seize. The nurse administered the Valium, that's it."

"Hmm."

Pickard scanned the monitoring equipment, they were beginning to return to more normal levels, the effects of the Valium he thought. He looked at the brain scan monitor and noted an anomaly or at least thought it might be an anomaly.

"It appears that something has changed regarding his brain activity, there are couple of traces that appear to be abnormal."

"I understand that you are going to do an MRI at 11:00, that should tell you more, right?"

"Hopefully, but there aren't any guarantees, you know that Jim. We will use nuclear tracers to see what shows up."

"Have you seen anything like this before?"

"Not really, Jim. I know that this vaccine is top secret, but I think we need to get Peter Mytryk in for a discussion. I need as much information as I can get about this situation if I am to be of any help."

"That's not a problem Cyril, I know you will respect the confidentiality of this whole matter. When do you want Mytryk here?"

"Get him in right away, it will be 2 to 3 hours before I get the results of the MRI, let's use that time to our advantage."

There was a telephone in the room; Nelson got Peter Mytryk on the line, "Peter, its Jim Nelson."

"How is Arnie doing, any improvement?"

"No Improvement" he said tersely.

"I need you to come over to hospital immediately and meet with me and Doctor Pickard, he needs more information on the vaccine."

"But Jim, this is highly confidential stuff..."

"Never mind all that crap, get over here now!" he slammed the receiver down.

"I can't stand that Asshole!" muttered Jim, not quite under his breath.

"He seems to have stabilized, at least for now. Come Jim, we'll go up to the conference room, I'll leave word at the switchboard to have Doctor Mytryk sent up to us when he arrives."

*

Mytryk grimaced as he hung up the phone; his anger showed on his face, it was fortunate that he had a little time on the trip to the hospital to compose himself and his thoughts.

He fully believed that, regardless of an overly generous salary and other perquisites, he got little respect from the principals of Soper Research Inc. His treatment by Nelson was just another manifestation of this lack of respect.

He had been the guiding force behind this new development, albeit Soper had the original hypothesis and was responsible for the direction that established the likelihood of a virus being the root cause of the disease. Mytryk believed that without his efforts, the company would not be in the position it was in today. He was bitter about the lack of personal recognition.

That son-of-a-bitch, he never had any respect for my abilities, always so self centred, So what if I managed to get a little back by peddling that patent information? I deserved that money, would never have seen any of it from Soper! Mahoney scares me though, nothing I can do, unless I was ever able to get that dossier. Fat chance! Even then, I had to split the money with him!

*

Nelson and Pickard sat in the conference room. Pickard sipping hot coffee and looking over the rim of his cup at the younger man opposite. "I take it Jim, that you are less involved in your medical practice these days than you are in business?"

"Yes, I have almost given up my practice, with a couple of exceptions like Arnie, although I still consider myself practising medicine today, just at a different level."

The conference room phone rang and the operator announced the arrival of Peter Mytryk.

When he came through the door, Nelson thought that the only thing less sincere than Mytryk's almost perpetual smile was his handshake, with these formalities over, they seated themselves at one end of the highly polished mahogany table.

Pickard, at Nelson's urging, gave Mytryk an update of Soper's condition, ending with the recent seizure.

"So, Doctor Mytryk, you can see, we need to have as much information as possible regarding this occurrence and the vaccine."

"Doctor Pickard, I really fail to see, from what you have told me, how there could be any connection between the vaccine and Doctor Soper's condition. We have had no such contraindication of this medication on all the animal trials or on any of the limited human trials, so I fail to see..."

Jim Nelson interrupted "Peter, none of that matters, except for background, please... just answer Cyril's questions."

Mytryk's face reddened slightly, but he fought to maintain his composure, "Ask away Doctor Pickard."

"Could you explain to me the modality of the vaccine, and a brief indication of the history of the discovery of the virus. I am unaware of any other research that indicates that the cause of Alzheimer's is indeed caused by a virus?"

"That is exactly what makes this discovery so exciting. Doctor Soper had the original flash of brilliance of this potential approach almost by accident. He was researching an entirely different disease when he came across a virus that he had never seen before. He was examining tissue samples utilizing polyacrylamide gel electrophoresis, used for examining protein fragments, an inferential method used to define viral elements.

He came across protein fragments that he did not recognize, consequently, using the company's extensive database; he began pattern-matching operations in order to find other occurrences.

To make a long story short, he was able to find these fragments in other samples. On further analysis, was able to establish a causal link between these protein fragments, and that all of the donors of the tissue had Alzheimer's in varying stages, as a common factor."

"Very interesting, but who carries this virus and how are people infected with it?"

"Interesting indeed, what we found was that almost everyone carries this virus."

"How do you explain the fact that only the elderly seem to be affected by the disease?"

"Very simple," he said with a smirk. "The virus is normally dormant and is only manifested when the immune system begins to deteriorate allowing the virus to utilize the protein in question in order to reproduce and manifest the disease."

"And of course that happens with advancing age."

"Yes, it is very symmetrical."

"And what is the modality of the vaccine?"

"The vaccine prevents the virus from utilizing this specific protein preventing the development of the disease. It cannot reverse the condition but it can halt it and if the process has not begun, it can prevent it."

"Amazing, how long is the vaccination effective?"

"Current test indicate that booster shots must be given every three months, a simple needle, with few or no side effects."

"That you currently know about."

"One other thing, the vaccine is "targeted."

"What do you mean, targeted."

"It is site specific, it is only effective in the parts of the brain that are normally affected by the virus."

"Is the vaccine based on "live virus?""

"Yes."

Peter Mytryk sat back in the swivel chair smiling broadly as though he had just shown everyone photographs of his only child.

Nelson looked at him with grudging acknowledgment. He was one of the top Microbiologists in the country; he was still a prick in his mind.

"Thank you Peter, we'll let you get back to your work now, unless there is anything else Cyril?"

"No, I think that will do for now, I know how to reach Doctor Mytryk if I need anything further."

When the two men were alone Pickard said "I can see the significance of this development, the opportunities for the future are fantastic, providing of course that the trials go well. Tell me what is the state of the patent?"

"Well in hand Cyril, we expect the granting of multi-national patents shortly, in fact our US attorneys indicate that it should be granted by the end of the month."

"This vaccine should be a "cash cow" for Soper, no one could afford to be without it and the fact that boosters are required every three months ensures a steady and phenomenal cash flow not to say profits!"

"Cyril, you can see why none of this business with respect to Arnie can get out, otherwise we could prejudice the whole thing."

"Jim, I understand completely, you can depend on me to be the soul of discretion."

"Thanks Cyril, and by the way, we look after our friends, once the FDA approve the release of the vaccine for full scale human testing we intend to take the Company public. I will make sure that will be an opportunity for you to have access to stock options at rather preferential pricing. If I am right in my assessment, the stock should sky rocket after trading opens. You should be able to make yourself a tidy sum"!

Pickard smiled broadly, Nelson figured he was likely doing mental calculations of his net worth already.

"Thanks for the consideration Jim, you can count on me, now I had better check on the progress of the MRI, I'll call you on your cell when I have anything."

Nelson knew that he had locked up Pickard by appealing to his greed, he also knew that he would keep the staff at the hospital under control. All of the special duty nurses had been arrange by Cyril, Nelson knew they would all be hand picked and as discrete as he could make them.

He made a mental note to get the names of everybody in direct contact with the case and to provide it to Declan Mahoney, just in case reinforcement of the confidentiality was required.

His mind was at work as he made his way into the centre of the city and his meeting with Ted Franklin. There was no way of knowing what the outcome might be to this whole situation; he needed to develop a strategy for any contingency. It was entirely possible that Arnie could die or be permanently incapacitated, he could not let either of these possibilities jeopardize his opportunity to acquire a fortune that would rival that of any other person in the country.

He was as greedy as the next guy was, but as Vice-Chairman of the Executive Committee, he now had the influence to manipulate people so that he would be assured of his rightful due.

After he finished his meeting with Ted, he would arrange to convene a Board Meeting next week. He would need to formalize his appointment as the new Chairman, at least under the guise of filling the gap created by Arnie's illness.

The Company, although doing over $450,000,000 in annual sales, was still a privately held corporation, there were six other board members, including Arnie's father-in-law Lester Coughlan. They were all independently wealthy; each had provided a portion of the "seed" money to start the venture.

The Board never caused Arnie any problems. As long as the dividends flowed, they were happy, they knew nothing and wanted to know nothing of the high tech side of this business. They were happy to leave this with Arnie, so therefore they were seldom ever consulted on any development matter and in fact were largely kept in the dark about all projects until after the product was launched. They knew nothing of the Alzheimer's Vaccine.

Arnie had been careful to maintain absolute share control of the equity of the company. All other directors, save Nelson, had only a qualifying number of common shares, the balance of their investment consisted of non voting preferred stock that generated rather large dividends to them on a semi annual basis.

Nelson had been able to establish himself with Arnie over the years as a friend and confidant; this resulted in him being able to obtain a 10% holding of common shares of the business. His net worth had appreciated considerably over the years.

He needed a game plan that would leave the status quo, except that he would make the critical decisions instead of Arnie.

As he neared the restaurant, a plan was beginning to take shape.

Chapter 3

What happened, bright lights, blurred images, now this, blackness, nothing but blackness, where am I? I can't feel anything; nothing seems to move, is my body here? It seems like I'm separated from myself. How can that be?

Was it a stroke? Remember Jim, then all this, why? What's going on?

Why is this happening?

Wait, there is some light, just a glimmer, Oh God! Am I dead? Am I asleep?

Get a grip! Don't go to pieces, rationalize. In some Cartesian sense, I know I exist. I think therefore I am. I can't be dead!

But then again, maybe I am dead, am I in an afterlife? Surely, one thinks in an afterlife. Could that be it?

Who spoke? Someone spoke! Can I respond, am I stupid to believe I can speak if my lips don't move? Hallucinations are a possibility, is that it, am I hallucinating?

There it is again! Through the darkness, a voice at once calm and yet insistent.

"Can I help you?"

"Who are you?"

"I am whoever you want or need me to be."

"I can't see anyone, where do you come from? Why are you here?"

"None of that is of importance, I just sense that you need help, why not let me help you?"

Try to see in the dim light, but see nothing, can't even tell the direction the voice is coming from. "Am I coming to pieces? Could it be the result of some kind of medication I'm being given?"

"Talk to me, tell me how you are feeling."

"I don't feel anything! That's my problem, at least if I could see my body I would know I was having an "out of body experience" maybe I'm asleep and just dreaming all this!"

"Do you have no sense of panic?"

Why do I have no sense of panic? Given the circumstances, that should be my normal reaction, but there is none! Valium that's it! They have given me Valium to attenuate the seizures that must be why!

"No.!"

"Why not?"

"Why are you asking all these questions, what's it to you anyway?"

"I said I wanted to help you?"

"What's in it for you? Why would you want to, you don't know me!"

"In many ways I know you better than you do yourself, so, do I take it that you want no help?"

Who is this person or thing that says he knows me, I can't even see his body let alone his face, just a disembodied voice that I don't even recognize. Christ! What is happening to me?

"I would be a fool to say I didn't want any help, given my circumstances, but I doubt that you can provide any, I don't even know if you are real!"

"You are sure of what reality is, then?"

"Is that your idea of help, to bate me?"

"Not at all, but if you doubt my existence how can I be of any help to you?"

"Who the hell are you! What's your name?"

"As I said, I am whoever you want me to be."

Chapter 4

"Il Dottore! It is so good to see you; it's been too long...I began to think you no more like my cooking!

"No No Rosa, I've just been to busy to get to your end of the city, but now here I am, looking forward to some of your Saltimbocca! Rosa, is anyone using your private room?"

"Nada. It is yours Il Dottore, follow me."

When he was seated, he asked her to send Ted Franklin back when he arrived.

"Would you like an antipasto or a drink while you are waiting?"

"Just a Compari and Soda would be fine Rosa."

He took a legal pad from his briefcase and began making some notes in preparations for the meeting.

He looked up as Rosa returned with his drink and Ted Franklin in tow.

"Hi Ted, can I buy you a drink?"

"Sure, Rosa bring me a Chivas, neat."

When they were alone Ted asked for an update regarding Arnold Soper. Before Nelson could respond, Rosa returned with his drink, She advised Nelson to signal her with the buzzer next to the door when they were ready to order, she backed out closing the door after her.

"Well things are not looking too good, he did regain consciousness briefly while I was with him. He asked for some water, but when I tried to give it to him he was unable to take it and spilled it to the floor. Shortly after, he had another seizure, they injected a dose of Valium into his intravenous and that stopped the seizure."

"Have they got any idea of what his problem is?"

"Not really, they are doing an MRI, as a matter of fact they probably already have by now, but it will be couple of hours before we hear the results."

"Great timing!"

" Exactly, that's why I called this meeting, we need to develop some kind of strategy on a worst case basis."

Nelson reviewed the few notes he had been able to jot down just before Franklin arrived. He began by describing a scenario whereby Soper dies in the hospital. In addition, just how the company would proceed with the FDA announcement regarding the release of the vaccine for extended human use.

The concern wasn't so much about the technical aspect of the release of the product itself. As much as, it was about the perception of the marketplace regarding the death of the company founder and leading scientist. Moreover, how this fact might effect the initial public offering of company shares.

It was essential that information regarding Soper's self-injection of the vaccine must be suppressed at all costs.

"How many people know that he took it?"

"I don't know, Mytryk told me, I have told you and Cyril, but I don't know how much further it goes, I am going to meet with Declan and get his thoughts on how to handle that specific situation."

"Declan. That guy scares me."

"He is discrete and very capable, we can count on him."

"Ted, where are we on the IPO, is anything compromised by Arnie's absence?"

" The Underwriter's are all set to go, we have pulled all the costs together, but we don't have a Board Resolution to proceed with the offering. Before all of this happened, that was a mere formality, you tell me, will that be a problem?"

"Shit! I should have remembered that, I agree with you it was a non-issue, but now I am not so sure. Share control rests with Arnie, he has almost 90% of the common shares, of course, each director has a qualifying share, and my own holdings have voting restrictions on them.

Given that Arnie has no Will, how are his assets likely to be divided?"

"The problem is going to be that we will have to go to Probate if he dies intestate, the court will decide. I can't even predict how long that might take, particularly if there are any challenges by family members."

"How is Ashley likely to be treated through such an exercise?"

"Well, there is nothing official about any divorce, so far as the court would be concerned, she would likely be considered a prime beneficiary of the estate. However, remember there is an adult son from the previous marriage as well as minor child from the current one. I don't know of any others that might have a claim, but you never know."

"So it will depend upon how the court rules in divvying up all his assets, at this stage we can't tell how his shares might get voted."

"Correct!"

Nelson continued writing notes as Franklin was speaking, jabbing the page with his pen after every comment written his increased frustration was becoming evident.

Franklin continued, "That may not be the worst case scenario. Consider what happens if he ends up in a coma."

"We may end up with no resolution at all! Is there no way around this situation?"

"We could get Ashley to go to court and have Arnie declared incompetent and convince the court that her interests are not being looked after and the value of her spousal share of the assets may be being diminished. But you need to know that the court may appoint a trustee, this would limit the board's ability to move quickly in any area, for example the trustee may not agree that the IPO is in the estate's best interest."

"Jim, it seems to me, that regardless of what happens to Arnie, short of a complete recovery, Ashley is going to be the key to all this. You are going to need her to vote her shares in favour of this endeavour whether she gets them by way of probate or having herself made Arnie's trustee. We need to get her on side with us, we cannot afford to alienate her, I know I don't have to tell you that she has access to financial resources that would allow her to hire first rate legal advisors"

"I think you're right, but you know as well as I do that she is more than a bit of a "firecracker" and given what Arnie set in motion, she may be somewhat unstable. I will make an effort to meet with her, as far as I know, she doesn't even know about Arnie's condition."

"The other thing Jim, is Bradley, Arnie's older son, we should also be trying to get him on side. Particularly if it comes down to having a trustee appointed, if he challenges the appointment of Ashley, we could be back at "square one."

"I haven't seen Brad since he was about 6 years old, do you have any idea where he is?"

"Not really, after the divorce I did set up a trust fund for the child, that was a condition of the settlement, I do remember that apparently Eve and Brad left the city for the West Coast."

"Another bit of work for Declan."

Jim Nelson reflected on Brad Soper and his mother Eve, he and his late wife had been good friends with the Soper family, he had particularly liked the boy, a bright precocious child.

Nelson could never account for the distance there seemed to be between father and son. He and his wife were childless and remained so throughout the marriage, he was jealous of Arnie and disappointed in his wife, although he took care and tried hard not to show it.

Brad must be 24 or 25 by now, he regretted not having taken the trouble to stay in touch with the boy, not so much because of the current situation, but more for the need of such a relationship.

"Are we going to have something to eat?"

Nelson started at the comment, being drawn back to the present. "Sure, go ahead and ring for Rosa, order me the Saltimbocca, I want to call the hospital and see what's going on."

He reached Cyril Pickard on his cell phone.

"Hello Cyril, what's the news?"

"Well it's not particularly good news Jim, it appears that he is in a coma as we speak and given the results of the MRI I am not sure he will recover from it."

"Cyril, I am just in the middle of a lunch meeting, is it possible for us to meet this afternoon, say around 3:45? I would like to get your complete prognosis"

"Of course I know how important this is to everyone, I will keep myself available, it will also give me more time to review the brain scans before you get here."

Nelson then called Declan Mahoney and arranged to meet him at his office after 5:00 PM, this was going to be a long day!

"Bad news I take it."

"The worst of the two scenarios seems to be what we will be facing, he is in a coma and Cyril thinks it unlikely that he recover from it."

"Shit!

The two ate without much further comment. Nelson barely tasted his meal; he knew it was good but he left half of it on his plate draining the Compari he left money to cover the tab and headed out to the hospital.

I'll be in touch Ted."

He met Pickard in the hallway just outside his office. "Come in Jim, your right on time."

"OK, lets have your prognosis on the patient."

"Well... I can tell you that there are no brain tumours, nor did he have any kind of a stroke."

"Let's dispense with what it's not and get to what his problem is!"

Pickard let the comment slide, no sense in getting involved in a confrontation, more important that he preserve the relationship they have been developing and get access to a business opportunity than to exercise his sharp tongue.

"There is a strange anomaly that I noticed when I reviewed all the test data, in certain brain areas there appears to be something attacking the myelin sheath around the nerves."

"You said in certain areas?"

"Yes, in the cerebellum, which as you know controls voluntary movement and in the parietal lobe and the occipital lobe. In fact the only areas that are untouched are the areas of the limbic system and hypothalamus that control memory and emotional centres."

"What is the cause?"

"We don't know for sure, it could be a number of things, but I would put my money on some type of virus, basically because there is nothing obvious. But if it is, it's one for the books, I have nothing on file that would help us."

"Antibiotics are of no use?"

"No and we have started treatment using known anti-viral agents and so far they are having no effect on him."

"Is he likely to die?"

"Well, we are going to put him on life support because I have concerns that involuntary body functions may shut down, in which case he would most certainly die. It will at least buy us some time as we try to develop a treatment regimen. However, I must tell you, that if we can't come up with something quickly, Dr. Soper's condition will not be reversible. Even if we can halt the disease' we may have a vegetable on our hands."

"That is a discouraging prognosis Cyril."

"No doubt, and one other thing, we have had to place him in isolation because we have no idea of what the mechanism is regarding infection, we just can't take any chances."

"I understand,"

"It seems to me that it might just be easier to withhold extraordinary treatment from him and let the disease take its course."

"Jim, we can't do that, ethically and legally we don't have a basis to do so. Remember he is not brain dead, there is no living will and family members must ultimately decide if we get to that."

"Is there anything else we can do Cyril."

"Well, there might just be something, Soper Research have a great deal of research talent on staff not the least of whom is Peter Mytryk. It might be an idea to have him in to consult on this matter and if there is any interaction with this new vaccine he would be most qualified to deal with it."

Nelson could not quarrel with this suggestion; although he detested the man, he was brilliant and he had after all spent months dealing with newly discovered viruses.

"Cyril, I agree, I will set it up. Is there anything else that I can provide for you?"

"Not at the moment, I will keep you up to date on the situation here."

Nelson entered the restaurant and saw Declan Mahoney sitting in a booth at the very back of the room. Mahoney was a square man nattily attired in a dark blue suit. He always wore a large sapphire ring on the little finger of his left hand.

Rumour had it that he was a former member of the IRA, and that he had a price on his head, consequently his departure from Ireland was not a decision he made entirely on his own. A loquacious man, he could draw a person into revealing things in conversation that were unintended.

Mahoney had a reputation of being ruthless in pursuit of his objective, but as Nelson knew, he was dependable, thorough and, expensive.

"Hallo Jim, it's good to see you again, but something tells me that this dinner isn't a social one. Sit down and tell me what we can do for you. First though, will you join me in a drink?"

Without waiting for an answer, he called the waitress to the table. "Sheila, see what my friend will have, for me it'll be a double Jamieson 1780 straight up!"

"Compari and Soda."

Mahoney stifled a sneer at the drink order, "A pansy's drink" he thought to himself.

"Well now Jim, we had best get to it, what's been going on since I last saw you?"

Nelson reiterated most of the information relating to Arnie's condition, except for the fact of the self-administration of the vaccine, the lack of a will and Arnie's threat to divorce Ashley. He wasn't sure why he withheld this information, instinct as much as anything he guessed.

"Now this is a right mess, what with the FDA ruling coming down and all. Since we are still unsure of the possible outcome of Arnie's condition, we need to prepare several cover stories that can be used when the situation becomes clearer. As I see it, we need a scenario based upon his death, reassuring the public of the continuity of the firm, how, while Arnie was the leader we have everything under control, you know, onward and upward."

"Yes, that would be important, I think we also need to confirm my appointment at least as acting Chairman."

"Let's play it that way for now Jim, although nothing is sure, the appointment would have to be confirmed by the board of directors."

"I am sure that is nothing but a formality." He watched Nelson's eyes flicker, and thought to himself "Not such a sure thing!"

"We also need to have a cover story right now covering his absence from the office, remember, he is in intensive care and as I mentioned, he has been placed in quarantine. I am not sure how you will deal with that, but if you could keep the lid on this until after the FDA announcement in would be helpful."

"That's a tall order, but let me think on it, I'll let you know what I propose in the next day or two."

Mahoney began to wheeze, his face became reddened, he reached in his pocket and retrieved his asthma inhaler, after two quick puffs, and his breathing was almost normal.

"Damned asthma! Its bothered me since I was a kid." He held up the inhaler, "but thanks to Soper, it's not nearly the problem it once was."

"I'm glad it works for you, but there is something else we must do, I need you to find the whereabouts of Bradley Soper, Arnie's son from his first marriage. All I can tell you is that he is about 24 or 25 and is likely living on the West Coast. Ted Franklin apparently set up a trust fund for him years ago, what is it they say in your business "follow the money.""

"Do you want me to get him back here."

"No, not at this time, I just want a method of contacting him. However, you give me a report on him, what he is doing for a living, personal relationships, general background information, that sort of thing."

"Done, I will get one of my associates on it immediately."

"One other thing Declan, is there any way you can put a lid on the gossip that will likely start coming out of the hospital soon?"

"The fact that he is in isolation will make that easier, perhaps we can alter the computer records regarding his admission, change the patient name, some thing like that. I will also arrange for some discrete discussion to take place with people who are aware of how he is and why he is there."

Nelson held up his hand. "That is much more than I want to know, I will say however, Cyril Pickard the Chief Neurologist is on-side with this situation, so you don't have to worry about him."

A sly smile played on Mahoney's lips, they are all squeamish when it comes to the specifics about how problems get solved, not to worry, whatever needs to get done will be done.

They ate dinner with not much more being said about Soper Research, Nelson was uncomfortable in Declan Mahoney's company, so he excused himself as soon as could decently do so.

As Jim sat in his car, he placed a call to Peter Mytryk; he answered on the second ring.

"Working late Peter."

"Hello Jim, I was beginning to wonder if I was going to hear from you, I called Dr. Pickard at the hospital. He told me that I should speak to you, no one is giving out any information on Arnie's condition."

"Sorry about that Peter, but we must try to avoid any kind of speculation in the media or the business community, don't take it personally."

"I understand... of course, it's just that I am concerned, can you tell me anything?"

Nelson repeated the facts of Arnie's condition as far as was known now, including Pickard's request for Mytryk's help.

"Of course, I would be most happy to be of any help that I can."

Jim could sense the elation in Mytryk's voice at having been asked to be involved in the case.

"Good, Peter might I suggest that you contact Cyril in the morning and set up the necessary arrangements. My thought was that it would be better if you went to the hospital to meet since all of the test data is there. Of course if you need to take Cyril to our lab, that's fine with me, if you have any problems with security, please call me."

"Of course, and thank you for your confidence Dr. Nelson."

"Ass kisser" thought Nelson as he closed his cell phone, he still had to call Ashley, but there was no point tonight, she would be well into the Manhattans by now.

*

Ashley looked at the blurred face of her watch as she listens to the persistence of her telephone ringing on the night table.

"Oh God, it's only 10:30, who the hell could be calling so early?"

"Ashley, its Jim Nelson, how are you?"

"I am afraid I might not be dead, such a hangover! After all these years why are you calling me, or did your Asshole boss put you up to it?"

"Then no one has told you."

"Told me what?"

"Arnie is in the hospital."

"It's fatal I hope."

"Ashley this is serious, he is in a coma, we are unsure of his prognosis, it well could be fatal."

There was silence on the other end of the phone, "My smart mouth has done it again," she thought.

"Ashley. Ashley, are you still there."

"Yes, Yes I am, when did all this happen?"

"Yesterday, listen, Ashley, we need to talk so I can fill you in, can you meet me for lunch, say 1:30 at Scaramouche's?"

"Jim, I am sorry for what I said."

"I understand, don't worry about it, I know you didn't mean it, can you meet me?"

"Yes of course."

What the hell is going on? Arnie in the hospital, maybe dying? No divorce now! What does Jim want, don't trust him, he failed me once, took advantage of me when I was down. Nevertheless, I have to go, have to find out!

Chapter 5

Was this some kind of test? Am I on trial here? What have I done in life to deserve this, it feels like an interrogation, I'm not a criminal.

"Is that how you feel Dr. Soper, like a criminal?"

Shit! Now he's reading my mind, or did I say it aloud?

"Tell me Dr. Soper, what would make you feel that way?

"You're beginning to sound like a Psychoanalyst, why all these questions?"

"At one time you were a Psychoanalyst, why would you ask that?"

"Let me ask you a question, am I dead?"

"You know that's not how these things work, I ask the questions, you give the answers, how many times have you told a patient that? But in this case I will answer you, no you are not dead."

"Are you here then to tell me that I am on the road to Perdition? Or perhaps I've stopped in Purgatory, on my way there?"

"It seems that you haven't forgotten your catechism, but you tell me where you are, I think you know."

Anger began to well up at being tested this way, I am sure that I can "will" this voice away, but to what end, I would be alone again. At least the voice is a diversion from the isolation.

"So I have to name you?"

"If you like. If it helps you."

"OK. Then you will be "Alfred" after the late Alfred Adler, your techniques seem similar."

" I am flattered."

"Then you know of him?"

"Oh yes."

"Modern psychology has shown us that the traits of craving for power, ambition, and striving for power over others, with their numerous ugly concomitants, are not innate and unalterable.

Rather they are inoculated into the child at an early age; the child receives them involuntarily from an atmosphere saturated by the titillation of power.

In our blood is still the desire for the intoxication with power, and our souls are playthings of the craving for power."

"I am impressed, a direct quote from Adler and from memory. So you are an Adlerian, a lucky guess on my part"

"Do you think the quote applies to you? Is your soul a plaything of the craving for power?"

"I don't believe in the concept of the everlasting soul, that is nothing more than a coping mechanism developed by an ignorant, unscientific people. Therefore the quote cannot apply to me."

"Then why did you first ask me if you were dead? Surely if you don't believe in the soul, your question would have been mute. Without a soul there would be nothing after death, consequently, you could not equate your current situation with death."

"Are you telling me there is such a thing as a soul?"

"I simply asked you what you thought."

"Tell me Dr. Soper, given these circumstances, would you not find some comfort if you held a belief in an afterlife?"

"Alfred, without doubt it would be more comfortable, but without the intellectual integrity of real belief it would merely be a fraudulent hope, a sort of insurance policy for the future just in case the belief was true! Surely if the belief was not truly held and then proved to be true, would I not be worse off. Would I not be seen as a dishonest opportunist covering all the bases?"

"A point taken. Would you like to talk about your family?"

"Not really." Soper recognized the not so subtle change in direction.

"Why not."

"Because I don't believe it is relevant to my current predicament."

"All right, then tell me, do you think that any part of the Adler quote could pertain to you?

"No, do you?"

"Dr. Soper, you know how this works, I ask the questions, you answer."

"Seriously, no I do not think the quote applies to me in any way. I have spent my life in helping others, curing disease, giving my patients their lives back. Frankly, I am offended at the suggestion."

"So, in your estimation, profit never entered into your decision to help others?"

"What's wrong with profits, without them research and development could not continue, profits of themselves are not inherently evil!"

"Then you are unaware of any individuals that may have been deprived of your treatments because they could not pay?"

"That is the responsibility for the larger community, the various levels of government for example. Alfred, you are beginning to sound like a socialist, you know that almost every socialist country has failed, individual enterprise is the only solution."

"Tell me about your first wife, Eve?"

"She was a good woman, she's dead, why do you ask?"

"Would you like to talk to her?"

"Don't you listen Alfred, I told you, she's dead, has been for almost 5 years."

There is someone else out there; I can sense it, who is it? I can feel anxiety rising in spite of any medication being administered. I would have run if I could, anything to escape this place.

"Hello Arnie."

"Eve, it is you, you look wonderful."

"Thank you Arnie, I wish I could say the same for you, I am sorry for the problems you are having."

"Eve, do you know Alfred? He is somewhere around here."

"There's no one here except you and I Arnie, who are you talking about."

"It's OK, just my imagination I guess, tell me, are you really here."

"I am here because it's what you wanted Arnie. How can I help you."

Help me, why? You were the one that hurt me, why do you want help me now.

"Can we really talk Eve? Is there enough distance now that we can do that?"

"That's really up to you Arnie, I have reconciled all that went on, I am at peace with myself, what about you?"

"I don't know Eve, I still have anger within me when I think back to what happened, so I would guess I can't say that I am reconciled, I still have a problem accepting what you did and forgiving you!"

"Arnie, I can understand your feelings towards me, but I had problems for many years dealing with the way you abandoned Bradley, that little boy idolized you."

"I believed that it would be better for Brad if I did not complicate his life by periodically reappearing, I knew you were a good mother, I felt he would be better off without me."

"It was your loss Arnie, Brad has grown into a fine young man, someone you would be proud to call your son. And yet you never maintained contact, you didn't care what happened to your son!"

Her beautiful face was passive, it registered no emotion as she spoke, her statements were really a matter of fact and not accusatory.

"That's not true, I provided well for you both you wanted for nothing!"

"He needed you, not your money, it seems that you still equate your relationships in dollars and cents. Why did you never attempt to visit him, to ask him about his interests, his problems?"

"I did have people check on his progress in school, I had periodic reports on how he was doing. He was an excellent student, he was doing well, thanks, I am sure to you. I lost all contact when you moved to Vancouver."

"Reports from strangers, do you think that makes up for your absence, did you ever visit with him, face to face like any normal father?"

"I told you why not."

"Your loss Arnie, as I said."

"Why did you move to Vancouver?"

"There was nothing here for either of us, and Brad had applied to UBC and was accepted, so we just left."

"Without a word!"

"Would it really have made a difference? You were so wrapped up in your work, you had even less time for anyone than you did when we were married."

"Tell me about Brad."

"He is a very bright young man, takes after his father in that respect, it certainly is not a gift from his mother, he has been accepted for a Doctoral Fellowship in the Ethics of Health Research at UBC. He must be very near completion of his Fellowship."

"I am impressed, but why ethics? Why not basic research, in medicine for example?"

"Who knows, perhaps he felt the family was a little short on ethics!"

Reconciliation? Doesn't sound like it to me. We were better off separated; we would have screwed up Brad's life too.

"Eve, you know full well what I was not the one who caused the break up in the first place, surely you will admit that!"

"I didn't come to blame you for anything, yes, I did something you found inexcusable, but if you were to ask me if I would do it again, I would have to tell you that under similar circumstances, I would. For one brief period, I was never happier in my life!"

"Frankly Eve, I don't see how any of this is going to help me, it seems more like punishment, I don't need that right now."

She didn't move her face still impassive, he knew he would never be able to reach her, to tell her his true feelings. Anxiety is rising, likely need more Valium, can't take anymore of this, just force them both out of my mind. Slowly her image began to recede; maybe I can sleep now. Sleep, will I know it?

Chapter 6

Peter Mytryk was escorted to Cyril Pickard's office precisely at 9:30, he had been 15 minutes early, but was kept waiting until the proscribed time. He took this as a personal slight, as he did most things that were not exactly as he deemed they should be.

He attempted to remove the scowl from his face, unsuccessfully, Cyril noted this and smiled inwardly, there was just something about this man that cried out to have his nose twisted.

"Dr. Mytryk, thank you so much for coming."

"Call me Peter, Dr. Pickard no need for formality."

Mytryk noted that Pickard did not make the same offer in return, this just added to his sour demeanour.

"Well, Dr. Mytryk let's get down to cases as they say."

"Firstly Dr. Pickard, could you please give me an update on Arnie's condition?'

"Of course, of course, well unfortunately there has been a change for the worse in his condition. He remains in a coma. We have had him moved to an Isolation Ward and with his declining situation, I have ordered him placed on life support. While he can still sustain some of vital functions, I thought it prudent to take this step.

"That is unfortunate news. Is there anything specific you can tell as to the suspect cause of his condition?

"The only conclusive thing I can tell you is that some thing, is attacking the myelin sheath in some of the nerve bundles in the brain, but at this point, I don't have any idea what that "some thing" is. That is why I have asked you to help, perhaps its an obscure or unknown virus, I know that is certainly your area of expertise."

Pickard could almost see the other man "puff up" at his comments.

"Perhaps a place to start would be to let me review the complete file on Arnie, including of course all of your test information, just to make sure nothing was missed."

It was Pickard's turn now to be annoyed, but he was more skilled at feigning a lack of regard for the comment."

"There is a small conference room adjacent to this office. You can use that to do your review, feel free to use anything in there that might assist you, there is a phone there, just dial 8 to reach my secretary of there is anything else you need. The only thing I ask is that you call my secretary if you need to see me. She will know if I am with a patient or not, I would rather you not enter my office unannounced and interrupt a consultation."

Mytryk could feel his gorge rising, he was being treated as an underling not a peer. "Why were people always treating me this way?" he thought.

He made his way to the conference room with his armload of documents, scans, traces and x-rays. He was pleased to see they had at least backlit panels for his use in reviewing the transparencies. Good thing he thought since the room was windowless.

Just remember Dr. Mytryk, dial eight for anything you need, even a cup of coffee, we aim to please here. I will try to check back with you in 2 or 3 hours and see how you are coming along."

With that, Pickard retreated to his office, closing the door to the conference room behind him. Mytryk, lay all of the material on the conference table and surveyed the room, he sighed, "At least there is a bathroom in here."

He busied himself, organizing all his material.

*

When Jim Nelson arrived at Scaramouche's, Ashley was already seated at his favourite table. He looked her over carefully; she was still a stunner, in spite of her drinking. I didn't hurt that she was likely wearing $5,000 worth of designer clothes. He wondered if she had had time to have her makeup professionally applied.

She extended her hand, "Hello Jim, it's nice to see you again, it's been such a long time."

Was he mistaken or did she actually flutter her eyelashes at him?

"Ashley, you look as beautiful as ever!"

"Liar!"

"You do, seriously, I think you are one of those women who will never get old."

"Such Bullshit, but keep it up it's good for girl's morale."

"I am just sorry that we have to meet under these circumstances, things do not look good for Arnie."

"Tell me Jim, just what has happened."

He recounted the facts to her as he knew them at that point in time. He told her, as well, about Peter Mytryk being at the hospital trying to help identify just what might be at the root of Arnie's illness.

He took care not to mention Arnie's self-administration of the vaccine.

"That creep! I have never liked that man, he gives me shivers!"

"I know what you mean, but there is no doubting his skill as a microbiologist, and with his research background, he is ideally suited to help out."

"I suppose you are right, as usual Jim. How about a drink?"

"Well it's a little early, but why not He waved discretely to their waiter and ordered a Manhattan for her and a Compari and soda for himself.

"It's flattering that you still remember, Jim."

"How could I forget?"

"I suppose that you have heard about Arnie and me?"

"You mean the divorce, yes I talked to Ted and he told me. Ashley I very sorry to hear about it, but it seems to be a mute point at this stage, given his condition."

"Well, we had grown apart to say the least, as you, particularly would understand, but I wouldn't wish this on him or on anyone else for that matter."

Their drinks came; Ashley removed the cherry and chewed it delicately, washing it down with a large sip of the amber fluid. He wanted her to stay lucid, so he hailed the waiter again and asked her if she would like him to order for her.

"Are you in a hurry Jim? Or is it just that you don't want to see me get drunk, do I really have that bad a reputation?"

"No, no, of course not, but we do have to discuss some serious things and both of us need to be on top of our game. I am afraid, as much as I would like to have it otherwise, this meeting is very much a business lunch."

You sit there, not even prepared to acknowledge what you have done to me! Fuck them and leave them, is that your motto Jim? Take advantage when I was vulnerable, when you got what you wanted, move on as though nothing happened.

What was it Jim? One up on Arnie?

"Go ahead then order for me, I guess I can trust you to do that much, at least I think I can. Can I Jim?"

He touched Ashley's hand trying to reassure her "Of course, you know that, Ashley we have been friends for a long, long time."

She pulled her hand away, finished her drink and asked him to get her another. He did so reluctantly; he ordered lunch and began where he had left off with Arnie's condition.

"I am afraid I have to say it, his prognosis is not good." He paused, "Ashley, there is a very high probability that Arnie will not recover and in fact he is more likely to die!"

"You know that Arnie and I have been pretty close since our med school days, frankly I have been devastated by what has happened." He stopped and took a sip of his Compari and continued.

"I would say you were close Jim, close enough to share many things I'm sure."

One mistake, will she ever forget? Just a slip, a temptation that couldn't be resisted, I let Arnie down! No! She led me on; she deserved what happened to her, it wasn't my fault. Arnie has everything, he didn't want her!

"Regardless of the outcome, there are issues that will need to be dealt with, I hate to have to raise business affairs with you at this time, but timing could mean everything, to you, to Ellis and to the Company."

"What do you mean?"

"Did Arnie ever talk to you about any of the research projects being carried out at Soper Research?"

"Well not really, but I could always tell when something big was happening or at least about to happen, he would get as grumpy as an old bear. And he sure has been grumpy of late!"

"What I am about to tell you must remain in the strictest confidence, can you give that assurance Ashley?"

"Yes, Yes, of course, just remember, I'm not the one that ever had a problem with trust."

Nelson tried to ignore her jibe and gave her a detailed explanation of the new vaccine and it's potential for mankind and of course for the profitability of the Company. Her eyes widened as she absorbed what she was hearing, her second drink had arrived, she knocked back a full two thirds of it in one swallow."

"That son-of-a-bitch! That's why he was dumping me! Get a settlement signed off before I knew about any of this and I get no share!"

"Ashley, calm down, to my knowledge, there are only four people who might know about Arnie's supposed intention to divorce you. That's you, me, Ted and of course Arnie! My advice to you would be forget you ever heard from Arnie, don't complicate the issue needlessly."

"I don't understand."

"Look, if Arnie dies or is permanently and severely disabled, there would be no divorce, so why make any noise about it?"

"I see what you are saying, just be the caring wife is that it?"

"It's more than that Ashley, I am afraid that Arnie never did prepare or execute a will!"

"What! Everybody makes a will, even I have one, you mean Mr. Perfect Business Man didn't have a will?"

"It means that should Arnie die intestate, his estate distribution will be determined by the Probate Court!"

"But why won't it just come to me, after all I am his wife?"

"You are forgetting Arnie's older son Bradley and of course there is Ellis, his interests must be looked after as well."

"I can look after Ellis, as for Bradley, I have never even met him, his father pretty much disowned him after Arnie divorced his mother, why should he get anything?"

"Trust me, he has rights and I am sure the court will provide for him, however, the more difficult situation would occur if Arnie remains in a coma for an extended period of time!

It would be better to petition the court to appoint a trustee for Arnie's estate, that way we would have continuity at the company, particularly as we bring the new vaccine to market.

I think as well, we could avoid any messy situation when Arnie does die, by having an agreement in place, created by the interested parties, namely you and Brad."

Business was not her forte, but she was shrewd enough to understand at least some of the implications of the approach that Nelson had advanced. While she had wealth in her own right, having even more was attractive to her. She was also spiteful enough to take some delight in the fact that she was "screwing" Arnie and getting something he was prepared to deny her.

"And who do you propose would be the trustee?"

"Ashley, you know that I am Vice Chairman of the Executive Committee, I have been Arnie's best friend, I have been close to you and your family, I really do think I am best suited to do this. We do not want any strangers involved in our affairs, don't you agree?"

She smiled to herself, she had guessed as much, but there was no way that she would ever consent to his appointment, not after what he did to her.

"I'll think about it Jim, this is all very sudden, I need outside advice before I can make a decision, but what about Bradley?"

"Once I locate him on the west coast, I will meet with him and see what can be worked out, I haven't seen him since he was six, he was a nice kid then maybe he still is."

"How old is he now."

"Oh he must be 25 or 26."

"Tell me Ashley, how is Ellis getting along?"

Her body visibly sagged at the mention of her son's name, she didn't respond immediately, her eyes welled up and she struggled to regain her composure then said.

"There really has been no improvement, he doesn't respond when I talk to him, he never looks at me. He spends weekends with me you know, I struggle to keep things orderly, he hates change, and the tantrums are very hard to deal with, some times I think he hates me."

"An autistic child can be a challenge, it takes time and you must develop coping skills to survive."

"Thank you Doctor!" She said with more than a hint of sarcasm.

"I am sure that people consider me a horrible mother having my child locked up 5 days a week in that hell hole full of disturbed children."

"Hardly a hell hole, I researched that facility for you myself, the have a great reputation!"

*

Cyril entered the boardroom and watched silently as Peter Mytryk studied the x-rays he had placed on the back lit viewers, sensing a presence he turned and faced Pickard.

"I didn't hear you come in."

"I am sorry, I don't mean to disturb you, how are you making out, anything remotely conclusive?"

"Well, I concur with much of what you have told me of your own observations, I see no tumours, no evidence on internal bleeding but there is some abnormality in the brain traces."

"Is there anything that does strike you as unusual?"

"Well, I have come up with what might be considered a working hypothesis, let me see what you think. I have noted that the brain wave patterns in certain areas of the brain are completely normal whereas they are completely abnormal in other areas. In the areas of cognitive thinking and memory, they appear normal and in fact highly active.

Those areas of the brain responsible for voluntary movement are however seem to have had the nerve bundle impacted somehow, I believe your assessment of the damage to the myelin sheath is correct.

What is very curious to me is that the pattern that I observe of the normal functioning nerve bundles coincide almost exactly with the targeting we expect from the vaccine we have developed for Alzheimer's."

"So then, what is this working hypothesis?"

"I wonder if it may be possible that this could in fact be viral. That somehow the vaccine, even though it was developed for an entirely different virus, may be protecting the same brain areas that we detect being attacked by the Alzheimer's virus?"

"That's astounding! Mind you, the whole idea of a virus causing Alzheimer's boggles the mind, so I would think anything would be possible."

Mytryk sat in a chair opposite Pickard and said quietly "You realize, if this is true, we have a "double edged sword" here. We may be able to keep Arnie alive indefinitely by administering the booster shot every three months, but we have no way to repair the myelin sheath, so there would be no improvement to his condition."

"Hobson's Choice!" muttered Pickard.

Chapter 7

More darkness, am I awake, how the hell can I tell? What day was it? What time is it? Moreover, what the hell does all that matter?

The discussion with Eve regarding Bradley, it all seemed so real, but it is just as likely my mind is playing tricks. Sensory deprivation could do that, was there any truth to what Eve had said about the course of study Brad was following? Where had that come from? Was it even true?

What does he look like? Does he take after his mother or me? How tall is he? I try but I cannot visualize anything except the tear-stained face of a six-year old boy clutching at my coat as he left that last time.

Remorse! I was the one that was wronged, why should I suffer any guilt.

I was embarrassed at being cuckolded, not by a younger man, but by a woman! Those feelings of shame, anger, betrayal, what did my friends think?

I had to control the situation; I had to protect my reputation, my image. The solution lay in the divorce settlement, Eve was not to contest the divorce, agree to a reasonable settlement and in return, I would not seek custody of Bradley.

Eve, knew my vindictive streak, knew I would charge her with being an unfit mother, she knew I would probably win and she would lose the child, so she agreed, I never saw my son again.

However, what have I lost? I had successfully removed Brad completely from my mind, or had I? Now all these thoughts are flooding back. Brad and I could have been involved in the business; I would have someone to pass it on to, something that I could never do with little Ellis.

Just imagine! A son that would take Soper Research to even greater heights; Brad could have made my legacy even greater!

"But not with ethics, there is no money in that, it is just another nuisance that people like me have to put up with," he thought.

"Ethicists, environmentalists, nothing but "bird watchers" and "tree huggers" I put them into the same category; basically distractions sent annoy and deter me from my goals."

Yes, maybe there was some remorse. However, it was Eve's fault not mine. She was the one that deprived me of my relationship with my son.

A faint glimmer of light again, the same voice again, what does all of that matter now, nothing can be changed will this all be over soon?

"Are you awake Dr. Soper?"

"Alfred, your still here I thought you had left me."

"No, I have been here all along, did you enjoy your visit with your wife Eve?"

"You saw her? But you didn't answer me when I called."

"Yes, I saw her, a lovely woman, I just didn't want to intrude."

"Yes she was beautiful, but a bitch!"

"I see you dismissed her then just as you did 20 years ago."

"She betrayed me, I can't forgive her."

"Did she?"

"Of course she did, she took a lover, and a woman at that!"

"And you have no responsibility for any of that?"

"How could I?"

"You don't believe that your neglect of her could have made her vulnerable, you don't believe that you could have made her susceptible to the advances of a more mature, caring, interested person. Male or female?"

"I thought you were Adlerian not Freudian, no, I do not believe that!"

"You do not believe that denigrating her before your friends, her son, or ignoring her interests, belittling her skills and achievements, played any part in this episode?"

"Skills, achievements, interests! Don't make me laugh, she had none!"

"You didn't always think that way."

That was true. It was a happy almost idyllic two or 3 years of marriage, before Brad was born.

Thinking back to when things began to change, yes, that was it! It was after the baby was born, she changed, it wasn't I. I was the one that was neglected not her, she doted on the baby, not on me, I no longer had a place

"If when you were still practising psychiatry, you had a patient that had those feelings, I hardly think you would have agreed with that patient, would you?"

As soon as Alfred had made the comment, I knew how ludicrous my thoughts truly were, but I also know, that was how I felt at the time.

"So instead of dealing with these feelings of abandonment, you threw yourself into your work and attempted to ignore everything else."

"And it worked too! If I say so myself I think I have achieved success, money, power. I can have just about anything I want."

"Can you."

"Yes I can!"

"Then why are you here? If you can have anything you want, would you not want to be out of this experience?"

"I am not in control of this situation, you know that, I can't get out of this situation, I have some kind of illness."

"Then, I would ask you, if you can't control this situation, what good is your money, your achievements, and your power?"

There was no answer to the question, Why am I being tested in this manner?

Was that yet another voice? Who's there he wondered?

"Hello Arnold."

"Pop. Is that really you?"

I wasn't even thinking about him, in fact I hadn't thought about my father in many years. There were not many happy memories of my father that is likely, why I repressed any thoughts of him.

If there was one word that always surfaced when I did infrequently think of the man, that word was guilt!

Pop had died before I graduated from Medical School. I believed then and still do, that my father died as a direct result of working 60 to 70 hours a week to help pay my tuition, even when he was in failing health, he never missed a day.

Not until the day he died that is, just three weeks before the graduation exercises, secretly, I was relieved that he wouldn't be attending my graduation. I could take no pride in having an uneducated immigrant for my father; I wanted a different image.

I could see he was dressed as though he had just finished his shift in the tannery. I was positive I could smell the urine emanating from his clothes.

"Hello Arnold."

"Pop, what are doing here?"

"Why I came to see my son the Doctor, what else!"

"Good to see you Pop."

"I am so proud of you Arnold, a doctor now! And famous too! It was all worth it, how we scrimped and saved your Mama and me, but you made it!"

My mother, she had died two years before his father, which very nearly killed the old man.

The white apron, the smell of food in the kitchen of the old house on River Street. I can visualize the gray hair pulled back into a bun on the back of her head; the wire rimmed glasses perched on the end of her nose. I remember.

I remember as a small boy, lying in bed at night in the back bedroom on the third floor, listening to the lions roar at Riverdale Park, these were the good memories.

The bad memories were the beatings I got if my school marks were not high enough, the times I wasn't allowed to play road hockey with frozen horse turds because I had to study.

I remember being ostracized by kids I wanted be friends with because they considered me, too smart, today I would be considered geeky.

I also remember, when I went to the University, how I never dared to invite any classmate's home on weekends, my parents embarrassed me. Not that I was overly popular anyway, the study habits and scholastic expectations placed on me by my father, left little time for any kind of social activity.

"Tell me Arnold, do I have any grandchildren?"

"Yes, Pop, you have two grandsons, the eldest is Brad, he is a grown man now and little Ellis he is just 6."

"Tell me Arnold, what do they look like, do they look like me, you, or maybe Mama?"

"To be honest Pop, I haven't seen either of the boys in some time. Brad's mother and I divorced 20 years ago and he went to live with her, As for Ellis, he is not well, he is in a special care facility most of the time, so I don't see him either."

"What! What kind of a father have you turned out to be? Two wives! Two children you don't see! A sick little boy! Why have you not cured him, smart man!"

"Pop, things are different now, marriages fail, it just happens. As for Ellis, he has a disease I know almost nothing about!"

"Shit! You are a nothing, it was always the same, if I wasn't there to kick your ass, you were a nothing!"

With that, the old man receded into the darkness and disappeared from my vision.

Get a grip! My emotions are getting hard to control, I don't think I'm, weeping, but do I really care?

"Are you depressed?"

"Of course not, this was the brightest part of my day!"

"It is still important to you, what your father thinks of you that is."

'More than I thought."

"Why do you think that is?"

"Any child seeks the approval of his father, if it isn't there, it is a confirmation of rejection."

"That's true I suppose, but how does that apply to your children?"

"What is this Alfred, a little salt?"

"Not really, but do you think about that?"

"I haven't up till now, and now it would appear to be too late to do anything about that."

"So that's it? Too late, too bad."

"Fuck off Alfred."

"I hit a nerve did I? Let's change the subject, what about Ashley?"

"That Bitch!"

"Your vocabulary is somewhat limited when it comes to women, isn't it?"

"It is with her."

"She seems to be a lot of things that Eve wasn't don't you think? She's beautiful, intelligent and let's not forget, rich."

"Alfred, I think you are losing your detachment, is this becoming a personal attack?"

"Maybe your right, I have no right to be judgmental, just tell me about Ashley."

"When I first met Ashley, she seemed to be the epitome of everything I wanted in a wife, she was, is beautiful, witty, well educated and had all the social graces one might want in a wife. And it didn't hurt that she came from a very wealthy family, but that was not a motivation for me, believe it or not."

"Then what happened to your relationship."

"She insisted on having a family."

"That seems perfectly normal."

"Except that we had both agreed prior to getting married, there would be no children, I wanted nothing to get in the way of my work!"

"And what happened?"

"She went off the pill without telling me, got pregnant and she had Ellis!"

"Why didn't you insist on an abortion when you found out?"

There was an extended pause while Soper considered his response; he had not faced this issue in 6 years.

"I know it sounds odd perhaps, but on reflection, I could not bring myself to be party to bringing a human life to an end. Remember, you have already determined that I was once a Catholic, it is ingrained I suppose or maybe it was just my Hippocratic Oath."

"Would you have changed your position had you known that Ellis would be born Autistic?"

"No! In spite of your opinion of me, I love that little boy. I am devastated by the fact that I am unable to cure him, my father was right."

"What happened to your relationship after that?"

"It slowly crumbled, I was immersed in Soper Research business, Ashley almost put herself in a mental institution trying to cope with Ellis, then the drinking started."

"Did you try to help Ashley?"

"I got the information on the clinic to help Ellis."

"But what about Ashley?"

"I guess I am truly my father's son, I threatened her."

"Did you beat her, like your father did to you?"

"Almost, but I did something she considered worse."

"What was that?"

"I just simply ignored her."

"Did it work?"

"No, I don't suppose anything would she's a drunk and until she decides on her own, no one can help her."

"What else happened?"

"She is in the process of screwing herself through Toronto's high society!"

"So you decided that the answer was a divorce?"

"Yes, I have enough on her that she won't be able to contest it, the whole thing has the makings of a sordid scandal. She won't do that to her father or Ellis, she won't contest it when she knows what I have on her."

"Why right now?"

"I am on the threshold of a major new product that will revolutionize the treatment of Alzheimer's. The profits from this new vaccine will dwarf anything Soper Research has ever created. It will be far greater than the total of everything we marketed to date.

The profits will be enormous, if I wait it could make the settlement much, much greater and I do not see where she deserves any share.

She is wealthy in her own right and I will make a reasonable settlement on her."

"And what about Ellis."

"He will continue to receive the very best treatment obtainable anywhere."

"That's not what I meant, was his relationship to be discarded along with Ashley's?"

Darkness, it seemed now there is comfort in the darkness, anxiety is rising again, need more medication. What the hell are they doing out there? Will I never escape this situation? Must have been this bad in Viet Nam, is Alfred trying to brainwash me or resurrect me?

Chapter 8

Jim Nelson answered his cell phone while driving westward, towards Soper Research on the Queen Elizabeth Way, not a particularly prudent thing to be doing. It was Declan Mahoney.

"Hello Jim, Declan here. How are you?"

"I am OK, all things considered, have you got anything for me?"

"I have located Bradley Soper, he is on a doctoral fellowship at the University of British Columbia."

"How can I reach him, do you have a phone number where I can reach him?"

"I do, but Jim if you are considering going to see him, I would strongly recommend that you do not!"

"Why would you say that?"

"Look Jim, I have some understanding of what you are trying to do and I certainly don't disagree with you. However, since no one including you, has seen him in more than 10 years, it would be better if we had someone profile him before you talk to him. In that way, you will have a chance to set your strategy before you meet."

"I have to admit, you make sense, as usual Declan. Do you have anyone in mind?"

"I have a bright young associate, about the same age, who would be perfect for the job!"

"OK, do it. I am sure I don't have to repeat the urgency on this, we are unsure how Arnie's situation may end up."

*

Bradley Soper was sprawled out on his sofa, reading a treatise on the ethics of dying, while he sipped appreciatively on Kokanee Gold.

He was a tall slim young man; in fact, he had considered basketball as a career, for at least a week, before he decided on applying for the Fellowship.

He had graduated with a Masters Degree in Sociology, took a year off to back pack around Europe and had somehow developed an interest in the emerging field of medical ethics.

The small apartment was sparsely furnished but it met his needs, besides, it seemed he spent more time at the University than he did at home anyway. He had rented the place because of the harbour, he enjoyed watching the small pleasure boats from the marina heading out or coming back from one of the islands.

His beer was empty, he decided to empty his bladder before enjoying another. He looked at himself in the bathroom mirror, straightening the blonde hair that seemed to insist on winding itself into tight curls, it did no good, the hair had a mind of its own it seemed.

As he moved back into the living room, the intercom system buzzed, he pressed the button. "Yes who is it?"

"Are you Mr. Soper, Mr. Bradley Soper?"

It was a woman's voice, but he did not recognize it.

"Yes it is, how can I help you?"

"My name is Janet Petersen, I am with a firm called Mahoney Associates, and I would very much like to talk to you."

"Look Ms. Petersen, I don't have any time for sales people, I am extremely busy I'm afraid..."

"I am not a sales person Mr. Soper! Moreover, I am a busy person too. I have come all the way from Toronto to see you regarding an urgent family matter."

"Ms. Petersen, I have no family in Toronto, are you sure you have the right party?"

"Your father is Dr. Arnold Soper is he not?"

He did not answer immediately.

"Mr. Soper, are you there?"

"Yes, yes, I am here."

"Mr. Soper, it is extremely important that we talk, may I come up?"

Without responding, he buzzed her in, what was this all about. He had not even thought about his father in years, his only knowledge he had of this man was what he read about him in the newspapers. He knew of course that this was not entirely true. However, he had trouble escaping the Soper name. He had even contemplated changing, but had to admit to himself that the name was a factor in being accepted for the Fellowship.

He could recollect little of his father. He knew he hated him because of how he and his mother had been treated by him. Right now, he had a problem trying to remember what he even looked like.

There was knock at the door.

He opened it to see this perky auburn haired woman, about his own age standing in the doorway. He was immediately taken with her wide blue eyes and when she smiled at him, she was radiant. He wasn't a stranger to the opposite sex, but he had never been in the company of any woman as attractive as this.

She was dressed in a navy blue business suit, obviously expensive, well fitted to a dynamite figure. She carried an alligator briefcase in her left hand.

"You might close your mouth, and invite me in!"

"Sorry, of course, please come in."

They sat in the small living room; he hurriedly picked the text he had been working on, offered the only chair while he sat on the sofa.

"Nice place, but I must admit I was expecting something a little more lavish."

Outspoken, not sure I like that, she looks great, but what does she want from me?

"What made you think that?"

"Well, you are a Soper!"

"I am not the one with the money."

He saw her eyebrow arch, but the smile returned to her face and he was unable to do anything but return the smile.

She liked what she saw, this lanky good looking, somewhat bookish guy. She could detect the athlete's body beneath the rumpled clothes and liked the way he moved about.

Without being obvious, she tried to determine his eye colour, she settled on gray, yes they were gray.

He broke the silence. "What is it you want Ms. Petersen?"

"Please call me Jan, may I call you Brad?"

"Of course, but please tell me why you're here."

She began by informing him of Arnold Soper's current condition, what his prognosis appeared to be and the fact that he was currently on life support. She was quite thorough in her recitation of all the facts she had been given; of course, she knew nothing of the Alzheimer's vaccine or the fact that Soper had injected himself with the vaccine.

Brad cupped his chin in his hands and seemed to be watching through the picture window, as the sailboats passed in the harbour, after several minutes he gazed at her.

"What does all this matter to me and why is it of interest to you?"

"Brad, my firm is on retainer to Soper Research, we handle most of the Public Relations issues for the company. It was felt that it would be better if you got this information directly, face to face so to speak and not through the media."

"There hasn't even been a whisper of any of this in the media, surely someone would consider this to be big news?"

"Well that is part of what we are hired for, to manage this kind of information, to protect the company and those involved when adversity strikes."

"I go back to what I said, what makes you think any of this is important to me?"

"Well, he is your father and. should he die, you stand to inherit a sizable fortune!"

"Look, as far as I'm concerned, my father ceased to exist when he dumped my mother and me when I was 6 years old, as for money, I don't have the same preoccupation with it as does my father!"

"Idealism! Nobody ever tell you that that is "old hat," everybody scrambles for the almighty dollar, but you are telling me you are different?"

"Believe it!"

She shifted gears immediately, with a toss of her pretty head she said.

"Hey, you wouldn't happen to have a cold beer would you?"

He was caught completely off guard; he couldn't help but smile in response to the cheeky request.

"Sorry Jan, I drank the last one and I don't have anything else in the place."

"Well then, surely there is a pub close by, how about buying a girl a drink?"

"Yes there is, but I think you are a little overdressed for it!"

"Let me worry about that, come on, are you game?"

"How can I resist such charming company."

As they were leaving, she linked her arm in his. "We'll take my car, then I know I will get back to my hotel."

"We'll have to, I don't own a car!"

She shook her head in disbelief, how could anyone exist in this day and age without a set of wheels!

They entered the Lion's Head. A quasi-British Style pub that proliferates the lower mainland. It was dark inside but she liked the comfortable smell of leather and was thankful that there was no odour of stale beer or urine.

They sat in a booth near the back, out of the traffic and away from the washrooms, their waiter approached and Brad could see him ogling Janet.

"Well hello Dr. Brad, what'll it be tonight?" He was almost leering at Janet.

"Brings us couple of Kokanee Gold's Mickey, and put your eyeballs back in!"

"Right you are, you don't blame me do you!" he said, winking shamelessly at Jan.

"What the hell is a Kokanee?"

"Oh yes, I forgot, you're from Toronto! It's OK you'll like it its a local beer."

"If you say so."

The beer arrived and Janet waved away the glass Mickey had brought for her, she joined Brad sipping it directly from the bottle. She seemed more than a little incongruous, this stunning girl, dressed in a $500 suit, swilling beer from a bottle, in a pub!

"So, why don't you tell me what this Fellowship is all about, But I gotta tell you, you seem a little old to be in school still, what are you, a slow learner?"

"Are you always this irritating?"

"You should see me on a bad day! Seriously, tell me about this Fellowship thing"

"Well if you are really interested... Its a Doctoral Fellowship in Health Ethics, I am just about finished, only my thesis left, I say that like there is nothing to a thesis, but I think it is the biggest part."

"So what do you end up doing with this Doctorate?"

"It qualifies me to be a medical ethicist."

"A what?"

"A medical ethicist, of course you know what that entails don't you?"

She tipped the bottle back and took a good swallow, "What you think I am uneducated, of course I do, but why don't you tell me your version anyway."

"Well I hope to become an ethicist in a major hospital or health care region, consulting on ethical issues relating to "end of life," new care techniques, heroic drug therapies and treatments, that sort of thing."

"How does that work exactly?"

"A number of ways really, I could be asked to render an opinion on withdrawal of life support systems where there is really no hope of recovery. On the other hand, I could speak out on controversial issues like cloning, T cell harvesting from fetuses, genetic manipulation, you know, all those sorts of things. More or less a patient advocate"

"What would ever motivate you to undertake that kind of thing, it sounds like a thankless task and it probably doesn't pay very well either?"

"Well, Ms. Petersen, I know this may come as a surprise to you, but not everyone is motivated by money, some would like to make a difference to society."

"Very lofty Mr. Soper! But are you sure that your motivation is not to prove that you are really a better person than everybody else, that you are sitting in judgment of others in order to prove your superiority?"

"Why is it I get the feeling that you are trying to bait me, or is it just that you like to argue?"

"No, not really." She said as a smile played on her lips. "Perhaps I am just a little jaded, I didn't think people like you existed, and I'm still not positive they do."

They finished their beer and Brad asked her if she would like another. "Sure but I think I'll have Heineken instead, your kokee whatever isn't really my kind of beer."

"Big City girl, I should have known better, imported beer tastes better and of course it's more expensive too."

"I'll pay!"

"I was only kidding, don't get sensitive, after all you have been poking at me ever since we got here."

"Now where were we, oh yes, you were saving the world from bad medicine!"

"Yeah that's me, do you think I'll need a cape?"

They both laughed, he swore the room got brighter when she did so, her giggle was infectious.

"Let me be serious for a moment. Doesn't the opportunity to run a company like Soper, give you a greater platform regarding medical ethics?

"I have never given that any thought, but what makes you think that that my be a possibility?"

"Your father has absolute share control, you are his son ergo, why wouldn't you be able to?"

"I have no reason to believe, that after all these years, that I would be in line to inherit anything. Frankly, as I have said, I don't want his money!"

"Look Brad, I am not supposed to tell you this, but your father, if he dies, will die intestate, you know what that means?"

"You mean he has no will? This business genius will die with no will?"

"Yes."

They both paused for another drink, Brad digested this news carefully, as though he was weighing his next statement."

"But he has a wife doesn't he, I seem to remember that, what happens with her interest in the company."

"None of that has been decided yet, not for either of you, it will likely be up to the courts, you need to consider that this company could end up in the hands of some multi-national. You father's wife has no experience in dealing at this level, she could be manipulated."

"I have no experience either, I have some esoteric opinions on ethical matters, but from a practical business standpoint, I am not sure I could cope either."

"So you are prepared to let this opportunity pass you by, by default, you won't even try?"

"I didn't say that, let me think about it." He then changed the subject abruptly, "How do you fit in all of this, you know an awful lot about me, but I know nothing about you?"

She picked up her beer and leaned back in the booth. "Well, by trade I am a lawyer."

"Oh poor thing, how did that happen?"

She laughed again and punched him in the shoulder. "I get no respect, anyway, I got bored with incorporation and litigation, then I was approached about this job. I have always been a business "junkie," and this gave me the opportunity of rubbing shoulders with the corporate elite. In the two years with Mahoney I have learned a great deal."

"So what is it exactly you think I should do?"

"Come to Toronto, meet with the stakeholders, work something out. You need to look after your own interests and perhaps the company's as well."

"But I hate Toronto!"

"Doesn't everybody out here? But there are two other good reasons come."

"Oh and what are they!"

"Well" she said, smiling slyly, "For one thing I live there."

She let that statement hang there for effect and then continued.

"And of course, you could meet your brother!"

"Meet my what?"

Chapter 9

Nelson returned to the hospital to meet with Cyril Pickard and review the progress, if any of his meetings with Peter Mytryk.

Pickard's secretary showed him into the same conference room that had been use by Mytryk in his review; Pickard was staring at the illuminated transparencies, seemingly unaware of Nelson's presence.

"Hello Cyril"

"Oh hello Jim, I didn't hear you come in, come sit down."

"What was Mytryk able to determine?"

"Well, he has a working hypothesis this is most interesting, he concurs with my initial evaluation regarding the destruction of the myelin sheath. Neither one of us is sure however, that this is a virus. But one thing he did determine is that the pattern of the unaffected brain area is similar to what he has seen in the tests he has conducted on Alzheimer's patients."

"I am not sure what you are getting at."

"What he says is, the Alzheimer's patients are affected in the same areas in which Arnie's brain remains unaffected. It's as though the vaccine he self-administered was protecting the nerves the same as it does for these other patients. If Arnie is suffering from a viral infection it may be a mutated variant of the same virus or some kind of close relation."

"That's a bit ironic, don't you think."

"No doubt, but it is an interesting supposition, but I did say we do not have conclusive evidence of this being a viral infection, it officially remains an undiagnosed condition. But that is not all bad, at least I am not required to report this to the Chief Medical Officer for the City."

"That's a relief, we need more time to deal with this situation!"

"Given that it has been over a week and we have not seen or heard of any other cases. In any event we are unsure of the method of transmission, if in fact it is a virus, I don't think there is much public risk."

"Just sit on it Cyril, you know how important this is!"

"Of course."

"So I take it there is no change in his condition?"

"Not really, we are seeing substantial brain activity in the unaffected areas, but he remains on life support, and in isolation. He has special nursing provided by your company and we have kept all other hospital personnel as far away from him as is reasonable."

"Good Cyril, I appreciate what you are doing, I won't forget it!"

"One other thing, Mytryk reminded me, that if he is right regarding the effects of the vaccine, we have to give him a booster shot every three months to maintain his condition."

"I guess that's right!"

As Nelson entered the hospital parkade he called Declan Mahoney on his cell phone, upon telling the operator who was calling he was connected immediately.

"Hello Jim, how are you?"

"Have you got anything for me on Bradley Soper?"

"Yes I have Jim."

"Good, I'll be right there."

It took him twenty minutes and when he arrived, the receptionist escorted him into Mahoney's office. It was on the 30th floor of the office tower, with a commanding view of Lake Ontario.

The office was efficient, well laid out, with surprisingly comfortable modern furniture, a full bar, stainless steel fridge and of course the requisite computer station along with several video monitors tuned various all news channels, fortunately the sound was muted.

Mahoney arose from a large leather swivel chair behind an oversized rosewood desk, all intended to impress, he extended his hand.

"Good to see you again Jim, take a seat."

"OK Declan, let's hear it."

"Jim, I think it would be best if I give you a verbal report, I have an aversion to committing anything much to paper, it tends to come back and haunt you." The smile that followed the comment was cold and insincere.

"Bradley Soper, as you already know I believe, is just finishing a Doctoral Fellowship in Medical Ethics at UBC, he is 26 years old, lives alone and appears to have no attachments."

"Attachments?"

"You know girl friends, wife that sort of thing, he lives alone in a modest apartment, has no car or much interest in material possessions. My operative indicates that he is an idealist. He has no great affection or interest in his father or his present condition.

He seems to be disinterested in Soper Research Inc., and the potential value this may represent to him, at least so he says."

"What is he living on? Sounds like he must be pretty frugally."

"You may be surprised to learn that his father established a trust fund for him as part of his divorce settlement and of course he had an inheritance from his mother, Eve I think it is, when she died. So in fact he is reasonably well off for a young man. Chances are, that he isn't even spending the interest on his trust, although the annual tuition for his studies is in excess of $20,000 annually."

"We have checked for any close friends, there seems to be few, but those he has seem to indicate that he is a solid citizen who is what he seems to be. We have also determined him to be heterosexual, no police record, save for one arrest for an environmental sit-in."

"An environmental sit-in?"

"Yes, he was arrested as a "tree-hugger" at Clayoquot Sound, it appears when he found out that some of the protesters were "spiking" the trees, he disassociated himself from the group."

"What do you mean, "spiking?""

"It's a practice that some protesters use to try to prevent loggers from cutting down trees. They drive large spikes into the tree trunk, when the unsuspecting logger uses his chain saw to cut it down, the saw engages the spikes, sometimes with disastrous results to the worker."

"You said he was almost finished his degree, how close is he?"

"Only his thesis and dissertation remain."

"What you are telling me then, is that we have an idealist, with no vices, who doesn't need any money or at least any more than he has. This does not sound promising, I don't see any way to get to him, to get him on side with what we are trying to do."

"No vices that we are aware of, but it's really worse than that, this appears to be an ethical man, a most dangerous kind."

"Do you have any suggestions Declan? We need Ashley and Bradley to concur with how Arnie's shares get voted in order to secure Soper research's future."

"While I am not prepared to share my ideas with you at present Jim, rest assured that I am working on a scenario that could end up giving you just what you need."

"When will I know?"

"Soon Jim, quite soon."

*

It was Friday afternoon and Ashley arrived at the entrance to Halton House, the private clinic where Ellis received treatment and lived for 5 days a week.

She parked her car on the circular gravel driveway and made her way to the front door of what had once been a fine country manor house. It had been converted into this clinic for treating autistic children.

The grounds are beautiful she thought, great old trees, well-manicured lawns, the shrubs were clipped into fantasy figures, everything seemed serene and in order.

However, the front door was always locked, she lifted the ornate door knocker and wrapped for admittance. Mrs. Fulton answered the door almost immediately. She and her husband Dr. Neil Fulton ran the clinic with the aid of several therapists and two nurses.

"Mrs. Soper, how nice to see you again, right on time as usual, please come in."

She nodded to the woman and walked inside, the foyer was retained in its original Victorian grandeur, "It must cost a fortune to keep this place up," she thought. "Stupid, of course it does, and I help pay for it!"

"Ellis is in the play room, do you want me to bring him out to you?"

"No, No, I'll go in and get him."

The playroom had once been the formal sitting room, it was just to the left of the foyer, there were six children in the room and three or four sat together playing with a variety of toys. One little girl sat clutching a doll and rocking continually back and forth; Ellis sat alone, away from the group.

He was a beautiful child, blonde curly hair, he had her features and skin, his eyes, big and blue, and staring. He didn't acknowledge she was there, even when she called his name, he just kept staring.

Mrs. Fulton came in and stood beside her, "It hasn't been an easy week Mrs. Soper. He seems more withdrawn; he had two full blown tantrums. We thought we might have to restrain him so he wouldn't hurt himself, but Dr. Fulton was able to bring him a round. I think he misses you."

"Oh if I could only believe that to be true." She thought.

She bent down beside him, taking his face in her hands and looked into his eye, those vacant eyes, absent of any liveliness, she kissed him, still no acknowledgment that she was even there.

There did not seem to be any improvement in Ellis' condition, even after 8 months in this clinic. She felt despair rising within her. She forced herself not to weep and pulled the boy up to standing position, "Come on Ellis let's go home."

She drove back into the city, Ellis sat in the front seat next to her, silently staring at the road, she could not hold back the tears, and she wept silently most of the way to the condo.

Even though she and Arnie were seldom in the apartment at the same time, she could not help but feel the emptiness of the place knowing that in all likelihood, he would never be back. She flicked on the lights; took Ellis by the hand, she had decided to surprise him by moving him to a new room that she had had redecorated. The room had been painted in soothing colours with pictures of storybook characters on each of the walls and a new bed that looked just like a racer.

When they entered the room and she turned on the light, Ellis stopped and looked all she had done and began to scream. He stamped his feet, and banged his ears with his hands and suddenly threw himself on the floor, kicking his feet and hitting his head.

She was stunned, she grabbed him and tried to make him stop. She shook him but nothing calmed him, in fact the more she tried the more violent he became, she was at her wits end. The only thing she could think of was to drag him into the living room, she sat down on the floor next to him and tried to hold him, he fought her, hitting her in the face.

Impulsively, she struck back, hitting him, hard across the face, she regretted it the moment that she did it, but it was too late. He went limp in her arms, she thought she might have killed him, but no, he was still breathing, what should she do?

She called 911, she could think of nothing else to do. She was almost hysterical when she was talking to the operator. Finally, she was coherent enough to give the woman on the other end of the phone the facts of what had happened, and her address.

It seemed like a lifetime as she waited, watching his still form on the living room floor, when the paramedics arrived she tried to regain her composure and give a rational explanation of the situation, including Ellis' autism.

The young medic checked the vital signs and lifted each eyelid checking the pupils with his penlight; the breathing and pulse seemed normal.

"The tantrum may have triggered a seizure. If we get him over on his side and watch him carefully, he should come out of it, he's breathing OK"

"A seizure?"

"As you may be aware Ma'am, autistic persons can be subject to seizures, not unlike some one with epilepsy. It just so happens that I have an older sister who is autistic. Tell me, is he on any kind of medication?"

"Yes, naltrexone."

"Do you have a supply on hand?"

"Yes I do."

"Well, we'll wait until he comes around and check him out to make sure he's all right, then I think you should give him some naltrexone, that should help with the tantrums. Tell me, has he been subjected to any kind of sudden change in his surroundings lately?"

"Why do you ask?"

"Well Ma'am that's a kind of trigger, they take comfort in sameness, a sudden change is threatening to them."

"Oh shit! Of course, that's it, how stupid of me, it's his new room. I moved him and had it all redecorated for him, I thought it would make him happy, what a fool!"

"Ma'am, don't beat yourself up, nobody knows how hard it is to deal with if you haven't been there."

"Thank you, you've been a great help, I feel lucky that you were the one to respond, how many of you have experience with autism?"

"Not too many I guess, look he's comin' around."

She held him close "Oh Ellis, I am so sorry, so sorry."

She barely noticed when the paramedics were preparing to leave, "Don't forget the medication."

"I won't and thank you, you were great."

She rocked him in her arms singing softly to him, thinking to herself, "Why me, why do I have to deal with all this, first Ellis and now Arnie, I don't deserve this!"

She went to the kitchen to get his medication, she opened the cupboard, the bottle of rye was in front of the pills, and she reached for the rye.

*

The telephone rang in Brad Soper's apartment; it took him several rings before he reached it.

"So, are you coming?"

"Who is this?"

"Who do you think it is you big dork?"

"Janet is that you?" smiling to himself, he was going to call her, but he was glad she phoned first.

"Of course it's me, did you think it was one of your many girlfriends?"

"Listen, I get so many calls from women that I was thinking of having my phone taken out!"

"Yeah, Yeah, your sex life is stellar I'm sure."

"What do you know of my sex life?"

"Nothing yet, but are you coming down?"

"That sounds like a come on."

"You should be so lucky, answer me! Are you coming or not?"

"I'm thinking about it, I did get a delay in my submission date for my thesis."

"Well what are you waiting for then? Get your round little ass down here!"

"You talk so nice, how could I resist, but I got to be honest with you, as pretty as you are, I probably wouldn't come if it weren't for meeting my little brother."

"You sure know how to make a girl feel good, you jerk!"

"A dork, a jerk, are you really sure you even want to see me?"

"Piss off, of course I do, if you want, I'll even try to set up a meeting for you and your little brother, how's that."

"That would be great, on that basis how can I refuse?"

"So, you're coming?"

"Yes, I bought my ticket yesterday, I'll be in next Wednesday!"

He thought he could hear the excitement in her voice, "You put me through all that, when you were coming anyway! You're not just a dork or a jerk you're an ass__."

"Don't say it, or I'll cancel my ticket!"

"OK, OK, tell your flight number and arrival time and I'll pick you up."

She made a note of the details and hung up the phone. She made another call, "Hello, Declan, he's coming, next Wednesday, yes I am picking him up at the airport.

Chapter 10

"Dr. Soper, are you awake?"

"Yes. I think I'm a awake."

"How are you feeling?"

"Physically, I feel nothing, nothing at all."

"What about mentally, what are you thinking about?"

"Lots of things."

"Would you like to share them?"

"What's the point, talking about them won't change anything, how long have I been here?"

"I am afraid I can't help you with that, I don't know."

"Tell me what you are feeling, at this moment."

"Depressed, I am depressed, can you think of any reason I wouldn't be?"

"Is that all?"

"No, I am angry, as angry as hell! Here I am in the prime of my life, with everything to live for and here I am, like a vegetable, lying here."

"Tell me why are you angry?"

"That's a stupid question! What did I do to deserve to be placed in this situation, why me! Why me!"

"You still think this is some form of punishment for things you either did or did not do in the past, is that it?"

"Are you telling me this is just fate, that I am just unlucky and that's why this has happened?"

"It's not what I think that is important, it's what you think, do you suppose that every accident victim "had it coming to him"? Is that your view? On the other hand, do you really believe that your situation is a part of some master plan, something that you do not understand? And that something or things you have done in the past have triggered your illness?"

"No of course not!"

"Then tell me what other reason there might be for you're being here, in this state?'

"I suppose that you are going to tell me that this is a kind of test, something that will show, by my actions and thoughts that I deserve to move on to some form of higher consciousness. Is that it?"

"Is that what you think?"

"Alfred, you can be very annoying!"

"I suppose that is true, would you prefer me to leave you... alone."

"Is that a pout that I hear Alfred, dear me I didn't mean to hurt your feelings!"

"Sarcasm has never done you much good has it Dr. Soper?"

"Look, Alfred, perhaps I am feeling sorry for myself, I feel I have reason for that. I do not believe that I have been an evil person, ambitious, yes, but not really evil. One can look throughout history and see true evil, some go through life oblivious to the turmoil they cause and yet live life to ripe old age and go unpunished to their graves."

"How do you know that?"

"What?"

"How do you know they go unpunished to their graves? It seems to me that that is an assumption on your part, since you have no way of knowing. Just consider, if your premise is true, that if your condition is a punishment, who else would know? Might not everybody think you went to your grave unpunished?"

"Are you saying I am going to die?"

"I don't know that Dr. Soper."

"At any rate, I am not an evil person!"

"As you know, my namesake had much to say about evil, he once said "The striving for personal power is a disastrous delusion and poisons man's living together. Whoever desires the human community must renounce the striving for power over others." So you see evil can be subtle, another psychologist has said that "Evil is simply the absence of empathy.""

"So, my sin is one of ambition, wanting power over others, is that it?"

"Would you deny that you have a lack of empathy?"

"Empathy! Sympathy! Words of weak people, without a single-minded focus on my goals, I would never have achieved what I have done. And the world would have been worse off had I evidenced such weakness, Many cures would have gone undiscovered, hundreds of people would likely have died, how can that be evil?"

"You deny empathy for others yet it seems to me you seek it for yourself."

"What do you mean?"

"You lay here and complain about your illness, sounds to me like you expect me to empathize with you, is that not so?"

"I said, I was feeling sorry for myself didn't I? I don't care if you empathize or not!"

"I didn't say I was not empathetic towards you, I was just..."

"Just shut up! Alfred, I get the message, there is no one who gives a shit about me, come to think about it, I doubt that anybody really ever has."

"I know of two who care about you."

"And just who might they be?"

"Your mother...and me."

"Well Alfred, my mother is long since dead and you are nothing but a figment of my imagination, so forgive me if I am not spiritually lifted by your statement of caring."

"But surely, you don't deny your mother,"

"No, but that was so long ago, now she had empathy! I could do no wrong in her eyes, she forgave me every bad thing or slight I may have done to her."

"Why don't you call her up, you can you know."

Oh God! It's her, she's coming towards my bed, what will I say?

"Hello Arnie, it's so good to see you, even like this."

She's touching my face, her hands are so soft and reassuring, her eyes were moist as though she had been crying, but she smiled down at me and she was radiant.

"Ma, you look good, I am so glad to see you, I've missed you very much. I have been thinking of you very often lately, thinking about the wonderful smells from the kitchen, my favourite oatmeal cookies."

"With the coconut."

"Yes, Yes, what I wouldn't give for some right now." Nostalgia is overwhelming, I feel as though I might cry, but nothing came.

"I understand I have two Grandsons now, Oh what I wouldn't give to see them, tell me Arnie. What are they like, what are there names, how old are they?"

"Well Ma, it's like two families, Brad, the eldest is 26, he is getting his doctorate in British Columbia, Ellis is only 6, he lives with his mother in Toronto."

"But Arnie, tell me who do they look like, I am sure they are beautiful boys, what sports do they play, does Bradley have a girl?"

"To be honest Ma, I don't see much of either of them, I am so busy and Bradley lives far away and little Ellis is not well."

"Not well, what do you mean, what's wrong with him."

"He is autistic, he has trouble communicating, it's a genetic thing."

"I am disappointed in you Arnie, how can you ignore family and particularly one who is not well?"

"Ma, as I lay here, I regret more and more the things that I have neglected in the past. It pains me to think that will not have the opportunity to make it up to them in the future, for I am not sure I have a future."

"Arnie, whether you have any future is not as important as making peace within yourself for all those things that you may have done that have caused hurt and anguish to others.

Do not leave this world burdened by such guilt."

"Ma, you don't understand, everything I did, I did for my business, aren't you proud of my success, Ma? I could buy you anything you want now! Money is no object. Just tell me you are proud of me!"

"Arnie, I have always been proud of you, proud of your schoolwork, proud of you becoming a doctor, but to let money be put ahead of your family, no Arnie, that I can never be proud of."

"But Ma, you don't understand."

"Arnie, it's you who doesn't understand, how do you put a value on all those things you have never experienced, time spent with your sons, watching them grow, experiencing their successes, not just your own, what's that worth Arnie?"

I could not answer and as I looked at my mother I could see her begin to recede, the light illuminating her began to dim,

"Don't go Ma!"

"I have to Arnie. I love you son." And she was gone.

"Nice lady."

"Yeah, she is or was, now I am more depressed than ever, I would like all this to be over."

"What do you mean Dr. Soper?'

"You know what I mean, can being dead be any worse than this state of limbo? At least then everything stops,"

"Does it?"

"Don't tease me Alfred, let me ask you a question, does life continue after death?"

*

A light rain was falling at Pearson International Airport; the Air Canada Airbus from Vancouver had just landed and was taxiing to a Jet Ramp.

Janet was waiting outside the arrival area of Terminal 2, she was a little early, but she was concerned about the rain slick 401 Highway coming into the Airport. She gave her head a little shake dislodging tiny rain droplets from her new short curly hair-do, she wondered of he would like it.

She had been thinking about him quite a lot since arriving back in Toronto, in fact, her heart was racing just a little, childish, she thought, just like a silly schoolgirl.

She caught a quick glimpse of him through the sliding doors as a fellow passenger came through.

Just as I remembered him, I wonder if this might lead anywhere. Not if Declan has anything to say about it! If only he didn't have such control over me! My fault should never have done it, too late.

When he finally exited the baggage area, he spotted her, gave a quick wave, hoisted his duffel bag over his shoulder and headed in her direction.

She had decided to "play it cool" and not rush up anticipating a big hug and kiss, instead, she held out her hand," Brad it's good to see you again."

If he was surprised at the greeting, he didn't show it, "Hello Janet, I like your hair."

She was pleased that he noticed, after shaking his hand she slid hers easily around his arm as they turned to exit the Arrivals area, arm in arm.

"My car is just over there, in the short term lot." She pointed to the silver gray Mercedes C320 sports coupe.

He let out a low whistle, "Nice Car!"

"It's just one of the perks, it goes with the job."

He eased his frame into the passenger seat after stowing his bag in the trunk, "Where are we going?"

She put the car in gear and pulled away from the parking stall with a squeal of rubber. "My boss wants to meet you and so does Dr. Jim Nelson, he's the Vice Chairman of the Executive Committee of Soper Research, they are both waiting at my office."

"Do you have any idea why they want to see me?"

"Well, you are a member of Arnold Soper's family, like it or not, and you know that he is incapacitated to say the least. By the way, why haven't you asked about him?"

"To tell the truth, I haven't thought about my father in so long, it's like he doesn't really exist, its not that I don't care, but really it would be like inquiring into status of a stranger. But to please you, how is he doing?"

She ignored his last comment. "There is no change, at least as far as I know, he is still in a coma and unresponsive. They have put him in isolated intensive care, really as a precaution, because they are unsure of what has caused his illness. It also has the side benefit of isolating him from any media hype."

"Why would the media be interested in my father?"

"I think the answer to that will be made clear when you meet with Declan and Jim Nelson."

"Declan?"

"Yes, my boss, remember?"

She changed the subject and asked, "So how was the trip?"

"What's this now? Small talk? Tell me something about my brother! When you left Vancouver, you left me hanging in limbo with your comment of my having a brother."

"So you didn't come just to see me?"

"Well that too. However, come on tell me about him. You have no idea how it feels to find out that you still have some family somewhere. For years, I have been under the impression that aside from my father, I had no one else. Jan, this is important to me!"

"OK, OK. Your little brother is named Ellis, he is 6 years old, and I am told he is a good-looking little boy. He must take after his mother. I understand that she is still a looker"

"What grade would he be in?"

"Brad, I am sorry, but you need to know this, apparently Ellis is autistic, he isn't in school, he's in a clinic through the week and spends weekends with his mother."

He was quiet for some time before he spoke again.

"Tell me Janet, how do you know all this?"

"I made a point of finding out, remember that is part of my job, but I figured this would be important for you to know."

She could see that he was lost in thought. She did nothing to disturb what ever was going on in his head. They continued to ride on in silence.

Ellis, autistic! How can that be? I've just found him and now this! It isn't fair!

Finally, he turned to her "And what about my father? Does he not have any involvement with Ellis?"

"Brad, I don't know that, but I am sure that you will meet with your, I mean Ellis' mother while you are here and she can fill you in more completely than I ever could."

"We're here," she said as they descended the parking ramp off King Street, one of the many office towers. She pulled into her parking spot, "You may as well leave your bag here, I'll likely be taking you to your hotel after the meeting."

"Where am I staying, I didn't think to make a reservation?"

"Kind of thought you might stay with me huh? No such luck my friend, the company has a suite at the Hamden Suites in the Research Park, they've put you in there."

"Sooner stay with you!"

"I bet you would." She said with a mischievous grin, she punched the 23rd floor on the elevator panel.

It was after 8:00 PM, the doors were locked, Janet entered her pass code, and the door lock buzzed and she pushed the heavy plate glass door open.

Brad couldn't help but notice the 3 security video cameras placed strategically around the lobby, their red LED's glowing in the half light of the area.

The front door had barely closed behind them, when a square figure of a man appeared from a hallway that ran off from the left side the receptionist's desk. He was broad shouldered, dress impeccably in a navy blue suit, highly polished wing tip shoes, and Brad could not help noticing the large sapphire ring on the pinkie finger of his right hand as he extended it.

"Bradley Soper? I'm Declan Mahoney, won't you come in to my office, it is a pleasure to meet you."

As Brad shook hands, he looked into the broad face and at once was fascinated at the teeth that smiled back at him. They were so regular that he thought they might not be real. The jaw muscles that he saw through the smile gave him the impression that the teeth could be lethal in any close combat.

The big hand that encircled his seemed as though it could exert crushing force should the owner ever want to do so.

The man meant to intimidate thought Brad, and he was doing a bloody good job of it too.

"Janet, that will be all for tonight, we'll look after young Mr. Soper tonight, leave his bag with the parking attendant will you? Thank you Jan."

Brad could tell that Janet was "pissed," but she wasn't going to show it.

They entered Mahoney's office, all the TV monitors were on but muted, the sunset over Lake Ontario was magnificent. The tall silver haired figure sitting in front of Mahoney's desk rose to greet him.

"Brad, it's good to see you again, I am sure you don't remember me, but I'm Jim Nelson, you know, Uncle Jim you used to call me."

Brad shook hands with the man, trying to recall ever having seen him before, there were some vague memories, but these would be boyhood memories and people change.

"Nice to meet you both. But frankly, I would like to know why I am here?"

"Well, Brad, you know about your father's situation."

"No, not that, I mean this meeting, why am I here?"

Mahoney gestured the young man to a chair, still smiling, those perfect teeth on display, "A man after my own heart! Direct and to the point, very good don't you think Jim?"

Jim Nelson nodded acknowledging Mahoney's comments and began to speak.

"Brad, you understand that your father is completely incapacitated at the moment, and his prognosis does not look good. You are likely also aware that your father is also the largest single shareholder in Soper Research. In fact, he owns almost 90% of the outstanding common shares of the business.

As one of his three heirs you would stand to inherit a substantial holding in the company upon his death."

"Hold on just a minute, I have never had any interest in my father's money or him for that matter, I find it hard to believe that I would be included in his will!"

"Brad, that may be so, but I doubt whether you are going to have a whole lot to say about that, you see your father, if he dies, will die intestate, there is no will. His estate will go to probate and a court will decide, in it's wisdom, what your rightful share will be.

However, a problem of greater significance exists, what if he does not die or lives on for an extended period? How are the beneficiaries of his estate protected?

In addition, how will the company continue to function? Yes we have a board of directors, including me, but if your father's common shares are placed in escrow, they cannot be voted. Hence, the estate and his heirs will have no say in decisions taken by the board."

"You obviously have not invited me here to give you an answer to that conundrum, I assume that you have a proposal?"

"Brad, I think the only thing to do would be to apply to the courts to have a trustee appointed. If the three interested parties agree on a candidate, the court would likely appoint the trustee of our choice. Otherwise I am afraid we would end up with some accounting firm being given this task. That would be cumbersome and I don't think it would be in the best interests of all concerned."

"I assume that there is a suitable candidate for trustee?"

Nelson coughed into his hand and looked into Brad's face. "Frankly Brad, I think it should be me, I am your father's best friend, we went through medical school together. And I have been Vice Chairman of the Executive Committee, I know the business!"

"Who else is on that committee?"

"Just your father and me."

"Then what role do the other directors of the Company have?"

"Each of the other directors have only a few qualifying common shares allowing them to vote, so depending on what issue is being dealt with, any shareholder vote is overwhelmingly controlled by your father's interest. There was never any real point in challenging what your father wanted done."

"In other words they are just a rubber stamp of my father's wishes."

"The important thing is that they have been a "rubber stamp" I give you that, but if your father's interest is put in escrow, the directors would not be obliged to follow your father's plans."

The room became quiet, and then Declan Mahoney spoke. "This might be a good time to take little break, can I get anybody a drink? A Compari and Soda Jim? What about you Bradley?"

"Yeah, would you have a Kokanee?"

"A what?"

"A Kokanee, a beer, a cold beer would be good."

"I have never heard of it Bradley, but I do have a Bass' Ale, will that do?"

"Yeah, Bass' would be second best. I enjoyed it when I was back packing around Ireland last year."

The beer was cold and bitter, he had not realized how thirsty he was, half the beer disappeared in almost the first swallow. He tried to belch discretely.

"Did you enjoy Ireland? Its where I come from you know, good people there, lots to see."

"I enjoyed the people and the scenery, but not the stupidity of the sectarian violence."

He noticed Mahoney stiffen at his words, he knew he had struck a nerve, but just as quickly he recovered and they returned to their original topic.

Brad began. "Why is this so important, I understand what you are saying Dr. Nelson, but what makes this issue so important right now?"

"Soper Research is on the verge of getting approval for a revolutionary new vaccine that will revolutionize the treatment of the most distressing diseases known to mankind.

It would be inopportune to say the least, not to be able to have direction for the company, to be able to adequately deal with this opportunity and anything that might serve to compromise our success,"

"What is this new product?"

"Bradley, I need at least your verbal undertaking to maintain what I am about to tell you in the strictest confidence, can you give me that."

"Yes."

"It is a vaccine that will prevent the development of Alzheimer's!"

"What? Since when did they discover the fact that Alzheimer's is caused by a virus, I have seem nothing in print or in any scientific journals that would have given any hint of this?"

"It's a discovery your father made, you may not appreciate it but it was stroke of pure genius on his part, and a great deal of effort on the part of the scientists at Soper Research.

We took great pains keeping the modality of the virus a secret. We are about to receive approval from the FDA in the US for clinical trials to start. Coincidental to that, world wide patents are being issued to us on the vaccine."

"That is astounding, I take it that this means the potential for making a great deal of money in the process as well."

Jim smiled at Brad, "You bet, this is a ubiquitous disease world wide, the potential is enormous and, this is most important, for the treatment to be successful, the patient needs a booster every three months! Think of it as a license to print money!"

Brad sat quietly watching, as Nelson became even more excited as he contemplated just how the money would stream in. He didn't notice how intently Declan Mahoney was watching him and his body language.

"So tell me Brad. Can I count on your support as your trustee?"

"Seems to me, that there are a couple of others that have to concur, do they agree to have you act as trustee?"

"I don't foresee any problem with Ashley and Ellis is a minor so if you and Ashley agree I think the court would feel that he was adequately protected."

"Dr. Nelson, is that a yes?"

"Well nobody has signed on the dotted line so to speak, but."

"Then I think I ought to reserve any decision until I have had a chance to meet and discuss it with the other parties."

"Fine, fine, I will set up a meeting, we can all get together and resolve this."

"Thank you Dr. Nelson, but frankly, I think I would like to meet with them on my own, now I would really like to get to my hotel if you don't mind. It seems I have a lot of thinking to do."

Chapter 11

B rad threw his bag on the luggage rack as he came through the door to the suite. This was not what he remembered of any Hamden Suites.

He guessed that this had been customized just for his father's use, the way he had been greeted at the front desk had made him feel like some head of state, he was uncomfortable with the treatment.

He did a quick tour, found the bar, complete with a full sized fridge, curious, he opened it and found it stocked with Kokanee Gold! Somebody had gone to some trouble on his behalf, maybe Janet.

He twisted off the top and drank from the bottle, Bass' was good, but this was his beer!

He went over to the desk and saw the message light blinking; he called the front desk. Janet had called and had left a message for him.

He took another sip of beer, smiled to himself and made the call, she answered.

"Thanks for the beer!"

"Oh your welcome, I surprised myself by finding it. So how was your meeting?"

"Frankly, it was uncomfortable, I felt I was being pressured to make a decision, I don't much like people trying to manoeuver me so that I do what they want, without having all of the background information to do so."

"Somehow, I don't think you are going to let yourself be pushed around!"

"Nope."

"What are your plans for tomorrow?"

"Jim Nelson is picking me up at 9:00 AM, he insists that I have a tour of Soper Research, I am to be duly impressed I suppose."

"Then what?"

"I want to meet Ashley Soper, do you have her phone number?"

"I can arrange it and pick you up and take you to her place if you like."

"Thanks, but no, I want to meet with her on my own, do you have her number?"

After a few moments fumbling with her address book, she gave it to him, he could tell that she was annoyed at not being included.

"How about having dinner tomorrow night?"

"First you all but tell me to mind my own business, then your all sweetness and want to take me out, what do you think, that I'm easy."

"Yes."

"Piss off!" Then she laughed, he could almost see the dimples and sparkling eyes as he heard it."

"Well, do you want to have dinner?"

"OK, when and where?"

"You know the best places, you decide, I'll call you at your office tomorrow afternoon and you can let me know."

They exchanged good byes; he hung up and then placed a call to Ashley. As the phone began to ring, he looked at his watch; it was after 9:00 PM, he hoped she was home.

"Hello."

"Ashley, Ashley Soper?"

"Yes, who is this?"

"My name is Brad Soper. I'm.."

"Yes I know who you are, I have been expecting your call, Jim Nelson said you might,"

"Ashley, I wonder if it might be possible for you and I to meet, say tomorrow afternoon, it would seem that we have some things to discuss?"

"It would seem so, but only on one condition."

"What's that?"

"Don't you dare call me Mom!"

He laughed "I promise!"

She gave him her address and some general instructions how to get there, she assumed that he had his own transportation. He hung up the phone and turned his attention back to his beer, but the bottle was empty.

He headed to the bedroom, remembering that he hadn't adjusted his watch after leaving Vancouver. It was after midnight here, time to turn in.

*

He stood out in front of the hotel, enjoying the early morning sunshine, a change from the drizzle he left yesterday. He could see Nelson's black Lexus approaching him, coming up the circular driveway.

Nelson stopped the car, leaned over and pushed open the passenger side door, "Morning Brad, sleep well?"

"The time change screwed me up a little. A good thing I left a wake up call!"

"One thing about staying here, we are only about 5 minutes from the office, it makes it very convenient when we have VIP's in town."

They pulled into the parking lot of Soper Research a modernistic 3 story building of stainless steel and green tinted glass, Arnie's car was still in it's parking stall, Nelson parked the obligatory one stall away from the Mercedes.

"Nice car."

"It's your father's, I was going to suggest that you use it while you're in town, otherwise I am going to have to find someplace to store it."

Brad thought to himself "The temptation of Brad Soper, hardly transparent."

"I am sure my father wouldn't approve!"

"Brad, I think you are being a little harsh, I am sure he would be pleased if you would use it and enjoy it while you are here."

While Brad didn't lust after things like a SL55, he did have a young man's interest in hot cars, with this one he could almost feel his testosterone level rising while he looked at it.

Besides, what could it hurt and he could see Janet giggling next to him as they sped off to dinner tonight. However, he would be controlled in his interest.

"We can talk about that later, but first things first, let's do the tour!"

Nelson explained the security system, Brad was impressed, he had heard about biometrics but this was his first opportunity to see how effective it was.

"Brad, this is very much a business based upon intellectual property, should a few sheets of paper or a floppy disk go missing, it could represent millions of dollars. In addition, we have a very sophisticated security system for our network and telephone system. What you are looking at is a building that is, how can I explain it? Like a building inside of a cocoon, protect from the outside world."

"Impressive, who designed the system, who maintains it?"

"You met Declan Mahoney last night, his firm has set this all up."

"But I thought Mahoney Associates was your PR firm."

"Well they are that too. You may not think so, but security and PR are not so dissimilar."

They proceeded through the retinal scanner and were going towards Arnie's office when Peter Mytryk almost ran them down as he rushed from his office.

"Peter, Peter, what's the big rush?"

"I am so sorry Jim, I didn't see you." He was obviously distressed about something and struggled to regain his composure.

"Peter, I would like you to meet Brad Soper, Brad is Arnie's eldest son, he is in from Vancouver. Brad, this is Dr. Peter Mytryk, he is head of research here and an eminent microbiologist."

Brad took the sweaty hand in his; the handshake was limp and insincere "Pleased to meet you Dr. Mytryk."

"Peter, call me Peter, I am so happy to meet you and I must tell you how sorry I am regarding your father's condition."

Mytryk stood like a black crow, shoulders hunched, head pitched forward and a nose like a beak. He was fidgeting from one foot to the other, truly not a likable man.

"Jim, may I have a private word with you?"

"Can't it wait Peter, Brad and I were just starting a tour?"

"I am sorry but it is very important!"

Nelson apologized to Brad with a shrug of his shoulders; he and Mytryk disappeared into the nearest office.

"What the hell is so important Peter?"

He left the shaken man and returned to Brad. "These brilliant people can be a pain in the ass, every little thing gets blown into a crisis."

Brad couldn't help but notice the stress in Nelson's voice, there was more to this than Nelson was letting on, but it had little to do with him.

They continued the tour, Brad was impressed, in spite of himself, and the sheer number of people employed in various types of research, the equipment including sophisticated electron microscopes astounded him.

"Very Impressive, but where is the manufacturing facility, you know, where you actually make the drugs?"

"Aside from making prototype batches for test purposes, we don't really manufacture the drugs, we license others to do that, in some cases they even do the marketing of the drugs. This allows us to concentrate on research."

"Is that how this kind of business is normally done?"

"Not really, it was your father's idea, brilliant really, we can move licenses around the world to take best advantage of lower cost areas, maximize our returns and play off the generic companies against the big multi-nationals. At the same time, we can employ our capital in basic drug research and not in manufacturing facilities."

"I see."

"Come, let's go up to your father's office, I arranged for coffee for us."

The office was impressive, walnut panelling from floor to ceiling, a massive desk, faced the large plate glass windows that overlooked the park with it's artificial lakes, water fountains and the requisite ducks swimming placidly in the water.

Nelson went to a wall panel to the left of the desk, pressed a button and the wall retracted silently into some kind of pocket in the wall. He flipped another switch that caused the illumination of the private laboratory that had been concealed by the wall.

"Arnie did much of his research right in there, I can't tell you how many original ideas flowed from that room. Brad, in many ways your father is a genius."

He went to the credenza behind the desk and poured two cups of coffee from the insulated carafe. "Cream, sugar?"

"Just black thanks."

He settled himself on the leather sofa; Nelson took his father's chair behind the desk and sipped on his coffee.

Looking over the rim of his cup he said, "So Brad have you had a chance to think about our discussion last night?"

"Yes, I have been thinking about it, but I am afraid I am no closer to a decision than I was last night. I have made arrangements to meet with Ashley this afternoon, I would really like to have her input."

"I see..., Brad, timing on this thing is extremely important, we need to lay plans for this business in the absence of your father."

"I understand all that, but I need to be sure that what is being proposed is good for all parties. With respect Jim, I don't really know you or any of the other players in this scenario. I think I deserve a little time to get comfortable with what's been going on."

"Of course Brad, of course, I don't mean to pressure you, take whatever time you need, I know you won't delay this unnecessarily."

Brad noted that Nelson had not volunteered the fact that he had called Ashley, was there a potential conspiracy there.

Nelson threw the car keys to Brad; he had no option but to catch them. "Use the car Brad, you will be doing me a favour, I won't have to find a storage space for it and it'll save you the trouble of renting one."

Brad accepted the keys without comment. He rose to leave, "Thank you very much Jim, I appreciate the time you have taken to show me around, be assured that I won't delay my decision unduly."

They shook hands and Brad left the office. Nelson called down to security to alert them that Brad would be leaving the building, then placed a call to Mahoney Associates.

"Hello Declan, this is Jim Nelson."

"Well James, what can I do you today?"

"Declan, I think we have a problem, I think we best discuss it face to face, can you come to the office?"

"I'll be there in 45 minutes."

*

Brad left the building stepping out into the bright sunshine; it was a beautiful spring day, barely a cloud in the sky. The car sat in the preferred parking stall, shining like a jewel; Brad couldn't help but notice that all three parking spots bore his father's name, with the car parked in the middle slot.

He walked slowly around it, admiring the sleek lines and quality that was evident, he finally put the key in the lock, unlocked and opened the door. "Like a bank vault." He thought.

He slid behind the wheel; the sensuous leather seats cradled his body in absolute comfort. He ran his hands around the slick steering wheel, all the while admiring all of the interior appointments. Everything had the look of having been hand crafted specifically for this one car.

After he inserted the key into the ignition, he found the convertible roof-retracting button, pressed it, he heard a low-pitched whirring sound and the roof began to open. It was completely automatic and the sun came streaming in, he lowered all the windows and was about to start the engine, when he realized he didn't know the city. He checked the glove box and found a Metropolitan Toronto map carefully folded there.

It only took him a couple of minutes to plan his route. Ashley's instructions had been very precise, and then he reached over and pushed the start button.

He was not completely prepared for the throaty sound of neither the engine nor the pulsing energy that he felt throughout his body, he was exhilarated!

"So cars aren't important to you right?" he thought. He pulled out of the lot, taking car not to burn rubber like a teenager

*

Declan Mahoney entered Arnie's office to see Jim Nelson still at the desk, "Takin' over already Jim?"

Nelson leaned back in the chair, ignoring Mahoney's comment, "Sit down Declan, we need to talk, we're secure in here aren't we?"

"I guarantee it! What's happened?"

"Peter Mytryk is becoming a threat to us, I think he is ready to use blackmail to get the Company "to give him his due" on the vaccine development. He's a greedy little bastard!"

"What did he threaten to do?"

"He says that he will send anonymous information to the authorities regarding our holdings in Grand Cayman, unless he gets "looked after.""

The smile on Declan's face did not change, but his tone of voice indicated his dissatisfaction with the response."

"Get that son-of-a-bitch in here, I need to hear what he has to say first hand!"

Nelson's complexion became somewhat ashen at this outburst. He did not like this man, but Arnie had picked him personally and trusted him with any sensitive issues. He had no option but to comply, he called Mytryk to come to the office immediately.

Mytryk entered, looking like a condemned man, trembling noticeably, he was wringing his hands nervously.

Declan; still smiling, said, "Sit down Dr. Mytryk. Tell me about the conversation you had with Dr. Nelson, just what exactly did you mean by "being taken care of"?"

The little man shifted uncomfortably in his chair, Mahoney frightened him, he groped for words, but none came.

"Did you not hear me Dr. Mytryk, shall I repeat my question?"

Finally Mytryk spoke; his voice was barely audible. "It's just that I have worked very hard on this development, I would like some recognition." His voice trailed off.

"What kind of recognition Dr. Mytryk? Your name in all the papers? Money? Just what is it you want?"

"All I meant was, everybody else is going to get rich, why can't I have a share?"

"You mealy mouthed little shit face! You've been paid handsomely for your part in all this, did you or did you not threaten Dr. Nelson and by extension, this Company, with revealing confidential information to outside interests?"

Mytryk was on the edge of a panic attack, he was so frightened, he tried to respond, and "I only meant that if…"

"Never mind what you meant! You get your sorry little ass out of here now! And if I ever hear a breath of a leak, I'll make sure you are "looked after," do you understand me?"

Mytryk stood up and backed shakily out of the office, a look of absolute terror on his face.

"What do you think Declan?"

"Jim that isn't for you to know, you need what is called ultimate deniability, you need a reason to remove Mytryk from the company and one that will discredit him. Just leave these things to me, you will know soon enough.

The only problem I see is that he is our Director of Research, what do we do for a replacement?"

"I had almost forgotten, one of the reasons Arnie was in Nairobi was to hire a new Director of Research, he called me from there, absolutely elated, he hired the top guy in the industry.

He hadn't decided how he was going to get rid of Mytryk though. The new man is to be here in a month, Arnie was working on a news release, I'll have a look around his office and see if I can find it."

Good, let me know when you find it, in the meantime, isolate the little son-of-a-bitch, he's not to have any information regarding Arnie, understood.

He nodded his understanding.

Declan left, Jim Nelson looked out on the park and a feeling of uneasiness settled over him, there was little doubt that Declan would handle the situation, but you could never be sure of the fallout.

Chapter 12

Brad headed east on the Queen Elizabeth Highway; he could see the Toronto skyline in the haze ahead of him. There was too much traffic to let out the SL55, although he was tempted by the muscular sound of the engine and the air rushing past him, even at the legal limit.

He pushed the CD into the player and was rewarded with the throaty sounds of Diana Krall; he was surprised that he and his father apparently had the same taste in music. "The last time he listened to this, he had no idea of what lay ahead," thought Brad.

He reflected on his visit to Soper Research. He thought that Peter Mytryk was an odd duck. Then most research types were weren't they. He wondered just what the crisis was.

He had to admit that he was impressed with what he saw. It was evident that it had taken significant investment to reach the level of excellence that Soper seemed to enjoy. The development of this new vaccine seemed too fantastic to believe, but he had no reason to doubt it. Particularly based on what he had just seen.

He began to think about Ashley Soper, he tried to visualize her, all he could see was some middle aged society matron, but that didn't square with the little he knew of his father. "No sense guessing he thought, I'm just about there,"

He entered the condo; "May I help you sir?"

"Yes, I would like to see Mrs. Ashley Soper."

"May I ask who's calling?"

"Brad Soper, she's expecting me."

The security guard called and announced him, he nodded to Brad and pressed the door release button, "Mrs. Soper is in the penthouse suite, take the elevator to the right, through the door."

Standing in the elevator, Brad felt a little anxiety, he was about to meet his mother's replacement, what would she be like?"

There really wasn't anyway that Brad could consider Ashley to be the "other woman." There had been a 15-year interval between his parent's divorce and his father's remarriage.

He stood in front of the door, hesitating before he knocked, he took a deep breath and wrapped, he thought, authoritatively.

It seemed a long time before the door was opened; Ashley stood smiling in the doorway, "So Brad, you found me." She extended her hand, he took it, she was gorgeous, not what he had expected at all.

"Come in Brad, and close your mouth."

He stammered "I'm sorry. I.."

"Not what you expected huh?"

"Frankly no, you're so young, I had no idea." He felt like a schoolboy, he felt his face redden.

She was enjoying his discomfort, she liked what she saw, maybe 6'-2," broad shoulders, probably a rower she thought. He was dressed in khaki Dockers, a beige golf shirt and sneakers.

"Well, I'm not old enough to be your mother!"

"Of course not!"

She reached up and touched his sun bleached hair, "You spend a lot of time outdoors, what do you do for a living?"

"I am, or will be in research."

"Not another one?"

"Not that kind of research, I am involved in medical ethics research."

"Sounds stuffy."

"Not really, I quite enjoy it."

"Sit down Brad, tell me why you are here, I know it has something to do with your father and his business. I don't understand much about these things."

"Well, I am sure Jim Nelson has talked to you about this business of having the court appoint a trustee. To protect your interest as well as mine and of course you son's, as it relates to his estate, primarily Soper Research.

"You know about Ellis?"

"Frankly I know very little, I just found out last week that I have a little brother, it's a bit of a surprise."

"Yes, Jim did talk to me about that, he also asked that I support him in being appointed the trustee."

"How do you feel about that?"

"I am not sure."

"You have some reservations?"

"You might say that, I don't trust the son-of-a-bitch!"

"What do you think Brad?"

"I really haven't formed an opinion yet, I have to be honest with you, my relationship with my father has been all but non existent up until this event. We were never close after he divorced my mother. I don't think I even saw him once after that. He didn't bother to come to her funeral. As a result I know little of his business, and even less about him or his associates."

"In a nutshell, you don't much care for your father?"

"That's about right."

"No matter, I think he's an Asshole too!"

That word coming out of that mouth seemed incongruous, "What did he do to you?"

"The night he took ill, he told me he wanted a divorce! He didn't even have the nerve to tell me in person, he told me on the phone!"

"I am sure that was a shock."

"The divorce, not really, but to be told that way, that was total lack of class, but then he never had any anyway. We had grown apart, particularly since the birth of Ellis, he didn't want another child, he was terribly angry when he found out I was pregnant. And when it was discovered that Ellis was autistic, well, that seemed to finish the relationship."

"But why would he have picked this time for a divorce, was there anybody else?"

"For Arnie his only mistress was his job, his company, no his reason became obvious to me when Jim Nelson came to see me."

"What do you mean."

"I mean the vaccine! Arnie intends or rather intended to take the company public coincidental with the announcement of the Alzheimer's treatment.

Jim Nelson says it will drive the stock prices up dramatically, they will all be rich and Arnie most of all. There was no way he wanted that as any part of a divorce settlement!

The greedy bastard!"

'Why is it that you don't trust Nelson?"

"I am not prepared to discuss that, just let's leave it that he knows why."

"Ashley, could you tell me more about Ellis. For years now, I have believed that I had no living relatives only to find out that I have in fact have a brother. I can't tell you how important this is to me."

"You mean a half-brother."

"I don't believe in hyphenated relationships, Ellis is my brother, neither of us may be happy with the blood we share, but we do share it."

"I am sorry Brad, I don't mean to be a bitch, its just been very hard dealing with Ellis all on my own. I found that I just couldn't cope on a full time basis nor did I possess the resources to help Ellis. I found Halton House, a place that specializes in autistic children, he gets special treatment and training, the staff seems very caring. But I still feel extremely guilty."

"Guilty of what?"

"Abandoning him, first his father ignores him, then I put him in a home."

He could see the tears welling up in her eyes, he went across to her, held both her hands, and looked into her face, "You haven't abandoned him, and I don't want to either."

"Thank you Brad, you're not your father's son, are you?"

"Not hardly!"

"I need a drink, can I get anything for you Brad?"

"Afraid it's a bit early for me."

She went to the bar and mixed herself a Manhattan; she took a chilled glass from the freezer and poured the drink from the shaker.

"Oh God, I needed that!"

"Ashley, do you think it might be possible to meet Ellis?"

"I have him very weekend, why don't you come over this weekend. However, I have to warn you; there may be an upset and tantrums. Because you will be a change that he has not anticipated. If you feel up to it, please come, it might do Ellis some good.

In fact why don't you spend the weekend? We have lots of space here, and it will give you a chance to get to know him.

And I promise not to try to seduce you, in case you have heard anything at all about my reputation, I am attracted to older men!"

They both laughed, but Brad not quite so heartily. I'm not afraid, I'll be here, thank you for the invitation."

"Brad what are you going to do about this trustee thing?

"I really haven't made my mind up yet, there is no question that it would be irresponsible to allow the situation to drift with so much important stuff pending. I wouldn't have a lot of confidence in an uninvolved third party being selected as trustee, conversely I know next to nothing about the parties that are involved.

I guess it is going to come down to gut instinct on my part."

"Then you are better off than me, I don't have any instinct when it comes to business."

"Tell you what, let's both of us think about this some more and when I come over on Friday, we can continue the discussion and I am sure we'll come up with something."

"You know Brad, I feel better just talking to you, I don't know what I expected when Jim Nelson phoned and said I would be hearing from you, but I sense that I can trust you."

"There you see, you do have good instincts."

"Sure you won't join me?"

"Thanks no, I have to get going, have you been in to see my father yet?"

"No and I am not sure I am going to!"

"I'm ambivalent about myself, but I think I probably should, I need as much background as I can get. Do you have Jim Nelson's number, I am sure he can arrange it?"

She gave him the number and he called, Nelson did not seem particularly comfortable with the idea, but promised to call Cyril Pickard and make the arrangements.

"See you Friday Ashley, I think you know, that you weren't what I expected either!"

*

He arrived at University Hospital; taking care to park the car so that no possibility existed that it would be accidentally scratched.

The receptionist paged Pickard and within a few minutes, Brad saw the balding old man in a white coat approaching him.

He put out his hand, "Dr. Pickard, I'm..."

Before he could finish, the old man grasped him by the arm and whisked him into an empty examining room close by.

Brad was taken by surprise, the old man had gripped him so tightly, and his arm still ached a little after being released.

"You are Bradley Soper, are you not? I am Cyril Pickard, sorry for the "cloak and dagger," but we need to maintain a high level of security in this instance!"

"Yes, I'm Brad Soper, what the hell is going on?"

"We have your father in an isolated intensive care unit, we are trying to protect his anonymity from the media as well as his exact condition. He has not been admitted as Arnold Soper, you understand don't you?"

"Not really, is this all necessary?"

"I don't know how much Jim Nelson has told you, but I will summarize, your father was brought in here 12 days ago, he was unconscious after collapsing at his office. He regained consciousness the day after admittance, but fell into a coma from which he has not recovered.

When he did wake from his initial attack, he was able to verbalize that he could not move any of his limbs. He had a seizure just before slipping into the coma again.

In a nutshell, that's it, he has some normal brain activity, as a matter of fact, parts of the brain involving memory, emotions and thought processes are, at times, extremely active."

"Do you have any idea what has caused this."

"As nearly as we can determine it is idiosyncratic."

"In essence, you mean you don't know!"

"Not definitively, it could be a virus, he had just returned from Africa as you likely know, in fact that is one of the reasons for the isolation, strictly as a precaution, but it also serves to protect his privacy."

"What is his prognosis?"

"I am afraid I have to tell you that it is not good, I can see no way that he will ever recover from this. Likewise, in spite of everything that has happened, I cannot tell you if or when he might die.

Come with me, I'll take you up in a private elevator"

He stood outside the room and looked through the viewing window at his father lying on the bed, connected to a variety hi tech monitors, intravenous tubes, catheter, and sundry wires and electrodes.

Nothing, I feel nothing at all for this man. Why is that? Shouldn't I at least have a sense of regret? But I don't, it's as if he's a perfect stranger. Well he is!

"You have him on full life support?"

"Yes, that started as a precaution, but as organs begin to fail, it becomes more and more necessary, in many ways it would be better if we could just withdraw all life support and let him die."

"But you can't, because of the brain activity?"

"Of course, but as you are aware I am sure, there are business reasons to keep him living."

"I am not sure I follow?"

"Didn't Jim Nelson explain it to you, if he dies it will trigger the requirement for a court appointed trustee to manage his estate. That may not be desirable to you and other members of the family. This at least buys some time to put a preferred trustee in place."

"How is it Doctor, that you know so much about his business and his state of affairs?"

The Doctor was taken off guard by the question; he was flustered. "Well, Ah, Jim Nelson gave me an overview, he thought it important to fill me in. As a member of the family, I didn't think I was violating any confidence in talking to you."

"Your not, I was just curious."

Brad could sense the tension in the viewing room; it seemed to him that more than family members had an interest in the right trustee being appointed.

There was not much more to be done here, he thanked the Doctor, excused himself and returned to the car, he needed time to think.

He drove up the 427 to the 401 and headed east on the 401 and then north on 400, the traffic was sparse.

It wasn't long before he was rolling along at 160 kph; he could see no patrol cars in either direction. The engine seemed to be loafing at this speed, he was conscious that the SL55 could do considerably more.

He eased back on the throttle, bringing his speed down just over the limit and reflected on what seemed to be going on, he liked Ashley, she had an obvious drinking problem, but who could blame her. She seemed genuine enough, from what Janet had told him, she was well off in her own right, she didn't really need more money. But was there a desire to punish his father even in absentia?

As for Jim Nelson, he felt uncomfortable with him too, just too slick, making too many assumptions.

He thought briefly about his father, Ashley had been right. His business was his mistress. He couldn't even die without the permission of his mistress.

He pulled over on the soft shoulder, put the car in idle and called Janet on his cell phone, how was it he had her number memorized?

"Janet Petersen."

He hadn't realized that this was her direct number.

"Hi there, so what about dinner?

"I was beginning to think I'd have to eat at the golden arches again!"

"No fear, where to you want to go and when would you like me to pick you up?"

"Pick me up, have you got a car?"

"Have I got a car? Of course, so?"

"OK, OK, I'll tell you what, if you're driving I can get mine in for service. Meet me at Alice Fazooli's, it's on Adelaide Street. Make it 7:30 is that OK?"

"Alice Fazooli, who's she?"

"Don't be dumb, its an Italian Restaurant, has great crab cakes too! You'll love it."

"See you at 7:30!"

She hung up the phone; Declan stuck his head in. "Who was that?"

"Just a date."

"Come into my office for a minute, please Jan."

He closed the door behind them; he motioned her to a chair in front of his desk.

"That was Brad Soper on the phone wasn't it?"

"Yes, so what?"

His smile never changed, but his voice was flat and hard. "Don't get cheeky with me girl! You do what I tell you to do when I tell you to do it! You understand that?"

She started to argue with him, he simply held up his hand, she looked at his face and stopped.

"Understand me Janet, I can fix it so that you never work again, I can even arrange to have you disbarred, should I choose to do so, cross me and you will have lots of time to regret it!"

She knew that he meant it, she felt the colour drain from her face, she knew also that he could and would do whatever he said he could do.

"I am sorry."

"That's better, I have no objection to you seeing the young Mr. Soper, providing I know about it and I set the agenda for what you are to do when you do see him. Is that understood?"

"Yes."

"What I want is for you to convince him that he should support Jim Nelson as trustee and that he should influence Ashley Soper to do likewise."

"But he doesn't even know Ashley Soper!"

"He does now, not only that, but he is going to spend the weekend with her!"

She tried not to let her surprise show, but she knew she would not be successful. He picked up on her reaction right away.

"Who knows, Brad might even get lucky, I understand she is quite a looker."

Bastard! Why do you treat me this way? Why is it necessary to be so controlling? If only I could get away from all this, but I can't, he has the upper hand.

She ignored the remark, or at least tried to. "How do you propose that I accomplish that?"

"OH I am sure that you will find a way, you're a good looking girl, use your assets."

He emphasized the first syllable of the last word, she hated the way he spoke to her, this was not the first time he had made the same kind of inference. However, there was little she could do, as perverse as it sounded; she needed to be here.

*

She watched him come through the door of the restaurant; he saw her, waved and gave her a smile. God, why does he have to be so nice? If only it was another time, another place, is there any hope?

"Hey this is a neat place!"

"Bet you haven't got anything like it on the West Coast?"

"Maybe not, but I can tell you that you wouldn't go hungry out there, we have some fantastic places too."

The waiter took their wine order, he had ordered a rather ordinary Merlot, and she let it pass without comment.

"So how was your day Brad?"

"Had a plant tour, visited my father and met with Ashley Soper."

"Sounds like a busy day, but why visit Ashley Soper?"

"Seemed like a good thing to do, we have some common interests, not just the business but little Ellis as well."

"How did it go?"

"She seems very nice, she is very attractive." He saw her shift in her seat at the comment.

"As is the present company," he added. She smiled; a little embarrassed that he had noticed it.

"Did you come to any conclusion as to what you might do, Declan had mentioned to me about the trustee business."

"Not really, I do know that she has some reservations about what is being proposed."

"Did she say what those reservations are?"

"Not really, we didn't get into it much, we spent more time talking about Ellis. You know I am like a little kid. I thought I had no family I now I find I have little brother. I can't tell you how much that means to me."

She knew that his excitement was genuine, she was glad for him, she just wished that her own circumstances were different.

"How do you feel about Jim Nelson as the trustee?"

"I haven't given it a whole lot of thought, I mean I only arrived yesterday, there is a great deal to absorb, is this thing somehow important to you Jan?"

He noticed my interest, not good, better back off.

"No, not really, I just know that this has to be a big issue for you and thought it might help to talk about it, that's all."

"I appreciate that, I'll keep you posted when I've made up my mind."

"Tell me all about Ellis."

"Ask me that after this weekend, I am going to stay with him and try to get to know him, Ashley has invited me to stay with them."

She didn't know if the weekend also included getting to know Ashley better as well, left to her, probably, and he was a man after all.

They drank the wine, she ordered the crab cakes, and he had the Louisiana Alligator, much to her dismay. He said it was delicious, but she doubted it and declined his offer to try it.

After dinner, they both walked to the parking lot where Brad had left the car, she walked instinctively to the Honda Civic rental, "No not that one, over here."

He was standing beside the shiny green SL55, "You gotta be kidding, this thing must be costing you a fortune to rent!"

"Naw, it's my father's car, Jim Nelson thought I should use it while I'm in town."

When they were settled in the car, her hands seemed to caress every part of the interior, she was just about speechless, but not quite.

"It looks good on you, I bet its a thrill to drive?"

"It is that, but you have to be very careful, it's not really for the novice driver, there's just more torque than one normally experiences, and everybody seems to want to drag you at every stop light."

"You don't oblige do you?"

"Of course not, I'm just a conservative hick from the west, well hardly ever!"

She laughed at the comment; "My car isn't going to be ready until tomorrow, could you drive me home?"

"Of course, but how do you get to work tomorrow?"

"Subway of course."

"Of course."

They bantered back and forth all the way to her apartment in Rosedale, she commented on the car and the way it handled, she wondered at how much it must cost. Finally, they arrived at her apartment.

"Just park it in that slot over there, it's mine."

He did so and as he put the car in park, she leaned across and kissed him full on the lips, it took his breath away.

"Would you like to come up?"

Chapter 13

Can't remember how long I've been here, hard to measure time, what is time anyway? Simply the measure of life? Theoretical, time doesn't really exist. A figment of man's imagination.

What the hell are they doing out there, there's been no change, is there nothing they can come up with? Someone's coming, good, can't stand this isolation!

"Alfred, is that you, I can't see you, are you there?"

"Yes, I am here Dr. Soper."

"Alfred, I asked you, is there life after death?"

"I honestly don't have any idea, but I believe it's what you think that is important, are you saying that it is nothing you have ever contemplated?"

"Maybe, when I was much younger, and impressionable."

"But no longer?"

"I don't really know, it was simpler when I was younger, everything was, maybe I believed it, once. As I grew older, it seemed irrelevant, I just put it out of my mind, but now, I must admit, I think often of death."

"Are you saying that, now belief in an after life has become important to you?"

"If life simply ends, so what, I will be unaware anyway, I just won't exist. It is the alternative that frightens me."

"Why would an after life frighten you?"

"I don't know"

"I think you do."

"What gives you the right to psychoanalyse me Alfred?"

"Dr. Soper, don't you remember, you invited me in."

"Yes, I guess I did."

"Can you answer my question Dr. Soper?"

"Alfred, a few days ago, at least I think it was only a few days ago, I was in complete control of my life, I was successful, at the peak of my powers, respected, I had everything I could want with more on the horizon."

"Do I hear a "but" coming?"

"But now, all of that seems meaningless, it's all gone!"

"That doesn't answer my question."

"My problem is, it seems to me, if there is a life after death, there also may be a judgment, perhaps I will be rejected and condemned to where I am now or maybe at that point it all ends."

"Back to the catechism are we?"

"Alfred, you seem to be enjoying this, I thought you were here to help me."

"I am Dr. Soper, I apologize if I have offended you, tell me, are there things that you done in your lifetime that you have come to regret?"

"Yes"

"Do you feel up to talking about them?"

"I don't know."

"Has it to do with your personal life?"

"There are things in both my personal and business life that I have come to regret."

"Maybe it would be easier if we talked about your business life."

"First do no harm!"

"What do you mean?"

"The most important precept of the Hippocratic oath, at least as far as I am concerned. I have always tried to live by that credo. I think I can safely say, that we never introduced drug whose side effects caused greater harm than the disease they were meant to control."

"That sounds laudable, but what about the other way 'round?"

"What do you mean?"

"What about drugs that you introduced that caused no harm but did little good either?"

"I don't believe that we ever sold a drug like that."

"You mean that you never developed a drug simply to compete with one that already existed?"

"It is part of business to match the competitors offerings."

"So you see nothing wrong with spending research money to simply develop a competitive drug that does nothing more than circumvent existing patents on a similar drug?"

This is a bullshit discussion, it's going nowhere, he doesn't understand, why do I waste my time? That's a joke, what else have I got to do with it?

"I don't want to talk anymore."

The phone rang in Jim Nelson's apartment; it was Declan Mahoney, "Have you got your TV turned on?"

"No, why?"

"Turn it to Channel 5, the 6 o'clock news is about to begin, when it is finished, come to my office, do not telephone," he hung up before Nelson could respond.

"The news at the top of this hour is a fast breaking story involving a prominent scientist with a large research firm here in the city.

Today, Metro Police have charged Peter Mytryk, age 48, Director of Research with Soper Research Inc., with possession of child pornography.

"Police raided his home a seized his computer, which informants say, contained over 100,00 graphic images, in addition, our sources tell us that the email files seized indicate that Mytryk may have been involved in worldwide trafficking. Also found were credit card charges and payment records showing he accessed several of the world's most notorious child porn web sites.

Here is what Inspector Fred Hoskins had to say."

The screen cuts to a plain-clothes detective, "We believe this is an important arrest in our continuing fight against child pornography and child prostitution, this is without doubt one of the worst examples of sick individuals exploiting little children. We intend to continue to prosecute anyone involved to the fullest extent of the law, we are committed to safeguarding our kids."

The reporter took back the mike, "Can you tell us how you came to know about this individual and his activities Inspector?"

"I am afraid not, we do not want to compromise other aspects of this case by releasing any further information at this time."

"Thank you Inspector, now back to you Allan."

Nelson, switched off the set and fell back on his sofa, he was stunned!

*

Nelson pressed the night button outside Mahoney's office and waited to be let in, he saw Mahoney come into the reception area and unlock the door. The ever-present smile was there, as always, "Come in Jim, good to see you."

Declan watched the man sitting across his desk from him, he looked sick enough to throw up, "Can I get you a drink?"

"Compari and Soda please."

"You look like you could use something stronger, are you sure?"

"Just Compari and Soda, thanks."

Nelson's hand shook as he took the drink from Mahoney; "You arranged this whole thing with Mytryk, didn't you?"

"Jim, I told you, don't ask about any of this, you do not need to know, in fact it is better that you don't, then you can truthfully say you knew nothing of this if and when you are asked.

You know Jim, truth is very important in these kind of issues." He smiled again, perfect teeth, ruthless face.

"Wait a minute, here's some more news coming in."

He flicked switch and the sound was restored to one of the monitors on the wall.

"This just in, a spokesman for Soper Research Inc. Says that "They are shocked and dismayed at the actions of Peter Mytryk, our former Director of Research. In face of the mountain of evidence obtained by the police, we felt it prudent to terminate our relationship with Dr. Mytryk as quickly as possible."

"The news release goes on to say that Dr. Mytryk's sudden departure from the firm will not compromise any current or developing products, a highly qualified replacement has already been engaged to fill this important position."

"Another part of this story, Peter Mytryk was released from jail this afternoon on $250,000 bail, his court date has been set for June 18th, 4 weeks from today."

"He's been released?"

"What would you expect, he's a first time offender, he hasn't even had a traffic ticket, but you got what you wanted, he has been discredited, he no longer works for the firm and he will never make a credible witness for anybody.

We need to get all of Mytryk's files cleansed; I want anything questionable delivered to me.

We don't need any more surprises, you had better do that yourself Jim and quickly."

"But did you have to go this far?"

"How far is far enough? Leave these matters to me; I know you don't have the stomach for it Jim. Just go with the events as they unfold."

"You don't leave me much choice Declan, I just hope this ends it."

"Maybe and then again maybe not!"

Nelson left Mahoney's office, his stomach was churning, he could sense that control of this situation was slipping from his hands and that he was simply being carried along by the course of events.

Mahoney sat behind his desk, his chest was constricting again. He drew a deep breath through his inhaler, almost instantly he could feel the airways opening up.

Damn asthma! Thank God for the inhaler, could be dead by now without it! I think Nelson is going to have to be dealt with, he's weak, and he's never going to pull this off, not in a million years! Lester Coughlan, that bastard! He's going to prevent Nelson's appointment. I know it. Can't do anything with him, too well connected, particularly with my old nemesis, those IRA bastards, if it wasn't for him, I'd have it all! Brad Soper must come on side, and then I have a chance.

*

Brad Soper had seen the same broadcast, he wondered if this is what Mytryk had wanted to discuss with Nelson, he shook his head and picked up the phone and called Ashley.

"Ashley, did you see the 6 o'clock news on TV?"

"No, why?"

He reiterated everything that had transpired Ashley let out a low sound.

"Jesus, can you believe it! If you're father knew he would be apoplectic! I always felt that Mytryk was a weasel, but not this! I hope they lock the bastard up forever, he should never walk the streets again!"

"So much for being innocent until proven guilty! He's only been arrested, not tried and convicted."

"Brad don't be naive, look at the evidence they've got, there are weird people out there."

"You are probably right, I know something was bothering him when I was on the tour with Nelson."

"What do you mean?"

He told her about the altercation in the hallway and Jim Nelson's response afterwards, he added that Nelson looked unnerved when he returned from speaking with Mytryk.

"You don't think Jim is involved in this thing, do you?"

"I don't know what to think. All I do know is that Nelson seemed upset, I've gotta go Ashley, I'll be in touch if I get any more information, let me know if you hear anything"

"All right, you're still coming on Friday?"

"You, bet, I'm looking forward to it!"

He then punched Janet's number into his cell, he knew she was still going to be ticked with him for turning her down last night, but he needed to find out if she knew anything about the Mytryk situation.

"Hello."

"Hello Janet" he said as brightly as he could.

"Who is this?"

"Come on Janet, give me a break, I told you I was still suffering from the time change, I just needed to crash, I was totally beat."

"Nice to hear I have that kind of effect on you!"

But she could not risk turning him off; she needed him on her side.

"OK, OK, can I get out of the doghouse now? It's important, we need to talk, did you see the news on Peter Mytryk?"

"Yes, and I think it's disgusting, I only met the man once and to believe I shook his Hand, Uh!"

He told her about the scene he had witnessed in the hallway, between Nelson and Mytryk, just the day before.

"Frankly, I thought both of them looked shaken when they finished their discussion, Nelson looked particularly ashen. You don't suppose that he is somehow involved in this ring do you?"

Janet had already figured out just who was behind this whole scheme, but she took care not to say anything that Brad might pick up on.

"At this point, I would believe just about anything, but I really don't know anything. I can tell you that I handled the news release, but that's as much as I've been told. Do you know anything about this new Director of Research?"

"No, I was about to ask you, I just assumed that Mahoney would be in charge of handling the PR on this. It seemed to me that they were pretty quick in dumping Mytryk do you really think that was such a great idea?"

"Brad, we needed to get out in front of this thing, from what I can gather, the police have a mountain of evidence, there really isn't any doubt that he's guilty. We couldn't be seen to be soft on what he has been involved in.

In any event, Mytryk was on his way out, your father hired this new man while he was in Nairobi, my understanding is the he is brighter than Mytryk so the company shouldn't suffer."

'You really didn't answer me, do you think Nelson might somehow be involved?"

"I don't know Brad, Declan has been handling the Soper file since long before I got here, I really only get to work on the periphery, so I don't really know the key players.

Is this episode having some impact on you regarding the consideration of Nelson as a trustee?"

"If there is any possibility that he is somehow involved, there would no way that I would agree to him representing me,

I am sure that Ashley would feel the same way, although I really can't speak for her,"

"I can understand, I think that would be my position too, if I were involved. But, and I don't mean to interfere Brad, I think it is extremely important that you resolve this estate fiasco as soon as you can. I think you can anticipate some uneasiness on the part of the board, the natives tend to get restless when no one seems to be in control."

"I hear you Janet, I want to spend more time talking to Ashley on this, before I make any decision, I can do that this weekend."

"You know Brad, I am a lawyer, if you want some legal advice, I would be glad to help you and Ashley too for that matter."

"I appreciate the offer Jan, but I don't want to put you in position of conflict of interests."

She could sense a hard edge to his response. She knew she had overstepped her bounds, again. She attempted to recover.

"Of course, you are absolutely right Brad, it was a dumb offer, I wasn't thinking with my head."

"Seems to me, that all of us have to be thinking with our heads!"

Chapter 14

"Declan, it's Jim Nelson, I just got a call from an Inspector Harris from the Metro Police, he's coming here to see me!"

"Did he say what he wanted?"

"Just that it has something to do with Mytryk, says he wants to have his forensic people look at Peter's work station."

"I figured they would, not to worry, my man will handle it, just turn him over to the network administrator, he knows what to do."

"Your man?"

"Of course, how do you think we control security over there?"

"Damn, why is this getting so complicated?"

"Relax James, nothing is complicated, this is a routine matter, they shouldn't be there more than 3 or 4 hours, there is nothing for them to see,"

The intercom light was flashing on his desk, "I've gotta go, that's probably him now."

"All right Jim, just be casual, be polite and turn him over to the network guy as soon as you can, call me when you get a chance."

The door opened and the secretary preceded Inspector Harris into the office, he was not what he had expected. He looked like a middle weight boxer, crew cut blonde hair, he seemed to bounce a little with each step as he came in the room.

His eyes were pale blue, unblinking, inquiring, he did not look like a man who ever smiled, not now at any rate.

"Dr. Nelson, Inspector Dave Harris, Metropolitan Police Department."

Nelson took the hand offered, the grip was tight, the hand seemed large for a man his size.

"How can I help you Inspector?"

He motioned to him to take the chair opposite, but Harris just remained standing in front Nelson.

"As I mentioned to you on the telephone, as a part of the continuing investigation of Peter Mytryk, it is necessary that we check his workplace for evidence of his trafficking in child pornography. I hope that you will cooperate with us; otherwise we will get a subpoena in order to proceed."

"No need to do that Inspector, we are prepared to do what ever it takes to help with this investigation. We are as shocked as anyone else, perhaps more so, given that someone we trusted and worked with is involved with such disgusting activities."

Harris sat in the chair that Nelson had originally offered; Nelson eased himself into his chair, relaxing slightly.

Never seems to hurt to get to the point quickly, threaten a subpoena, get immediate access and establish the authority. Nelson looks nervous, is there something else here? Let's find out.

"We appreciate your cooperation, I have one or two questions that I would like you to help me with before I turn the Forensic team loose on your system."

Harris could not help but notice Nelson stiffen in his chair, a normal reaction? Maybe something else? The probing began.

"First, I will need a list of any fellow employees that he might have been close to, and as well if you know of any close friends, that information would be most helpful as well."

"Dr. Mytryk was very much a loner, frankly, I know nothing of his private life. In fact I don't know of any social contacts he may have had either within the company or outside it."

"Do you know of any particular habits of Mytryk that may have struck you as odd, perhaps something you remember after his arrest that did not seem significant at the time?"

"No, as I say, he kept very much to himself."

"In his job here, was he a part of a closely knit team? I would suspect that he did not do his research in isolation."

"You're right, he did head up a team of scientists, I will certainly get a list for you, but surely you don't suspect anyone here do you?"

"Dr. Nelson, I must investigate all avenues, we suspect he was part of a larger ring of paedophiles, it's my job to track these individuals down and arrest them. In the case of his fellow workers, consider that we are just as interested in clearing them of any involvement as well."

"Yes of course, I see."

"Now then perhaps we can get started in his work station?"

"Let me get the Network Administrator to lead you through your examinations, frankly, I have never mastered the mysteries of our computer system. But as you might imagine, in this kind of environment, security is a major issue, against both internal and external potential threats."

"Do you employ a Security Manager, given the sensitivity of some of the work you do here?"

"We do have security people on the premises of course, but in fact, the security arrangements are contracted out to our consultant, Mahoney Associates, you must know them."

Mahoney? Why Mahoney? Something he couldn't remember niggled at him in the back of his brain.

"Yes I do in fact, very thorough I understand."

Nelson called the Network Administrator and asked him to come to his office, the voice on the other end asked, "The police are here then?"

"Yes."

"Declan filled me in, I'll be right up."

"I had one other question for you Dr. Nelson, I was hoping to meet with Dr. Soper, but when I asked for him I was told he was unavailable and that I should see you. Where is Dr. Soper and when might I meet with him?"

He had so much on his mind, he had almost forgotten about Arnie, "I'm sorry, Arnie is away ill."

"Nothing serious I hope?"

"Some sort infection I think, there may be risk of him spreading it around so he decided it was better to stay away from here."

"Any idea when he will be available?"

"Not really, but I will contact you as soon as I know anything."

The administrator arrived, "Fred, this is Inspector Harris, he wants to check on Peter Mytryk's work station, it's in connection with this terrible business he's got himself involved in. Please give Inspector Harris your complete cooperation"

"Sure thing, but I can tell you right now, you won't find a thing, I take great pride in the security of our system here at Soper, if anybody even gets to surfing the web, I know about it. Our system prohibits all non essential web site activity and we maintain an activity log for every employee with computer access."

"I am sure you are right, but we have to check, I will also want to look at those logs as well Fred. I have a team of forensic computer chaps with me, where can we go to set this investigation up? "

"Come on down to my office, I have everything you will need right there."

Pat answers! Haven't even asked my questions yet, why is he so prepared? Why did Nelson get so uptight when I asked about Soper?

The two men left Nelson's office; he immediately shut his door and called Mahoney.

"Hello Jim, well how did everything go?"

"I don't like it Declan, everything is OK I think, with respect to the computer system, but he is inquiring about Arnie, he wants to see him!"

"What did you tell him?"

Nelson went over everything that had been said, "So, what do you think Declan?"

"I think we are going to need to resolve this situation regarding Arnie very soon."

*

Brad drove the SL55 into the parking stall that Ashley had arranged for him at the condo, he sat in the car after turning off the engine, why was he so nervous, this is just another kid.

No it wasn't just another kid, it was his brother, aside from his father, who barely counted, and this was his only living relative!

Suppose he doesn't like me? How will I deal with the autism thing? Researching it is one thing, but experiencing it is another. I want this thing to work, wait ease off, and take it one step at a time.

He gave his head a shake, no point in delaying further, he entered reception area and gave the security guard his name and who it was he wanted to see."

"You may go up Mr. Soper."

He stood outside of the penthouse door, screwing up the courage to knock, when the door opened, Ashley looked marvellous. Her radiant smile welcomed him in.

She reached up and kissed his cheek, "I thought I heard the elevator, come, put your stuff in the guest room, Ellis is having a little nap, then we can have a few minutes to talk before he gets up."

"You look great Ashley, nice to see you again."

"I've been looking forward to your coming Brad, I just hope everything goes well. Change is a difficult thing for Ellis."

"Ashley, I don't want to cause you any trouble, if it gets difficult, I can leave, the last thing I want to do is upset Ellis."

"I am sure it'll be OK, I just worry too much sometimes. Come, let's sit in the family room it's cozier."

"So tell me Brad, what have you been up to since we last talked?"

"Well, I went to see my father."

"You did!"

"Yes, I thought that I should at least do that much, in spite of everything, he is still my father."

"How was he?"

"They have him in isolation, did you know that?"

"I don't think they told me that, why?"

"Apparently they are not sure if, whatever it is he has, is communicable or not."

"And they don't know specifically what it is that he has?"

"No, it is kind of a tragic thing to see, he's hooked up to life support systems, monitors of all kinds, but he's more dead than alive. Except for parts of his brain, which seem to be working, there is apparently, a lot of brain activity."

"Wouldn't it be simpler to just eliminate the life support systems and just let him die?"

"Simpler for who? If he was brain dead, clinically brain dead, then that would be a consideration, but who is going to make the decision? The doctors will be concerned about legal charges. And then there is the company."

"What do you mean, the company?"

"I get the impression that his condition has complicated things at the company, what with new products being released, the possibility of the company going public and the fact that there is no will."

"So you believe that is why we are being pressured about the trustee thing?"

"Yes, the way I see it, should he die and is intestate, then this whole thing would be forced into probate. That could mean an unpredictable result with respect to share control for the company. If however, they can get us on side to support Jim Nelson as trustee, that would give Nelson control of the company and there probably is good chance that it would pertain after my father's death.

At least it would until you or I decided to test it in court, should we be so inclined."

"All this business crap just makes my head swim, I have other things to think about, have you come to any decision about what you are going to do?"

"Not really, but you had said earlier that you don't really trust Nelson, can you tell me why?"

"Brad, I would rather not get into it, just let's leave it as a personal issue with me, it has nothing to do with whether or not Jim would be capable of looking after our interests in the business."

Brad decided not to pursue it any further, he really didn't know Ashley that well and felt uncomfortable prying into any personal areas with her. He heard a slight noise behind him; he turned to see a little boy standing in the doorway of the bedroom, clutching a well-worn stuffed animal in one hand.

He looked at the floor with downcast eyes, he stood motionless, his mother called to him, "There's my big boy! Come over Ellis there is someone I want you to meet."

He moved towards the sound of his mother's voice, but avoided eye contact with her, she encircled him with her arms, turned him around to face Brad and said "Ellis, this your brother Bradley, he's come to see you."

Still no eye contact, Brad didn't speak, unsure of what to say he just looked at this little boy with the curly hair and vacant stare, and Ashley gently pushed Ellis towards Brad. Suddenly the boy screamed! He ran from the family room back into the bedroom and threw himself on the floor, both Ashley and Brad Followed."

Ellis was yelling unintelligible words and banging his head on the hardwood floor, Ashley looked stricken, hand over her mouth as though stifling a scream herself. Brad was at the boy's side in an instant, he scooped him up in his arms and struggled to hold the flailing child.

He placed a hand behind his head and encircled the little body with his other arm; he appeared to squeeze the child tightly. The struggle continued, but Brad persisted, whispering in the boy's ear as he continued applying pressure to the little body.

Gradually, these actions seemed to calm Ellis, his head lay on Brad's shoulder and as the flailing ended, Ashley could see both of Ellis' arms around Brad's neck, he was hugging Brad back.

The three of them returned to the family room and sat on the large sofa together, "Brad, how did you know to do that, and more importantly, what was it you said to him?"

"It really wasn't anything I said, it's really a case that he felt threatened by a change in what he expected when he came into the room.

By hugging him and talking quietly to him, he sensed that I was in fact protecting him, comforting him. The trick seems to be getting just the right amount of pressure, too little it has no effect, too much and you could cause more panic, I just got lucky I guess."

"But where did you learn all this?"

"When I heard Ellis was autistic I did some research so I might be better prepared when I finally got the opportunity to meet him. I found out that Hug Therapy is one method that has been tried as a treatment for autism.

You might find it hard to believe, but they actually manufacture a hug machine, intended for adults or more mature children, even in a classroom setting. Whenever they feel threatened, they can climb in and apply the pressure or "hug" to themselves.

It was nothing more than intuition on my part to try it with Ellis, and it appears to work."

"It certainly seems to, just look at him, he seems so comfortable with you, I can't believe it. You know Brad, the last time this happened here, he went into seizure and I had to call 911, I thought I was going to lose him!"

Brad leaned back on the sofa, Ellis was still holding tightly to his neck, but his body now seemed completely relaxed.

"Ashley maybe you could turn on the TV, I have also read that colour images and music have a calming effect as well."

Ashley clicked the remote and before she could switch to the cartoon channel. The local news came on.

"A late breaking development in the Peter Mytryk case, Channel 5 News has just been alerted that Peter Mytryk has been found dead in his home in Forest Hills. He is the victim of an apparent self-inflicted gunshot wound.

You will recall that Dr. Mytryk had been arrested concerning possession of child pornography and as suspect in an international ring of child prostitution and pornography.

His trial was scheduled to begin June 18th, again Peter Mytryk dead at 49 of a gunshot wound, an apparent suicide victim. More news at 10:00."

Chapter 15

Inspector Dave Harris sat in the office of Chief of Detectives Michael Fast, he had just concluded an oral report of his findings at Soper Research.

"So, there was nothing there?"

"No, but not a great surprise, frankly I would have been more surprised had we found anything, the security is very tight on their network, the forensic guys were very thorough,"

"You heard that Mytryk "pulled the pin"? "

"Yeah, just couldn't take the heat I guess."

"Shit, he hadn't even felt the heat yet. I had hoped he might lead us to others in this ring; you haven't interviewed all the other members of his research team have you?"

"No, I have that set up for tomorrow, but I haven't been able to track down Dr. Arnold Soper yet, he is apparently away sick."

"You better find him, no one gets excluded from this investigation!" He could see the agitation begin to show in Harris' face, "Fuckin' MBA cops, don't like to be told nothin'" he thought.

"Nelson seemed a bit evasive when I asked about Soper, something may come up on that front, I intend to keep chasing it."

"Good, just understand, we don't close this case just because Mytryk off'd himself, we may just get lucky, connect up the dots, you know, I am sure they taught you all that stuff at university."

Harris controlled his temper as best he could, Fat-assed Fast, that's what everybody on the force called him, sugar glazed doughnuts and coffee, that was police work to him.

He returned to his desk, he would try the direct approach, he'd call Soper's wife, and she should be able to tell him where he was.

*

"Oh my God! Did you hear you hear that Brad, Peter Mytryk is dead!"

He was still cradling Ellis in his arms, he was quiet now, but he still had his arms around Brad's neck, as though he was afraid he might lose him if he let go.

" Yes I heard, but let's not discuss it in front of the little guy here."

Brad sat on the floor, still holding Ellis; he picked up the stuffed toy from where it had been dropped during the outburst. "You know Ellis, I would really like to know who this is, will you tell me?"

Brad tried to turn the boy's head and make eye contact with him, but Ellis just squirmed away, looking at the toy.

"That's OK Ellis, I know that you will tell me his name when you are ready."

He played on the floor with the child for almost 2 hours, while Ashley was busy preparing dinner in the kitchen. Periodically she peered through the doorway at the two of them, Ellis actually seemed engaged in the play, she had never seen that before, he was always so withdrawn when she had seen him during playtime at Halton House.

The phone rang, Ashley decided to take in the study, when she returned she seemed shaken.

"What's wrong?"

"Shit, I think I might have screwed up!"

"What do you mean, who was on the phone?"

"It was the police! An Inspector Harris, he said he was working on the Mytryk case. He wanted to know how to get in touch with Arnie, wants to talk to him he said."

"What did you tell him?"

"I said he was ill."

"Was that all?"

"No, he kept pressing me, I admitted he was in the hospital, I told him he was in University Hospital!"

"Ashley, I wouldn't worry about it, it's going to come out some time, and you can't really lie to the police."

"I know, it's just that Jim Nelson made such a thing about keeping all of it confidential, he was afraid the media would get a hold of it."

"Given the current situation, I don't see how he could hope to exclude the media in any event, besides, I doubt the police are much interested in giving anything over to the press."

"You're probably right, it's just that I really don't know what to do next, this is becoming such a mess."

He put his arm around her, simply to reassure her, she turned her face towards his as if anticipating a kiss, instead he asked. "How's dinner coming?"

She composed herself and quickly looked away. "Be ready in a couple of minutes, it isn't much, but I hope you'll enjoy it, how about mixing us a drink before we eat?"

He moved quickly to the bar, glad to have the opportunity to break the tension, he would have to be more careful in this relationship. He didn't want Ashley to misunderstand his interest.

He carried her Manhattan into the kitchen; he had managed to find himself a beer in the bar fridge. Ashley said his Manhattan was superb, he was sure she would have said that regardless of what she really thought.

Ashley proved to be a rather good cook, he enjoyed the experience.

Ellis still sat quietly with eyes unfocused on the dish in front of him; he pushed some of the food around his plate eating very little.

"He has never been a very good eater I'm afraid."

"Well, he certainly doesn't look underfed to me."

They finished and Ashley began clearing the table, immediately Ellis moved to Brad's side and clung to his arm.

"He's afraid you are leaving, looks like you've made a real friend."

"I hope so. Come on Ellis, if you and I play, I can get out of doing the dishes"

*

Dave Harris dialled the University Hospital switchboard and asked the operator about the condition of Arnold Soper, he was surprised when the operator responded after a long pause, "I'm sorry sir, we do not have a patient by that name, are you sure you have the right hospital sir?"

"Perhaps I am mistaken." He hung up the phone and called Jim Nelson's home, there was no answer, he decided against leaving a message on his voice mail.

Declan Mahoney and Jim Nelson were holding a meeting at that moment, in Arnold Soper's office.

"Christ Declan! Mytryk's dead, this whole thing has gotten out of hand, you should have known he was unstable!"

"James, you are the one that is beginning to become unhinged, just because a pedophile decides to take his own life as a result being caught out, you think the wheels have come off."

"Is that it, you are saying he was a paedophile? You had nothing to do with this; it was just a convenient event?

"Of course, and mark me James, that's the way you are going to play it or you may come to regret it." The smile never left his face, but his eyes were flat and soulless, Nelson was sure that he would not hesitate in dealing with him as he had Mytryk.

"Just don't lose your head, remain calm, act reasonable, and there will be no problem. You know nothing more than you have read in the papers or heard on TV, just respond to any questions as directly as you always do."

"This officer, Inspector Harris, he is not a slow witted individual, I worry about him sniffing around."

"Just do as I say and he will be no problem. He found nothing when he was out here and that's the way it's going to stay"

"But he was asking about Arnie, how are we going to handle that?"

"That's the real reason I am here, we need to formulate a plan to deal with Arnie's condition and we have to get the new Director of Research in place and get a positive spin on all of it."

"I found his professional profile in Arnie's files." He passed the rather thick dossier over to Mahoney.

He skimmed through the background information and found a summary that gave him all of the salient information, "Very impressive, I am amazed that he has been able to accomplish all of this and by the tender age of 42 at that! Let's see, he's single, that's not so good, heterosexual, good!"

He continued with his review, he made notes on his PDA as he went, "So much for Dr. Nazir Monpetit, what is he, French I take it?"

"I am not sure, as I said, Arnie did not confide in me on this, the whole thing was very hush hush, Arnie handled it all directly himself, I was not privy to any of it. All I know is that he was with one of the major pharmaceutical companies, You can see from the compensation offer in that file, he is a very expensive acquisition!"

"I didn't see any photograph in the file, do you have one?"

"No, unless there is one somewhere in another file, but I didn't see anything else."

"When is he arriving in the city?"

"According to what's in that file, the announcement was to be made in mid June, I know Arnie would want him here for orientation and staff meetings about a week before that. He could be arriving anytime now."

"Well doctor, I would suggest that you get on it, finalize the details and be prepared to answer any questions he might have regarding what has transpired here. My guess would be that this has gone through the whole industry, he likely has heard about Mytryk.

The best approach in my opinion would be to handle it just as I have suggested you do with the police, the company knew nothing of these activities, certainly, had we known he would have been terminated immediately. You could even imply that perhaps Arnie might have had an inkling of what was going on and that was the reason for making the change.

Of course you would express surprise and dismay at his suicide, and just let it go at that."

Nelson didn't like taking instructions from Mahoney, but he knew had no real choice in the matter.

I'll get on it right away, but what about the situation with Arnie?"

"You had better convene a board meeting next week and have yourself appointed Chief executive Officer."

"But what about Arnie's holdings and the idea of my getting appointed as trustee?"

"Given your singular lack of success in getting either of Arnie's beneficiaries on side, I don't think we can afford to screw around much longer with this matter.

You should be able to sell the board on the need to have a new leader appointed to ensure continuity of the business during these stressful times and with a high profile Research Director to come on board.

You are the most likely candidate, a simple majority of the directors is all that is required, surely you can call in some favours on this?"

"I have no reason not to believe that I can, but nothing is certain, they are a greedy lot and you never know what they are thinking, particularly Lester Coughlan!"

"Then you had better start politicking, line up your support, if you don't see a clear majority in your favour, we will need to see how we can manage to control a shareholder meeting.

*

Dave Harris called his friend Ruthie, a nurse at University Hospital, "Hello Ruthie, how are you?"

"Dave, Dave Harris is that really you?"

"None other, thought it was time to phone my best looking nurse friend."

"Bullshit, you must want something, it's the only time I hear from you!"

"Come on Ruthie, it's not as bad as all that, is it."

"You want something from me, it's gonna cost you dinner!"

"OK, all right! It's a deal."

"And drinks too!"

"Sure, you bet." That could cost him more than the dinner he thought.

"Well what is it?"

"You got any special patients around the hospital these days?"

"What do you mean?"

"You know, somebody that jumped the queue, special duty nurses, that sort of thing."

"We aren't supposed to talk about it."

"So you do! Who is it?"

"I don't know, he is in isolated intensive care, nurses are from outside."

"Can you find out the name on his chart?"

"John Doe."

"John Doe?"

"That's what his chart says."

"What floor would that be?"

"He is on the six floor "E" wing, but you'll never get near him"

"Thanks Ruthie, you've been a great help."

"So when are we going out?"

"I'll call you, soon, I promise."

He hung up the phone, it could be worse; at least she had a great figure!

Chapter 16

"Dr. Soper, why don't you want to discuss it?"

"Discuss what?"

"We were talking about duplicate drugs that you may have released to the public, you said you didn't want to talk about it, why?"

"You don't understand how this business works."

"Then explain it to me."

"We spend millions, literally millions of dollars on research, we can only recover those costs from sales made, there have been times when we end up with a miserable failure and we are forced to absorb the development costs.

It should be understandable then, that we need revenues from products that are similar to existing drugs. Besides, competition helps drive down the price of such drugs for the consumer."

"I am sure then that you would make all of the authorities aware of any shortcomings of any of the drugs you have developed and ultimately the public, would you not?"

"Look my job is to keep the company viable so that we can continue to develop new products that will aid mankind. This is a heavily regulated industry, the regulators bear most of the responsibility of informing the public and releasing new product for use."

"Have you ever tried to influence the regulatory agencies to overlook their responsibilities?"

"I have "wined and dined" influential people, that's a normal business practice."

"You know that that is not what I mean."

"You need to know the serpentine nature of the bureaucracies involved in this business, it helps to have someone in the department smooth the way, to assist us in getting approvals, that sort of thing."

"You do not see any conflict of interest on the part of such an individual?"

"He is paid to overlook his own ethics!"

"That's very cynical."

"What now Alfred, you're being judgmental, that's hardly professional!"

"You're right, I apologize. But tell me about your own ethical stance in these matters."

"Ethics are a luxury, business is like war, if you are not scrambling forward you are falling back, after a while it becomes like a treadmill, sometimes you can't be sure that you aren't just running to stand still."

"In case you haven't noticed, you appear to have fallen off the treadmill now."

He was right, I am off the treadmill, time to reflect, what have I really accomplished? Hindsight that's what this is, aside from making money what have I achieved? There is no future, that's becoming ever more evident.

Has all of it really been for nothing? Surely not, I made some significant contributions to mankind haven't I? Drugs and treatments I was responsible for that eased the life of my fellow man. Yes, I had profited greatly as a result, but isn't that my right?

"Dr. Soper, are you asleep?"

"No, at least I don't think so."

"Do you feel any remorse regarding decisions or actions you have taken in the past?"

"Does it make any difference? What's done is done."

"The important thing is do you think it makes any difference?"

*

Ashley returned to the family room after checking on Ellis asleep in his room, "You're a "big hit" Brad, I have never seen him as comfortable with anyone, thank you for coming."

"Hey, I've enjoyed it, I've had as much fun as he has."

"He certainly went to bed well for you, I anticipated more anxiety from him when you put him down, he seemed to understand that you weren't leaving. But I am worried about your leaving on Sunday and his having to go back to Halton Hills."

"Well, tomorrow, I plan on taking him out in the SL55 for a drive, I am sure any kid would get a thrill out of that, we should be able to have the top down too, it's supposed to be a nice day. You'll come, won't you Ashley?"

"Brad, I don't want to interfere with your time with him, maybe you should go, just the two of you."

"I am going to try to make sure that I am going to be a permanent fixture in his life, maybe that will lessen his apprehension about Sunday."

"Does that mean your not going back to Vancouver?"

He hadn't given that any thought when he spoke of his relationship with Ellis, he had a great deal going on in his mind, his father, the business, Ellis, Janet. He needed more time to think he knew that he was going to have to make some difficult decisions.

"Ashley, I am really unsure of what I am going to do, even in the short term, let alone the rest of my life, I just know I want Ellis to be a part of it."

"Brad, I have been thinking about the trustee thing, I think I would be more comfortable with you as the trustee and not Jim Nelson." There, it was on the table, she had said it.

He looked at her in surprise; he had never even considered it.

"I'm not qualified, what the hell do I know about business?"

"Maybe not, but your honest and trustworthy, I know that, I also know that Jim Nelson is not!"

"How do you know I am all those things? I appreciate your confidence, but we barely know one another."

"I just know, that's all. Will you do it?"

"Ash, it's not something I really want to do, aside from the competency thing, how can I have meaningful role as an ethicist, if I end up actively involved in a drug company? I can't imagine anything being a greater conflict of interest, I would be a laughing stock in my chosen field."

"It would seem to me that Soper Research could do with a healthy dose of ethics!"

"Maybe so, but why me?"

"Brad, please promise me that you will at least consider it."

"OK, but please understand, it may not turn out the way you want it to, tell me, why don't you trust Nelson?"

"I am not sure I want to go into all that, it's personal and I was hurt deeply by what he did, can we just let it go at that?"

The next day was bright, sunny and warm a perfect day for touring, he buckled Ellis in and put the top down, the boy was intrigued by the roof mechanism, watching intently as the roof opened and the blue sky appeared, he clapped his hands in glee.

Brad fired up the engine and he watched Ellis' eyes grow large as the powerful engine roared to life. It was only 9:00 o'clock on Saturday morning, but Brad guessed correctly, the 401 was already heavy with traffic, he wondered if there ever was a slow time, he exited to the collector lanes where there seemed fewer cars.

They headed north, he though Lake Simcoe would be a nice little day trip, too bad he didn't know this part of the country better, he would do the best he could to see that Ellis had a good day. He looked over at the youngster, blonde hair blowing in the wind, he was staring intently ahead but sensed Brad looking at him, he turned and looked into Brad's eyes, and smiled.

Brad could hardly believe it! Ellis was making eye contact with him AND smiling, this was going to be a great day!

*

"Janet, it's Declan, could you come to my office, right away."

No "please" she thought his demanding tone angered her, but she had no option other than to say "Right away."

Saturday, her day off, it didn't matter, if Declan wanted her, she went. She arrived 30 minutes later and entered his office.

"Jan, have a seat, we have some things we need to go over with respect to the Soper account. You are aware that Arnold Soper had retained the services of a new Director of Research."

"Yes, do we know when he arrives in town?"

"He's already arrived, he is out at the Bristol Place, near the airport, would you arrange to pick him up and bring him down here. We need to arrange for all the usual announcements and perhaps a press conference, we need to prep him."

"There goes my weekend," she thought.

"Certainly, what's his name?"

"Nazir Monpetit, he is expecting you, just ask at the desk and they will ring him, I hope you are free this evening, I'd like you to take him to dinner."

I have to take control of this situation now, can't depend on Nelson, he'll likely screw it up. I need a face to face meeting with Monpetit, I've only had telephone conversations, and I don't know him that's dangerous. I can't let this opportunity slip through my fingers!

She answered with an affirmative nod and left the office, fuming.

She wondered why Declan could not have told her all of this on the phone, it would have saved her the trip downtown, she knew why, and to prove to her who had the control.

She parked the Mercedes in the lot and proceeded to the front desk, "I'll ring Mr. Monpetit's room immediately." She wondered if the piercing bothered him as he held the phone to his ear, she tried not to think of what other body parts might have had the same treatment.

She walked over to the elevators and waited, there was only one elevator that appeared to be moving and it was coming down. "Must be him."

The doors opened, she looked at the occupant and then looked away. "Ms. Petersen?"

He stuck out his hand, but she stared in disbelief, this was the biggest man she had ever met! He must have been at least 6'-8" tall, broad shouldered, fit and as black as could be!

"M... Mr. Monpetit?"

He threw back his head and laughed loudly, showing large, pearly teeth, "Not what you expected I take it!"

The accent was vaguely French, but cultured, he was a very good looking man she thought, she had trouble tearing her eyes away from his face, but finally she grasped the hand that had been offered. Or more to the point her hand was swallowed by the massive paw, yet it was a gentle handshake.

"I am sorry, I really didn't mean to stare it's just that,... just that..."

"I'm so big and soo black." Again a laugh rumbled from his chest. "It's OK, happens all the time, most people think I

should be a football player or a weight lifter, not a scientist."
His smile was dazzling; his presence was overwhelming.

Regaining her composure "I am very happy to meet you Mr.
Monpetit."

"Just call me Naz, all my friends do, and I think we are going
to be friends aren't we?"

He had an uncanny knack for keeping her off balance, she
hadn't met anybody like this before, and she couldn't help but
wonder how Declan was going to deal with him!

They got into the car, she with ease, he with great difficulty,
folding his great body to try to fit even with the seat all the way
back. Finally he was in, but he occupied more than just the
normal passenger space, his shoulders forced her against her
door, his head rubbed the headliner.

"You're going to have to get a bigger car if we are going to
do this again Ms. Petersen, sorry if I'm invading your space."

He twisted his upper body so that his back was more or less
to the passenger window, she was sure that it was not
comfortable for him, but she felt less claustrophobic.

She headed back towards the office, "So, Naz, where do you
come from?"

"That's a long story, but as to the name, my father was
French and my mother was Moroccan, I was raised in Paris and
attended the Sorbonne."

"Your English is very good."

"It should be, my father sent me to public school in
England, I also got a degree from Oxford."

"So what prompted you to leave, where was it? And come to
Soper Research."

"I was in Belgium, working for Zaltech Inc., I met Dr. Soper
and he made me an offer I couldn't refuse, tell me, are you
always so inquisitive?"

"Sorry Naz, but I am one of the people who will be
responsible for introducing you to the industry in this country,
and in the US of course, so it is more than idle curiosity."

"So you are a PR person?"

"That and more!"

"How much more?"

*

Brad pulled the car into the Dairy Queen pick up window and got them each a soft ice cream cone. He wondered just what his father would think of his offspring eating ice cream in his SL55, he could guess.

He watched Ellis' face when he handed him his cone, he was beaming, he attacked the cone and ended up with more on his nose than he got in his mouth. It was such a simple pleasure but it seemed to Brad that no ice cream had ever tasted so good!

If he returned to Vancouver, he could kiss these kind of days goodbye, and while he would miss them he would get over it, but he seemed to be making progress with Ellis, he knew it wouldn't be fair to him to leave. And yet, what about his own future? Should he attempt to become involved with Soper?

"To hell with it!" He grasped Ellis' knee and squeezed it, "What do you say little fellow? Let's have some fun, he spun the tires and sprayed gravel as they got back on the highway. He thought he heard Ellis laugh.

Chapter 17

Janet watched the look on Declan's face when Nazir followed her into his office, it was obvious that he was not what was expected, she had never seen Declan at a loss for words, but now his mouth was silently open.

"Declan meet Nazir Monpetit, Nazir, this is Declan Mahoney, he is the CEO of Mahoney Associates.

She watched as Declan's hand disappeared in the handshake. Nazir towered above Mahoney by a good foot; it was obvious that Naz was not going to be easily intimidated. Jan hoped that she was going to get to stay for the meeting. But such was not to be the case; Mahoney dismissed her and closed the door behind her.

"Well Dr. Monpetit, it is a pleasure to meet you at last, I have heard nothing but good things about you from Dr. Soper."

"Thank you, but please, just call me Naz, frankly I am surprised that Dr. Soper isn't here as well, will he be joining us?"

"Ah no, not today. He is ill and can't be with us."

"That's unfortunate, nothing too serious I hope?"

"Well, as a matter of fact, it may be very serious, we are not quite sure of just what his problem is. At present he is in University Hospital after collapsing at his office three weeks ago."

"Three weeks ago and there is still no diagnosis?"

Mahoney had no option but to continue with his outline of Soper's condition, but he avoided any mention of the self-administration of the vaccine.

"Good God! I can't believe it; we were just together in Nairobi, his attack must have occurred just after he returned here.

Tell me, who is in charge at Soper Research in his absence, I must talk to someone about my status, this is incredible!"

"Not to worry Naz, Soper Research is far too big a company to be dependent upon one man, even a man like Arnold Soper.

Dr. James Nelson is acting CEO at present, he was Vice-Chairman of the Executive Committee, he's a brilliant man and fortunately he is right on top of all aspects of Soper Research.

Have the two of you ever met?"

"No, I'm afraid I haven't, what is his specialty?"

"He is a well known MD here in the city and a long time personal friend of Arnie's, they have been almost inseparable, the company is lucky to have Jim in place, there will be no break in the continuity."

"I look forward to meeting him, I am sure we have a great deal to discuss, do you have any idea when we can arrange that?"

"I will get him on the phone as soon as we finish our meeting here, there are several things you and I need to discuss."

We provide Public Relation Services for the company and it's executives, and we also handle all security issues such as protection of intellectual property owned by the company, building protection, network protection that sort of thing.

There is one other issue I must discuss with you, and it's a sensitive one at that.

How well did you know your predecessor, Dr. Peter Mytryk?"

"Not at all, except of course by way of the papers he presented to the International Institute of Microbiology. He seemed bright enough, although there must have been some shortcomings based on Arnie's desire to replace him."

"Well, it has come at an unfortunate time, but Peter Mytryk is dead!"

"Dead?"

"An apparent suicide, this is the difficult part Naz, he was arrested last week for possession of child pornography, the police felt he might have been part of an international ring of paedophiles, and that he might have been trading or selling kiddy porn!"

"Shit! What have I gotten into here, first Arnie Soper is in a coma and now Peter Mytryk turns out to be a pervert that commits suicide!

"Naz, calm down, neither of these things reflect on the integrity of the company or the opportunities that Arnie discussed with you, they still exist, in fact, they probably have increased, given the turn of events.

In fact, it is entirely possible that these events will serve your ends even better than might have been anticipated"

"How do you figure that?"

"Look Naz, the job you were hired for is a very prominent one, but with the number one man incapacitated, can you not see that enhancing your role here and achieving the goals we have discussed over the phone?"

Of course the same thoughts had already occurred to Monpetit, he felt sure that he was in an excellent position to up the ante for him with the company in such a vulnerable position.

"I must tell you that all of this does not make me happy, but for the benefit of all concerned, I will make my best effort to make this work."

"Good, I am glad that you still consider this to be a great personal opportunity, let me layout for you how we plan to introduce you to your new position and to the rest of the industry in North America."

Mahoney then proceeded to make his presentation; it was impressive. Media releases meetings with investors, television interviews magazine articles and receptions.

"This is going to be the making of Nazir Monpetit" he thought, yes this could be a very good thing in spite of some initial messy business, but he could handle that.

When Mahoney finished, he felt a flush of satisfaction in the toothy grin he saw on Naz's face He had him hooked!

"Naz, I am going to suggest that you relocate from the Bristol Place to the Hamden Suites in the Research Park, it is much closer to the office, it would make a good base for you until you find permanent accommodations.

I'll have Janet drive you back and get you settled in. I am sure you are anxious to have a look around the facility, I'll arrange for Jim Nelson to meet with you for breakfast, then he can take you on a tour and introduce you to your staff, we may as well get the ball rolling."

The thought of spending more time with Janet pleased Naz, probably more than the prospect of seeing yet another lab setup.

"Anything you say Mr. Mahoney."

"Declan, please Naz."

He buzzed Janet and gave her the instructions he wanted followed, no please, no thank you.

Now what the hell is going on? If all of this is true, it may make my plan even more achievable. I don't trust Mahoney, but I need to use him. Maybe I can use Nelson too! In the meantime, Janet my girl, let's have some fun!

*

When they had left, Mahoney called Nelson and filled him in, not on all of it, he may as well get a surprise too.

"By the way Jim, I understand that Ashley is trying to convince Brad Soper to be the trustee, apparently she doesn't trust you, She says it's personal and that at one time you hurt her deeply, I guess we both know what that is all about don't we?"

"How do you know all this?"

"It doesn't matter, what matters is I know about it, if you can't swing your appointment by way of the board of directors, we will have to deal with Ashley, one way or another."

He replaced the phone, "That son-of-a-bitch! He must be bugging the condo. I had better be careful, this place is probably bugged too, the office certainly."

*

Janet and Naz had made peace with the space available in her car and she headed back up to his hotel, he watched her manoeuver expertly in and out of the heavy traffic, he was impressed with this good looking girl.

"So Janet, tell me about yourself, what do you do at Mahoney Associates?"

"Haven't you noticed, I am the resident cab driver!"

"He pisses you off huh?"

"You noticed did you?"

"Yes I did, but don't avoid my question, what do you do at Mahoney?"

"If you promise not to make unkind comments, I will tell you."

"Me, unkind, to you, never!"

"Well I'm a lawyer in real life, got tired of corporate law and this job promised some excitement, you know, moving among the heavy hitters."

"I knew you weren't without talent, but a lawyer, I would not have guessed that, do you get to do any lawyering at Mahoney?"

"I get to give opinions on issues that come up, develop scenarios so that we stay out of legal troubles, give informal advice, that sort of thing."

"I sense that you are not fond of Mr. Declan Mahoney?"

"Naz, it is better not to foul one's nest don't you think?"

"I'll take that as an affirmative answer. Can you tell me why Declan seems to have such a prominent role in Soper Research?

I get the feeling that he is calling most of the shots since Arnie has been incapacitated?"

"My understanding is that Jim Nelson is supposed to be calling the shots, as you say, I can only assume that Declan is carrying out instructions from him. I do know that there is a contractual relationship between Mahoney Associates and Soper Research Inc. Although I have never seen the contract."

"What do you make of this business with Mytryk?"

"It was a shocker to say the least, nobody that I have talked to had any idea that he was into that kind of thing, I think it's just horrible! I can't say I am sorry the bastard is dead, anyone that takes advantage of little children should be castrated at the very least."

"You know, there are usually some signs that are evident when deviant behaviour of this kind is involved, I just find it strange that no one noticed anything."

"Are you trying to tell me that you also have a degree in Psychology on top of everything else I've read about you?"

"You've read about me? I'm flattered, but yes I do."

She smiled at him, she liked him, and she felt she could trust this individual, some anyway. They stopped at the hotel, he checked out and put his baggage in the trunk, he seemed to be travelling pretty light given that he was moving permanently to Toronto.

"That's all you have?"

"I'm like a gypsy, don't need much more than the clothes on my back, in fact the rest of my stuff has already been shipped, it's to be held in storage until I can find a place, maybe you could help me do that?"

"Maybe."

She drove him past Soper Research so he could have a look before checking in to the hotel, he had to admit to himself, it was impressive, he began to feel more comfortable with the move."

She had intended to just drop him off at the Hamden Suites, but before he got out he asked, "how's the food here?"

"Food? Remember this is a Hamden Suite. There is a pretty good steak house not far from here, just ask for directions to The Bum Steer"

"The Bum Steer? You pulling my leg?"

"No seriously, that's what it's called, you'll like it."

"May I buy you dinner? Come with me, remember I've no car."

She thought "What the hell, why not. Brad was likely shacked up with Ashley, besides if Declan finds out I just dumped him, I'll be in trouble."

"Sure, I'll come in while you check in, I need to stretch my legs."

*

Brad returned to the condo and parked the car. Ellis had nodded off to sleep. He had had a busy day.

He carefully lifted the little boy out of the seat, Ellis' arms twined around his neck, he kicked the door shut with his foot, locking and setting the car alarm with the key fob.

Ashley answered the door, she had been fretting about any problems Brad might have had with Ellis, the relief showed in her face when she saw the two of them standing there.

"I've got one tired little soldier here Mom."

"You were gone so long I started to get worried, but it doesn't look like I needed to."

"Let me just put him on his bed, you can undress him and put his PJ's on, he doesn't need dinner, nor do I for that matter, we stopped at McDonalds. I hope you don't mind, but he had a blast in the play centre and he liked the food."

"Of course I don't mind, just go on and sit down, get yourself a beer if you like, I won't be a minute."

He looked in the bar fridge and sure enough, Ashley had bought some Kokanee, he took a long pull from the frosty bottle and settled onto the sofa.

Ashley returned.

"He's dead to the world, Brad thank you so much for doing that with him, I'm glad there were no upsets, I hope you had fun too."

"You bet I did, you know Ashley, he laughed, he actually laughed! It was so great to hear, we had ice cream, we went to the beach, we wrestled it was just great!"

"You went to the beach? Where?"

"Lake Simcoe, it was crowded but he held on to my hand, never left my side, I don't know if he had ever seen that many people,"

"I don't think so, what an adventure for him, thank you Brad." She sat beside him taking his hand in hers, "You don't know what this has meant to me too."

"The least I could do for my little brother!"

She got up and made herself a drink and returned to her place, "Brad, have you thought any more about what I asked you last night?"

"You mean about the trustee thing?"

"Yes."

"After today, I am thinking about being in Toronto permanently, I don't want to be too far from Ellis, remember he is my only family. But I am torn with what it is I planned to do with my life and what you are asking.

Mind you I could still follow my original career plan here in Toronto, I don't have to go back to the West Coast."

"Brad, I know you love Ellis, you need to think of him in this instance too, Soper Research could have a big influence on his life, remember, he will be the major beneficiary, along with you of course."

"I am trying not to be selfish in this matter, but don't you think that Jim Nelson would be more qualified to protect your interest better than I and Ellis' too for that matter."

"I have given this a lot of thought, I would sooner see the court appoint someone other than Jim if you won't do this. I have told you I cannot trust that man."

"But why?"

Chapter 18

Lester Coughlan was on the other end of the phone when Jim Nelson answered it, there was no question that Coughlan had the uncanny ability to unnerve Nelson simply with his tone of voice, it didn't really matter what he said, it was how he said it.

"Nelson, tell me what the hell is going on at Soper, first Mytryk is arrested, then he commits suicide and now I can't find Arnie!"

Nelson went through the normal pleasantries of taking the phone call in order to try to collect his thoughts as to how he should answer.

"Forget the bullshit, just answer my questions, everything seems to be going to ratshit there!"

"Lester, calm down, it's all under control, Declan has everything under control, the media..."

"Fuck the media! Fuck Mahoney, I don't trust that creepy bastard; I don't know why Arnie ever hired him!"

I've got a small fortune tied up in that company, I don't intend to see it pissed away by incompetents! Where's Arnie?"

Nelson really had no option except to tell Coughlan about Arnie's current state, but was careful to omit any references to the new vaccine or that Arnie had taken it himself. He left the impression that Arnie's predicament was possibly related to a virus he picked up in Africa.

"Stupid son-of-a-bitch! Why the hell was he in Africa anyway? This is a sorry mess, we'd better meet next week, we can't leave things as they are."

"Lester, I couldn't agree with you more I was just about to call you and arrange a meeting, when you called me!"

"Contact the rest of the board and call me back with the date, can you do that much?"

Nelson could feel his blood pressure going up, he fought the urge to respond with an invective and instead said "Yes Lester, I'll get right on it."

Coughlan hung up the phone.

Mahoney, that sneaky bastard, he's up to something I'm sure, I can't forget the look on his face when he found out that I was on the board of Soper. Still don't know why Arnie hired him, had something to do with Mytryk I know that much.

Got to admit, I was surprised too, this informer and thief right in our midst. I fixed his wagon, a few words in the right ears back to my old stalwarts in Belfast! He's lucky they didn't kill him. I would have, if I'd been younger.

They'll suck him dry before they do knacker him; his life is the only thing more important to him than money!

Could be that he's behind whatever has happened to Arnie, I wouldn't put it past him, I must watch and be careful.

*

Mahoney sat at his desk looking intently at his computer screen; he saw that the voice-activated microphone hidden in Ashley Soper's home was active. His computer was storing whatever was being said, he selected an option with his mouse and the speakers on his desk allowed him to listen in.

He could hear Ashley's voice, she was talking to Bradley, "Brad, please understand, I don't want Jim Nelson to run Soper Research, as I said I don't trust him, I have a very uneasy feeling about this whole thing.

"I don't understand just what you mean Ashley, I can't make an intelligent decision without having all the facts. You tell me you don't trust him, but you won't tell me why. You say you have an uneasy feeling about all of this, but again you tell me nothing.

Ashley, I don't think it's reasonable for you to expect me to change my career course on the basis of your intuition!"

"Brad, I'm asking you to trust me on this, I told you I had a hurtful experience involving Jim Nelson, I don't want to reopen old wounds."

He could see she was about to cry.

"Ashley, I don't mean to hurt you by dredging up some past sins, real or imaginary."

"Oh they were very real Brad!"

"OK, I won't press you any further, just know, that I will understand and respect anything you tell me, whenever you want to tell me."

"Thank you Brad, but I'm serious about this, if you decide that you are going to support Nelson, I will fight you on it, in court if necessary."

"Fucking Bitch!" Mahoney's eyes were narrowed slits, his teeth clenched, "We'll see how much you change your tune when I get finished with you!"

He clicked the mouse button and the speakers fell silent, but the recording continued, this system automatically scanned for key phrases. He knew he could retrieve any important information, without having to listen to every word. In fact, this system could dial him on a secure telephone and play back significant parts on any conversation that met the surveillance criteria.

"Jim, its Declan here, have you arranged the board meeting as I requested?"

"As a matter of fact, I just got off the phone with Lester Coughlan, he's available and I've just finished rounding up the balance of the directors."

"I can't believe it, you've actually moved your ass on this, good!"

Nelson bristled at the treatment, yet he said nothing, he could say nothing, Mahoney had him by the short hairs, as much as he detested the man, he acquiesced. Nelson knew that this coarse man could destroy him in an instant and likely take pleasure in the act.

"Will Tuesday be OK?" He tried to keep any hint of sarcasm out of his voice; Mahoney's bad temper was legendary.

"Good! And James, it will be in your best interest to be successful, you may find our alternatives somewhat distasteful."

The Directors filed into the boardroom, there were 8 of them, not including Nelson, all were in their sixties, all prosperous, each had a sense of their own importance, this sense Nelson concluded seemed proportional to their bank balances.

Nelson took the seat at the head of the table, it was Arnie Soper's customary chair, even when Nelson occasionally chaired a meeting in Arnie's absence, he never used his chair, the board members sensed that something had changed.

Lester Coughlan, Ashley's father took his seat to the right of Nelson, Jim knew that he was the key to this meeting, he was a very successful businessman, others viewed him as having the "Midas Touch." It seemed every venture was successful, every investment paid dividends, and therefore people wanted to emulate him.

This was largely the reason that the other board members, like lemmings, had made their investment in Soper Research; he was without doubt their leader, the fact that Coughlan followed Soper's every lead didn't matter to them.

Coughlan was older than the rest; he was a large man with a leonine head of white hair, half glasses perched on the end of his nose, he looked more like a University Professor than a tycoon.

Nelson was nervous and fidgeted with a file folder in front of him, the corporate secretary sitting to his right, nodded to him to indicate she was ready. He began.

"Gentlemen, the secretary will note that the meeting was called to order at 1:30 PM on June 6th, 2003, with James Nelson as acting Chairman.

The purpose of this meeting is two fold"; he paused and took a drink of water. In the first instance, I must advise you that the Chief Executive of the firm, Arnold Soper, has been incapacitated."

Immediately he had their attention, "What do you mean he's incapacitated?" asked Coughlan, just as though he had never heard about it.

"On his return from Nairobi, he was taken ill and collapsed in his office, subsequently, he was taken to University Hospital, where he remains in a coma."

The questions came thick and heavy, mostly from Coughlan, Nelson did the best he could in response to all of them, but it didn't help much to have such a speculative diagnosis nor much of a prognosis either. These were all laymen, so he tried to keep this discussion at their level, but fell into the trap of being condescending.

"Look here Nelson, don't try to bullshit us or talk down to us, just give us the facts. What is the likely outcome of Arnie's condition? Will he recover, will he die, will he be somehow handicapped should he recover?" His glasses slipped further down his nose.

"We just don't know, the best I can do is to give you my sense of the situation, I don't believe Arnie is going to recover, at least not to any significant degree. He is on life support; his nervous system has been irreparably damaged. Full recovery is out of the question. Will he die? That depends on your definition of life, as far as I am concerned, Arnie is already dead, there is brain activity, but nothing else, remove the life support and he will die."

"Then why don't they let the poor son-of-a-bitch die? Take away the life support, what good is he in this state, to himself or anybody else?"

"That's not our call, there are legal implications involved, it could take a court order to remove life support."

"First we have Mytryk charged with being a paedophile, then he blows his brains out, now this! What the hell is becoming of this company? I have sunk a small fortune into this place, it all seems to be going into the Shitter!"

Nelson couldn't help but note that the concern was money not Arnie's condition nor Mytryk's misfortune, it was money, just money, and nothing else mattered to them. They had already written off the man who had built up the business, the man who had given them an exceptional return of their investment every year, he obviously was no longer an asset to them.

"As you are aware, Arnie had already made arrangements to replace Peter Mytryk, in fact Nazir Monpetit is here, now, I met with him yesterday. We will be making an announcement as to his appointment shortly."

"Well, that's something at least, as I remember Arnie stole him from one of our competitors, in Europe wasn't it?"

"That's correct, he was Chief of Microbiology research at Zaltec in Belgium, Arnie felt it was a real coup to recruit him."

"He better be as good as Arnie anticipated, as I remember, he's going to cost us a fortune."

It was the way every board meeting went, Coughlan asking the questions and his sycophants nodding in approval or muttering the occasional "that's right!"

"Dr. Monpetit's credentials and list of accomplishments are substantial, I am sure that he will prove Arnie right. Arnie always said, "Superior skill sets don't cost, they pay!"

"We'll see, now, tell me, what's happening to the investigation of Mytryk's death, all I know is what I read in the papers or see on TV?"

"There is little more to report, the police were here, checking Mytryk's workstation, I suppose to see if he was using our facilities here in his dirty business. Of course, we got a clean bill of health. As far as I am concerned, the case is closed, I believe the police are inclined the same way."

"Maybe, maybe not! We'll see. I can tell you that I have great concern given that we are about to release a new vaccine that will revolutionize medicine, and make us all rich in the process. We can ill afford any bad press, we need the media on side, who's going to look after that, Arnie was a past master at getting his way with is message?"

"Actually, Lester, that brings me to the second reason for this board meeting."

"And what might that be?"

"I would propose that the board of directors elect me as the Chief Executive Officer of the firm. I think it is desirable that we have strong direction for the company during this turbulent period, critical decisions must be made, I think I'm the man to make them and lead the company forward!"

"Are you quite finished?"

Nelson looked at Coughlan and nodded, he could see hatred in the man's face, the hard eyes stared back at him, and he raised a bony finger and pointed in Nelson's face.

"There is no way in hell that you will ever head up this company, as long as I am involved here.

I know of nothing that you have ever said or done that would qualify you for this position. As long as Arnie was around, you were a protected species, trust me, you are no longer!"

"Lester, Lester, where is all of this coming from? I am the most qualified for the job, I worked closely with Arnie, I am well connected with the industry, I have been dedicated to this company, at the expense of my own practice I might say!"

"Nelson, I don't trust you, never have. I move that we form a committee of three of our number, excluding you, to act as a search committee to find a new CEO. This committee to report back to the board by July 15th."

The motion was seconded and an affirmative vote of 8 to 1 was quickly recorded, a second motion adjourning the meeting was past in a similar manner.

Nelson sat with his mouth agape, he had not anticipated this, and he was devastated.

"Lester! What have I done, what have I ever done to cause this lack of trust?"

"I don't need to answer that, you know full well what you have done!"

The 8 men filed out of the boardroom, Jim Nelson sat by himself, and even the Corporate Secretary had abandoned him. He slumped in his chair, head in his hands.

His cell phone rang; It was Declan Mahoney.

"I wouldn't call that a very successful meeting James, would you?"

How did he find out so quickly? Was even this room bugged? It must be, the ubiquitous Mahoney seemed to be everywhere, seemed to know everything!

"You heard it all?"

"Yes, every last word, I can't say you are well liked can I?"

"I don't want to hear any more of your crap Mahoney!"

There was a silence on the other end of the line, then "Listen to me you ass-hole, don't blame other people for your own shortcomings, if you could have sold yourself at that meeting, you would have guaranteed a place for yourself near the top of the heap. Now you will be lucky to be on top of the dung heap!"

Nelson could feel anger and resentment rising within him, but he knew he could not afford to vent his anger. He hated this man, with all his being, but Mahoney had control over him, a well-placed word, a file placed in the wrong hands and he would be destroyed.

He took a deep breath, suppressed his emotions and asked, "What do we do now?"

"We need to get Ashley to change her position with respect to supporting you as trustee, we need her to influence young Soper as well."

"What good is that going to do, by then there will be a new CEO at Soper, I am sure of it?"

"The motion that was passed today won't mean a thing if we can move quickly and get control of Arnie's shares. We will convene a Shareholder's Meeting, with share control we can rescind that motion and appoint you as CEO, it's that simple."

"But how are you going to influence Ashley?"

"I have enough on her and her activities over the last 6 or 7 years, Arnie had me collect it in case the divorce settlement became difficult, if I released even half of it she would be completely destroyed and she would surely lose custody of her son!"

There was little doubt in Nelson's mind that he was dealing with evil, this man would achieve his ends regardless of the means, without remorse, and without regard to the havoc he creates in the process.

"So you will talk to Ashley?"

"I will have a word with her, but I know that you have some significant history with her, just understand I will use that information if I have to."

"If you make that information public, it will destroy her!"

"That's not my problem."

Chapter 19

D ave Harris entered University Hospital and proceeded to the room his friend Ruthie had indicated was Arnold Soper's. It had cost him a dinner and then some, but he had gotten his information and then some, he figured he got his money's worth.

There was a man in a dark navy suit standing outside the door to the isolation ward; the man stopped Harris with an outstretched upturned palm.

"Sorry Sir, no visitors are allowed!"

Harris flashed his police badge, "This says I'm allowed!"

"I'm sorry detective but I have my orders, no one gets in without authorization, sir."

"Who the hell says so?"

"Mr. Mahoney sir, he's in charge here."

"Like hell he is, if you do not want to be charged with obstructing a police investigation, get the hell out of my way!"

The man reached in his pocket and retrieved his cell phone; he punched the speed dial and reached Mahoney's direct line.

The man explained the situation to Mahoney and then handed the phone to Harris.

"Detective Harris, is this really necessary, Arnold Soper is in a coma, he can offer nothing to your investigation?"

"Look Mahoney, I am investigating a suspicious death, it is essential that I determine the whereabouts of all the actors in this picture. If you hadn't played "cloak and daggers" by hiding Soper in the manner you did, it would likely not be necessary for me even to be here."

"What do you mean "suspicious death," I thought you were investigating Peter Mytryk's suicide?"

"His death has not been officially ruled a suicide, now, are you going to force me to get a warrant to enter his room?"

"There is nothing to hide here, that won't be necessary, however, if you want to enter into Mr. Soper's unit, you will have to accept the hospital protocol regarding, gowns, masks, head coverings etc. They have no idea if Mr. Soper is Infectious or to what degree, this would be for your own protection.

Your option would be to view him through the observation window from the ante room, I could authorize that right now, otherwise, we have to involve the appropriate hospital authorities."

"That may be adequate, providing I can see his face for identification purposes, who is his attending physician, I'll want to see him too!"

"Dr. Cyril Pickard is in charge, he is the chief neurologist there."

"Tell me Mahoney, why all the secrecy? Why is he in here under an assumed name? What's he or you got to hide?"

"Inspector Harris, neither Arnold Soper or I have anything to hide! We just needed time to try to determine how serious his situation is; we didn't need the media swarming all over this thing! Is there anything else, I have other calls holding."

"Just get you man to let me in!" He handed the phone back to the blue suit.

The man nodded to the phone and unlocked the door. "Sorry Inspector, but it's my job."

Harris ignored the comment and brushed passed by him, into the anteroom. Although he knew that the unit was being ventilated under negative pressure, he was sure that he could smell the smell of imminent death, but then he always seemed to smell that smell, an occupational hazard.

He moved to the viewing window and observed Soper on the high hospital bed, it was draped in white and it reminded him of a catafalque holding some dead warrior. The lights in the isolation chamber were set to a low level that cast a greenish hue over everything the light touched.

From where he was standing it was not possible to hear the sounds of the ventilator supplying and expelling air from the patient's lungs, nor could he hear the electronic beep of the monitoring equipment. There seemed to be clear plastic tubes in every orifice, intravenous solutions were being metered into his left arm, a urine bag hung from the foot of the bed.

"Poor son-of-a-bitch!" he thought, however, he could not make out the man's identity, his face was obstructed by the ventilation mask, he would have to get a statement from Pickard as to the man's identity.

It was clear to Harris that this was not some sort of scam, it seemed obvious to him that this man was on the verge of death.

Cyril Pickard picked up the wall phone and responded to his page, it was Declan Mahoney.

"Cyril, just a "heads up" Inspector Harris knows about Arnie, in fact he is in the viewing area of your isolation ward right now. He indicated that he wants to interview you afterwards."

"Why is he here? What has any of this to do with the police?"

"Harris is investigating Peter Mytryk's suicide, when he tried to contact Arnie, as Mytryk's employer, he found out that he had been taken ill. I really think it is just routine. He is just being thorough, just answer his questions as directly as you can, but don't volunteer anything about Arnie taking the experimental vaccine OK?"

"Yes, of course, I was shocked by Mytryk's death, to think that obscene little man was here, right here in my hospital, using my computer and office." Mahoney could not hear his shudder.

"Cyril, give me a call later and let me know how things went."

Harris left the viewing area and proceeded to the reception desk, he asked for Dr. Pickard, the bored receptionist looked up at him from behind the glass partition, "What is this inquiry in regards to?"

He flashed his ID, "It's official business, just get the Doctor for me."

Pickard ushered Harris into his office. The decor reflected his status within the hospital hierarchy, the dark walnut panelling glowed with a patina that spoke volumes as to the cost, the oversized matching walnut desk with an imposing throne like chair, might give one the impression of conversing with God, when sitting opposite.

However, Harris was not so impressed. He seated himself and as Pickard settled into his chair asked, "So, Dr. Pickard, is Dr. Arnold Soper a patient here at this hospital or not?"

"Yes, Yes he is, why is that significant to you?"

"Dr. Pickard, this interview will be shortened considerably if you just understand, I ask the questions and you answer. Not the other way around."

"Of course, please continue."

"Is the man in Isolation Unit 4E in fact Dr. Arnold Soper?"

"I have already told you that!"

"Just answer the question Dr. Pickard!"

"Yes, Dr. Soper is a patient in this hospital and he is in 4E Isolation unit!"

"Thank you Doctor, now tell me, why is he registered under an assumed name instead of his own?"

"Jim Nelson and Declan Mahoney requested that he be admitted under an assumed name to prevent the media from getting hold of this situation and sensationalising it.

We have had other celebrities in here from time to time, it makes it difficult for the staff to do their jobs when there is media harassment, it can get to be a zoo!"

"I can understand that sort of thing with film stars and the like, but what's so special about Soper, why does he get this special treatment?"

"You obviously don't read the financial pages, rumour has it that he is about to take his company public, this kind of news would be detrimental to that, besides he has been a major benefactor to this hospital. It seemed the least we could do, until we had a definitive diagnosis of his condition."

"Sounds like two tier medicine to me doctor."

"Look, there is no cost to the government, there is no cost to this hospital, all we are trying to do is aid a man who is obviously dying. Besides which, what has any of this to do with the death of Peter Mytryk, I understood that to be the thrust of your investigation."

"Well Doctor, my informants tell me that you had Peter Mytryk in here consulting on Dr. Soper's condition, to me that indicates some sort of nexus that requires I investigate, as I mentioned earlier, we have not officially ruled Dr. Mytryk's death a suicide.

What can you tell me about Mytryk's presence here, why was he involved?"

"Dr. Mytryk is or rather was a renowned microbiologist, I asked him to review the tests we had conducted to determine if it might be some form of virus causing Arnie's problem. He has done considerable research in this field in his position with Soper Research, Jim Nelson recommended him most highly."

"And what was his conclusion?"

"There really was nothing he could tell us that we didn't already know, he merely confirmed our own observations, if it is a virus, it is very obscure, there seems to be nothing in any of the medical journals remotely like this."

"Tell me Dr. Pickard, just exactly is Arnold Soper's condition?"

"It appears the myelin sheath is being damaged, almost stripped away from specific nerve groupings in his brain."

"Excuse me, myelin?"

"Consider it like insulation on an electrical wire, if the insulation is damaged, then short circuits occur, in your house, a fuse would likely blow, in Dr. Soper's brain, permanent brain damage is the result."

"Are you telling me that Soper is brain dead?"

"No, in fact far from it, there is evidence of high activity in certain areas of the brain, those areas responsible for long term memory and other cognitive functions. But in other areas, those that control certain basic functions such as vision, hearing and smell for example, are not functioning at all. It's as though we are watching someone in a deep sleep with very high REM activity."

"Is this activity going on all of the time?"

"No, there are periods of what we assume is rest, where the brain activity slows down."

"Hmm, very interesting, and what do you believe his prognosis is?"

"To put it bluntly, he has no future, if we remove life support he will die. The brain damage that has occurred, is irreversible, his is a hopeless case."

Harris sat quietly pondering all that he had heard, he was unsure if there was any connection here with Mytryk's death, but something niggled at the back of his brain. He decided on another tack with Pickard.

"Tell me doctor, what was your impression of Peter Mytryk, did the recent revelations surprise you, or had you ever heard any rumours pertaining to him?"

Harris noticed Pickard's eyebrows twitch suddenly, had he touched on something? Did the Doctor have something to hide?

"I had never met him prior to his coming here to consult, as I told you, it was Jim Nelson who recommended him. I am offended that you would even consider that I might know anything of his sordid pastime! Perhaps you should direct that question to Dr. Nelson."

Another tack.

"Why have you not removed Soper from life support, if his case is hopeless would it not be more humane to allow him to die with some dignity?"

"First, there are legal implications, he is not technically brain dead, secondly he did not provide a "Living Will" thirdly his next of kin have not requested that he be removed from life support."

"By next of kin I assume you mean his wife?"

"Or his son, his eldest son, he was here to visit his father a week ago, there is also a minor child, but he would not be of consequence in such a decision."

"His son was here?"

"Yes, I believe his name is Bradley, Bradley Soper, Jim Nelson made arrangements with me to let him in to see his father."

Harris continued making notes as he had throughout the interview, he double underlined the name Bradley Soper in his notebook.

"Do you know where I might find Bradley Soper?"

"Not really, but I am sure that Jim Nelson does."

"Thank you doctor, I appreciate your time, I shouldn't have to bother you further, I hope to wrap this matter up in the next few days."

He watched Pickard exhale suddenly, was that relief? Was there something else he should have learned from him?

"Just one final question, is there anything that I haven't asked about that you think might be relevant to my investigation?"

His eyes flickered, "No nothing."

Harris closed his notebook, "Oh yes there was, and he would find it.

Chapter 20

Brad responded to the knock at his hotel room door, when he opened it he stood with his mouth agape, staring at a rather formidable black man, standing there with his hand outstretched.

"Brad Soper I assume? My name is Nazir Monpetit."

Brad shook his hand, almost absently, making an effort to close his mouth. He was not expecting any visitors; to say he was surprised would have been an understatement.

"May I come in?"

"Perhaps you could just tell me what you're doing here?"

"Of course, I am sorry to have startled you, I am the new Director of Research for Soper Research, I just assumed your father might have spoken of me."

"I see, please come in."

Brad watched as the big man moved to the sofa, he was at least a head taller than Brad and moved with a grace that seemed at odds with his massive size.

"I am sorry Mr. Monpetit, but I am afraid that my father did not tell me anything about you, in fact I have just recently arrived here from the West Coast and know little of my father's business."

"Please, call me Naz, I don't mean to intrude upon you, it's just that Jim Nelson had mentioned you were staying in this hotel too, and I thought we might share a drink and perhaps get to know one another."

Sensing that he had been less than gracious, Brad said, "I didn't mean to be so abrupt, it's just that you're visit was unexpected and I have had a great deal on mind over the last few days."

"Of course, I understand, now, what about that drink, shall we go down to the bar and get properly acquainted?"

There was something about the man, the openness of his face, the infectious smile, showing perfect rows of teeth; Brad caught himself smiling in return.

"Sure, why not, but I must warn you, I know nothing of microbiology or the drug business!"

"Well you know, those are not my only areas of interest, I am sure we can find other topics more to your liking" He winked broadly and stood to leave.

The bar was almost empty, the piano player had just finished a set so that the room was quiet, an attractive short-skirted waitress took their drink order and they both settled into the comfortable swivel chairs.

"So tell me, Naz, why did you want to meet me?"

"Is that so strange, I got to know your father quite well over the months that we negotiated my joining his firm, I like him, it's a tragedy what has happened. I just thought it appropriate to at least introduce myself to you and express my regret."

The comment seemed so sincere that Brad almost immediately regretted his brusque manner. The waitress arrived with their drinks, a Kokanee for Brad and a Glenfiddich for Naz.

"This was your father's favourite drink, but then I assume you know that."

"I'm afraid I know less about my father than you do, he left us when I was 6, I never saw him after that."

"That's too bad, as I said, I like him, he seemed to me to be interested in what you were doing.

"He told you about me?"

"Of course and your brother too, I can tell you, he was or is very proud of you, we talked about you at some length, is that a surprise?"

"I didn't think I even existed as far as he was concerned, he certainly never was in contact with me over all those years."

"I can't pretend to know your family history Brad, I just know that he followed your progress, even it if was from a distance.

Brad was surprised at this information, shocked more to the point, feeling uncomfortable with the probing of his life he turned the tables.

"Obviously, you also know more about me than I do about you, tell me something about yourself."

Over the next two hours and several drinks the two talked about the past, Naz talked about his early life in Morocco, being shipped of to France for his education, life in boarding schools, and the loneliness. Brad became aware of the similarities between them in spite of the obvious differences, he felt at ease with Naz.

"So Brad, why did you give up on the environmentalists, you were involved with a group against logging in, Ah where was it?"

"Clayoquot Sound, out in British Columbia, yeah I was a tree-hugger for a while, we were going to stop clear cutting, we were successful to a degree too. I even went to jail." He said somewhat proudly.

"So why did you give it up?"

"Some dumb son-of-a-bitch decided to "spike" the trees!"

"Spike the trees?"

"Yes, they drove large spikes into trees that were due to be harvested, when the cutters came in with their chain saws and began to take down the trees, the spikes were supposed to cause the saws to breakdown."

"Didn't it work?"

"The first cutter to hit a spike with his chain saw, watched as his saw ripped out the spike and drove it through the head of another cutter, killed him instantly!"

"Shit! You were there, you saw this?"

"Yeah, I was there, I vomited on the spot, but believe it or not others were actually cheering, can you believe that?"

"What happened after that!"

"The police rounded up everybody at the site, we were all charged, all kinds of media coverage, but ultimately, no one was charged in the death because no one admitted to driving the spikes into the trees and the police had no proof. We all got off with a fine and an admonition."

"Is that when your interest in Ethics reared its head?"

"I suppose so, all I can tell you is that, that whole episode caused me to rethink what I was doing with my life. I began asking myself questions that I came to believe should be addressed to the population at large."

"OK Naz, now you, what made you give up that cozy job in Belgium to come and join a much smaller firm here in Canada?"

"When I met your father, I was intrigued by the strategy that he had developed for his Company. I don't have to tell you that one can get stifled in a large bureaucracy. Initiative is not necessarily rewarded. Internal politics are a fact of life, the bigger the company, the more intense the politicking.

Your father had a different mind-set, in spite of what you might think or have heard, I don't really think he was as much driven by the generation of wealth for the sake of wealth, as he was solving problems using unique and often radical approaches."

"You better not have another drink Naz, I think they're going to your head. Either that or your not talking about my father, as far as I am concerned all he ever thought about was money, the greater good was not in his vocabulary!"

"Sounds like you think you know a great deal about your father, but remember, you're the one that said I knew your father better than you! Could it be that you might be wrong in your assessment of him?"

"Bullshit! I know what I know!"

"Better change the subject, tell me Brad, do you intend to take over Soper Research from your father?"

Brad was jolted by the question and he was somewhat annoyed by it, what right did Naz have to even ask it? He realized that he probably had every right to ask it given the current circumstances, with his father's condition, and Peter Mytryk's suicide. There was a possibility he supposed of some instability within the company because of these factors.

"No, I have no plans to do any such thing, my field is medical ethics, its what I have been trained for, its what I want to do with my life."

"Why would your interest in ethics preclude you from heading up Soper Research? Do you not think that the pharmaceutical industry could not benefit from a strong dose of ethics?"

"That's a pipe dream, a fairy tale, who would listen?"

"I think it's a better platform than writing Letters to the Editor!"

"Besides which, I have no experience in running a multi million dollar corporation, I would drown in the detail, I would never get time to learn how,"

"A very good point, but my young friend, I do! We could make a very good team!"

"So now we get down to it, this is why you wanted to meet me, get to know me, you're on the make like the rest of them!"

"Piss off Brad! I meant what I said about your father and you for that matter. As for being on the make, understand this, I don't need your money or your father's my net worth is substantial. Yes, I like money, but like you, my work is the important element in my life."

"OK, OK, I am sorry if I offended you, it's just that I have people hounding me about this business thing, I sense that most of them are trying to take advantage of the situation."

"Do you want to tell me about these people, maybe I can help you, I'm not trying to pry into your affairs, I would do it for your father."

"Because my brilliant father made no Will, Ashley, his wife, wants me to go to court and get appointed as a trustee for my father's estate and administer it on behalf of her and my brother Ellis."

"So what's wrong with doing that?"

"Aside from the fact that I don't want to run the company, as I have just said, there is nothing wrong with that. But Jim Nelson wants me to support him in the same role, but Ashley wants no part of it, she says she doesn't trust Nelson."

"Does she say why?"

"She won't tell me, but she is adamant!"

"Brad, I really think you should give Mrs. Soper's request some serious thought, we both know that the prognosis for your father is. If you don't arrange for a trustee before your father dies it will mean that the estate will go to probate with all the uncertainty that such delays will cause.

You need to think of your step mother and step brother with respect to these matters, you don't appear to be a selfish individual to me and certainly your father didn't think so."

"I hear what you're saying, the last thing I want to do is cause problems for Ellis, he has enough in his young life as it is.

I promise you, I will make a decision one way or the other very shortly, even if it doesn't satisfy everybody."

"Good! Brad, have you given any thought to your father's situation, I mean, what about the life support decision?"

Brad felt comfortable enough with Naz that the question did not bother him as much as it might, had someone else posed it.

"Believe me Naz, I have been wrestling with that since I first saw him in the hospital.

The decision would have been infinitely simpler had there been a Living Will, also he is not clinically brain dead, so that also mitigates against termination of life support.

I suppose that the hospital could petition the courts to end the extraordinary treatment, Dr. Pickard does not appear to be so inclined, frankly I am not sure why, he is definite enough about his prognosis.

It may come down to me having to make that decision and going to the courts myself, this whole thing is pretty crappie, a month ago I was a graduate student, now I have been dumped in this pile of shit!"

"Let's have another drink! Let's talk about something even more serious!"

Brad was already feeling the effects of his 4 beers, but he didn't resist the suggestion.

"What could be more serious?"

"Women of course, what do you know about Janet Petersen?"

"You son-of-a-bitch! How do you know Janet?"

Chapter 21

"Alfred, are you still here?"

"Yes, Dr. Soper, I'm here, what can I do for you?"

"I've been doing a great deal of thinking Alfred."

"I might guess that you have been, is there something specific that you want to talk about."

"Yes, while I can't tell how long I have been in this state, it seems to me that nothing is happening externally. One would think by this stage any potential treatment they might be applying, should be showing some kind of result or change to my condition and yet I sense no change.

That could mean that they are unable to diagnose or treat whatever it is that I have contracted.

It also appears to me that the conditions is serious and likely irreversible."

"You might well be right Doctor Soper, so tell me what you think is the likely outcome of all this?"

"I think I am going to die!"

"Then you believe that whatever it is that you have is fatal?"

"Either that or I may on a life support system that will be withdrawn, either way I will die."

"That's a very dim outlook Dr. Soper, are you really sure that the outcome will be so bleak? Can they just arbitrarily withdraw life support?"

"There is a limit to everything, this won't go on indefinitely, I am enough of a realist to know that, I'm just taking up bed space!"

"But what about your family? Won't they have some input regarding the life support issue?"

"My family! I can just imagine, Ashley would pull the plug with her own hands!"

"But what about your son Bradley?

"As ethicist, he may have some problem with the whole end of life thing, however, just remember Alfred, I'm worth a whole lot more to these people dead, than alive.

"What I regret is the fact I did not see fit to create a Will or directives regarding end of life issues. Now all of that will likely be left to the courts to decide. For the first time in my life I have no control over myself, my company or anything else for that matter."

"And you truly believe that you had control over all these things in life?"

"There was never any doubt in my mind! Of course I was in control, now I lay here, waiting for my terminal experience!"

"Tell me Dr. Soper, how do you feel about your life, about your past actions, your relationship with others?

"Alfred, if you are looking for a death bed confession, you've come to the wrong place, I don't think I have done any worse than lots of others and better than some.

I feel an overwhelming sadness that the end has to come this way; I would have been better off dying suddenly. Hit by a truck or something. Laying here, not far off being a vegetable, reflecting on what might have been, there is no doubt that this is my purgatory!"

"So, what you are saying is that you are without remorse for any act that you committed, there is no one for whom you have any empathy based upon things you may have done, you are totally at peace with yourself?"

"I admit that I'm not perfect, I also recognize that you continue to work your views on evil into these discussions. I am not an evil person, I'm as empathetic as the next guy, but when tough decisions must be made, I didn't shirk them, does that make me evil?"

"Then you also must admit that you had remorseful feelings after some of these "tough decisions.""

"Of course! But those feelings did not change the ultimate decision that's only human. It's the weak that fail to take action for the common good based upon a preoccupation with the welfare of the few!"

"That sounds a little like "The end justifies the means," tell me how your dealings with your wife Ashley, how did they contribute to the common good?"

"You know Alfred, you can be a real Asshole sometimes, there are things that occurred between Ashley and I that are none of your Goddamned business! I thought you were here to help me, not abuse me!"

"Temper tantrums won't help you either, I am here to try to help you, but you know better than I do, I can't help you if you don't confide in me, you were a psychoanalyst long enough to know that!"

"Just leave Ashley out of these discussions, I don't want to go there at least not now."

"Alight, then what about your son Bradley? Do you think you have done well by him?"

"I made sure that Bradley was looked after, he has a sizable trust fund, I have followed his activities with great interest."

"So that's it? You made sure he had enough money, you checked on his grades. Tell me how your abandonment of him was to the common good?

Why did you not seek custody or at least visitation rights?"

"Alfred, you are beginning to sound judgmental, why are you harassing me? I told you that I felt it better for the child to be with his mother, if he had stayed with me, he would have been raised by a nanny, would that be as good as his own mother?

Remember, I was just getting the business started, I travelled a great deal, and Brad would have been deprived of both his mother and father.

As for the greater good, he stands to inherit a large portion of my estate; he will be a wealthy man. If I had been a single parent instead, he would not have this opportunity today.

As for visitation rights, I decided, rightly or wrongly, that I would have been a disruptive influence in his life if I was constantly appearing and disappearing, I believe he had a great deal more stability in his life living with his mother."

"Dr. Soper, why is it that you continually confuse materialism with your relationships? Is it not possible that Brad might have valued you in his life more than your money?"

"Whether you believe it or not Alfred, most of my life has been dedicated not just to the pursuit of material things, but also to provide for my family. Your point regarding Brad is well taken, I regret not having the relationship that many fathers have with their sons. Had things been different, I might have had the opportunity of bringing him into the firm, grooming him to take it over, watching him succeed."

"You mean, if that's what he wanted to do with his life?"

"Yes, of course."

"That sounds like remorse to me Dr. Soper."

"Maybe it is."

"And what about you're other son, Ellis?"

"What about him?"

"Were you not about to abandon him as you did Bradley?"

"That is totally different."

"In what way?"

"Ellis is not my son!"

"What do you mean, he is not your son?"

"Have you suddenly become hard of hearing Alfred, I said Ellis is not my son!"

"But your name is on the birth certificate is it not, so how do you know he is not your son?"

"Believe me, I have irrefutable proof, but I am not prepared to pursue this any further, just leave it be."

"Just tell me why you acknowledged the child as yours then?"

"I just could not see Ashley destroyed, I knew I was at least partially responsible for her predicament, my long absences, working late, she had a sense of abandonment as well.

In addition, she thought he was my child, so I made no issue about the birth certificate, it just seemed easier for all concerned, we had grown apart by that stage."

"Does Ashley now know that Ellis is not your son?"

"NO!"

"Is there anything else you want to talk about Dr. Soper?"

"There is much more I would like to talk about Alfred, but I need more time to think and I find myself getting tired more easily now, I'd like to rest.

I can't handle much more of this, here I lay, a shell, with a functioning brain, well almost functioning, I have no control of my future and the past is past. I'm in limbo, can't go forward and can't go back. I think I want to die.

Chapter 22

Brad had picked up Ellis at Halton House and headed back to Ashley's condominium, she had called him earlier in the day to ask him if he pick the boy up. Her car was in for servicing and they didn't have a courtesy car available.

Brad was happy to do it, it gave him even more time with Ellis, and he glanced over at the youngster playing happily with the new plush toy he had given him. Looking at him one would be hard pressed to consider there was anything wrong.

It looked very much like it was going to rain, Brad had the top up on the SL55, and it was still a pleasure to drive even with the top closed. He punched the radio button and listened to some light rock on the superb audio system, life he decided was not too bad, even the traffic was relatively light on the 401, relatively being a relative term.

He pulled off the highway and proceeded to the condo, Ashley told him to use her spot in the underground garage, that way they could avoid getting wet.

He gathered up Ellis' backpack and took him by the hand to the parking garage elevator, Ellis held on tightly to his new toy with one hand and clutched Brad's hand with the other.

Ashley let them in, giving a hug and a kiss to Ellis and a respectable peck on the cheek for Brad.

"Come in, come in, how are you sweetheart? And you too Brad its good to see you again, I am sure Ellis was glad to see you at Halton House."

"Yeah, he was standing just inside the door, all packed up before I got there."

"And what have you got Ellis, is that a new toy, did Brad give you that?"

The boy looked into her face and nodded excitedly, he held the furry creature up for closer inspection, a smile wreathed his face."

"You're a lucky boy Ellis, that was very nice of you Brad."

"Nothing's too good for my favourite little brother." He said tousling his hair; Ellis was beaming up at him.

"Thanks for picking him up for me, it would have been a hassle having to rent a car and all."

"No problem, what's wrong with your car anyway?"

"Frankly, I have no idea, just that it refused to start this morning, I had CAA come and they couldn't start it either, they towed it into the dealer, but they didn't have a courtesy vehicle, at least that's what they told me.

But I'll bet if it was Arnie, they would have found him a car!"

"Oh well it all worked out and gave me some extra time with Ellis."

"Brad, supper isn't started yet, if you and Ellis want to go down to the pool for a swim, there will be lots of time."

It had been muggy all day and a swim sounded like just the thing, he knew that they would likely have the indoor pool all to themselves. The tenants seldom seemed to use it.

"Hey sport, do you wanna go for a swim?"

Ellis began to jump up and down with excitement.

"I'll take that to be a yes! Come on squirt, we'll get your bathing suit on."

The door closed behind the pair of them, Ashley could not help but smile, Brad had certainly made a major difference in Ellis' life, he was like a different child.

At that moment, the telephone rang, she went into the family room to answer it, and she sat on a barstool and picked up the phone.

"Ashley, this is Declan Mahoney."

She was startled to hear his voice, he always seemed so sinister, and she disliked him, although she had had little to do with him.

"What do you want Mr. Mahoney?"

"My, my, you sound a little testy today."

"I said, what do you want?"

She never quite understood why Arnie had hired him, or really what it was that he did for the company, but plainly he made her nervous.

"I have something important to discuss with you, may I come over?"

"No certainly not! It isn't convenient, what could you have to discuss with me anyway?"

"Let us just say that this is an urgent family matter, it concerns you and your son Ellis."

She could feel her heart thump, she almost dropped the phone, he made the words seem ominous, and there was silence for a moment before she could respond.

""What do you mean an urgent family matter?"

"I'm not prepared to discuss it over the phone, but believe me, what I have to say to you could change your son's life forever." He added, "And not for the better either!"

"Do you mean that Ellis may be in some kind of danger?"

"You might say that, meet me in half an hour, at the White Swan, I think you know it?"

"Yes, yes I do, I'll be there." The phone went dead in her hand, her mind was racing as was her heart, "What does all this mean, what's happening to my life?"

She finished her drink in one swallow. She had no car! She could borrow Brad's. It was as much hers as his anyway and she was sure he wouldn't mind. She went through his pants pockets and found the keys, she would leave them a note. With any luck she might be back before they finished their swim.

She hoped she wouldn't meet them coming back up in the elevator to get something from the condo, but luck was with her, no one saw her.

She was glad that Brad had put the convertible top up. It was raining hard now and she would not have known how to put it up herself. She unlocked the car and settled into the sumptuous bucket seat. She inserted the key and tried turning it, but it would not start.

She was in near panic until she noticed the small round button on the dash, she pressed it and the big engine thundered to life, she sighed and settled back in the seat. She had never driven a car like this before; the sheer energy the car possessed seemed to frighten her a little.

She put the transmission selector lever in Reverse, took her foot off the brake and gingerly pressed the accelerator, the car leapt backwards with a sudden jolt. She hit the brake pedal causing the car to come to a quick stop, but the brake pedal was close to the accelerator and even with her small foot she managed press the accelerator again by mistake. The car lurched again, tears welled up in her eyes, she was distraught, she took a deep breath and tried again, this time she backed up more smoothly and she was able to navigate out of the parking garage without further incidents.

She knew that the White Swan was just south of the 401 on Kennedy Road, she had some trepidation about driving this car in the kind of traffic that always seemed present on the highway, but she knew of no shorter route.

She eased the powerful car onto the entrance ramp, she accelerated as the merging lane end was visible up ahead, the car responded, she had no trouble moving into the collector lane traffic.

Feeling more confident as she drove, keeping her speed just at the cruising speed that seemed to be favoured by the majority of the traffic, the trip proved to be less eventful than getting the beast out of the parking garage.

Exiting at Kennedy Road, she headed south for the two blocks and saw the White Swan Tavern on the right hand side. Fortunately, there was lots of parking. She selected an area with few other cars close by and brought the car carefully to a halt. Turned off the engine and heaved a sigh of relief.

It was now raining heavily, she was glad she had thought about the umbrella, she struggled to open it while sitting in the car with the driver's door open, finally she was able to get out, lock the car with the key fob and enter the Tavern.

She hadn't been in this place for some time, it mostly catered to the blue collar crowd now, it had once been an upscale watering hole frequented by her and her college friends, she could not help but think that the place had fallen on hard times since.

But at least she didn't have to worry about being seen with a creep like Declan Mahoney; nobody in here would know her.

As her eyes became accustomed to the dim light, she saw Mahoney in a booth near the back of the bar, he rose to greet her, his teeth seemed to flash as did his pinkie ring on his extended hand.

"Ashley, so good of you come."

"I didn't have any choice, based on what you said on the phone, did I?"

"Ashley. Let me buy you a drink, a Manhattan I believe?"

"Make it a double!"

The waiter brought her drink, she sipped it immediately, feeling the warmth of the liquour soothe her insides, she put down the glass, and looked directly at Mahoney, the liquid courage seemed to help.

"Why are you making threats against me and my child?"

"Ashley you are mistaken, it is not I who is making threats against you and your little boy, I'm merely trying to help you don't you see?"

"You didn't make it sound like help on the phone, that was a threat pure and simple." She picked up her glass and had another swallow of the liquor.

"I am simply trying to give you some very good advice so that you might avoid substantial future unhappiness, you and your little family that is."

"And what advice might that be?"

"I want you to support Jim Nelson as trustee for Arnie's estate and I want you to convince Bradley Soper likewise."

"There is no way on this earth that I'm going to do that, I have made that clear to Jim, I told him face to face, he knows where I stand."

"If you do not do as I have requested, then you will, unfortunately, suffer the consequences."

"Such as?" she sipped again at her drink, emboldened now as the whiskey suffused her body.

"There is a very real possibility that news might leak out that Ellis Soper is not Arnie Soper's biological son, how do you think young Mr. Brad will take that. And what do you suppose that will do to your son's claim on a share of the estate.

In addition, people may become aware of just who the real father is, and wouldn't that create something of a scandal?"

"What do you mean, Ellis is not Arnie's biological son? What kind of crap is this?"

"Are you trying to tell me Ashley that you are unaware of the little surgical procedure that Arnie had some 6 months prior to you getting pregnant?"

"What procedure?"

"Why the vasectomy of course. There is no way that Arnie could have fathered that child!"

"What? I don't believe you, you bastard!"

"Oh it's true all right, I have the proof, you see the surgeon that performed the surgery was none other than your dear friend, Dr. Jim Nelson!"

She was stunned; she was having trouble catching her breath.

Arnie never told me, the son-of-a-bitch! What am I going to do? Nelson! He did that and never told me! What a fool I've been what a mess I've made. What am I going to do?

"And another thing Ashley, I have DNA evidence as to just who Ellis' father really is, just in case you don't know, I'd be happy to share that with you."

"You smarmy Asshole! Arnie is Ellis' father, you're lying!" She was almost yelling in his face, he reached across the table a gripped her forearm painfully.

"Keep your voice down slut! Unless you want to broadcast all your seamy activities to the barflies in here!"

I should think you would only be too anxious to help out Ellis' real father in his time of need, all you have to do is see he gets your support for the Chairman's position at Soper."

The tears were flowing down her face, her mascara was beginning to run in streaks, she was shaking uncontrollably, "Why are you doing this to me, I have never caused you any trouble, why me and why my little boy?"

"Ashley, Ashley, you are doing this to yourself, it doesn't have to turn out this way, it's really up to you, just do as I asked."

I don't believe you have any proof of any of this, nobody does, I deny everything you say!" She was becoming more agitated, she finished her drink, Mahoney signalled for another. Her hands began shaking, tears were welling up in her eyes, she struggled for self-control.

He reached out and tried to touch her hands, but she withdrew them, the second drink arrived, she gulped a considerable portion of it.

"Ashley, you know that Arnie was planning on divorcing you before his unfortunate incident, just who do you suppose was gathering up information to support his position should you decide to litigate?

I have enough information, including, shall we say, some compromising photographs of you and some of your friends. He leered when he said the word "friends" Not only to win any court case, but also to have you declared an unfit mother and have your son taken away from you by the authorities.

Do I make myself clear?"

By this time the tears were streaming down her cheeks, her whole body was wracked with shaking sobs.

She picked up her glass again as though to drink, but instead pitched the contents into his face and threw the glass at his head catching just above the left eyebrow, she saw blood spurt on his immaculate white shirt.

She ran from the tavern, forgetting her umbrella into the rainstorm and dark of the evening, her hair was drenched and her clothes soaked through by the time she found the car, she pressed the key fob, unlocked the doors and quickly entered the vehicle.

She pressed her head to the steering wheel, the horn suddenly blared loudly, and she snapped her head back as though the wheel had burned her. The taut blue canvas roof of the car reverberated with the sound of pounding rain as though it was some kind of jungle drum or tom-tom, the noise was almost deafening.

She started the engine and moved out on to Kennedy Road North, and then to the 401 westbound, between the rain on the windshield and her tears it was difficult to see clearly. All she knew was that she had to escape, to get away from Mahoney, to get away from everything.

She had made so many mistakes in her life, now her actions were going to hurt the two people she loved most, how could she ever go back to Brad and reverse her position, more importantly, how could she ever support Jim Nelson after what he had done?

She wove in and out of the traffic, the alcohol in her system giving her a confidence her skills did not match, her speed began to climb 140, 150, 160 kilometres per hour, things were rushing by, the speed was exhilarating, could she leave her problems behind?

Her speed climbed even higher, the car moved effortlessly, the engine barely straining as she raced forward in the high-speed lane.

The rain hammered down on the roof, she sobbed and wiped tears from her eyes and she pressed on even faster. As she was entering the area known as "spaghetti junction" because of the convergence of collector lanes and on off ramps for several north south highways, she came over a small rise in the road.

Why is this all happening? Why to me? How could Arnie do this? It can't be true, that bastard Nelson, he knew, he did it! He didn't tell me, screwed me and didn't tell me! Nelson can't be Ellis' father, he can't be!

As she reached the crest, she was unaware that all four wheels of the vehicle had momentarily lost contact with the road. Consequently, the highly sensitive safety sensors detected this event and automatically triggered the roll over protection bar behind her head.

She was startled by the sudden explosive deployment of the roll over bar, she reacted to the sound instinctively turning to look, inadvertently turning the steering wheel at the same time.

She turned back in time to see the car heading directly for a row of concrete safety dividers, she tried to brake, but her foot slipped off the brake onto the accelerator.

The left front tire caught the base of the divider, the car to climbed it at full throttle, causing the airbags to deploy as the car began what seemed like a slow motion barrel roll. The vehicle turned a full 360 degrees, the car shot into the air and tumbled end over end crashing into 4 other cars in the process.

Car parts were strewn everywhere, tires screeched, smoke billowed and steam hissed, with the darkness and the rain and people screaming, it seemed like a small glimpse of Hell.

It took almost 40 minutes for the police to arrive at the scene; the westbound lane was shut down completely with traffic backed up for 8 kilometres with bumper to bumper vehicles.

Rescue equipment had to be brought in by using the east bound lanes and crossing the centre median to get to the accident site.

The final count was 8 dead, and 12 sent to hospital with a variety of injuries, at least 4 of them in critical condition.

Little remained of the SL55, the police however managed to retrieve the rear bumper and license plate, the remaining pieces were almost indistinguishable as automotive parts,

Ashley's body, or what was left of it, was sent to the morgue to await positive identification by the next of kin.

A police cruiser was dispatched to the address obtained as a result of the license plate search, it was 4 hours after the fatal crash, when the cruiser pulled into the condo driveway.

Chapter 23

Brad and Ellis entered the condo after spending and hour and a half splashing about in the pool, Ellis still clutched his inflatable toy as Brad called out for Ashley.

There was no response, he looked through the apartment, and he saw her empty glass on the bar but no sign of her. He found her note on the dining room table, it was storming out, she had obviously been drinking, and he couldn't help but worry about her ability to control such a powerful vehicle, even on a good day.

The note said she wouldn't be long, he looked at his watch, considerable time had already elapsed, where was she?

He got Ellis changed into his pajamas, they watched TV for awhile, Brad paced the family room, looking out the window, but she nothing of the car, just rain and sudden bursts of lightning.

It was getting late and still no sign of Ashley, in spite of the apprehension he felt, he knew he had to get Bradley something to eat, he settled on a couple of boiled eggs and some toast.

The boy ate the last of the impromptu dinner, he rubbed his eyes, it had been a long day and all the activity in the pool was catching up with him. Brad got him into bed and lay beside him, he had promised to read a story, but by page three Ellis had drifted off.

He returned to the family room and reread the note, it said she would be right back, where in hell was she?

What was so urgent that she had to go out on a night like this? She was drinking, could have been picked up, maybe she had an accident with the car. I don't need this crap! What can I do?

He could feel the knot in his stomach growing; he had an ominous feeling that something terrible had happened.

At just past midnight, the intercom buzzed, Brad sprang to answer, and instinctively he knew this was going to be bad news. It was security in the lobby.

"Mr. Soper, I'm sorry to disturb you I know it's late, but the are two Metro Police Officers here looking for Dr. Soper, I told them he isn't here but they insist on speaking to someone in the apartment."

"That's OK Dennis, put one of them on."

"This is Officer Parker of the Metropolitan Toronto Police Force, who am I talking to?"

"I'm Brad Soper, Dr. Arnold Soper is my father." As he said the words he felt strange saying them.

"I understand your father is not there, where is he?"

"In the hospital, he is ill."

"I see, may we come up sir?"

"Can't you just tell me over the intercom?"

"Afraid not sir."

His heart sank, he anticipated the worst and he was afraid he was about to hear it."

"Come ahead."

He opened the door and admitted both of them, they stood in the foyer, the younger man stood behind the man who was obviously Officer Parker. Their faces betrayed the fact that both of them would rather be somewhere else, but this was a necessary part of their duty.

Parker launched into a speech he had made to many times, "Mr. Soper, I regret to inform you that Mrs. Ashley Soper was killed in an auto accident on the 401 highway at approximately 7:30 PM tonight."

The words struck as though he had received a punch to his solar plexus, he sucked air into his lungs instinctively. Although he expected the worst, hearing the words caused him to fall back slightly against the wall.

"Are you all right sir, can I get you anything?"

"No, No, it's just such a shock, that's all, I'll be OK. How did it happen?"

"Well sir, the accident team have not completed their report yet, but on a preliminary basis, it appears that she lost control of the vehicle, hit a concrete safety barrier, rolled over, end to end, several times. I'm afraid the car was totalled."

"Shit!"

"One other thing sir, we will need you to come to morgue, tomorrow if possible, we need a positive ID."

Brad noted the younger officer looking at something behind him, Brad turned and saw Ellis standing in the doorway of his bedroom, a stuffed animal in his left hand, his eyes staring at the two officers. How much had he heard? His concern now had to be Ellis.

He agreed he would do as they asked, the officers turned to leave, the younger one finally spoke, "Sorry for your loss sir."

He gathered Ellis up in his arms, deciding the best approach was not to explain the presence of the police in the event that he had not heard anything. Ellis clutched Brad around his neck, he didn't cry, so maybe he hadn't heard.

He put him back in his bed and lay beside him, he picked up the book again, but Ellis just turn his face to the wall, he either went back to sleep or pretended to. After a time, Brad left the boy and went into the family room.

He sat at the bar, the tension had not left him, his stomach was still churning, he reached for the Glenfiddich, his father's drink someone had told him, he poured about three quarters of a glass, added some ice and sipped it neat. The liquor burned all the way down; he hoped the amber fluid would calm the inner turmoil he was experiencing.

"What would have possessed her to go out in a storm, to drive a car she was not experienced enough to drive, where was she going?"

The note was an obvious lie, there was plenty of food in the house, and she didn't need to buy more, what had happened while he and Ellis were at the pool?

Too many questions, and no answers. He reached for the phone and dialled, a sleepy voice answered.

"Hello, who the fuck is this?"

"Jan, it's me, Brad."

"It's 2:00 o'clock in the morning Brad, couldn't you wait till a more civilized hour?"

"She's dead Jan, she's dead!"

"What, Brad, who's dead!"

"Ashley, she's dead, killed in a car accident!"

"Oh! Jesus, when?

"About 6 maybe 7 hours ago."

"Where are you?"

"I'm at Ashley's condo, I have Ellis with me." Before he could say more she responded.

"I'll be right there Brad, it'll take me 40 minutes, I'll be there."

He hung up the phone and took another sip of whiskey, he didn't know whom else to call, he needed someone to talk to, and there was no way he would sleep.

He considered all of the things that had happened to him since he had left Vancouver, Things were so simple back then, was it only 5 weeks? It seemed like a lifetime, was all of this real or just a dream?

He went to look in on Ellis, no at least this was not a dream, his brother seemed to be sleeping peacefully, he was grateful for that. What Brad couldn't see, because the boy faced the wall, were the open, unblinking, staring eyes.

The intercom buzzed again, it was Janet, he told Dennis to admit her, and he was waiting in the doorway when the elevator arrived, and she ran to him and hugged him tightly.

"Oh Brad, I am so sorry," she kissed him and he pulled her inside.

Once inside, he gave her all of the details he knew, they sat together on the sofa, she held his hand.

"What are you planning on doing now, Oh, that's a stupid question, you've barely had time to think."

"That's OK, in fact that's just exactly what I've been sitting here doing until you got here, I guess I should call her father, but I don't even know how to reach him."

"My guess is that the police have already notified him, they generally do all of that before anything gets released to the media. So don't worry about that Brad."

"Yeah, the media, I hadn't even thought about them, I suppose this will set off a feeding frenzy, Jan I'm afraid she might have been drinking. She didn't have anything while I was here, but when we came back from the pool, I found a glass with the dregs of at least one drink."

"Face it Brad, there will be an autopsy, if she was over the limit it will come out, we need to worry about the things we can control."

"What do you mean?"

"Look Brad, the media have not found out about your father yet, when this hits the news, everybody is going to looking for your father to get a "sound bite," the hounds will be on the loose!"

Janet looked at Brad, she held her finger to her lips, she shook her head, he looked at her quizzically, but before he could speak she said,

"I could do with some fresh air, look the rain has stopped," she continued to hold her finger to her lips and guided him by the arm to the balcony doors.

Once outside she slid the door shut, "What the hell is going on Jan!"

"There is a very good chance that the condo is being bugged, we should be OK here, but don't talk too loudly, the equipment of choice is very sophisticated."

"But who would do this?"

"Mahoney has had this place "bugged" ever since your father decided to divorce Ashley, I know this is not what you want to hear, but Ashley's reputation with other men is common knowledge in certain circles in this city. I certainly don't mean to judge her, but we don't need to be captured on tape either!"

The air had become much cooler since the rain had ended, Jan shivered slightly and Brad moved to put his arm around her, she smiled up at him. The condo was a penthouse suite facing south from the highest piece of land overlooking the city.

The lights twinkled below and at another time it could have been appreciated as a romantic setting, but Brad was consumed by his current situation.

"I don't know what I am going to do about Ellis, perhaps his grandfather will want custody of him, he needs to be cared for, doubly so now."

"Does he know about Ashley?"

"I'm not sure, I don't think so, he did get out of bed when I let the police in, but I don't think he heard the conversation. I was able to put him back to bed and he seemed to drop right back to sleep again."

"Well, that's a blessing for now at least, as for Grandpa Coughlan, remember he is almost 80, the rest of his offspring have amounted to less than nothing, the other daughter is in a mental institution and the son is a crack addict, not exactly the potential for guardians."

"Well, I'm certainly not equipped to be his guardian either, I still have my dissertation to do, I have a life back in Vancouver, this last month has been a nightmare."

"Then that would mean that Family Services will have to step in, in fact they will likely have to do that initially in any event, at least to set up care in the short term until something permanent can be worked out."

"Goddamn it! He doesn't deserve that! You're a lawyer; can't you do something? I need your help Janet."

"Brad I can't act for Ellis, it would be a conflict of interest because of the work I do on behalf of Soper Research, but I can arrange for somebody I trust to look after this thing. But, Brad, you need to consider your own position on Ellis' future, if you appear to be abandoning him now, there will be no going back at a later date."

"I hear what you are saying, I will try to have an answer for your lawyer friend when I meet with him."

"OK, I will get on it first thing in the morning, in the meantime, we need to make some plans regarding Ellis and what we do with him over the next two days. Tomorrow is Saturday; all hell will break loose on TV. Ashley is "copy fodder" because of the other loss of life and the potential for a drunk driving charge. The coverage will be intense. You don't want Ellis exposed to that, at least on Sunday you can get him back to Halton House, I could likely arrange security there. He will be back in an environment that he knows and trusts, that will buy us some time."

"Jan, I really do appreciate what you are doing and the fact that you came right over here, I couldn't do this without you, you're a real friend.

"I intend to be more than that!"

The next day, every channel ran footage of the crash scene, the traffic tie ups, the ambulances, with sirens blaring rushing casualties to the hospital, the "jaws of life" attempting to remove survivors or more likely mangled bodies from the wreckage. Police directing operations, their yellow "ponchos" slick with the rain.

Footage of Ashley attending various society functions was also aired, along with pictures of her and Arnie in happier times. The voice over commented on the fact that Dr. Arnold Soper was not available for comment, but that they expected an official announcement from him or his spokesman shortly.

The commentator finished with the routine observation that is was yet to be determined if alcohol played a factor in this dreadful accident.

Declan Mahoney sat in his office early Saturday morning, he watched the all news channel on one of the monitors, last nights accident played out as he sat there.

"Stupid bitch! Stupid drunken bitch!" he said aloud.

There was a knock at his door; his secretary stuck her head in. "Mr. Mahoney its Dr. Nelson to see you, May I send him in?"

He muttered to himself, "That's all I need."

"Yes, Yes, send him in."

Nelson stood in front of Mahoney as the door shut behind him.

"What have you done? You were only supposed to talk to her, now she's dead!"

His eyes glittered with suppressed tears, he repeated, "What have you done?"

"Listen you weak kneed little turd, I didn't do anything to her, yes we had a talk, she left me she was fine, a little drunk perhaps, but then you knew she was a drunk didn't you. Don't try to make me responsible for her whoring or drinking! You are the one responsible for her death, if you had convinced her to support you, none of this would have happened, it's all your fault!"

"You bastard! I curse the day I ever got involved with you! You're the one that should have died! Not her!' He moved towards Mahoney as though to threaten him, Mahoney stood up and came from behind his desk, towards Nelson.

"What are you going to do Nelson, beat me within an inch of my life?" Come ahead Asshole, I'll swat you like the little insect you are!"

Nelson knew he was no match for the bigger tougher man, he knew of his reputation as a street fighter. He stopped his forward motion and spun around and abruptly left Mahoney's office.

As the door slammed behind him, he could hear Mahoney, "Like I said, you're a weak kneed little bastard, you've got no guts."

He could hear Mahoney's laughter ringing in his ears as he continued down the hall.

"That son-of-a-bitch will pay, Oh yes! He will pay! He wiped away the tears with the heel of his hand.

Chapter 24

Janet had spent the rest of the evening of Ashley's death with Brad and Ellis, they slept little, but as nearly as they could tell, and Ellis slept soundly. They checked on him several times and on each occasion he remained still and apparently asleep.

They watched the sunrise from the balcony, the disaster of the previous evening pressed in on them in spite of the freshness of the air and the brightness of the sunshine. They sat quietly, not speaking for long periods, until, finally, Janet spoke.

"Brad, we need to make some plans, this is going to be a tough day, for you and Ellis, but I know you will get through it.

First, Ellis is going to have to be made aware of his mother's death, the sooner the better, I think it would be wrong to delay, it will only make it that much tougher.

You need to meet with my lawyer friend to decide the best approach for Ellis' future care, even if you can't bring yourself to make a final decision on your own role, you need to know the options. I can look after Ellis while you two meet, I am sure I can handle that.

We need to get you some transportation; we can pick up a rental vehicle so that you can be mobile.

And Brad, I know you probably don't want to talk about this right now, but maybe when you meet with the lawyer, you should look at your options regarding the trustee thing, whichever way you decide, you need legal advice."

Brad lifted his head, she wasn't sure he had been listening to anything she said,

"You make it all sound so cold and calculating."

"Sorry Brad, I guess that's the lawyer in me, I am sensitive to what has happened, it isn't like I don't care, you know that don't you?"

"Yes, of course I do, and I appreciate everything you have done for me, I know what you say is right and all of these things need to be done, but it seems that we have simply dismissed this life as though it had never happened,"

She reached out and lifted a lock of his hair that had fallen over his left eye,

"Brad, you are a good and caring man, just don't take all of this on your back as though you were responsible somehow for the horrible outcome of last evening. That won't do you or your little brother any good.

We need to get some food into you and Ellis, me too come to think of it, Let's wake up the little guy and head out to McDonald's, it ain't classy, but it's quick and I'm sure Ellis will enjoy it!"

"Yeah, I guess, it would be better to get some food into him, before we talk to him about his mother."

She touched his hand, and looked up into his face,

"Brad, it won't be we, it's going to have to be you, I will be with you for support, but you have the relationship, I think the only way to do this is to be direct and then try to handle any fallout afterwards, he trusts you. We want to be able to reassure him as much as possible, we don't want any sense of abandonment to occur."

He smiled at her, he knew in his heart that she was right, but he could not overcome his sense of dread in anticipation of the boy's reaction to all this.

Brad entered the boy's room, reached down and tousled his hair and said,

"Come on sleepy head, let's go to MacDonald's for some breakfast!"

Ellis opened his eyes and smiled up at Brad, he jumped up and grabbed Brad around the neck, holding on for dear life.

"Hey, Buddy, don't choke your only brother." He tried to peel the boy's arms away, but finally had to give up for fear of hurting the child. He carried him through to where Janet was.

"Hey Bud, I want you to meet a friend of mine! Ellis, say hello to Janet, isn't she pretty? She's going to join us for breakfast, would you like that?"

The boy stole a look, nodded his head and returned his face to Brad's neck,

"Tell you what, I'm going to grab a quick shower, change and then we'll go OK? In the meantime you can get to know Janet."

He wouldn't release his hold, Brad sat down with him on his knee, Janet leaned down and touched the little boy's head, "Hi

Ellis, why don't you come over and introduce me to that "stuffy" you're holding. I really like stuffed animals; I have seven of them. Do you believe that? Come on over and I'll tell you all about them."

Slowly Ellis relinquished his hold on Brad, he held out the stuffed animal at arm's length for Janet to see, she reached for it but he pulled it back, he giggled and continued to tempt her.

Brad, slipped quietly into the bathroom, he let the hot water beat on him. He tried washing away everything that had happened; it didn't work. He dressed quickly and returned to the family room, he hadn't been gone more than 15 minutes, Janet was holding Ellis and hugging him tightly, the boy was crying.

"What happened Jan, it looked like everything was under control when I left?"

"As soon as you went to shower, he began running from room to room, looking for something or someone more likely, he ran faster and faster and when he couldn't find what he was looking for, he began screaming.

The only thing I could think of was to pick him up and hug, you know to try to reassure him."

"You're not only pretty, you're smart, that is actually one of the therapies that is used with the autistic, hug them and reassure them, it works, most times for Ellis anyway."

Janet called her lawyer friend, explained the situation and they agreed Brad could come to the office at 11:00 AM, The lawyer estimated that an hour would be good enough for at least a quick overview of the options available. Brad could schedule more time later when he was in possession of more facts.

She handed Brad one of her cards on the back of which she had written the lawyer's name address and phone number,

"L.J. Phillips, what's he like?"

"Competent!"

The breakfast was uneventful; Ellis was delighted with cheap plastic toy that came with his MacHappy meal. He showed it to Janet, even letting her hold it.

"Looks to me like you have made a real friend there Jan, he really likes you!"

"More than his big brother?"

He laughed, "Maybe, but I doubt it." They both chuckled, for the first time in hours; it was understood that Brad would wait until after the meeting before talking to Ellis about Ashley. It wouldn't have been fair to Janet to have to deal with any aftermath.

She dropped him office at the Royal Bank Office Tower and imposing building of shimmering golden metal and glass that seemed to rise forever from the pavement. The cavernous lobby had people bustling through even this early on a Saturday, he took the elevator to the 32nd floor, there was no receptionist at the desk, but he did find a small bell.

He hit the bell twice and waited. A frosted glass door to one side of the reception desk opened a statuesque woman in designer blue jeans that fit every curve as did the powder blue pullover she wore with them. Her blonde hair was pulled back into a ponytail, she was "Drop Dead Gorgeous!"

She held out her hand, "Brad Soper? I'm Leslie Phillips."

He sensed that he was standing with his mouth open, he snapped it shut causing the lawyer to smile slightly.

"Come on back to my office, as you might expect, we don't have very many people in on a Saturday morning, mostly just us partners."

The office was as elegant as the occupant, floor to ceiling windows on her left gave a great view of the city skyline, she dropped into a trendy leather chair, he sat opposite and watched as she propped her stiletto shod feet on the desk.

"Well at least I understand what Janet meant, now that we have met!"

"What did Janet say?"

"Told me to keep my hands to myself"

His face reddened, he was beginning to understand how women felt when men made such comments about them.

She observed his discomfort and smiled and said "Not to worry, why don't you just fill me in on everything and what concerns you the most?"

She was all business now, the flirting was over and he felt more at ease, he reiterated everything including Janet's trip to

Vancouver, his father's condition, Jim Nelson, Ashley, Ellis, all of it.

She asked for clarifications regarding the lack of any Will, what Ellis' age was and spent some time on his own personal background, which surprised him, a little.

"Well, what Janet has told you regarding Ellis' and the Family Services department is correct, they are going to have to be informed and at the very least they will be looking for someone to take temporary custody of him. Logically they would look to family members, either you or the Grandfather, that sort of thing, is there any other family members that you are aware of?"

"Janet mentioned two siblings of Ashley, but one is in a mental institution and the other is a drug addict, she also says the Grandfather is 80 years old, that's all I'm aware of."

"Do you think the old man will object to you having at least temporary custody, or for that matter, are you willing to do so?"

"Look Ms. Phillips."

"Leslie, please."

"OK, Leslie, Ellis is my only living relative, of course I would take temporary custody, I'm not completely sure of the longer term, I'm not sure I'm equipped to handle it, I have never had that kind of responsibility. I'm single, I don't really have a job."

"It would appear to me that your future is pretty well assured given your father's estate, there is only you and your half-brother to share in it, your financial situation seems to have great potential."

"When my father dies, that may be true, but for now."

"But from what you have told me, he has suffered irreparable brain damage, you would have every right to seek the right to administer yourself or appoint an administrator to look after the estate."

"To be honest, I am not sure I want anything to do with the Company, it's not the kind of thing I've been trained for, I have no experience and I had other plans for myself."

"It seems to me, that you have much more to think about than just what you want, you have an autistic child to consider."

He hung his head, of course she was right, but still.

"Tell you what, let's take this one step at a time, I will go to Family Court and arrange for temporary custody on Monday, you go home and think about these other matters. Then you can let me know what you want to do."

He could do nothing but agree, she showed him out of the office, she told him to call her on Monday afternoon, and he nodded.

Janet and Ellis were waiting in the lobby when he stepped of the elevator, "So, how did it go? What did you think of Leslie?"

"You didn't tell me that she was uh, that she."

"That she was a good looking woman? Look she is a hell of a lawyer, you will be well looked after."

"That's what I'm afraid of!"

Janet smirked.

They returned to the condo after arranging for a rental car, Janet followed, Brad had to deal with Ellis and the death of his mother, he could avoid it no longer.

Brad took Ellis on his knee and held him close as he struggled to tell him his mommy was dead, the boy averted his eyes, he would not look into Brad's face, his body stiffened, he was afraid the boy might go into seizure. He hugged him tight and told him what had happened the night before; Brad was surprised at the lack of reaction.

But then Ellis slipped of his knee and began running from room to room, flinging open doors, closets even the kitchen cupboards, he began to scream, unintelligible sounds

"I think he understands what I told him, but he appears to be in some kind of denial, I think he is looking for her!"

"What do we do Brad?" Janet stood stunned in the middle of the family room, one hand clasped over her mouth in disbelief of the outburst.

"All I can do is try to reassure him, tell him that he is OK, that I'm here, you're here, that we won't leave him!"

"Jan, his medication is in the medicine cabinet in his bathroom, would you get it please?"

Ellis finally threw himself on the floor, kicking and screaming, Brad sat next to him and tried to soothe him, Jan handed him the prescribed dosage of the medication and held a glass of water ready when he needed it.

He gathered of the flailing body and pressed him to him, whispering in his ear that everything was going to be OK, but was it?

Finally, he was able to force the tablets into the little boy's mouth and with some coaxing got him to swallow them. He held the child for what seemed like an eternity, but the drugs eventually had the desired effect and the boy began to doze.

"OH, Brad! I've never seen anything like that before, how are you ever going to cope?"

"Well, this is about what I expected, but I dread tomorrow when I have to take him back to Halton House, frankly Jan, I feel absolutely trapped!"

Chapter 25

The funeral was held on Thursday, it was a beautiful sunny day, no smog was apparent and after the weekend rain, everything seemed fresh and clear. The funeral home chapel was filled to overflowing; Janet had come with him, that way she was able to point out people in attendance that he did not know, besides which he needed her support.

There had been a scene with Ellis when he returned him to Halton House, perhaps not quite as bad as he had anticipated, but he knew he would receive the care he needed from people that seemed to care about him. At least as much as people in such facilities can spare, given the number of children there. Dr. Fulton had advised against Ellis attending the service, Brad would be eternally grateful for that recommendation, time enough in later years for such things.

They had arrived early and sat in the back of the chapel, Janet whispered the names and occupations of the notables as they arrived.

She pointed out, Lester Coughlan, Ashley's father, an old man with red rimmed eyes, leaning heavily on a walking stick. A slim, younger man, with skin that looked like early days of jaundice, aided him.

"That's his son the junkie," whispered Janet. "The sister is in a loony bin! Some family!"

Brad poked her in the ribs with a well-placed elbow and shushed her.

Jim Nelson came in, alone, Brad was startled at his appearance, normally impeccably groomed, he looked like he had been on a 4 day bender, he noticed has hand shaking as he reached for the back of the pew to steady himself.

He was surprised to see Nazir enter the already crowded chapel, "What's he doing here?"

"You mean my old friend Naz? Remember, in this circle it pays to be seen at appropriate events, this is one of those,"

With that, Brad noticed some men ejecting a photographer as he attempted to gain entry, "Some of your people I assume?"

"This is a private service, they have no right to intrude!"

"I happen to agree!"

"Yeah! Well all bets are off when we hit the streets after this thing is over!"

The service was mercifully short, the body had already been cremated, and the graveside service was for immediate family only.

Although they were at the rear of the church, the pastor had asked everyone to wait until family members exited before leaving; consequently they were among the last to leave. They had come in Janet's car because parking at the funeral home was limited, she had told him where to stand on the curb and she left to get the car.

There were times when she annoyed him with her directives. However, he wasn't prepared to walk so he did as he was told.

Hordes of reporters were about to encircle him, when a voice said, "If your smart you'll get in!" The tinted window of the stretch limousine was only partially opened; he couldn't see who spoke, to avoid the media he did not hesitate.

Once in the car, he realized he was sitting opposite Lester Coughlan, Ashley's father, his hand was extended, "You're Arnie's son I understand."

"Yes, Brad Soper sir, I'm sorry we have to meet under such circumstances."

"Me too, but that was not of our choice now was it?"

The man was impressive in spite of his age; he had a presence. He was sure of himself and obviously was used to commanding respect.

"I just wanted to have a few words with you, I assume that you won't be at the graveside service?"

Before he could respond Coughlan continued, "No need really, what's done is done and no words can undo it!

Before she died, Ashley told me about you, she very much liked you and for some reason, trusted you. Mind you her assessment of men was not among her greatest assets." He said wryly.

"She also told me that you were very good with my grandson, that unfortunate child seems to be the story of my whole family. Disappointments all! Save Ashley, Oh, she had her faults I am very aware of that, but she did shine! Now she's gone and what am I left with, a worthless drug abuser for a son, a daughter in an asylum and a defective grandson!"

The words made Brad bristle with anger, "This self centred son-of-a-bitch! Has he no feelings?" he thought.

"I seem to have touched a nerve, have I? I'm a plain spoken man, more than a little bitter about they way things have turned out in my life, I'm afraid I'm all out of compassion Brad.

But that's not what I wanted to speak to you about, Ashley told me she was trying to get you to become a trustee for your father's estate and that you were resisting, is that true?"

"Yes, I promised her I would consider it, but frankly it doesn't fit into what I want to do with my life."

"I once felt the same as you, but, I must tell you that events have more to do with shaping your life than your own plans do, trust me, at my age I can reflect on my own life and I tell you that is a truth."

"Perhaps, but I choose not to be a fatalist!"

"One thing Ashley was adamant about, was that she did not want anything to do with Jim Nelson as a trustee, I assume you are aware of that?"

"Yes, but she never shared with me what caused this lack of trust "

"Nor I, but it became almost a fixation with her, frankly, I have never much cared for Nelson, I know he was a close friend of your father's, but to me he seemed more a hanger-on than a doer. I never say anything behind anyone's back, so Nelson is fully aware of what I think of him."

"Tell me, Mr. Coughlan, what are your plans for Ellis?"

"I don't have any, I rather hoped you might have some, particularly since you are now, aside from me, his only blood relative!"

"Are you telling me you don't care what happens to your grandson?"

"Mind your manners kid! I never said that!" The red rimmed eyes were flashing now.

"Just understand, you cannot absolve yourself of responsibility for my grandson, just because it doesn't fit you plans! Grow up young fella! I am going to be 81 in September, you know the situation Ellis' with his other relatives, who do you think has the greatest responsibility here?"

Brad could not really argue with the logic, but he felt like a condemned man with the noose tightening on his neck

"I have made application for temporary custody of Ellis, really just to forestall any action by the Child Welfare people, at least that will buy me some time until I can figure out what to do!"

"Good, I agree with that, now you can see what I mean about events shaping your life! Brad, it isn't that I want no part in what happens to Ellis. I am talking about the reality of the situation. I will be there with financial support; his future will be secure in that regard. But as to his emotional needs, they will have to be met in other ways and by people other than me."

"I hear what you are saying sir, there has been so much going on."

"I know all that, now let's talk about Soper Research, I want you to know that I have told Jim Nelson that the Board has struck a search committee to find a new CEO and that he will not be considered. Since ultimately you will end up with de facto equity control of this business, sooner rather than later, I feel I need to discuss this with you."

"I don't know what help I can offer, I don't have any experience in the business, it isn't my background..."

"I know what your background is, so let's not waste time here, we are not looking for a research type, we are not looking for MBA's with the world's greatest business plan, frankly we got those kind of people coming out our Ying yang!

What we need is someone with the strategic ability to point the company in a direction for the future, we need a thinker, like your father, we need someone who can see trends emerging in the health care field, including, God forbid, even medical ethics for the future.

"I think you have the stuff to do that, Ashley did too, I should be around long enough to teach you the "street stuff" What do you say, are you interested?"

Brad was stunned, how could he answer, it was like being trapped by the onslaught of an avalanche. "Ah, Ah, I really need to think about this Mr. Coughlan!"

"Good, Good, that's all I ask, call me Lester, you look like you could do with a drink, he opened the sliding door to the mini bar. "What's your pleasure?"

Janet had already left, as had virtually everybody else, with the exception of the man he saw standing in the alcove of the funeral home, it was Jim Nelson.

When Coughlan's car had pulled away from the curb, Nelson approached him, "Hello Brad, sorry to meet you again under these circumstances."

Nelson looked like he had slept in his clothes, whenever it was that he last slept, he was dishevelled, they shook hands, and Brad could not help but note the clamminess.

"Brad, I need to talk to you, it is extremely important can you spare the time?"

He took pity on the man and nodded in agreement. "I can give you a lift if you need, it appears that your ride has left you?"

"Thanks, I would appreciate that."

Nelson looked over his shoulder and then said "But, Brad, we can't talk in the car, we need a public place, we'll go to the zoo,"

"But why can't we talk on the way?"

"I am sure my car is bugged, so say nothing!"

The drove in silence to the zoo, it was no great problem for Brad to sit quietly, his head was swimming with all that was happening, and now this, was it a dream? Was all this really happening?

They walked from the parking lot to the Great Primates cages without speaking, Brad watched as an orangutan picked nits from the armpit of his mate and ate them, "My life should be that simple!" he thought.

They sat on a secluded bench, it was still early and there was no crowd, Nelson spoke.

"Brad, I need to tell you some things, that I feel you need to know. You know, I think that your father and I were good friends going back to med school days. I can't tell you how distressed I am with respect to the events of the last few weeks concerning first you father, then Peter Mytryk and culminating with the tragedy last Saturday.

You must find all of this as overwhelming as I do! But I need to warn you about Declan Mahoney, he is a dangerous man and you must take care where he is involved, he is totally immoral and will stop at nothing to get his own way."

"But what has Mahoney to do with me, isn't he just the P.R. guy for the company and I understand that he provides security as well, tell me how he figures in all this?"

I'll get to that, but first, I need to tell you about my relationship with your father, as I said we have been best friends since college, I have always admired him he was always so able, you know only some his achievements, there is so much more to know."

Brad interrupted, "Look Jim, if this is some kind of testimonial for my father, please stop, I don't need to hear any more."

"I understand your bitterness Brad, believe me I do, for in spite of my friendship with your father, I have to confess that I was also very jealous of him, he had everything I wanted. He became famous, he became rich, and," he hesitated, becoming agitated he began wringing his hands, "I also envied him Ashley!"

"Ashley?"

"Yes, Ashley."

"You were in love with her?"

"Without question, so you may understand my distress at her horrible death!"

"But Ashley told me that she wanted nothing to do with you, that you the last man on earth she would trust, how do you reconcile that?"

"I can't, I can only tell you what caused that lack of trust, then you may see why I couldn't overcome it."

"Please do!"

"After your father and mother divorced, your father became even more immersed in Soper Research, he wanted no distractions, he withdrew from society, he saw no one. He was deeply hurt by what your mother did, I think that was a large part of what drove him."

"What was it that my father thinks she did to him?"

Nelson paused, unsure of how to proceed; he finally breathed a sigh and continued.

"Your father did not leave your mother, it was the other way around, she left him."

"What? Was there another man, who was he, I never saw him, I don't believe this!"

"No it was not another man, it was another woman!"

"I don't believe a thing you're saying!"

"You should, because the other woman was my wife!"

Brad was stunned, he had never heard any of this, but he did recollect a favourite aunt living with them for a few years, he also remembered the impact her sudden death had on his mother.

"Frankly, I blamed your father for many years, perhaps if he had not neglected your mother for the sake of the business, none of this would have happened, but then I guess I have to bear some of the responsibility too! In any event, your father brought me into the business with him, my practice was not doing all that well, even though I have continued as a practicing physician, my only real patient ended up being your father.

I became a man Friday for Arnie, a gopher, I did anything he asked of me and I gradually accepted that he was not responsible for the breakup of my marriage. There were signs that I missed in our relationship, that might have warned me, but I suppose the result was inevitable."

There was a pause in the conversation, Brad wasn't sure if that was all, or if there were more revelations to come, and then Nelson continued.

"And of course, as you already know, Ashley came into Arnie's life, I think your father was mesmerized by her, he was truly infatuated despite the age difference. Moreover, I have to admit; I was smitten as well.

It was a whirlwind courtship, they married in less than a year, they seemed immensely happy, at least in the first couple of years.

The business grew dramatically, there came a time when there was a need for additional financing, that's when Lester Coughlan, Ashley's father, entered the picture. With the addition of substantial capital investment by Coughlan and his cronies, the business just started to take off.

Your father had a genius for the business, he worked very hard, and he seemed to have everything in his life.

Nevertheless, things began to change in the relationship when Ashley started to press about having a family.

Arnie wanted no part of having a family, as a matter of fact he came to me to perform a vasectomy, he felt that strongly about the issue."

"And did you, perform the vasectomy I mean?"

"Yes."

"When?"

"It was 6 months before she became pregnant with Ellis!"

He was thunderstruck! If true, that would mean that Ellis was not related to him, he no longer had a little brother.

"I can't believe all this, it can't be true!"

"Sadly it is, there are medical records to prove that the surgery was performed.

"Was Ashley aware? Of the surgery I mean?"

"No."

"You mean there was no spousal conference in advance of the surgery?"

"No, your father forbid it, and once the surgery was performed, I was bound by doctor patient confidentiality, not to reveal it."

"That's bullshit! You had an obligation to inform the spouse!"

"That hardly matters now does it?"

"Then who is the father of Ellis?"

Nelson sat quietly as though carefully considering how he might answer; the pause seemed interminable.

"Did you hear me? Who is Ellis' father?"

"All I can tell you is who Ashley thought it was? Although I don't necessarily accept it"

"Who?

Again silence, then finally Nelson looked into Brad's face and said,

"Me, she thought it was me! But frankly, my sperm count was is so low, I do not consider it much of a possibility,"

Brad was having difficulty taking in all he was hearing, "But you did have sex with her?"

"Only once, it was a weak moment for the two of us, I told you, I was in love with her, it was just a spontaneous thing, it's not something one can undo!"

"Did my father know?"

"That it might have been me? No, at least I don't think so; he never gave any indication at any rate. Our relationship continued as it always had, but, as might be expected, the relationship with Ashley was virtually destroyed when he found out she was pregnant."

"What did he do?"

"That's really the strange thing, he did nothing, at least nothing officially, for all intents and purposes, he accepted the child as his, legally. They remained married but the situation was strained. But Arnie wanted no scandal, he also had a concern for her father, they had become very close and he didn't want to see him hurt."

"We started this discussion with your warning me about Declan Mahoney, what has he to do with any of this?"

"He is at heart, a blackmailer, he found out about all that I have told you, I don't know how, but he has used it to blackmail me. On the night Ashley died, I know he called her to arrange a meeting, I believe he was going to threaten her with the release of all of the information I have related to you.

That would have destroyed Ashley, your relationship with her and Ellis would come crashing down. I blame Mahoney for Ashley's death!"

"That son-of-a-bitch, why, why! What would he do all this for?"

"For some reason he wants share control of Soper Research, that's why he was pushing me forward as a trustee, that's what he wanted from Ashley.

Another thing, I don't believe Peter Mytryk's death was a suicide, I think somehow he crossed Mahoney and was murdered!"

"Why haven't you gone to the police with all this?"

"Mahoney is too crafty, I have no direct proof, I would be dispensed with just as easily as Mytryk!

Let me drive you back to your car, but remember, I suspect my car is bugged, so we can't continue our discussion, just sit quietly until I get you back."

Brad's mind was whirling with everything that had happened to him today, but the was one question he had to ask, as they walked back to the parking lot, "Tell me Jim, where does Janet Petersen fit into the scheme of things."

He was sure he saw a flicker in Nelson's eyes at the mention of the name, "I know of her, but aside of some occasional work she did directly for the company, I had no involvement with her.

Just take care Brad, of anybody involved with Declan Mahoney!"

Chapter 26

Dave Harris sat at his desk reading the accident report concerning the death of Ashley Soper; he had heard first word of the accident on his car radio as he came into work. He thought to himself.

"The husband is in a coma, the Director of Research has apparently committed suicide and now the wife is dead, so much for coincidences, somehow there must be a connection, but what is it?"

The ringing of his phone interrupted him; it was his boss, Chief Inspector Fast.

"Harris, take line 3, it's your best buddy from the Mounties, seems they would like your help, when you're finished come and see me." The phone was disconnected by a loud click in his ear, it seemed that Fast could do or say nothing without some kind of sarcasm.

He punched line 3, it was Dwayne Hitchcock, he was assigned to the commercial fraud department of the RCMP, they had been classmates together on the MBA course, in fact Hitchcock had tried to recruit him to join the force, but Harris had resisted.

"Hello Davey! How's the sleuthing business?"

"Hi Dwayne, the sleuthing is more interesting than that crap you do! How can I help you?"

"Well, I had a call yesterday, from the FBI in Washington, they are looking into a potential fraud case involving a federal employee of the Food and Drug Administration."

"What's that got to do with us up here?"

"I am not really sure at this point, but it appears that this individual was in direct contact with senior members of a Canadian Corporation, namely Soper Research Inc., they suspect that this guy might have been receiving payoffs for "fast tracking" a drug approval.

I heard that you were investigating the suicide of the late Director of Research at Soper, it's probably just a coincidence but I thought it might be worthwhile to run it past you."

"I don't believe in coincidences Dwayne, and if I did, there have already been too many as far as this outfit is concerned." Harris briefed Hitchcock on what he knew so far regarding the events relating to Soper.

"I see what you mean Dave, I can only gather that the U.S. feds don't have enough to make an arrest and are fishing in our waters to see if they can establish any factual basis for charges."

"For your information, I haven't closed the case on Peter Mytryk's apparent suicide, there is something bothering me about it, and now these other events have occurred, I think I am going continue my investigation and maybe widen it a little."

"Would you keep me up to speed Dave?"

"Yeah, I will, but my priorities are somewhat different to those of the FBI, if I come across anything I think will be useful, I'll let you know."

"That's all I can ask for, thanks Dave."

"By the way Dwayne, do you have anything on a Declan Mahoney?"

There was a silence on the other end of the phone, Harris waited, "Dwayne, are you still there?"

"Yeah, I'm here, Dave it's not my area, but I've heard that he is under surveillance, but not by us."

"Who then?"

"CSIS! You know that we don't necessarily get along, but there are a couple of good guys over there, but they don't like to share"

'Can you guess why he is under surveillance?"

"Not really, but you know he is an Irish Immigrant, and as near as I can tell, he was involved in some kind of IRA activity there. About all I know is that Mahoney is a bad actor, we've had active investigations on him and his company in the past, but there never was enough evidence to lay any charges."

"Why are CSIS involved, are you still actively investigating?"

"No, apparently there is a directive from Foreign Affairs, highest level, we are to stay out!"

"Can I get a copy of your file on Mahoney, it might save me some time?"

"No can do, it would be worth my job, besides, I can't access it anyway."

"I understand Dwayne, I'll let you know if I come up with anything that might interest the FBI, maybe we could have a drink sometime."

"Good enough Davey, See you soon, we can chew over old times, maybe I can even convince you to move over and join us."

He detested the diminutive use of his name, before going to see Fast, he fired off a fax to Interpol, asking for any information they might have on one Declan Mahoney.

He entered Fast's office just as his superior stuffed the last of a glazed doughnut into his mouth; he was unable to talk, so he motioned Harris to sit. He watched as the food rolled around in the man's mouth, it took him two swallows before he could speak.

As he wiped the sugar coating off his chin and jowls he said, "So now the Mounties are working for the FBI, what do they want from us?"

Harris explained the purpose of the call and told Fast only as much as he deemed necessary, he did not bring up Mahoney's name or his fax to Interpol.

"Look, Harris, this is a simple suicide, why are you turning it into something it ain't, close the fucking thing, we have other cases to deal with!"

"Mike, I am not so sure it was a suicide and given some of the other things that have happened, I think there is more to this situation."

"What makes you think it wasn't suicide, college boy?"

He ignored the taunt, "Well for one thing. The gun was unregistered, how would a bookish scientist know how to acquire that?" Secondly, if this guy was a paedophile and had over 100,000 porno images on his computer, how come he slipped right beneath our own radar.

To have collected that many and to have had memberships in as many web sites as was apparently the case from his hard drive transactions, would have taken months.

Many of those sites have been under surveillance and vice has knocked off several individuals therefore, why not Mytryk? Something just doesn't smell right!"

The fat man reached into the Tim Horton box on his desk and retrieved a jam buster, taking a bite, the jelly squirted down his chin. He took a crumpled napkin and wiped his face, "Theories, nothing more, what facts have you got to support your hunches?"

" I admit, not much, but I am not prepared to close the Mytryk case just yet."

"Listen to me Harris," gesturing with the remainder of his doughnut. "You got just 7 days to wrap this thing up! You got that?"

"Yeah! I got that!"

He left Fast's office, maybe he should join the RCMP Commercial Crimes Unit, and at least he'd be rid of "Fat-Assed Fast." He knew he wouldn't. However, it was pleasurable just thinking. Of telling Fast what he could do with his job.

Brad sat in his hotel room; he was deep in thought about all of the things that had happened in his life since Janet first contacted him. His father was in a coma; his newly discovered brother was likely not his brother after all. Ashley was dead; all of it seemed to be a blur.

It looked like Lester Coughlan was right, events were shaping his life, and he seemed to have lost control over the direction he had planned for his future.

The phone rang.

"Brad, it's Naz, how are you doing, I saw you at Mrs. Soper's funeral, I tried to catch up with you afterwards, but you seemed to disappear."

"Yes, I saw you as well, I got involved with Ashley's father, sorry I missed you."

"I assume that he took it pretty hard, her father I mean."

"Not so you'd notice, he's a tough old man, he'll get through it."

"But how about you, it seemed the two of you and the boy of course, were getting pretty close?"

"Yeah, we were, it's Ellis I'm worried about now." He saw no reason to explain his decision to seek temporary custody of the child.

"Brad, have you made any decision with respect to your involvement with Soper Research?

"Not really, but there is lot's of pressure being applied, I don't need any more right now Naz!"

"Sorry, I don't mean to press you, it's just that I need to talk to someone about things here, would it be possible for you to come in so that we can have a discussion."

"Why don't you just discuss them with Jim Nelson, he's your boss isn't he?"

"I don't want to discuss it over the phone Brad, and some of what I have to say involves Nelson, I would appreciate it if you could come here."

Brad resigned himself to another unforeseen event, "OK Naz, I'll be there in about half an hour."

"Good, I'll arrange with security, see you then."

Mahoney clicked the mute button on his computer screen; something was up, what did Naz find? The situation was getting out of control, he was going to have to do something about Nelson, and he was becoming a significant liability!

He punched the intercom button and asked his secretary to locate Jim Nelson for him, 15 minutes later Nelson was on the line.

"Jim, I'm glad I caught up with you, something has come up and it's important, would you be good enough to come to my office tonight, say about 10:00 o'clock? I know that's rather late, but I have to attend several meetings and that's the very earliest I can be available."

"What's all this about Declan?"

"I can't discuss it on the phone Jim, all I can tell you is that it is in your best interest and for that matter the best interest of the late Mrs. Soper too."

"What could this meeting possibly mean to Ashley now, she's dead!"

"Then let's just say, it could impact on how she is remembered!"

"You bastard Mahoney! Can't you just leave her in peace?"

"That's exactly what I am trying to do Jim, but that is entirely up to you, will you be here?"

"Yes, I'll be there!"

"Good, and Jim, there will only be the two of us, just ring the buzzer at the door and I'll let you in."

*

"Brad, thank you very much for coming, I know you are dealing with someone difficult issues, but I need to talk to someone about certain things that I have uncovered since I came here."

"Naz, before we start, maybe you could show me around a little bit, the last time I was here, I must admit I didn't really pay a whole lot of attention."

After he finished speaking he held a finger to his lips before Naz could respond, Naz looked at him quizzically for a moment, then his eyes narrowed and he said,

"Sure Brad, let me give you the $20.00 tour."

Brad remembered a staircase that lead to the roof of the building, service personnel used it when any of the environmental air handling equipment was in need of servicing.

They both stood in the bright sunshine; they could see most of the Research Park from this vantage point.

"Why are we up here Brad?"

"I have reason to believe that someone is utilizing electronic eavesdropping techniques in order to take advantage of or compromise what we say, we should be OK up here."

"Shit, Brad, what is all this cloak and dagger stuff, where is all of this coming from?"

"Ashley was convinced that my father's apartment was bugged, likely still is, it seemed reasonable to me that if that was happening in his home why not here.

The other thing is that Ashley didn't trust Nelson, for reasons I won't discuss with you, so I can understand your reticence in wanting to go to Nelson with whatever you wanted to discuss with me."

"You think Nelson is behind the "bugging"?"

"Could be, but who knows, what was it you wanted to discuss?"

Just then, Naz' cell phone rang.

"Monpetit here, - who? He's asking for me? I'll be there in a minute."

He closed his cell phone and looked puzzled, "I don't know what the hell is going on here?"

"What do mean?"

"That was the switchboard, because of size of the plant we use cell phones instead of extensions, saves a lot of steps, She says there is an Inspector Harris from the Metro Police Department here to see Jim Nelson, but he isn't in. The detective then asked for the next in line, she figured that to be me."

"What does he want?"

"He wouldn't tell the receptionist, I'd better see to it, want to sit in?"

"Why not? My day is screwed up anyway."

He sat in Naz' office waiting for his return. He had to admit, his curiosity was piqued, what the hell was going on?

Naz returned with the detective, Brad was introduced; they shook hands, he and the detective sat opposite Naz.

Naz leaned back in his chair and asked, "Tell me Inspector Harris, why have you come?"

"Well, Dr. Monpetit, this is my second visit, initially I came with respect to our investigation into the death of Dr. Mytryk, your predecessor I believe."

"Yes, he was, but my understanding is that his death was a suicide, is that not so?"

"We have not closed the file on his death, so there is as yet, no decision with respect to whether it was suicide or if foul play may have been involved."

"You said your initial visit was related to Dr. Mytryk's death, is that still the reason you are here?"

Harris ignored the question and turned his attention to Brad, "Mr. Soper, I would like to extend my condolences to you, both in the instance of your father's condition and on the recent death of your step-mother."

"Thank you for your concern."

"It seems that Soper Research and your family have had more than their share of tragedies, I suppose that one could consider all of them to be unrelated coincidences, but I must admit that most people in my line of work abhor coincidences much as nature abhors a vacuum."

Naz looked surprised at the detective's comment, "What are you implying?"

Again his question was ignored; Harris leaned back in his chair and watched both men carefully before he asked his next question, he wanted to see the reaction to it.

"The reason that I am here today, is to ask you if you have any personal knowledge of a situation that has come to our intention, involving this company and a foreign government agency."

"I don't understand."

"It appears, that as a result of an FBI investigation in Washington DC, that someone in this company may be in collusion with a senior employee of the Federal Drug Administration. This possible collusion may involve illegal payments to the said employee in return for preferential treatment of approval applications for controlled substances.

Please be careful in response to my next question, your answers could be used against you in a court of law, should subsequent events indicate that your answers are untruthful.

Do either of you have any direct or indirect knowledge of any such arrangement?"

Chapter 27

Brad sat in the large, over-stuffed Victorian chair next to the gigantic Grandfather Clock that was ponderously ticking his life away as he awaited the arrival of Lester Coughlan. He had been invited to lunch with the old man at his club, the exclusive Greystokes Men's Club.

He was unfamiliar with the location, consequently, not wanting to be late, he had arrived almost 30 minutes early. When he entered, he met a stiff little man who looked as though he had stepped in something unpleasant. Brad mentioned that he was to meet Lester Coughlan for lunch, the name had the desired impact and he was allowed to enter and was placed in this chair.

Across from him was a wide, winding staircase with an enormous banister, ornately carved hand rails all in dark walnut that glistened from the many hands that had polished it over many years.

He could only guess at just how much money it cost for a membership here, but the opulence of the place made it obvious that it would be very substantial.

He tried to get comfortable in the very uncomfortable chair, the clock continued to remind him of just how early he was and how much longer he was going to have to wait.

He thought back to the meeting with Detective Harris and Naz, he felt that Harris found it hard to believe that neither of them knew much about the workings of Soper Research, even when they told them that they were both new arrivals on the scene.

As for Naz, after Harris left, he found it strange that he no longer wanted to discuss whatever it was that was so urgent on the phone when he had called, in fact he seemed anxious to get away from him.

Naz suggested that the matter could wait and perhaps they could get together for dinner this evening, maybe he would find out then, just what was bothering Naz.

He continued to roll over in his mind all of the events of the last few weeks, trying to make some sense out of them, he was deep in thought when a voice broke into his reverie.

"A penny for your thoughts is probably not enough, is it?"

He looked up suddenly; the old man seemed to loom larger than he had remembered.

"Sorry Mr. Coughlan, just daydreaming I guess."

"Make it Lester son. Even in here I'm not much on formalities, come on let's go up for lunch."

They made their way up the staircase, Brad marvelled at the thickness of the carpet, he guessed that this was one of the things contributing to the sheer quietness of the place.

The formally dressed waiter deposited a drink for each of them on the linen covered table and left as silently as he had come, leaving menus for each. Brad noted quickly that no prices were shown, I guess if you were concerned about the price of anything here, you shouldn't be a member.' He thought to himself.

"So tell me Brad, how are things proceeding with young Ellis?"

"Well, as I mentioned, I have made an application to the court for temporary custody, my lawyer says it is merely a formality. I may have to make brief appearance in court later this week, just so the judge can put a face to the name I guess.

My lawyer says that they will almost always side with relatives as opposed to taking the child into the system."

"Good, Good, but what about the long term, are you prepared to become Ellis' legal guardian?"

"Honestly? I don't know, I hardly think I am qualified to be a parent as well as a brother."

Brad had decided not to mention his discussion with Jim Nelson regarding the paternity issue, he was surprised at his own feelings upon discovering Ellis was not his half-brother. That is, if Nelson was telling the truth.

"Do you think you could just abandon Ellis to the Child Welfare system in this province? You know there will be little likelihood of any adoption of a child such as he."

"Lester, I am fully aware of all that, I've lost a lot of sleep over it frankly, all the things that have happened since my father's illness are more than somewhat overwhelming. It just seems that I'm getting pressure from all sides, frankly, I don't much like it."

"At least you are not saying you won't become Ellis' guardian, right?"

"That's right."

"OK, let's change the subject, what about taking over at Soper Research?"

"More pressure."

"Yeah, more pressure. Frankly if you can't take the pressure you're the wrong man for the job. So what have I got to lose?"

"There are some things I want to discuss with you that may help me clarify what direction I should take. Right now I have more questions than answers."

"Fire away, I'll answer all your questions, directly and honestly, if I can. I mean if I know anything your talking about."

"I spoke to Jim Nelson last week, he told me he has no intention of trying to get your support regarding the Chairman's position, in fact he no longer wants the job."

"He knew he would never get the job anyway, that wasn't a question, tell me what you want to know."

"In that same meeting, he warned me about Declan Mahoney, who is Mahoney, and why is he involved with the Company?"

"First, why is Mahoney involved with the Company? About 10 years ago there was a costly security breech within the Research Department, a competitor, "scooped" us on a patent application, got it entered before we could. Later it became obvious that it was all of our research and techniques that had been used by our competitor.

However, we couldn't prove it. Your father, and rightly so, went ballistic, he went looking for a security consultant to prevent that sort of thing from happening again. Also to find out where the leaks were and stop them.

That's when Declan Mahoney entered the picture, his firm analysed all of our procedures such as they were, and recommended the necessary changes. Mahoney also had a division that would implement the new procedures and provide ongoing supervision for a fee of course.

In addition, it turned out that Mahoney could also provide Public Relation Services as well, it was quite an attractive package."

"And did Mahoney ever discover the source of the leak?"

"Apparently so, there was a shake up in the department. People were let go, and I can tell you, no such thing has occurred since Mahoney Associates came on the scene."

"But no prosecutions I take it."

"Not enough evidence for a court of law, but enough for your father.

"But just who is Mahoney?"

"A good question, and I am not sure anyone really knows, personally I don't like him, never have, but he gets the job done. He reminds me a little of J. Edgar Hoover, I am sure he has a file on everyone he ever had contact with, including you and me. If he could turn a buck using that information, I believe he would.

Word has it that he had to get out of Ireland, he's the kind that would play both ends against the middle, got into some kind of trouble with either the Loyalists or the IRA, I don't know which, and had to get out."

"Nelson also told me that he doesn't believe that Dr. Mytryk's death was a suicide, he believes he was murdered."

A little smile played briefly across Coughlan's lips, "I had wondered about that myself, you know, he was part of the research department that was leaking information, as a matter of fact, he was one of the few left untouched after Mahoney got finished.

Frankly, I found that a little odd, so did your father, but because of the lack of evidence and in the interest of continuity, Mytryk remained. But I must tell you, he did not have your father's complete confidence, in fact I think that was the real reason behind hiring this Monpetit fellow."

Brad had already said more than he had had intended to, but he sensed that the old man had integrity and that he was someone he could trust, so he decided to continue.

"Nelson also told me that he believes that Ashley was meeting with Mahoney the night of the accident, in fact he seemed to imply that Mahoney may have in some way, been responsible for it."

Coughlan looked directly at Brad, "Brad I have no knowledge of anything that Ashley might have had to discuss with Mahoney, but as I said, he had files on everyone." His eyes narrowed and his tone became harsh. "But, I can tell you this, if I ever find out he had anything to do with Ashley" death, I'll kill the bastard myself!"

Brad fully believed what Coughlan had said, even if he was too old to actually do it himself, there was little doubt he could have it done.

He took a deep breath and continued. "Lester, were you aware that my father was about to divorce Ashley just before he took ill?"

"Sadly, yes. Ashley had told me about it just after she found out, it was just after your father had his problem. It's sad really; I don't know what happened between them, I just know that I cared for both of them. I know Ashley seemed to be on a self-destruct course and I know your father could be a hard man, as can I but-."

The words just hung in the air, Brad regretted almost immediately, having raised the issue

"There is just one other thing Lester, are you aware of any kind of arrangement with an employee of the FDA in Washington, involving illegal, under the table payments for preferential treatment of an application concerning the new vaccine?"

"No, I am not! Why would you ask me that?"

"Naz Monpetit and I were just questioned by a Detective Harris pertaining to an ongoing FBI investigation that apparently involves Soper Research and some unnamed federal US employee in such an activity."

"I can tell you that no such request ever came before the board!"

"I doubt that it would, it would seem to me that, if it was done at all, it would have to be with great secrecy, even I know that such an approach is illegal."

"There was only one thing that I remember happening that seemed questionable, but I'm sure it would have had nothing to do with this."

What was it Lester?"

"Well, I noticed a change to the Balance Sheet on the interim financial statements, your father explained it to my satisfaction, so I just dropped it."

"What was this change?"

"The Company had apparently invested in a startup company, the equity we had purchased was shown as an asset on our statements. When I questioned your father about it he simply said it was something he was interested in having a stake in, something about the development of a new sunscreen chemical.

I said to him that I thought that this was a major deviation from our normal focus and that it seemed too speculative to be considered an asset and should probably be simply expensed.

He surprised me by agreeing without argument and said he would look after it."

"And did he?"

"Come to think of it, no. This conversation took place just before he left for Nairobi. He wouldn't have had time"

"What was the name of this company?"

"There is no name, it was a numbered company."

"Located where?"

"The Grand Cayman Islands!"

"So, Lester, you might understand my reticence about getting deeply involved with the company, it seems to me that I really don't need all the baggage associated with it, not to mention the potential risks involved."

"Yes Brad, I do understand, I must admit that I was not aware of everything that you have experienced and I can see where you see the West Coast as a safe haven. But, as I have said before, events have overtaken you, yes you can walk away from what is now part of your personal history, but you cannot alter that past, it is what it is, you can only affect the future by your actions.

"But why should I?"

"You're the ethicist, why are you asking me, you have the opportunity to change lives for the better, young Ellis for one, but what about the millions of people that could benefit from this new vaccine?

Oh yes, another company could acquire it, but you could have control of availability, pricing, supplies to under developed countries, future product developments and research projects. Can you turn your back on all of that and still consider yourself an ethicist?"

Chapter 28

It was just approaching 10:00 o'clock as Nelson entered the lobby of Mahoney's office building, it was getting dark, not much twilight in this part of the world he thought.

Ever since he had received Mahoney's call, Nelson's mind was in turmoil trying to determine just what he might be up to, it was useless trying to second guess what someone as amoral as Declan Mahoney might do next.

Nelson had made his mind up that he would have to try to put an end to this whole affair, he could stomach no more and he had an idea of just how to do that. A smile played on his lips, as he stood ready to press the buzzer outside Mahoney's office, yes he had an idea.

Mahoney appeared almost as soon as he released the button, he had obviously been watching for him.

"Hello Jim, thanks for coming."

"What's this all about Mahoney?"

"Come into my office so we can discuss it, we can be more comfortable there."

Once again he sat across from this man he had come to detest, he just hoped that he could maintain his composure, losing his temper would only complicate what he was here for.

"Can I offer you a drink Jim, a Compari and Soda I believe?"

"Yes that would be fine."

He watched Mahoney as he turned his back to him and proceeded to mix a drink at the bar, continued talking as he mixed the drink and poured a neat shot of Jameson's for himself.

"Jim, the last time we met you were very upset, you seemed to be blaming me for Ashley's death, I think you know, deep down, that that is not true. I liked Ashley; I wouldn't want to hurt her by any means.

You know better than anyone, that Ashley was not a particularly stable person, the purpose of my meeting, as you well know, was simply to convince her to support you in a bid for the Chairman's position."

Nelson could feel the anger rising within him, he had to fight to keep from shouting at the man, cool it, and take it easy, he's trying to goad you. He tried to speak in a level voice, controlling his emotions as much as he could.

"Are you telling me that weren't trying to blackmail her? That all you did was have discussions with her in support of me?

You will understand if I don't believe a word you are saying, won't you?"

"You know she was a drunk Jim, she was likely drinking before she met me, she must have been because she only had one drink with me!"

"What did you say to her?"

"I told you! I didn't ask you to come here and rehash what was said when we last met, all I want to know is, are you still interested in going forward with our original plan?"

"No! I want out, the whole thing is out of control, there is no plan!"

Nelson knew that he was probably signing his own death warrant, but strangely a calmness came over him, he felt suddenly relieved, he sipped his drink.

"You stupid son-of-a-bitch, you don't just quit on me! There is no way to get out, you're in this as deep as anybody!"

His face was distorted with anger, his eyes glittered with hatred of the man before him, suddenly his chest constricted, he couldn't breathe, and he reached for his asthma inhaler on his desk.

He took a deep breath inhaling the medication deep down into his lungs and almost instantly he could feel the vice gripping his chest begin to loosen. He began to breathe normally once more, but his anger had not subsided.

"Get the fuck out of here" he rasped "We have nothing more to say."

Nelson rose and quietly left without a word, Mahoney failed to see the slight smile on his face.

Mahoney used his inhaler again, he was able to breathe in even more deeply the second time, he held the inhaler in his hand and wondered how many times it had saved his life in the past. He had been an asthmatic since childhood; the doctors had told his mother that he might never reach maturity because of his illness.

He had fooled them all, he remembered too that this disease is what first had led him to Soper Research. It was Arnie Soper's discovery of a new more effective dilator that had likely saved his life. In addition, it had probably just done that again.

Nelson decided not to use the expressway to get home, instead he drove through the downtown area, it was bustling with life even at almost midnight. He failed to notice the headlights that were following him, his mind was somewhere else, the smile still on his lips.

When he turned on to a deserted side street, he noticed someone was following him, he speeded up and so did those following him, when he turned, they turned,

He frantically tried to get back into a heavier traffic area, but mistakenly turned onto a dead end road, the car pulled up beside him and forced him to the curb. He knew he couldn't outrun them, there was no one to hear him if he shouted, it was over.

The bigger of the two men pulled him from the car; the second shone a flashlight in his face.

"Yeah it's him!"

They pulled into a dirty little alleyway, he was paralysed with fear, his bladder emptied involuntarily.

"Do it, the son-of-a-bitch pissed himself!"

The larger man slipped the wire around his throat and within minutes, without a sound, life slipped from Dr. James Nelson.

*

Dave Harris' phone rang waking him from a sound sleep; he groped for the phone.

"Hello, who is this?"

"Sorry to wake you Dave, it's Bill Martin, we just had a unit call in with a homicide and I thought you should know about it."

"What the hell time is it?"

"It's 3:30 AM."

"Shit, it's the middle of the night couldn't it wait?"

"The victim appears to be Dr. Jim Nelson, you know, a big cheese at Soper Research. You're still on that case ain't ya?"

Suddenly Harris was wide-awake, "Yeah I'm still on it, sorry Bill, I appreciate the call, I was half asleep is all. What have you got so far?"

"Well, robbery's a possibility, wallet gone, no wrist watch, we ran the vehicle plates and came up with the name. But the death seems a little odd for a robbery gone bad, he was garroted with a steel wire!"

"Where was the body found?"

"That's the other odd part, Cherry Beach!"

"What the hell would he have been doing down there? I assume there is no time of death yet?"

"Not yet, it just came in, the crime scene unit is on the way, the coroner should be there shortly too."

He got the exact location from Martin, dressed quickly and was on his way in a matter of exactly 11 minutes, 28 minutes later he was at the scene.

Harris recognized the young uniformed officer talking to the crime scene investigator.

"Hi Terry, what have you got for me?"

"Sixty-ish male, no sign of a struggle, appears to have been strangled using a wire, it seems to be imbedded still. No wallet, no jewellery, probably just a mugging gone bad."

"Where's the body?"

"Still in the alleyway, the car is on the street there, the driver's door was open when we cruised by, my partner and I saw the interior light on and then found the body."

"Thanks Terry."

He went into the alley, bent down and lifted the covering away from the face, the smell of urine hit him as he did so, and it was Nelson all right!

The eyes seemed to bulge out of the sockets, even in this light he could see the wire ends protruding from the neck, he couldn't have cried out, no one to hear him anyway, he thought.

"What brings you out Dave?"

It was the coroner, he always reminded Dave of the actor John Carradine A walking cadaver himself. Suited for the job he thought.

"The Vic is Dr. Jim Nelson, he is or was a subject in an investigation I'm conducting at Soper Research."

"So you know him?"

"We've met, but no I don't know him, not yet anyway."

"Let me have a look, I don't know how much I can tell you before we have a post mortem, I might be able to give you an idea of approximate time of death at least."

"Thanks Henry."

He went over to talk to the crime scene people, they were good at what they did, he knew that they didn't need any direction from him and would probably resent it if he gave any.

"See anything I should know about?"

The man in the white coveralls responded "Not much Dave, you've seen the body, you know how he died, we're covering the whole area in case the perps left something behind for us. I doubt it though, it looks pretty professional to me."

He returned to the coroner, "Anything for me Henry?"

"I would estimate the time of death to have been 4 to 6 hours ago, not much else until after the autopsy."

"Thanks, I'll check in with you later today and see if you can come up with anything else."

Harris headed towards his favourite diner for some breakfast, it would give him a chance to roll over this new event in his mind, besides, his stomach was rumbling.

He parked his car in the diner lot, turned off his engine and removed his electric shaver from the glove compartment. It was still dark, but with the help of the illuminated visor he managed to do a credible job of removing the stubble.

He rubbed his finger over his teeth to remove the sour tasting scum from his teeth, must have slept with my mouth open he thought.

He was the only customer in the diner, the only waitress sidled up to him, filled his coffee cup and asked "Sausages and eggs Dave?"

He nodded and she turned to walk back to the kitchen, was he that predictable? So what? He liked sausages and eggs!

He took out his note pad and made a list. He always made a list.

1. Arnold Soper – Coma

2. Peter Mytryk – Dead - suicide?

3. Ashley Soper – Dead – Car Accident

4. Jim Nelson – Dead – Mugging?

5. FBI Investigation

6. Nazir Monpetit – Mytryk's replacement

7. Bradley Soper – Arnold Soper's son

8. Declan Mahoney - ?

Three deaths and one in a coma, coincidence? No bloody way! Soper Research is the common thread here, what am I missing?

I need more information on Monpetit, and Bradley Soper for that matter! I'll check and see if either of them have any involvement with the authorities.

He made a note to follow up with Interpol, maybe there was a response waiting for him now, he knew that Mahoney was somehow involved, but how?

His sausages and eggs arrived, his stomach overtook his mind and he turned his attention to the plate.

Chapter 29

"Brad? It's Naz, have you heard the news this morning?"
"No, as a matter of fact I just got up, what is it?"

"Jim Nelson was found dead, murdered, last night sometime. Brad this is really disturbing, I don't know what's happening. All these people, Mytryk, Ashley and now Nelson! All dead" He could hear Brad's startled intake of air at the news.

"What the hell is going on, you're sure it was Jim Nelson, you said "murdered" it wasn't an accident?"

"Not according to the news channel, said he was murdered, strangled was what they said. The media are going to be all over this, you know it won't be good for the company. Have you got any ideas of how to deal with the situation?"

"I guess the best thing to do is call Janet, they are supposed to be the experts at public relations, let's see what they come up with, do you want me to call her?"

"Would you mind, I'm spending most of my time putting out fires here, maybe the two of you could come here and we could put out some kind of an announcement or something. Call me after you talk to her."

He hung up the phone before he remembered to ask Naz, what it was he wanted to see him about before Harris had interrupted their meeting. Well, that could wait for now.

When he reached Janet, he found she was aware of the situation. She seemed as shocked as he was. She was in general agreement with what Naz had suggested; except that she felt it should be a full blown press conference and that Naz, Brad and Lester Coughlan should attend.

She wanted this done so that the press conference coverage would coincide with the 6:00 o'clock news.

"Can you come to my office Brad? There are a number of things we have to go over, I would like to meet with you alone first, then Naz and Lester. If you could come now, I'll contact the other two, will you come?"

"I don't see where I have any option, I'll be there shortly!"

*

Dave Harris was already in the middle of a media scrum concerning the late Dr. Jim Nelson a crowd of reporters shoved and pushed at him, sticking microphones and tape recorders in his face. This was a part of his job he disliked the most, in his mind the public's right to know was a questionable premise, particularly at this stage of his investigation.

Relieved, he saw the police media information officer come into the room, an attractive 28-year-old brunette, she took over the scene and read a prepared statement concerning the previous evenings police activities.

She left the murder to the last, after a string of arrests for petty acts of burglary and house break-ins, Harris ducked out, glad that there was no necessity of being polite to the media vultures nor to answer their inane questions either.

He returned to his desk and found a sheaf of reports that he had requested the day before, "Let's see what we can out about this cast of characters."

He read the Interpol response on Declan Mahoney, then sat back in stunned silence, the report could not gave been much shorter, there was no match on the name! They had not a thing on a Declan Mahoney; it was as though he never existed!

"What the Hell! He checked the spelling to make sure. It was correct! Nothing!

He slammed the folder down on his desk in disgust, he picked up the folder marked Nazir Monpetit, here was a different story, and there must have been twenty pages on Monpetit, starting with his parents.

The father was a French national, now deceased, the report indicated that he had been involved with the Algerians in their confrontation with De Gaulle. It looked like he must have been on the government side, While the report was not specific; the father may have been supplying intelligence regarding any insurgence that was planned.

The father relocated to Morocco, the birthplace of his wife, during all these events, the son Nazir, was in school. First in France, only the most prestigious it seemed, then to England and Oxford, then back to France, finishing at the Sorbonne. Harris did not even attempt to read all of his qualifications; it made his lowly MBA seem paltry by comparison.

There was on bit of information however, that struck him or rather the lack of it did, he noted, no degree in microbiology!

How could that be? He was supposed to be the new Director of Research at Soper, a position that clearly should have required such a qualification. He combed over the records again in case he had missed it, no, nothing about microbiology.

The report did confirm his previous employer as Zaltec Inc, but not only was he an employee, but he was a significant shareholder, in fact such a significant shareholder that Harris wondered why in the hell he worked at all!

He closed the folder, put his hands behind his head and leaned back in his chair, "Shit! All this has done is raise even more questions, all I know is something isn't right in all this!"

He opened the folder on Bradley Soper, surprise, surprise, one arrest and a misdemeanour, public mischief, not much else, still waters run deep!

*

Janet met Brad at the front desk, "Brad, you can't go on TV looking like a college under kid, come with me!"

She led him to a small room, without windows, just some clothes lockers and a couple of benches to sit on.

She reached into one of the lockers and removed a suit of clothes, a shirt, tie and matching socks, "I guess the shoes will have to do, get dressed, I'll be back in a minute, and hurry we don't have much time.

Annoyed, he did as he was told, after all he considered, this is why they were on a retainer; she obviously knew what she was doing.

Moments later, after a quick knock, the door opened and Janet reappeared, just as he slipped the jacket on. "How's the fit?

"Pretty good, whose is it?"

"Yours, I bought it after we talked this morning, just in case you showed up looking like a drifter, and you did." She smiled and reached up to push back a lock of hair that had fallen over his forehead, "Hmmm, you clean up pretty good!"

Before he could comment, she grabbed him by the arm and pulled him behind her, back to the conference room where they had started out.

Naz and Lester were already there, awaiting Mahoney.

Popular or not, the death of Jim Nelson had effected those present, they all sat in stony silence each contemplating how best to deal with the situation.

The conference room door opened, Mahoney entered, his eyes seemed glazed, he was walking with some difficulty, he guided himself to his seat by sliding his hand on the edge of the large conference table. He grasped both arms of his chair and lowered himself into it slowly, grimacing as he did so.

Janet spoke "Declan, what's wrong? Are you OK?"

"A touch of flu I think, I'll be OK. My stomach doesn't feel so good and I ache in every joint." He began to cough and his breath came in rasping gasps, he took his inhaler and held it to his mouth breathing deeply.

When he finished, his body was wracked with a fit of hacking coughs, his eyes watered, he wiped them with his handkerchief.

"Janet, I think maybe you better take this meeting, I feel the need to lie down for a bit, you know how to handle the situation, just as we discussed."

Janet could not believe the change in Declan from just two short hours ago when they held their preliminary meeting.

"Declan, do you want me to call a Doctor?"

"No, No, don't fuss, it's just the flu, I'll be right as rain tomorrow, just help me get to my suite."

Mahoney kept a suite of rooms in his office, Janet was unsure if he ever lived anywhere but there, he was always on call it seemed.

He leaned heavily on her, Brad attempted to help the man but he shrugged him off, "No, Janet can do it!"

In her absence they spoke among themselves, Lester spoke, "I've never seen him in that kind of shape before, I did know about his asthma, but I didn't think it was that bad."

"That was more than just an asthma attack, what do you think Brad?"

"I have no idea, he certainly seemed to be the picture of health when I saw him a month ago, but who knows."

"You must be Nazir Monpetit, I'm Lester Coughlan," the old man held out his hand,

"Oh Lester, I'm sorry I just assumed the two of you had met before this."

"That's all right Brad, I must say he looks big enough for the job at any rate!"

Naz' smile lit up the room, "I'm pleased to meet you Mr. Coughlan, I've heard a lot about you."

Janet returned before the conversation could continue, "OK let's get on with this, we have a press conference scheduled in this room for 3:30 PM, that will give us a crack at the 6:00 o'clock news slot. I have prepared a written statement which I will read, a copy will be provided in the media pack for each reporter.

You will find in your folder, a copy of the statement, perhaps you could each read it and let me have your comments, there is still time to modify it before the press conference, if it's OK with you then we can proceed on to the next order of business."

Brad was surprised at her presence; she had taken control of the meeting from the first words she uttered. She was in control; he was impressed.

They read through the document in silence, it was well written it described each of the events starting with Arnie Soper's illness and ending with the murder of Jim Nelson. The statement was a straight forward telling of the facts, stressing that there was no connection, at least as far as the people at the company were concerned, between any of these rather sad occurrences.

Unfortunate circumstance was the key premise, that and the steps taken to ensure continuity of the company were the keystone elements of the statement, there was no speculation contained in it.

Lester spoke, "I think it says it all, it's well done, you did this Ms. Petersen?"

She nodded in acknowledgment, "What about you Brad, is it OK?"

"Yeah, it tells it like it is, I don't see where it requires a whole lot of "spin.""

Naz also concurred with the statement, Janet continued.

"OK then, that's the easy part, now for the question and answer session!"

"Question and answers?"

"Yes Brad, the reporters are going to have questions that they want answers to, I will attempt to act as sort of the Master of Ceremonies and field the questions and deflect those we don't want answered. However, the three of you can't sit there like the 3 monkeys; you will have to take at least some questions.

Mr. Coughlan, it would be helpful if you could take some of the early questions, you're an old hand at this and it would give Naz and Brad a bit of an opportunity to sort of get a feel for the flow and dynamics of the press conference"

"Yes of course, I can do that, I know many of the people who will be here, we've jousted before."

Brad looked concerned, "What are they likely to ask?"

Janet smirked, "With you, likely what colour shorts you are wearing or even if you are wearing any, at least the women might, come to think of it, some of the men too."

The ensuing laughter seemed to ease the tension in the room For everyone except Brad he just blushed.

"Seriously, we can't be sure of just what they are going to ask, take a moment to reflect on the question, but not too long or they may think you are lying to them. You can always fall back on "No Comment" if the questions are too uncomfortable.

Just remember, I will be there to help where necessary, why don't you all grab a cup of coffee and relax, we should be set to go in about 20 minutes."

She turned to leave and Brad grasped her arm stopping her, whispered "Janet, what's up with Declan, he looked terrible?"

"I'm not sure, he seemed OK first thing this morning, he was coughing a bit, at first I thought it was just his asthma, the smog was pretty bad. But the joint stiffness and stomach discomfort, I saw that for the first time when you did."

She left quickly, he assumed that she was going to check on Mahoney, but he realized that she had lots to do relating to the press conference, he admired her confidence and composure.

A man in uniform came in and brought a lectern complete with microphone that plugged into a wall outlet, and 4 additional chairs, he arranged them at the end of the conference room.

Janet returned a few minutes later, she tapped the microphone, blew into it a few times, then switch it off.

She explained the seating arrangement to each of the participants and said, "Are you all ready? Just remember, follow my lead and if you find me stepping on your words, just shut up as quickly as you can. That just means you are straying into areas we don't want raised here. OK?"

No question, she was in control and she seemed to enjoy it, a ball-breaker thought Brad!

As if on signal the door opened and the receptionist stuck her head in, "Ready?" Janet nodded.

In total there were 27 media members that filed in, 14 women and 13 men of that total about half seemed to be camera and sound people predominantly the male contingent.

As the camera lights were switched on Brad began to squirm in his seat; a stern look from Janet stilled him.

She moved to the lectern and with a clear confident voice she began the press conference.

"Ladies and Gentlemen, thank you for coming today, as a responsible member of our community, Soper Research Incorporated felt that we should meet with you and share our concerns regarding the loss some of our best loved associates.

In fact, I would like to ask you for a moment of silence for the loss of our founder's wife, Ashley Soper in a tragic car accident and now the untimely death of our Executive Committee Vice-Chairman, Dr. James Nelson."

She bowed her head, as did the rest at the head of the table, but lights continued shine and cameras whirred, other than that, the reporters maintained a respectful silence.

Janet then commenced to read from the prepared statement. She read it with conviction, clearly trying to distance the corporation from these seemingly unconnected tragedies. This of course was not what the media had come for, they were anxiously waiting for the question and answer session they had been promised.

She concluded her remarks and introduced Brad, Naz and of course Lester Coughlan, then the questions started.

Janet made a vain attempt at trying to force those asking the question into some kind some kind of rules based behaviour but it was a losing battle, chaos soon became the order of business.

Just as pandemonium appeared ready to break out, Naz stood up, he towered over everyone, and he held up his arms like a Baptist preacher and shouted loudly.

"HEY!"

"IF YOU DON'T SHUT UP THIS MEETING IS OVER!"

There was absolute silence, they all stood or sat with mouths agape.

"That's better, now you heard what the lady said, we want to try to answer your questions, but if you don't behave, we can't even hear them, how the hell can we answer them?""

Janet smiled in acknowledgment to Naz, he shot his sleeves and sat down, he was an intimidating presence, but almost instantly a radiant smile broke across his face that nearly outshone the klieg lights.

The group seemed to relax as one, the first question was directed to Brad. A pretty redheaded intern smiled at him as she asked.

"Is it true that you came out from Vancouver to be at your father's bedside during his illness?"

Dumb question! "Yes."

She followed quickly with "Could you tell us, just what kind of illness your father has and what his prognosis is for recovery?"

Janet jumped in "We are unsure of just what Dr. Soper's ailment is and consequently, we are not in a position to speculate on his recovery."

The red head persisted, "Mr. Soper, can you tell us something about your father's condition? Anything at all? He hasn't been seen in public for weeks, we of course were aware of his trip to Nairobi, could he have caught something there?"

Janet was about to respond, but Brad put his hand on her arm, "My father is in a coma, the cause of which has yet to be determined, he hasn't regained consciousness in the past several weeks. We have been given no reason to suspect any specific infection nor any other ailment for that matter.

All I can tell you is that his condition is not improving with time."

A voice from the back "Do you believe that the illness of your father, the suicide of Dr. Mytryk the death of your step-mother and now the murder of Dr., Nelson are not somehow connected in some way?"

This time Janet fielded the question, "We cannot comment on ongoing investigations being conducted by the police. All we can tell you, is that as far as we are concerned, we are not aware of any connection between these sad events other than of course the personal relationship between them."

An overweight reporter with an unlit cigarette in his mouth was next "Dr., Monpetit, I understand that you left a senior position at Zaltec in Europe for your new position here, given what has transpired, any second thoughts about your career move?"

"My reasons for coming to Canada were personal, but one of the main ones was to have the privilege of working with someone as eminent as Dr. Soper. Do I have regrets? Of course! I would hope that Dr. Soper does recover and that we can work together. If not, I guess, just like the rest of you, I'll have to wait and see."

They were peppered by questions concerning Ashley's accident. Did they believe Mytryk's death had been suicide, Brad was grateful that Ellis had been left out of the discussion. Janet skilfully handled all the questions, when she had finished responding to any question. Her answers were seldom challenged, but Brad noted that she had told them very little.

They were nearing the end of the allotted time for the press conference, when the little red head piped up again. "Mr. Soper, given the fact that the Chairman of the Executive Committee is incapacitated and the Vice Chairman had been murdered, can you tell us who will be put in charge of the Company?

Brad was stunned, he was not prepared for the question, but before he could even think of a response, Lester Coughlan was on his feet.

"Young lady, I think your question is better directed to me, as Chairman of the Search Committee, it is my responsibility to recommend such a replacement to the Board of Directors."

"Well sir, then I redirect my question to you, who's the new man? She smiled sweetly.

Coughlan looked at the other three, cleared his throat and said, "While it was not the Board's intention to make this announcement at this press conference, I do think it important that the public knows that the company is not leaderless, we have continuity, continuity of program and of purpose.

I am pleased to announce that the Board unanimously endorses Mr. Bradley Soper! As the new Chairman of the Executive Committee of Soper Research Inc!"

Brad looked like an animal caught in the glare of oncoming headlights, Naz stood immediately and started to applaud, joined by Coughlan and even though she had been blind sided by the announcement, Janet couldn't help but applaud as well.

Coughlan, pleased with himself and the spontaneous applause asked, "Perhaps we could have a few words from the new Chairman?"

Brad paused for a long minute before getting to his feet, realizing that once more, events had taken control of his life. He sensed that there was no backing out, he gave a very brief acceptance speech and tried to catch up with Coughlan before he left.

Chapter 30

Dave Harris entered the bar, it took a few moments for him to become accustomed to the dim light and smoky atmosphere, but he spotted Dwayne Hitchcock sitting at the bar, holding his drink and puffing on a rather large cigar.

He touched him on the shoulder; Hitchcock turned, broke into a smile and said.

"Hello Davey! I'm glad we could finally hook up." He reached inside his jacket pocket, "I got your application form right here, why not sign up tight now?"

Harris gave him a playful shove, "Now why would I want to join a second rate team?"

They shook hands and Harris' face conveyed the seriousness of this meeting, "Dwayne, maybe we could move to a booth."

"Sure, sure." He motioned to the bartender, indicating they were moving to the back booth and to bring a round of drinks, all by using what seemed to be an international bar sign language.

When they were seated, Harris began,

"What's with this Declan Mahoney guy, I went through Interpol and came up empty, there wasn't even a file on the guy, nothing, like he doesn't even exist?"

Hitchcock looked around him before answering, in low voice he said. "He doesn't."

"What the fuck are you talking about?"

"I said he doesn't exist, he's a figment of the imagination of MI-5"

"British Intelligence?"

"None other."

"What is he, in a witness protection program or something?"

"It's "or something," apparently Mahoney, or whoever he is, saved several prominent asses in the UK, the relocation is some kind of pay back."

"Do you know what it was that he did to earn this kind of set up?"

"Only pieces of it, but Dave you need to know that I could get really jammed up on this if anybody ever finds out that we have even been talking about this!"

"I understand, this will go no farther, but I have 2 potential murders on my hands and perhaps more, I need whatever you can give me."

'Well, my understanding is that Mahoney was in the upper level of the IRA, he had access to financial accounts, you know, money coming from overseas to support their activities. Apparently he got greedy and decided to divert some for personal use.

Someone got wind of the shortfall, Mahoney knew that they were going to able to trace it back to him, his only option was to get out of the country, go as far as he could to start a new life."

"OK but why would MI-5 give shit whether Mahoney buys it or not?"

"Here is where it gets interesting, Mahoney makes contact with an MI-5 field operative and offers to defect with some critical information that will be of interest to them. They bring him in."

"Presto, Declan Mahoney is born, but what the hell did he have to trade for a new life?"

"The rumour is that he knew the details of a plan to assassinate most of the Royal Family on a visit to Brighton, you remember, they blew up the hotel but none of the Royals were there.

It turns out that intelligence had no idea of the plan until they did the deal with Mahoney."

"But why Canada?"

"It's far enough away, Toronto is big enough he wouldn't attract attention and for some reason, it's where Mahoney wanted to go.

In addition, MI-5 had a good relationship with CSIS, so they could make all the immigration issues go away. I can only assume that CSIS owed MI-5 for some past favours, that's the way these things work."

"So that's the reason Foreign Affairs says "hands off?"

"You got it Davey!"

"I assume that he also got a cash settlement from the crown to help him on his way?"

"You betcha! AND he got to keep whatever it was that he stole from the IRA!"

"Is there anything else I should know Dwayne?"

"I think that's everything I know, except for the fact that I think Mahoney has been feeding CSIS with information regarding some of the companies he does work for.

We have had some of them under surveillance too, but without much success, in this business, the right hand seldom knows what the left hand is doing."

"Do you think he was on CSIS' payroll?"

"Could be!"

"Thanks for the info Dwayne, I gotta go."

"Dave, one quick question."

"Yes."

"You wouldn't be wearing a wire would you Dave?"

*

Brad entered the Law Courts Building, he located the Family Court location from the information board and proceeded to it, he was to meet Leslie Philips there regarding Ellis' temporary custody hearing.

Leslie had said it was a mere formality, she said it wouldn't take more than 15 minutes, the way his life was going in recent days, he was unsure if anything could go according to plan.

As he approached the doors to Family Court, he could see Leslie standing outside talking on her cell phone.

She looked even better than he last remembered, gone were the designer jeans and pullover, replaced with a well tailored outfit in black, jacket and skirt, no minis here, but short enough to display great legs.

She was preoccupied with her phone call and had not noticed him approach, he continued his appraisal, she still wore high heeled shoes that accented the legs, she wore little jewellery, no rings at least. Her blonde hair was pulled back at the temples and was held at the back with some kind of clip that allowed her hair to flow down her back until just below her shoulders.

She suddenly noticed him looking at her, she smiled and he blushed like a schoolboy caught doing something he shouldn't have, she gave a little laugh.

She closed her cell phone "Hi Brad, you're right on time, let's go on in."

"I understand congratulations are in order Chairman of the Executive Committee! That's quite a lot of responsibility, but I am sure you're up to it."

Before he could answer, the clerk asked everyone to rise, the judge entered, a fat woman of perhaps 60, she motioned everyone to sit.

The clerk announced the purpose of the hearing, then a caseworker from Children's Aid was called, and she supported the placement of Ellis with his brother.

The judge called upon Brad to stand and asked him if he were prepared to undertake this responsibility, he answered in the affirmative, the judge hammered her gavel.

"So Ordered, a court date for 90 days hence will be set to decide on permanent custody for the minor child Ellis Soper."

The whole thing took even less time than he had imagined, the future of a young life may have been decided in a little more than the blink of an eye and the boy had no input.

They left the courtroom, Leslie looked at her watch, and "It's just after 12, have you got time for some lunch?"

He nodded.

"Good, follow me, we can walk it's not far and parking is such a bitch down here."

They entered an office building and descended into the lower regions to a small bistro called The Mermaid, it was very crowded.

"We'll never get in."

"Sure we will, Henry, Henry, is my table ready." She waved her hand at I little bald headed man he took to be either the owner or the maitre de or both.

"Of course Miss Phillips, as always, please follow me."

They squeezed past some unhappy potential diners and were escorted to a comfortable little booth out of the main traffic area.

"There, see, I told you we would get in, this is a nice little place, I come quite often, I'm sure you'll enjoy the food.

Henry approached a left the two menus and took their drink orders, a beer for Brad, no Kokanee unfortunately and a Shiraz for Leslie.

"You know, I meant what I said about congratulations on your new job, how do you feel about it?

"Well it seems to me that I didn't choose the job so much as it chose me, I didn't feel like I really had much choice in the matter."

Their drinks arrived, they ordered the special, Leslie said it was good so he went along, seemed like that was all he was doing lately.

"I know you said that this process was going to be quick, but I still can't believe fast everything really happened."

"Brad, there is really no way that the courts want to put a child into the child welfare system if it can be avoided. They much prefer to place the child with a relative, unless there are some extenuating circumstances, which of course is why you had that meeting last week with Caseworker.

Which you passed with flying colours by the way. The court sees you as an upstanding individual, with a good job and you so obviously care about the boy.

The care that he is getting at Halton House and the home you are providing for him, after all that, as they say, it was a "slam dunk."

"The ninety day thing bothers me."

"Is there any doubt in your mind that you don't want permanent custody Brad?"

"It's not that, it's just that I'm so unsure, unsure of my ability to provide the care that Ellis needs, unsure of whether or not that I can cope with everything that is going on.

Essentially, I will have to be a father to Ellis, never having had one, how do I know what to do. Will I be any good at it? What if I fail?"

"You sound like any expectant father, you'll do OK, I just know you will. The 90 days is like a cooling off period, it allows you and the system to re-evaluate the placement. Don't worry, you'll do just fine."

"Yeah, maybe, but I feel the same way with respect to taking over the company, what the Hell do I know about business?"

"Brad, this is a successful business, it's well organized, you have trained staff at your disposal, the day to day stuff will get looked after, you said Lester Coughlan would be your mentor. He's been a fantastic success, its going to work out, you'll see."

"You're quite a cheerleader Leslie, I wish I could be as enthusiastic, but then you don't know all of the stuff that's been going on."

"You want to talk about it, I'm not just a cheerleader, I'm a good listener too!"

"I don't know Leslie, I just don't know who to trust in all of this."

"Give me a Loonie!"

"What?"

"I said give me a Loonie, that'll be my retainer, then all these conversations will be privileged, I won't even be able to tell my priest!"

"He reached in his pocket and retrieved a coin, "Here take this Toonie, it's all the change I have, now you will have to be twice as quiet!"

They both laughed.

"So tell me, what's bothering you?"

For some reason, he felt that she was trustworthy, he felt comfortable in discussing almost anything with her, and besides he needed to talk to someone.

He reiterated all that had transpired with Inspector Dave Harris and the inquiries coming from the FBI regarding some kind of collusion that may or may not have taken place between a federal employee at the FDA and Soper Research.

"That's a pretty serious situation, if it in fact is true, I can only assume, since they did not make a direct approach to the Company, that they don't have enough evidence to lay any charges."

"I suppose that that is true, but nevertheless, it is a cloud hanging over the company and I'm not sure how to deal with it."

"I take it that you think if it happened, that Dr., Mytryk may have been involved, I assume he would be a principal contact with the FDA?"

"Or my father!"

"In either case, the trail goes cold, your father is incapacitated and Dr. Mytryk is dead, no way to get testimony from either of them. Sorry Brad, I didn't mean to be so unthinking."

"It's OK Leslie, I know what you mean."

"Have you been able to determine if any moneys have been paid out in any extraordinary fashion?"

"Leslie, I haven't even put my first day in yet!"

"Of course, sorry, my tongue is getting ahead of my brain!"

He laughed at the comment, he was beginning to like this very attractive woman, and she was bright too, he could talk to her, he was beginning to feel better.

"Brad, if it's OK with you, I'm going to do some digging into this matter, I think we need more information, we need to develop a strategy for dealing with whatever surfaces."

"You're my lawyer, it's OK with me."

They finished their lunch, leaving the business and matters relating to Ellis for another time, instead, they flirted.

"Brad, I would very much like to meet Ellis some time, maybe we could do a picnic or something, whatever he might like."

"That's a good idea, he likes pretty girls! As does his brother."

"It was Leslie's turn to blush, he never thought he would see that.

They left the restaurant and went there separate ways to their respective cars. As Brad sat contemplating what had just happened, he made a decision, he called Inspector Harris.

Dave Harris answered his phone, surprised to hear Brad Soper's voice on the other end.

"Inspector Harris, Brad Soper here, I wonder if we might arrange a meeting."

"Would you mind telling what this meeting might be about?"

" I want to discuss my last meeting with Dr. Jim Nelson."

"Where do you want to meet?"

"I'm heading to the office, could you meet me there?"

"I'll be there, and by the way, congratulations on your appointment."

Chapter 31

Asleep? Awake? Dreaming? It seems all the same now, still no anxiety, good old Valium. At least I'm lucid, ... Am I? That odd light, what is it? Is someone looking into my retina? That's it! Maybe they are actually going to do something! Is there some hope..... No, light's gone!

"Alfred, Alfred, are you still with me?"

"Yes Dr. Soper, I'm still here, I have not left, what can I do for you."

"I have a question for you Alfred."

"Dr. Soper, you know better than anybody how this works, I don't provide answers, you do, otherwise I lose my objectivity."

"Screw your objectivity! I want an answer!"

"Ask your question then, perhaps in asking it the answer will become evident to you."

"Alfred, has anyone told you that you are a very annoying person, it's like having a conversation with a puddle of quicksilver!"

There was no response in the darkness, Soper waited, and there was only silence.

"Alfred, you still there?"

"I'm here, but if you are intent upon insulting me I don't see how I can be of any help to you."

"If I have hurt your feelings I apologize, but frankly given our relative positions, I don't see that you have much to complain about,

Here I lie, perhaps in my own offal, unable to communicate with anyone or thing except you! I can't see or hear I can't smell, taste or touch. I can only think.

I know that you are likely nothing more than a figment of my own imagination, and yet you tell me I have insulted you! What about the insults dealt to me?

"I think your reaction to your predicament is perfectly normal, you say to yourself "Why me?" Neither one of us can answer that; it is just what is.

Is that your question?

"No!

"Then what is it?"

"Since we have started these conversations, you have talked to me about things that I did or did not do and the impact these things may have had on others."

"Yes we have."

"And then you seemed to lead the conversations to any feelings of remorse that I may or may not have had or that I may be feeling now."

"I don't know where you are going with this tack Dr., Soper, but yes, go ahead."

"As I remember, repentance is supposed to follow remorse, tell me Alfred, given my condition, how would you suggest I accomplish the act of repentance?" He added, "If I were so inclined."

A period of considerable silence followed, Soper could not tell if Alfred was struggling with an answer or if he was simply awaiting Soper to continue.

Finally Alfred responded. "Dr. Soper, you must agree that to repent or not is a personal choice, to whom or what, one might repent is also a personal choice. Moreover, of course the need to repent rests with the individual.

You must look into your inner self to determine the answer you seek, there is no right or wrong answer, it must be based upon what you determine to be your personal truth."

Silence again.

This time it was Alfred who spoke first, "Dr. Soper, do you understand what I was trying to say?"

"Yes."

"Dr. Soper, how are you feeling, do you want to rest now?"

"I think so, I feel a little like a cheap little toy whose battery is running down, I feel like I might sleep but I have much to consider."

"I'll leave you then."

"Wait Alfred, I realized as we've been talking I don't even know what you look like, before you leave, could you come closer so I can see your face before you go?"

The figure moved closer to the bed, into the greenish glow cast by the monitoring equipment.

He looked up into the face and a dawn of recognition crossed his face.

*

Dr. Pickard lifted the strip chart generated by the EEG machine attached to Arnold Soper; he rubbed his beard absently and then scanned all of the other monitors.

"Nurse, I think it is time we notified Dr. Soper's son, I believe he is the only next of kin, the patient seems to be failing faster than I originally anticipated. I see no point in prolonging or adding more heroic measures to extend his life, if one could really call it that.

Try him at Soper Research, he may be there or they will know where to reach him, when you get him, see that I am paged. We need a family consult.

*

Dave Harris entered Soper Research and stopped at the reception desk, the uniformed security guard took his name and punched a number into the switchboard console.

"He'll be right down to get you."

"Thanks, some security system you got here, is this all handled by Mahoney Associates?"

"Yessir, including me, I work for Mahoney too."

Brad appeared on the winding staircase leading to the second floor; he motioned for Harris to come up.

They stopped in front of a Retinal Scanner; Brad peered into the blue light and then asked Harris to do the same.

"Sorry about that, but security you know.

"I can understand you on the scanner, they have records of you but what about me?"

"As I understand it, my retinal image is compared to those on the database, when there is a match, I am allowed in based upon pre-established permission levels. A visitor is scanned and his image is stored, in your case it is linked with mine.

If you come back another time, the system will identify you as being linked to me, then the system will notify me and I come down to let you in, or not."

"Pretty slick. So you have logs of all visitors, when they enter and leave the building as well as their sponsors so to speak?"

"Yeah, all the comings and goings of employees and visitors are recorded complete with time and date stamps."

"Impressive."

Brad had taken over his father's office, at the insistence of Lester Coughlan, he felt it was necessary for Brad to put his "stamp" on the company as soon as was decently possible.

He still wasn't completely comfortable with the opulence of his surrounding and was almost apologetic to Harris as he showed him around.

But before Harris could take a seat, Brad grabbed him by the arm and said, "Come, I'd like to take you on a little tour."

Brad whisked Harris up to the roof next to one of the building ventilation fans, "We should be OK to talk here."

"What the Hell is this all about Soper?"

"Naz and I are convinced that the whole building is bugged, I didn't want our conversation overheard."

"Bugged by who?"

"Declan Mahoney!"

"What was it you wanted to talk to me about regarding Dr. Nelson Dr. Soper, it is Dr. Soper isn't it."

"Almost, but not quite, I still have my Doctoral Dissertation to give."

"Close enough then, Dr.."

"I met Jim Nelson at Ashley's funeral, he requested that we go somewhere that we could talk in private, he seemed obsessed with the fact that someone was electronically eavesdropping on him. And it appears he was right."

"Did he say who might be doing that?"

"Yes, Declan Mahoney."

"To what purpose, did he say?"

"He said that Mahoney is a blackmailer, he was attempting get some form of share control of this company through Nelson. He said he believed that Mahoney was responsible for Ashley's death, Nelson said that Ashley and Mahoney met the night Ashley was killed.

Nelson also told me he didn't believe that Peter Mytryk's death was not a suicide, he was convinced he was murdered."

"Why didn't he just come to us with all this?"

"He said Mahoney was too crafty, he had no proof, he was afraid you wouldn't believe him, maybe he believed it would get back to Mahoney."

"Why are you telling me this now?"

"Originally it seemed pretty fantastic, but when Nelson was murdered, I thought you should know."

"I understand that Mahoney Associates has control of the security system for this building."

"Yes, and I'm not happy about it, I was going to review the contract and see if I can terminate it."

"I would suggest that at this point you use all caution in dealings with Mahoney, I would not recommend that you take any immediate action.

If Mahoney is behind these things, you could be putting yourself in personal danger."

"Of course, whatever you say, let me know if I can help."

"What I would like is to have one of our computer forensic people come in here, undercover and obtain a printout of those logs we spoke of earlier, they can also do a scan of the premises and confirm if in fact you're being bugged.

A good cover would be that you are making space for a school buddy as opposed to going through Human Resources."

"I guess I can do that, might be interesting to see if I really can pull a few strings."

"No point in having it if you can't flaunt it!"

"That's about all I had to tell you." He left out Nelson's news that Ellis was not his real brother, he knew that he would if he had to, but why complicate things now?"

"Let's go back to your office, if you are being spied on, we had better keep my visit believable, I'll question you about Mytryk, that was the initial reason for coming here after his arrest and death."

Once settled in Brad's office, Harris turned his attention to questioning Brad about Mytryk's death, they both went through the motions, covering ground that had already been dealt with, Harris was about to take his leave when Brad's phone rang.

"Dr. Soper, one moment please, I'll connect you with Dr. Pickard."

"Dr. Soper, Cyril Pickard here, it's about your father."

"Yes, has something happened?"

"Not yet, Brad, but I regret to tell you that he appears to be failing faster than I originally thought, there is really no additional course of action available to us. Even what we are doing now is not something that would be considered a normal treatment level.

In fact, in some circles, our current course of treatment could be considered inhumane given that his condition is absolutely irreversible.

I would recommend to you that we withdraw a life support from the patient and let him die a peaceful death.

Of course, the decision is yours."

Brad was stunned, he knew that this moment would likely come sooner than later, but he still was unprepared.

"Dr. Soper, are you there?

"Yes, Yes, I'm here."

"Can you come down to the hospital…now."

"Yes of course, I'll be right there."

He had forgotten Harris' presence in his office.

"Problem?"

"Yes, my father, the hospital wants me to take him off life support.

"Shit!"

Chapter 32

Dave Harris entered the Coroner's office to find the sliim emaciated man standing staring out his window with his back to the door. He turned when he heard Harris come in.

"Hello David." The deep voice seemed at odds with the physical stature of the man. "What brings you down here?"

"Dr. James Nelson, or rather his recent death does, I thought I should see your report on the autopsy."

"Nothing startling I'm afraid, death by strangulation, obviously murder, not much else to tell."

"Did the crime scene boys leave anything of interest with you?"

"You can have a look if you like, I've put the stuff in a storage locker until you fellows are finished investigating, come I'll show you."

He handed Dave a pair of surgical gloves, donned a pair himself and retrieved a large polyethylene bag with a zip closure, and dumped the contents on a table. The smell of stale urine permeated the small space they were in; Dave breathed through his mouth and sorted through the meagre items collected at the scene. Clothes, no wrist watch, no wallet, some kind of medication.

Harris was sure that this was not a mugging, why use a garrote?

"Anything show up on the tox screens?"

"Nothing, a small amount of alcohol, maybe the residue of one drink, no drug residue, he was as clean as a whistle!"

"Was there anything at all that seemed odd, out of place?"

He scratched his chin, and replied, "You noted the medication, it's an asthma inhaler."

"Yes, so what, lots of people use them."

"Usually only people that need them, the autopsy revealed that Nelson's lungs were in perfect condition, for his age, he had no need for the inhaler."

"Maybe it wasn't his, where did they find it?"

"It was in his suit jacket pocket, before you ask, yes his prints were on it, there may have been others, but nothing clear enough to identify."

"Well thanks Fred, I'll let you know when we are ready to release the body."

Harris left and headed back to his office, he was convinced that this death was a "hit," but ordered by whom and why?

*

Declan Mahoney was doubled up with stomach pain, he couldn't even stand up, he screamed in agony, but no one could hear him in his sound proofed office, he couldn't straighten out his arms, the joints in his elbows were seized as were his knees.

He was sweating profusely; his clothes were soaking wet from his perspiration, although he had no way of knowing it, his temperature had soared somewhat.

Panic seized him, he was struck with another coughing fit, he struggled to reach his inhaler, but could not, he did manage to press the intercom button to Janet's office. She responded, but all he could do was to gurgle and cry out "HELP ME!"

Mahoney's office door flew open and Janet stood there, horrified as she watched Mahoney struggle to his feet, he opened his mouth to speak, but a gush of blood and phlegm rushed out staining the carpet at her feet.

She screamed just as his bowels released a profusion of blood and excrement, he collapsed in a heap, into the stinking red stain that spread out before him.

Janet ran from the room screaming for somebody to help, "Dial 911, get an ambulance, hurry, something's happened to Declan!"

*

The Emergency Department at The Toronto General Hospital received Mahoney within 20 minutes of the 911 call, they worked feverishly trying to determine what was wrong with him, they tried anti-viral drugs anti-biotics, combinations of drugs, all to no avail.

They ran blood tests, nothing showed up that would give them the slightest hint of what was effecting him, and they did internal examinations, again, nothing. Virtually every type of test was run, without ever gaining any insight that might have aided treatment.

Mahoney's condition worsened, 6 hours after admittance to hospital, he died of multi organ failure.

The Head of the Internal Medicine Department placed a call to the Metropolitan Toronto Police Department to report a suspicious death; he then placed a call to a friend of his at the Virology Lab in Winnipeg.

"Ben, this Ian Henderson in Toronto, how are you?"

"Ian, it's been a long time my friend, I'm fine, how are you and Ellen?

"Great, Great Ben, but I'm afraid that this isn't a social call, we have just had a very strange occurrence here at the hospital."

He described all of the things that had happened with respect to one Declan Mahoney, the fact nothing showed up on any of their tests, none of the medications had any effect.

"That is very strange Ian, it is not often one comes up against anything like this, as a matter of fact I have only heard of one other."

"Where and when was that Ben?"

"Well, it was during my time in London, I was studying at a hospital there. You may remember the case yourself Ian, it was Georgi Malenkov, the author."

"The name sounds familiar."

"Yes, he was making life difficult for Soviet authorities with some of his writings and broadcasts to those behind the iron curtain. They ended up assassinating him, using a poison, rather bizarre as I remember, it was administered by umbrella."

"What was the poison?"

"It was ricin, a derivative of the castor bean plant, highly toxic, no known treatment and it leaves no trace. The quantity required to kill a man is about 60 micrograms, less than would be held on the head of a pin.

You will also remember that just recently, several people, terrorists I think, were rounded up in London for making the stuff."

"This Malenkov, he was injected with ricin, my patient exhibited no injection sites."

"The other ways of getting this poison into your system would be by ingestion or inhalation. Inhalation would by far be the most effective method of introducing this toxin into the body."

"Ian, my guess is that your patient was murdered, I assume you have contacted the police, no one would commit suicide in this fashion, it can take up to 4 days to die from it and the death is extremely uncomfortable. It would be highly unlikely to be accidental as well."

"As a matter of fact, I reported the death to police even before I called you, I know they will have some questions for me, I just needed some background, none of us likes to admit we don't know what the cause of death is."

"Anytime I can be of help Ian, give Ellen a hug for me!"

*

Harris had just settled into his chair when someone stuck his head through the doorway and said "Hey, Dave, Fast wants ya in his office, right away!"

"Yeah, Yeah, thanks Eddie."

There were no doughnuts on Fast's desk this time when Harris sat opposite.

"What's up?"

"This Soper thing is starting to get complicated, I don't like to admit it, but I think you're right, there may be more to this thing than Mytryk's apparent suicide."

Harris smiled to himself, not bad, first I'm right and secondly, it's now an apparent suicide.

"You mean because of Nelson's murder and the car accident that killed Mrs. Soper?"

"Yeah, that and somethin' that has just come in."

"What?"

"Declan Mahoney's dead!"

"What the Hell? He was one of my main suspects!"

"Doctor at Toronto General called it in, says it was a suspicious death, you better get over there and see what you can find out, his name's Ian Henderson"

"OK, I'm on it."

"Oh, by the way Harris, I've authorized up to 3 more investigators to work on this with you, don't screw up and don't blow the budget, get this cleaned up as quick as you can."

"But I'm still the lead, right?"

"Yeah, Yeah, now get the Hell outa here, go arrest the bad guys!"

Harris sat in his car and reviewed his notes and his list; he couldn't help but notice that the victim list was getting longer as the suspect list was getting shorter. "At this rate, the case may solve itself and I just have too arrest the last man standing." He thought to himself.

He was glad Fast had increased the staffing for the case. At least he wasn't going to have to bend any rules for the young officer he had planted at Soper Research.

Brad Soper had come up with a good idea for his cover as a Market Research Assistant, nebulous enough, nobody ever knows what those guys do anyway,

He called Toronto General on his cell and asked to speak to Dr. Ian Henderson, the operator began the usual dance, but Harris cut through the crap by brusquely telling her she impeding police business. Henderson answered almost immediately, he agreed to see Harris as soon as he could get there.

Henderson gave Harris a complete rundown of what had transpired with the arrival of Mahoney in emergency to his death some 6 hours later, he also volunteered the information that he had obtained from his friend in Winnipeg. Harris appreciated the forthright manner of the Doctor; he didn't have to pry information loose, he was happy to give it.

"Doctor Henderson, you say there is no way to confirm that poison was ricin, surely there must be some way or someone that can? What about the CDC in Atlanta?"

"After I called my contact in Winnipeg, I went on the Internet and did a little research, based on CDC's own statements, I don't think anyone can definitively say it was ricin. Except for the symptoms demonstrated that is."

"Why would anybody have this kind of stuff around anyway?"

"There are a few legitimate uses, such as bone marrow transplant research, there may be others, I certainly don't pretend to be an expert."

"Bone marrow transplant, Jesus, wouldn't that just kill the patient?"

"I understand it's used for experimental purposes, and in vitro at that."

"In vitro?"

"Sorry, not in the body, outside, like in a dish."

"Oh, I see, would the hospital here say, have any ricin on hand?"

"No, I shouldn't think so, we aren't doing research of that type, I would think a Research Lab would be your best bet. However, I'm sure you heard the news reports about the terrorists arrested in London, they were making their own, it really isn't that difficult."

"Yeah, I do remember that, but given that it is easy to make and it's in the hands of terrorists, why haven't we seen incidences of ricin poisoning on a larger scale?"

"Well, I'm not an expert on that either, but it seems to me that it is better suited for assassinations than it is as a weapon of mass destruction."

"Why do you think that?"

"Distribution is a problem, there are three ways to administer the poison, the most lethal way is by injection, difficult if not impossible to do on a mass basis. Inhalation is next best, but how to deliver it, released into the atmosphere, it would be unpredictable because of changing air currents, variable concentrations etc.

The third way is by ingestion, it is the least successful of the three and not always fatal and again distribution becomes a problem.

"I see what you mean, so your guess is that Mahoney inhaled the ricin as opposed to the other two methods."

"Well, there were no puncture wounds anywhere on the body that might suggest injection sites, given his condition on entering the hospital, I would doubt he had anything in his stomach, he hasn't likely been able to eat in the last three days. Your pathologist will likely confirm all these things."

"And you say that 4 days would likely be as long as he could survive after having inhaled the poison."

"Maximum."

"Thank you doctor, I really appreciate your help in this matter, I'll arrange for the transfer of the body to the City Morgue as soon as I can."

"Inspector Harris, would it be possible to get a copy of your pathologist's report, I would appreciate it, it would help close the file on this situation."

"I'll see to it, thanks again."

Chapter 33

Harris knew he had to act quickly, he needed a search warrant for Mahoney's place of business, he called ahead and alerted Chief Inspector Fast. The Chief had already heard about Mahoney's death and was one step ahead.

"I've already sent Tim Cassidy over to Mahoney's office, he has a warrant, I was about to call you, get your ass directly there, we don't want anything touched!"

It always annoyed Harris when Fast spoke to him this, like a raw rookie, but then again annoying Harris seemed to be one of Fast's great pleasures in life.

He arrived at the site and was surprised to see several RCMP cars outside the building; he double parked next to one and put his Police Card on the dash.

Once inside, he punched the elevator buttons several times as though that would speed up the arrival of the car, finally, one came. When he arrived at Mahoney's floor, he could see Cassidy in an argument with his friend Dwayne Hitchcock.

"What the Hell is going on Dwayne, what are you guys doing here?"

"Hello Davey, well as I was trying to tell your partner here, the Toronto Police Department has no jurisdiction in this matter."

"What the fuck are you talking about? We're in the middle of a murder investigation here, this may be the scene of the crime, who says we can't come in and investigate? We've got a legal warrant!"

"The Solicitor General of Canada, that's who!"

"Shit! Are you trying to tell me the feds've got jurisdiction here?"

"Yep! Don't push it Davey, you can't win on this!"

"What makes this a federal issue? I'm investigating a murder, that's not federal."

"I don't need a lesson in the law Harris, all I can tell you is that we are taking this action under Bill C-36."

"Terrorism? What the hell are you talking about?" Harris could not mask his astonishment.

"I have no more information for you Dave, other than the Police Department is specifically excluded from any involvement, we have taken possession of all evidence and have all suspects under arrest.

It may be that when we are finished with our investigation, some information may be released to you, but for the moment that's it and no interviews with any suspect will be allowed."

"So much for due process!"

He knew there was no point in pursuing it with Hitchcock; he had his orders. He also knew he would not be the only one prohibited from seeing any of the suspects, and their lawyers wouldn't either.

They would languish somewhere at the whim of the Attorney General. "What the hell is going on here?" he thought to himself.

He signalled to Cassidy and they both left the scene and returned to their cars.

On the way down in the elevator, Cassidy asked, "What do you make of all this Dave?"

"Buggered if I know, all I've got is a victim, I'm going back down to the morgue, you head back and report all of this to Fast. If he has anything to shed light on this schemozzle, tell him to call my on my cell."

*

Naz burst into Brad's office without knocking, Brad was just about to leave for the hospital.

"Brad, I just heard that Declan Mahoney has been taken suddenly ill, they've just rushed him to the hospital."

"How did you hear about it?"

"I was talking to the security supervisor here, he had been talking to his office when the paramedics arrived and took Mahoney away.

I just tried to get hold of Janet, but their phone system is down for some reason"

"That's interesting Naz, but I'm not quite sure of what it has to do with us." He motioned to Naz, reminding him that their conversation may be bugged.

"I'm just on my way down to the hospital as I mentioned, I'll try Janet from there when I get a chance."

"Of course Brad, good luck with that, would you like me to come with you?"

"No, but thank you, this is something I have to do alone."

Brad got into his car and thought about his last comment to Naz, maybe he shouldn't be doing this alone. He decided that legal advice might be in order and called Leslie, when she picked her phone and spoke. Brad's spirits were lifted at once.

"Hi Brad, nice to hear from you, what can I do for you?"

He explained to her the reason for the call.

"I know you are very busy, but do you think you might be able to meet me at the hospital? I might be in need of legal advice, depending on what I find when I get there and what Dr. Pickard has to say."

"Of course I can." She said without any hesitation whatsoever. "It'll take me about half an hour to clear my calendar and about another hour to get there. Don't do anything or say anything until I get there. You have to remember that Pickard will be looking after his best interests and those of the hospital."

"OK counsellor, thanks Les."

*

Harris encountered Fred in the lobby of the Morgue, he looked up and spotted Dave coming towards him, there was anger in every step.

"Hello Dave, is something wrong, you look like a bear with a sore arse!"

"Nothing that a change in government wouldn't cure!"

"Can't help you there, cadavers, the dead kind, are my specialty, the live ones, well you'll have to seek help elsewhere."

Dave couldn't help but smile, "OK Fred, I understand that you have a new one for me, Declan Mahoney."

"OH yes, Mr. Mahoney, a strange one indeed."

"What do you mean a strange one."

"Well I've been around here for more than 20 years and I've never come upon one like it before. His internal organs had virtually disintegrated or very nearly so, and yet no trace whatsoever of any cause."

Harris shared with the pathologist, what he had found out in his discussion with Dr. Henderson at the General.

"He might well be right, but I don't know how you would ever prove it, if we knew the method by which the ricin was introduced and could find a needle or pellet, there might be enough residue left to identify the toxin."

"Tell me Fred, in your opinion, could the ricin been introduced into his system by way of an inhaler?"

"You mean like an asthma inhaler?"

"Yes."

"That would be a very effective way of introducing it, but there would be requisite skills required to particulate the ricin finely enough and you would need equipment handle this fine powder and to introduce it into the container with the appropriate propellant."

"In your estimation, who could do that?"

"It would take some sophisticated lab equipment, a knowledge of how inhalers work and of course a source of the ricin."

"Would it have to be scientist, a microbiologist say?"

"Not necessarily, a good lab technologist could do it. Mind you that is just my personal and not my professional opinion."

"Not to worry Fred, I somehow doubt that this situation will ever see the inside of a courtroom."

Fred looked quizzically at Dave, but said nothing.

Harris thanked him and was about to leave when his cell rang; he excused himself and went into the hall to take the call. It was Chief Fast.

"I heard what happened at Mahoney's office, it looks like we can wrap this whole thing up and just leave it all to the feds."

Harris knew that Fast would be relieved that his precious budget would not suffer because of this case, but he was not about to give it up that easily.

"Chief, this is a murder case, pure and simple, I think the feds are involved in some kind of cover up, we just can't let this fade away, we need to pursue it!"

"Listen college boy, and listen good, if I say it goes away, it goes away! You got that?"

Harris knew there was no sense in getting into "a pissing contest" with him. He wouldn't win it anyway.

"Yeah, I got that."

"Good, just clean up any loose ends, so we can't be criticized, let the Mounties come up with a press release and you walk away, OK?"

"OK!"

Of course Harris was not about to do that, at least not yet, after terminating his call he headed to Soper Research Inc.

Naz greeted him in the lobby, he informed him that Brad was at the hospital visiting his father, and he did not elaborate on the reason.

"Dr. Monpetit, I have a few questions for you, might I have a few minutes of your time?"

"Of course, anything I can do to help Inspector."

They sat in Naz' office, it was a large office, but the man seemed to dominate it with his sheer size.

"Dr. Monpetit, there are a few things that I need to know, they may seem a little strange but it would be very helpful in my investigation if you can provide me with some background information."

"Fire away!"

Harris leaned back in his chair alert for any response he might get from the big man, that might signal something other than a direct response.

"Does Soper Research maintain an inventory, regardless of how small, of a material known as ricin?"

"I believe that we do, it is generally used for in vitro treatment of bone marrow containing cancer cells. One of our research projects concerning leukemia treatments."

"Does Soper Research have facilities to produce asthma inhalers?"

"As a matter of fact, we have several patents on asthma products, using some proprietary dilators, while we do not manufacture any product here, we do maintain facilities for doing prototype work on new products."

"So your answer is yes?"

"Yes."

So far no indication of any surprise at the line of questioning, either a very truthful man or an experienced liar.

"To sum up then Dr. Monpetit, since the materials are all here, and the equipment to produce prototype inhalers is present, would I be correct in assuming that an inhaler containing ricin could have been manufactured here?"

"The only trick would be to aerosolize the ricin, but that could be done here as well."

"He not only appears truthful, but he is volunteering information as well, I wouldn't have known to ask that."

"May I permitted to ask what this is all about Inspector?"

"I appreciate the way you have answered my questions Doctor, but I'm afraid I'm not at liberty to answer yours, at least not at this time."

He took his leave of Monpetit and proceeded to the parking lot, he had, by prearranged signal, set up a meeting with the young officer that he had planted at Soper. As he pulled out of the parking lot and proceeded east on the Lakeshore, he noted a car fall in behind him when he passed the second intersection.

Harris pulled into a roadside fast food outlet, ordered a burger and a drink; it took several minutes to complete his order. He returned to his car with his food, a manila envelope was on the front seat.

He settled in, munching on his burger as he read, he smiled, "Good work," he thought. His plant had been successful in getting a copy of the security log for the day that Jim Nelson had been murdered, and sure enough, there it was, Nelson had been there that day.

Not only that, but the record showed that he had entered the lab area after the offices had closed for the day, he was there for two and a half hours, was that long enough and did he have the skills?

He needed to place Nelson at Mahoney's office that same day; he wouldn't be able to confirm that at Mahoney's office, not now. He called Soper Research and was successful in locating Nelson's former secretary, he explained to her, just who he was, she was shaken at the call.

"Ms, Kelley, could you tell me of any appointments that Dr. Nelson may have had for the day he died" he couldn't remember the specific date and knew his reference to his death would upset her further, but it couldn't be helped.

"Well" she hesitated "The only one that stands out was the appointment Mr. Mahoney was trying to make with him, he can be a very rude man Inspector. I was finally able to get the message to him before I left for the day, but I couldn't tell you what time they were to meet."

"But as far as you know, it was for that day?"

"Yes, yes, Mr. Mahoney was very insistent, but it must have been after business hours I would guess."

"Thank you very much Ms. Kelley, you've been a great help."

"You're welcome, I do hope you catch whoever did this terrible thing, he was such a nice man."

*

Brad was allowed into his father's room, he stood at his bedside, with all of the medical apparatus connected to him. It was hard to recognize him as anyone he knew.

The monitors issued periodic beeps, the lung machine hissed like the bellows on an old organ, bags of fluid were draped from an assortment of stands, and it was like a scene from some old "B" Horror Movie.

He could see his hands, crossed over his chest, which rose and fell in rhythm to the lung machine, instinctively, he reached out and touched the hand. Surprisingly it was warm, why did he think it would be cold?

He was overwhelmed by feelings he had not anticipated, what might have been, under different circumstances. He had a sense of loss, not just the loss of a father, but of the loss of past opportunities, never to be regained.

Someone is out there! I can sense it! Who is it, a nurse, or a doctor? Who's there?

"Alfred are you here, Alfred, I'm apprehensive!"

"I'm here Dr. Soper, what's wrong?

There is a terrible sense of sadness out there! What is it? Valium must be low, need more?

"Alfred come closer."

"I'm right beside you Dr. Soper."

He reached out and found Alfred's hand, Alfred recoiled from the contact as though burned.

"What is it Alfred? What have I done?

"Nothing its nothing, you just startled me, that's all."

As he stood there, trying to see his father's face beneath the mask and feeding tubes, he felt something, could it be true or was it just his imagination! He wasn't completely sure, but he felt something, yes! His father was squeezing his hand, ever so slightly.

He pulled his hand away in shock!

Or was he just imagining it.

Chapter 34

Harris sat in his car and he traced back the events in this strange case, somehow he knew that they were all connected, but how?

He was sure that the death of Peter Mytryk, Jim Nelson and now Declan Mahoney were a part of this puzzle, perhaps even Ashley Soper and while he wasn't dead yet, Arnie Soper as well.

Why were the RCMP and the Department of Justice involved with this thing, if the D.O.J. was involved could CSIS be far behind, not likely e thought.

Soper Research seemed like an odd client for Mahoney, but then who knows? It was obvious to him that Brad Soper was not the one to ask who then?

"Lester Coughlan, that's who, let's just see what he has to say!"

He looked back in his notebook and found the number, he punched it into his cell, he got some officious broad on the other end, he silenced her with, "It's the police, tell him it's Inspector Harris calling, tell him it's urgent!"

Coughlan came on the line, clearing his throat as he did so. "What is it you want Inspector?"

"I want to come and see you, NOW!"

"No need to get testy with me, I'm not your problem you know, come ahead if you like, I've nothing to hide."

As he closed his cell, he thought about that comment, what in Hell did he mean, if anything, this case was getting on his nerves?

The old man greeted him in a large, almost Victorian office, complete with tea service and a secretary with a bun, a bun in her hair that is. "Would you like some tea Inspector, she smiled sweetly at him through yellowing dentures.

"No thanks!"

She left the two of them alone and backed out of the room, old Lester sat like some potentate from a bad fairy tale, he coughed into a non too clean handkerchief.

"Now, what's so all fired important?"

"Perhaps you haven't heard, Declan Mahoney is dead!"

He thought he caught an imperceptible smile.

"Dead you say? How'd he die."

"I'm here to ask the questions."

"Then ask away, I haven't heard one yet."

"I would like to know how Mahoney became involved with Soper Research in the first place."

"Simple enough, he was hired by Arnie Soper after a very significant security breach at Soper, That breach cost the company several millions of dollars."

"How was that."

"One of our competitors got wind of a patent application we were about to file and they beat us to the punch. They got the patent, we didn't, and we lost a small fortune and didn't even recover the cost of development. Arnie was furious, as was I."

"I can imagine, did Mahoney ever uncover who the culprit was?"

"If he did, he never told me, Oh heads rolled, but I don't think the kingpin was ever found or if he was, was never disciplined."

"Did you have a theory as to who was guilty?"

"As far as I was concerned, it had to be Peter Mytryk, as you people would say, he had means, motive and opportunity."

"But he was left in place, why?"

"You'd have to ask Arnie that."

"Do you have any understanding of how Mahoney and Soper came together on this arrangement."

"Not really, I just assumed it was by word of mouth."

"Did you know anything of Mahoney's personal history, after all you are an officer and a significant shareholder of the company?"

The old man paused, poured himself some more tea from the elaborate pot and sat back in his chair and observed Harris for a moment.

"I did know this man you call Declan, from a past life if you like. Inspector, you have probably noted from my accent that I'm not Canadian born."

"I've noticed, I have always assumed you were from Ireland."

"Yes, I came out in 1962, and never looked back, a land of opportunity it is."

"Then you knew Mahoney back then, before you came out?"

"Yes, we had some similar political ambitions then, we were both interested in a United Ireland, strange how important that seemed back then."

"Still does, to some people."

"Yes, yes, I know, well at any rate, we were both involved in the IRA and came into contact occasionally with one another, I didn't get involved in much of the thrilling stuff, I just raised money for the cause."

"Thrilling stuff, you mean the murder don't you?"

"Just remember, there was killing on both sides, then and now, I gave up trying to justify any of it."

"Are you saying you just walked away from it, that's not my understanding of how it works?"

"More or less, I did, mind you I wasn't very high up, I knew little so I was neither a great threat nor a great loss, Mahoney however, now that was a different story."

"What do you mean."

"Mahoney was what I think you call a mover, he was ambitious, he wanted to move up in the organization, he undertook dangerous missions, murder was not beyond him and he was trusted. That was the important thing.

They put him in charge of some of there business fronts, you know semi legitimate businesses, selling insurance for example so your business never got bombed.

He did well at it but he had sticky fingers, he couldn't resist taking a little for himself, that would have been unnoticed, but he got greedy."

"And they caught him."

"Not quite, almost by accident, he found out they were on to him, he would have been summarily executed as an example, except for the fact he overheard a discussion that implicated him."

"So how did he escape?"

"Simple, he turned informer, because he had been trusted, he knew of several plots, one of which was the plan to kill several members of the Royal Family on a visit to Brighton.

He traded that information for his relocation to Canada, a new identity and he got to keep the money he stole from the IRA."

"Why Canada?"

"Why not? It's not a particular hot bed of political intrigue, he could get lost very easily and besides, there was a family connection here."

"I am surprised that you are being so forthcoming, I appreciate this information, but tell me, why are you telling me all this?"

"In case you haven't noticed, I'm a very old man, I have just lost the only one that meant anything to me."

"You mean your daughter Ashley?"

"Yes, the rest are wastrels and worse. I'm not particularly proud of my part in all of this, but if what I tell you helps in anyway to avenge my daughter's death, I will die happier than I am now.

Going back to my story, you might guess my surprise when Arnie introduced me to the owner of the new security firm that he had hired. I recognized him instantly, but I suppose I had changed enough over the years that I was a complete stranger to him."

"What did you do after that?"

"I placed a Trans-Atlantic phone call to one of my old contacts and let them know what I had discovered."

"Why would you have done that?"

"Old loyalties die hard. He was a thief, he had violated a trust, I felt it was my duty."

"I'm surprised he wasn't exterminated!"

"No, No, they turned him into an asset, they sent a team over and explained how he could continue with his life uninterrupted if he agreed to their terms or how his life would be extinguished if he did not agree. He agreed!"

"What was it that they wanted from him."

"They became his business partners, he became a front for some of their illegal business activities, money laundering etc.

His surveillance activities were also of interest to them, they could use his expertise and connections to watch key figures and maybe even extort money for their cause."

"Money Laundering?

"Yes, it's quite a business really and not just drug dealers, but terrorists too, everything he laundered, Mahoney Associates got a percentage, not unlike a bank really."

'You said he had family here in Canada?"

"Yes, he was estranged from his wife, she left Ireland and came to Canada, I think the wife had a sister here too, at any rate the wife died 5 or 6 years after he arrived."

"Is there anything else you can tell me?"

"Not much else, if I remember anything significant, I'll call you."

Why is it I sense he is not telling me everything he knows? He obviously had no use for Mahoney. Based on what young Soper had to say, perhaps it was Coughlan who ordered up the hit on Mahoney.

But then again, Old Lester, wouldn't be the only one interested in seeing Mahoney dead!

"Thank you for your help Mr. Coughlan, I'll see myself out.

*

Brad needed time to think, although he had not been close to his father, making a decision to end his life was not going to come easily. He left his father's room and entered the family lounge at the end of the hall; fortunately it was empty.

He took a chair facing a window that looked out from the 6th floor, he watched the people below as if they were totally unconnected with his world, he was startled when his cell phone rang. He had forgotten to shut it off on entering the hospital.

He looked furtively around and answered it trying not to be too obvious it was Janet.

"Brad, Oh, Brad Thank God I got you!" She sounded like she was close hysteria; he was having trouble making out what she was saying.

"Janet, slow down, what's wrong, speak slowly, I'm having trouble understanding you."

"Brad, it's Declan, he's dead, they've killed him and now they're after me!"

"What do you mean he's dead, when, how?"

"No time, no time! I have to see you, please, please, meet me, now!"

"Janet, I can't, I'm at the hospital, my father is dying."

"Brad, if you don't help me, they will kill me too!"

"Janet, who's trying to kill you? What's this all about?"

"Can't talk here, meet me, please!"

"OK, OK, do you remember that place where we had dinner?"

"Yes, Yes!"

"Meet me there in half an hour."

"Thank you Brad! And Brad."

"Yes."

"Don't tell anyone about this call, not Naz, not Inspector Harris, no one, do you understand?"

"I understand."

However, he didn't understand, that was the problem, he quickly switched of his phone and put it in his pocket. She was obviously terrified, so unlike her, he could only hope that his father could hang on a while longer.

Secretly, he was relieved that any decision he might have to make regarding his father was suspended. He had to do what he could to help her.

He walked into Alice Fazooley's and spotted her almost immediately sitting in a booth near the back of the restaurant. She looked distraught; eyes red rimmed, like some trapped animal he thought.

Then she saw him; she brightened considerably; she rose to greet him, hugging him tightly to her.

"Nobody followed you did they?"

"No, of course not, what the Hell is all this about Janet?"

"I told you Declan is dead, it was horrible, I don't know how they did it, he was always so careful, but somehow they got to him and the murdered him!"

"Who Janet, who?"

Instead of answering him, she told him what she had experienced at the office, the horror of what seemed to have happened to Declan Mahoney, tears streamed down her face.

He ordered a glass of Cognac for each of them, maybe it would help steady her, he needed some steadying too; he had never seen Janet in such a state.

She told him that she had followed the ambulance to the Emergency at The Toronto General Hospital, they wouldn't allow her to accompany him into the emergency department, nor would they tell her anything about his condition.

Their drinks came and she took a large swallow and began to cough almost immediately.

"Easy Jan, easy." He reached over and took her hand.

"I decided to go back to the office, I really didn't know what else to do, I tried calling you but your line was busy. When I got there, they were already there!"

"Who was there Janet?"

"The RCMP, those bastards killed him, I know it!"

"Janet, calm down, the RCMP don't go around murdering people, you're mistaken!"

Her eyes glittered with tears, her mouth became a hard line "How the fuck would you know!"

"Janet, take it easy, please."

"I tried to reach someone in the office by phone, the Mounties answered, I tried reaching them at home, no answer. I have kept trying still no answer, the phones into the office have been disconnected, they are after me too, I know it."

"Janet, why in the world would the RCMP be after you?"

"Because, Declan Mahoney is my father!"

Brad was stunned; he had a sense that Mahoney was holding something over Janet, but never this!

"Jan, you better start at the beginning."

Chapter 35

Harris took a sip of his drink, the straight liquor burned on its way down, it burned just like he burned, he thought. He waited for his friend Dwayne to make the first move; there was an awkward pause before he spoke.

"Look Dave, I'm sorry about yesterday at Mahoney's place, but there was nothing I could do!"

"Why not?"

"It wasn't my show, you know that, we were just there to exercise the warrant."

"Then whose show was it Dwayne?"

"CSIS."

"CSIS? What the Hell were they involved for, this is a murder investigation, I had jurisdiction?"

"Dave, you know the spot you're putting me in, I could be up on charges if anyone knew we were talking, but believe me, they had no interest in your murder investigation. They were operating on a different agenda."

"Dwayne, I know all about Mahoney's connection with the IRA, but to my knowledge they aren't on the terrorist list, so how the Hell does CSIS get away using Bill C-36?"

"How'd you find that out Dave, I never told you, I didn't tell anybody."

"Take it easy Dwayne, I'm not wearing a wire, anything between us stays with us, you know that."

They weren't his only partner!"

"Who else?"

He had a pained expression on his face, he hesitated before he answered, looking around the half empty bar, and no one seemed even remotely interested in them.

"CSIS for sure and maybe MI-6 and even the CIA!"

"What?"

"You don't really believe that you're free and clear after one of these relocation things do you? Once CSIS found out that Mahoney was being muscled by the Irish fellas they decided to turn him as a double agent if you like.

He had valuable information on what he was doing for the IRA and they wanted it, they threatened him with exposure, which would have meant certain death, if he didn't go along."

"What was it he was doing for the IRA?"

"Well, as you might have heard, their funding had largely dried up, particularly out of the US after 9/11, they had to develop some imaginative ways to raise the cash they needed."

"Such as?"

"Money Laundering, Blackmail, Extortion.

They handled drug money, money from the Middle East destined for terrorist cells around the world, with a little domestic blackmail thrown in"

"I assume Mahoney got a piece off the top?"

"You bet! He did very well for himself.

"So I take it the warrant was for aiding terrorist organizations?"

"You got it! A quick trip to a sympathetic judge and its "Slam Bam thank you Ma'am," assets frozen, records seized arrests made, took less than two hours!"

"No legal counsel, no phone calls, all neat and tidy."

"Except for one thing."

"What was that?"

"That crafty bastard, Declan Mahoney, had installed a Latency Virus on his computer system."

"What the Hell is a Latency Virus?"

"Well, it's a little program that runs on his network, as long as he personally is logged in and indicates activity by way of key strokes or mouse movement, nothing happens.

If he is logged out for more than two hours or inactive for one hour, the virus kicks in, it very quickly destroys all of the data stored there, all the terminal hard drives are shared, therefore all the local data is destroyed as well."

"Where'd you find out about all this stuff? Last I heard, when it comes to computers, you couldn't find your ass with both hands!"

"Up yours! I talked to one of our computer forensic guys."

"So what you are saying is, after all this trouble, you've got no evidence!"

"Given Mahoney ran a paper less office, more or less, I'd say yes!"

"But surely your forensic guys can salvage something off the hard drives?"

"Apparently everything on the system was 1024 bit encrypted and as the virus cleaned off the disks, it overwrote all available space in some kind of gibberish."

"And I think I have problems!

Just wait a minute! There has to be a backup of all that data, Mahoney would never have trusted this latency system completely."

"You're not as dumb as you look Davey. You're right, but we need to find it."

"Dave, what do you know about Mahoney's daughter?"

What daughter? I didn't even know he had a daughter, Shit! Got to play this one carefully, if Dwayne finds out I know nothing, that's likely the way it will stay, gotta bluff this one.

"Why should I share that with you? Tell me what you know, I'll see if I can add anything."

"What kind of Bullshit is that, if you show me yours, I'll show you mine? Seems to me this communication thing has gotten pretty lopsided!"

"Never mind, just tell me what you know, you're the guys interfering in my case."

"OK, OK we don't know all that much about her. Just that she seems to have been into this thing right up to her eyebrows, in fact it appears that she was responsible for the movement of large sums of money. She's a lawyer you know. My guess is she handled the laundering aspect while Mahoney himself looked after more of the dirty work."

"So you have her under arrest, does she know where the backups are?"

He recognized instantly, that he had gone too far. Dwayne's eyes hardened, "That's all I've got to tell you, I've said too much already."

He got up to leave; Harris grabbed him by the arm. "Thanks buddy, I appreciate what you have done for me, trust me, it'll go no farther."

Hitchcock pulled his arm away, looked him in the eye and said, "You owe me!"

Harris sat alone, he took another sip of his drink and retrieved his list from his pocket, and he spread it out before him, took his pencil and began adding the new facts and contacts–suspects he had just learned about.

He scratched his head in puzzlement, "How the Hell does all of this tie together?" He ordered another drink, turned the paper over and started his scratchings all over again. Moreover, just who is this daughter of Mahoney's? What's her name?

An hour and two drinks later, he was still no farther ahead, he was getting tired, better head home he thought, start fresh in the morning.

He unlocked his apartment door and was hit with the odour of 10 day old lasagna, "Shit, I thought I threw that out last week!"

He opened the fridge, the smell almost made him puke, breathing through his mouth he carried the container to the garbage chute and disposed of it, he couldn't help but think of the supers reaction when he came to put out the garbage.

He returned to his apartment and as he closed the door behind him he was jumped from behind, he turned with a start. It was his cat Max!

"Max, I'm too tired to play "silly buggers" with you tonight, he scratched him behind the ears, the cat responded with deep throated purring.

The one white paw scratched at him playfully, Harris had not turned on the light when he came in but Max' white patches seemed to glow in the dark, the black patches seemed to leave just the white floating in the dark.

'I bet you're hungry; too bad you didn't say something sooner. I had some nice lasagna for you!"

He mixed up some yogurt and Special K for the cat." There that should help your urinary tract!" He added fresh water to his water bowl and returned to the living room and his list once more.

He switched on his reading light and sat in his leather recliner, he poured over the list, and still nothing connected in his mind. Usually he could find reason and purpose in any crime; here he had too many reasons, too many purposes, what the Hell was going on?

Sometimes it just worked best if he tried to empty his mind; he stretched out in the recliner, Max bounded up onto his lap a curled up contentedly.

*

"Janet, tell me what's happened, why are you so frightened?"

"OH Brad! It was horrible, I knew something was wrong with him, he hadn't been himself for several days, but he wouldn't see a doctor, and I saw the whole thing he was dying right in front of me!"

She repeated to whole spectacle she had witnessed in Mahoney's office, it was indeed a grisly experience thought Brad. He tried to calm her, she was anxious to talk.

"Nobody understood him, I don't mean that he was an easy man to understand, he was hated by many, but Brad you need to know what had happened to make him the way he was.

In the beginning he was a patriot, yes a real patriot, he fought to unify Ireland, he was respected back then, I can barely remember that time, it was before my mother and I had to come to Canada."

"Had to come to Canada, why?"

"The English had a price on my father's head, he felt that his family was also at risk, he loved us and didn't want us exposed to the violence, there were great arguments between he and my mother, but of course, he won out.

We came to live in Toronto, with my Aunt Agnes, but both of us, my mother and I, were heart broken, we didn't think we would ever see my father again.

Three years later, my mother died of cervical cancer, I was devastated, my father couldn't even come to the funeral. He would have been arrested at the airport.

It was a terrible time, please understand, my Aunt Agnes was wonderful and caring, but she wasn't my mother, I felt abandoned, alone."

He could empathize with all these feelings she must have had, for his, if not as dramatic, were much the same.

"Then how did you're father finally get to Canada?"

"There had been some kind of falling out within the senior leadership of the IRA, my father being one of the group was singled out on some trumped up charge of stealing a large sum of money under his control. It was lies all lies! But they were going to kill him, no judge, no jury, just an execution!"

"What did he do to escape?"

"He did something he hated, he turned informer!"

"I don't understand?"

"I told you he was in the senior ranks of the organization and in that position, he was aware of almost all of the plots for various attacks against the "occupiers." He made a deal with the bastards! He had to, he had no choice other than to die and it wouldn't even have been a martyr's death.

My father was a clever man, his price for the information was safe passage to Canada, a new identity and to be allowed to live out the rest of his life in peace."

"The information he provided must have been very significant, to have been given such a deal."

"It was, if you count the Royal Family as being significant!"

"What do you mean?"

"You probably are too young to remember, as I was, the bombing at a hotel in Brighton, devastated the hotel, but there were no significant injuries. As it turns out the major part of the Royal Family was to have been in that hotel that night. Only by the grace of my father were they not!"

"My God!"

It seemed as though she was not there with him as she spoke; it was as though she was reciting the actions in a movie she had seen.

"He came to Toronto as Declan Mahoney just shortly after, I was ecstatic, he came to see me and Aunt Agnes, he brought gifts and made me laugh, I was only 10 years old.

We didn't see much of him in the early years here, he was busy starting his business, he stayed in touch and when the time came, he helped me get through law school.

His business was doing well by then, I had finished articling and had been working for a prestigious law firm for a couple of years when he approached me to join his firm.

I was thrilled, not only to have my Dad back, but to be able to work at his side everyday, I was overjoyed."

"But it sounded to me like you didn't much care for Declan when we first met?"

"That largely depended on the day, he could be an overbearing tyrant one minute and just Dad the next. He was also a sexist; he had his own idea of my limitations because of my gender. I don't really suppose it is much different for anybody who works for his or her father.

Unfortunately you will never have that experience I suppose."

"OK Jan, but what gets us to where we are today?"

"It was that son-of-a-bitch Coughlan!'

"What?"

"Your father had decided to retain Mahoney Associates after a rather serious security breach at the lab, I'm sure you heard about it. We were recommended by a mutual business acquaintance that was impressed with my father's work.

In the process of being retained, Declan met Coughlan, quite by accident, on site, he thought he looked familiar, but couldn't place him. Coughlan had no such problem, he remembered my father from his IRA days and promptly let his contacts in Dublin know what he had found out."

"Then what happened?"

"What do you think, within days of the chance meeting, my father was visited by two men, senior in the organization, the proposition was simple, keep your life and take us in as full partners or you die. And oh! By the way, so does your daughter."

"No choice at all!"

"No. He knew they meant it, life means nothing to them."

"Jan, I can understand your fear of them but why the police?"

"I'm coming to that, within two months, my father was paid another visit, this time by two Canadian thugs! From CSIS, they had been watching him all this time, the IRA visitors were known to them. They drew the correct conclusion and made my father a second offer he couldn't refuse. In essence, they made him a double agent by threatening to expose him and extradite him back to England to stand trial for some unsolved bombings."

"And you think CSIS or the RCMP killed your father?"

"Yes, Yes I do, who else could it have been?"

"But why do you think they are after you?"

She smiled a wan little smile, "Because they didn't get what they were after when they shut down our offices."

"Janet, this is like pulling teeth, finish the story please."

"All of the evidence was destroyed automatically, just after my father died, they have no case, ours was a paper less office, everything was electronic, and it's gone!"

"So what's the problem then?"

"Like any good business, we backed up all our data scrupulously, and I am the only one that knows where that backup is

*

Harris awakened with a start and dumped Max from his lap.

"Shit! That's it. There is no connection between these cases, accept for the nexus of Declan Mahoney. I've been trying to connect dots that don't exist, how stupid!

Chapter 36

"Janet, you are upset, that's understandable, but you can't really think that the authorities would be involved in something like this?"

"Brad. Don't be so naive; it wouldn't be the first time would it? Look I need your help! Will you help me or not?"

"How do you want me to help?"

"I need a place to stay, I can't go back to my place, Brad I don't know where else to turn, please help me!"

He looked into her face, she was absolutely terror-stricken, she should turn herself in, he knew that, but he also knew she wouldn't. If she were guilty of any of the murders, he would become an accessory; he tried to reason with her.

How much of what Jan has told me is true? Declan Mahoney, a blackmailer, extortionist, maybe murderer, even involved in Ashley's death. How much does she know about all of this, I can't get involved? Must try to get her to turn herself in. She has deluded herself where her father is involved.

"Jan, you are asking me to be a conspirator in all of this, as much as I would like to help you, I can't do that.

Let me get hold of Inspector Harris, I trust him, turn yourself in, he can protect you."

This forlorn girl that he thought he knew suddenly erupted with anger, he eyes no longer full of tears were blazing, she was almost shouting at him.

"You gutless Asshole! Just forget it! Forget it! All you do is think about yourself, I thought there might have been a possibility that we could have had something together.

Instead you are ready to throw me to the wolves, well FUCK YOU! I'll look after myself like I've always done!"

She sprung out of her chair and left the restaurant almost running, nearly knocking down a waiter with a tray full of water glasses.

Brad was left speechless, he half rose from his chair, but he was too late to stop her, she was gone!

The outburst had attracted little attention, the place was almost empty, the waiter, the near victim of the collision, stopped at his table.

"Looks like you could use a drink sir."

"Yeah, make it a double, Glenfiddich please, rocks."

As he sat contemplating what had happened, his cell rang, it was Naz.

"Brad. It's Naz, have you heard what's happened at Mahoney Associates?"

"Yes, Yes I have."

"It's completely shut down, their offices I mean, I was trying to phone Janet to see that she's OK, but the message just says the phones have been disconnected, do you have any idea where she might be?"

"As a matter of fact, she just left here, she was in quite a state, she's afraid someone is after her, that she might be in danger."

"But who would want to hurt her?"

"I am not sure anybody really does, she believes that Declan Mahoney was murdered and that she may be next."

His drink came, he took a small sip and felt the pale liquid warm his insides, Naz persisted.

"Who is supposed to have done all this?"

"She wasn't really coherent, besides I don't think we should be having this conversation over the phone."

"Surely you're not worried about eavesdropping, remember Mahoney's been shut down."

"Nevertheless, cell phones are notoriously easy to listen in on."

"OK, why don't I meet you, where are you?"

"Alice Fazooley's, come down and I'll by you dinner."

"That's a deal, be there shortly."

Brad dialled Dave Harris' number; he answered on the second ring.

"Harris here!"

"Inspector, its Brad Soper."

"How can I help you Dr. Soper?"

Brad repeated everything that had happened during his confrontation with Janet; he tried to be careful in his retelling of the episode, leaving nothing out.

"I appreciate your call, and if you had any concern, you did the right thing, if she is involved in anything illegal or criminal then you certainly would have implicated yourself.

Did she give you any indication of where she might go? Who she might contact?"

"No, she just stormed out when I refused to help her with a place to stay."

"So she wanted you to put her up?"

"Yes, tell me do you want to arrest her?"

"What I would like is the opportunity of questioning her, the result of that questioning may or may not lead to charges being laid and her subsequent arrest. But of this moment there is no outstanding warrant for her arrest."

"What about her concerns about any government agency being out to kill her?"

"Dr. Soper, I think you know that that is out of the question, as far as I'm concerned conspiracy theories don't belong here. If you are asking me if her life is in danger, that's a totally different matter, somebody did murder Declan Mahoney, depending how deep her involvement in his affairs goes, its possible."

"What about this backup business, do you think that could be the basis of the threat she seems to feel so strongly?"

"I'm afraid I can't comment on that matter, that is a different case and is not within my jurisdiction."

"Shit, then it could all be true, her life is in danger and I turned my back on her!"

"I told you, you did the right thing in refusing, with all due respect, this no place for amateurs, if she contacts you again, I want you to contact me immediately, do you understand?"

"Yes Inspector."

"Where will you be in case I want to contact you?"

"Right now I'm at Alice Fazooley's, the restaurant, I'm going to have something to eat and then go see my father at the hospital."

"OK, I'll call you if I have any news."

Harris hung up; at least I know who Mahoney's daughter is! A piece if luck, finally!

When Naz arrived, Brad was on his second drink, a single this time, he could see that Brad was upset.

"Ho there Brad, what no beer tonight?"

"Just felt the need for something stronger, I think I've let down a good friend and I don't quite know what to do about it."

Naz ordered a drink, "So tell me Brad, who does Janet suspect is behind the killing of her father?

""It sounds like an Oliver Reed movie, she believes government agents did or failing that, some IRA extremists and that she is next on the list."

"Sounds like a stretch to me, what reason would they have?"

Brad went over the whole story again, it seemed to get more bizarre with each telling, when he had finished, the large man opposite looked at him sadly.

"I can see why you look depressed, but for what it may be worth, I think you did the right thing."

"That's exactly what Harris said."

"You told him you met with Janet?"

"Yes, why?"

"Nothing, I had just forgotten for a moment what an ethical man you are."

Brad was not sure how to take this last remark, but was relieved when he saw a late smile bloom on the face across from him.

"Come on let's order, I'm starving, maybe some food will help cheer you up!"

"Naz, why did Janet ask me not to tell you about the fact that I was meeting her here?'

Why the surprised look Naz, something is going on here, what kind of involvement have you had with Janet? I'll just keep poking.

"I Uh, I really don't know why she would have said that Brad. I think you know I would be on her side, you know that don't you?"

"I would have thought so, but look at me, I let her down didn't I, did you do that too, did she call you as well?"

"Yes she did! I'm sorry Brad, I should have told you that, frankly I told her the same thing you did, she wanted to come and stay with me, but I couldn't let that happen."

"So much for being second choice!"

"She was likely afraid if you told me where you were meeting her, I might have tipped off Harris, that's the only reason I can think of."

Brad rotated his drink between his hands, he did not look up at Naz when he asked, "So then Naz, did you sleep with her?"

*

Harris sat in the library at York University, at one of the tables, with his yellow legal pad, yet another list having been completed.

He pushed back in his chair, a smile spread over his face, the puzzle pieces were beginning to fit together, he thought, a scenario that might explain the events of the past several weeks.

Once he had separated the death of Nelson from that of Mahoney and the aftermath of his death, things seemed to fall into place; he of all people knew that things were seldom what they seemed to be.

However, it was a long way from a hypothesis to an arrest, he needed to be able to corroborate some fact in order achieve that.

He had to find Janet Petersen, but where? Was the aunt still alive? If so where was she? It would be too obvious for her to hide out with her, but the aunt might be able to shed some light on her whereabouts.

He left the library and from his car he phoned a friend of his in Missing Persons, maybe he could come with an address for the aunt.

"Hi Pete, its Dave Harris here, need a favour."

He explained what it was that he wanted, the officer on the other end suggested that he might be able to at least get a last known address from Case Worker's file that handled the case after Janet's mother's death, it could be a starting point. It might be possible that the aunt still lived there. He promised he'd call back as soon as he could and yes, he understood it was urgent.

"Thanks Pete."

He was going to put out an APB on her car but thought better of it, the Mounties were probably monitoring the Metro Police radio frequencies, no sense in antagonizing them and Fast as well.

He wondered if Soper was still at Alice Fazooley's, perhaps there was more he could remember about his meeting with Janet. Besides, he hadn't had dinner anyway.

He drove to the restaurant, on his way his friend Pete called back, "Dave, Pete here, I got lucky, there was a Break and Enter file right here. Apparently some kids broke into her house years back and scared the bejeesus out of the old lady. The kid phoned it in so her name was on the B & E sheet.

Good thing we got all these things on E-file now saves a lot of time."

"Great Pete, let me pull over so I can write it down, what's her name?"

"Agnes, Agnes McNally, lives down in Cabbage Town, been there since before it got trendy at 34 Spruce Street. I hope it works for you Dave, she's got to be in her late seventies or early eighties, could be dead too."

"Aren't you just a little ray of sunshine! Anyway Pete, I owe you big time thanks."

"You bet."

"And uh, Pete, can you put a lock on that file, I'll let you know when you can take it off."

"OK Dave, but now you really owe me!"

"You want my first born Pete?"

"Ruthie's number would be good."

"Bugger off Pete! He hung up still smiling; "We're movin' now!"

He turned the car around and headed back downtown. He needed Janet Petersen!

*

"Why should my private life be any of your business Brad? She wasn't your private property was she? As a matter of fact, she told me that you apparently had no interest in her as a woman!"

What! I never said that, is that what she really thinks, we just never had a chance that's all. Who knows what might have developed? Not now, not ever.

"Calm down Naz, you're right it's none of my business, I apologize, let's just drop it."

Brad and Naz finished dinner in silence and ordered a liqueur. Naz felt compelled to tell Brad of Harris' recent visit and questions about ricin, how he wanted to know if Soper had ricin in the lab.

"What the Hell did he ask that for?"

"Just remember, he asks the questions, at least that's what he told me when I asked him the same thing."

He also asked if we had facilities to produce asthma inhalers and would it be difficult to aerosolize ricin and place in an inhaler."

"And what did you tell him?"

"I told him yes on all counts."

"I know very little about ricin, other than it's a deadly toxin, what's it doing in our inventory?

"It's used in research, particularly involving bone marrow transplants."

"What's your best guess as to why he was asking these questions?"

"Well he's a policemen, people have been dying, my guess is he suspects this might have been some kind of murder weapon."

"Shit! How did we become involved in all this, this is the last thing we need?"

"Calm down Brad, we aren't the only lab in the city with ricin, as a matter of fact you can find out more than you need to know about it on the Internet."

They finished their drinks and Brad told Naz he was going up to the hospital to see his father.

"How are things there?"

"Not good Naz, they want to remove life support, but they want my permission. OH Shit! I just remembered, I was

294   NJ Matthews

supposed to meet Leslie Phillips there, my lawyer. Then I got Janet's call and it completely slipped my mind dammit!"

"I'm sure she'll understand Brad, you've had quite a day, call her, I'm sure she'll still meet you there.

In the meantime I have to leave, believe it or not, I have a date!"

"Why isn't that a surprise, thanks for coming Naz, I'll see you in the morning."

He called Leslie, he got her answering machine, no way of knowing if she was there or not, he left an apologetic message anyway asking her to meet him at the hospital again.

Before he could hang up, she lifted the receiver "So you just plain forgot about me, after I cleared 4 appointments with paying clients to come to your side, some gratitude!"

"Les, I'm truly sorry, I've had a terrible day, won't you please meet me at the hospital, I can explain, really I can!"

"You sound like such a poor little boy, how can I refuse, I'll meet you there."

He felt like a weight had been lifted off him. She's so normal he thought; at least I think I still remember what normal is.

Chapter 37

Brad headed west on the Queen Elizabeth Highway; the traffic was heavy but moving steadily.

He was deep in thought about all that had happened in his short time in the city, he was particularly concerned with his actions with respect to Janet, in spite of the assurances of others, he still felt like he had abandoned her.

That word played on his mind, abandonment, he knew the feeling first hand, so did Ellis and it was evident, even before her father's death Janet had experienced it too. His death simply compounded her hurt, and now he had abandoned her too!

He searched in is mind for an answer, was his a moral and ethical decision or simply one of non-involvement, and was he simply "covering his own ass

Strange how much simpler things seemed in the abstract world of the University, where he could hypothecate on the moral high ground, without getting hands dirtied by being involved in the actual events?

The same was true with respect to dealing with his father's situation, is it just as simple as "pulling a plug?" That one act would end his dilemma, or would it?

Did anyone have the moral right to take the life of another despite the circumstances?

On the contrary, could he avoid the decision just because it was easier to do so, he had no idea if his father sensed anything, was he in pain? What is the definition of life anyway? Can it be quantified? Can you write an algorithm, so that you can just plug in all the variables and let the computer decide?

In his heart, he knew the answer to the last 3 questions. No, you could not!

Before he realized it, he was at the Hospital Parking Lot, as luck would have it, he saw Leslie pulling in just ahead of him. They were able park along side each other, they got out and embraced, she kissed him even before he could speak.

"God, Brad, you look awful, what the Hell has been going on?"

He reiterated everything that had transpired, he told her about Janet, his discussion with Harris and finally his meeting with Naz, he ended by repeating his apology for standing her up.

"I didn't believe for a minute that you did that intentionally, but this stuff with Janet, that's hard to believe, I had no idea of any of this, she never even mentioned that Declan Mahoney was her father!"

"I wonder why not?"

"I don't know, we have been friends since law school, we graduated together, even articled for a while. We did the usual things, we even double dated once, but you never got to get really close with Janet, not even with me.

She was pretty much a loner, just she and an old aunt, Aunt Agnes; I met her once, a dear old soul, a little dotty I thought, Janet looked after her, it seemed more like a mother daughter relationship. Which it was I guess, since she raised her after her mother's death.

Incidentally, you did the right thing in not aiding her; this is your lawyer talking now. I know it sounds harsh, but Janet's problems are not of your making. In the end, you would not only have compromised yourself, but likely you would just have delayed the inevitable, the police will find her."

"I guess you're right."

"That's what you 're paying me for, that whole Toonie!"

It was strange, in just a few minutes she was able to lift his spirits, he grasped her hand and gave it a squeeze, and it seemed she understood and smiled that dazzling smile at him in return.

"You know, I never did understand why Janet gave up the law to go to work for a PR firm, the fact that she went to work for her father makes more sense now."

Brad pressed the elevators button for his father's floor, as they got in, Leslie said, "Brad, do not be rushed into anything here tonight, if you need time to consider the options, just take it. The hospital will be anxious to get off the hook for any potential liabilities, they will be just as anxious to transfer those potential liabilities to a family member."

"Are you saying that there may some kind of hidden liability here?"

"Not necessarily, but neither party wants to be charged in a mercy killing,"

They stood before the Intensive Care viewing window, the special care nurse was fussing about the bed trying to assure his father's comfort, nothing seemed to have changed since he was in last.

The nurse noticed them at the window, she signalled that she was coming out.

"Dr. Soper, we missed you earlier today, Dr. Pickard was looking for you."

"I'm sorry nurse, I was called away on another emergency, would you be kind enough to let Dr. Pickard know that I'm here?"

The nurse nodded and headed down the hall.

"What's this Dr. Soper Business?" She looked at him quizzically.

"Not yet, but it's a Ph.D. not an MD."

"In what."

He took a deep breath before responding "Medical Ethics."

"Seriously!"

"I'm afraid so."

"And here am I, blabbing to you about what little I know about end of life situations, and here you are, an expert!"

"Not hardly, I do know some of the legal pitfalls, but most of my time has been spent on issues other than end of life as they pertain to the practice of medicine and drug therapies.

Just remember, I asked you to come with me."

At that point, Pickard arrived, "Brad, I'm very glad you're here, we missed you this afternoon."

"Sorry Dr. Pickard, I'm afraid it was unavoidable."

"At any rate, as I told you this morning, your father's condition has worsened even since you were here last. Frankly, I have never really had a hope that he might recover from whatever it is that has attacked his system.

The best we could hope to do was keep him as comfortable as possible and look forward to the faint hope of some kind of treatment that would help him.

But I must say that from the second day he was here, there was irreversible organ damage, even if we could have arrested it, there was no way to repair the damage.

It is my opinion that we crossed the boundary of heroic efforts in simply sustaining life for the sake of sustaining life, I do not think we are serving your father's best interest in prolonging his ordeal just because we can."

"Is it the cost of doing so?"

"Young lady, that never has been the case, I'm sorry, we don't seem to have been introduced."

"I'm sorry Dr. Pickard, this is Leslie Phillips, a good friend."

"And attorney" added Leslie

Pickard's head bobbed perceptibly at Leslie's comment, but he continued.

"You may not be aware Brad, but Dr. Nelson arranged for full payment outside of the Insurance system, paid for by your company I might add.

However, you should know that other cases are being blocked from this facility, because of your father's case."

"I see, but one thing Dr., when I was here earlier, he seemed to respond to me."

"Impossible! How do you think he was responsive?

"When I touched is hand, he uh, he seemed to squeeze my hand."

"Well I'm sorry to tell you that that was likely nothing more than an involuntary muscle spasm, believe me, he is beyond hope.

No one spoke for what seemed like hours, silence hung about them like a shroud. Finally Brad spoke.

"Would the two of you mind, I would like a few minutes alone with my father."

Leslie asked, "Brad let me stay with you."

"No it's OK, really, I just need a couple of minutes, then you can come in all right?

She nodded and he entered his father's room.

He looked down at the pathetic figure on the bed, how is it he had such intense feelings about somebody he barely knew? Was this some kind of long repressed desire for family, was it anger at having been deprived, was it the fact his father had ignored him, abandoned him?

*

"Alfred have you gone?"

"No Dr. Soper, I'm still with you, how do you feel?"

"That's my problem, I don't feel."

"I don't believe that you're telling me the truth."

"Can't fool old Alfred can I?"

"No, you can't."

"Well then, how should I feel? I can tell you that I feel that this thing is about over."

"And how does that make you feel Dr. Soper?"

"After all this time, can't it just be "Arnie"?"

"How does that make you feel Arnie?"

"Regret for things left undone, regret for things done, a hope that on balance, I have done more good than bad."

"You said earlier, that you felt remorseful for some things, do you remember?"

"My son, I feel remorse that I abandoned him, and his mother too. Then I have failed him; I see that now.

We have both paid a heavy price, and it is all my fault, I have been selfish and centred only on the material aspect of my life, how could I have been so stupid?"

"And Ashley?"

"Yes, and Ellis too, even though he wasn't my son, I could have made him so and didn't, I have left a heavy burden for those that I left behind, uncaring, unthinking, self-centred!"

"Are you ready to leave?"

"To go where?"

"I don't know."

"Will you come with me?"

"Of course, just as I have always been with you."

This is it! Surely it is over now. But wait, —— why wait? Go now, no, can't go yet, something is holding me here, waiting, but why?

If only I could tell Brad how much I care for him and what a fool I've been not to see it before. Could Brad love me? In spite of the years of neglect? Perhaps never, but I must wait, —— why must I wait?

What is that I feel? Like a warm breeze on my body, but how can that be? I can't feel, — and yet...

Is this how life ends, euphoric sensations? No... It can't be, and yet it's like a weight being lifted from me. My heart is full!

"Arnie are you ready?

"Alfred, will you take my hand?

"Of course!"

*

I can't see his face for all of the equipment, but his body seemed to have shrunk, he seems smaller than I can ever remember.

I am trying to remember things from my boyhood, things we did together, but nothing comes. Why then am I overcome with these strong emotions, this man was almost a stranger, why do I care so.

Why would I be conflicted about ending a life that isn't really a life at all, and might that action not save another life that might otherwise be ended because of the lack of this facility?

All of this was just so much logic, I know that, there is no comfort for me in sterile logic.

He thought about the people who spent a lifetime trying to find birth parents who had abandoned them, why?

I know this is my fault, why didn't I attempt to re-enter his life? What have I missed because of my determination to hate this man and what he did? I must take responsibility for my own despair.

I know nothing of the good things he may have done; I have simply manufactured him in an image on which to heap my unhappiness. Unfair of me, childish of me.

Why do I care so? There can be only one answer —— because I love him, and now I will never be able to let him know that

Was this a primal force that moves me in this way? Were these then selfish feelings, mine alone? What about my father, does he deserve release from the hopeless abyss he was in?

I know what the answer truly is, but I can't bring myself to say it, the answer was there though, it just wouldn't go away.

He reached for his father's hand, it was warm to his touch, the moment seemed almost electric, like a release of pent up energy, and he was almost overcome.

"Dad, I love you, I'm so sorry I didn't get to tell you that before all this, it's my fault!"

Like a flood, it's washing over me, he loves me, – I know it! Some strange force, how can this be? My father loves me!

His heart soared, was it a miracle, had some kind of communication happened?

Suddenly alarms began to sound, Pickard and the nurse rushed to the bedside, Pickard's head dropped and he removed the mask and tubes from his father's face, he looked into the eyes, pulling the eyelids up for a better view, shining his flashlight into the unseeing orbs. Arnold Soper was dead!

"I'm sorry Brad, but he's gone, a blessing really, no decision required now, nurse, we'll leave for a few moments, show Miss Phillips in."

He became aware of Leslie standing next to him; he was not surprised to see tears streaming down her face as she cried silently.

"He loves me, my father loves me, he let me know that —— somehow.

"What?"

"Somehow he let me know that he loved me, and now he's gone without me being able to tell him how much I love him. I will carry that guilt forever.

She turned him to her and kissed him gently, the tears came as he buried his face in her neck. She held him for what seemed a long time, trying to reassure him that he should feel no sense of guilt

"Brad, let's go somewhere, I think we could both use a drink."

"Leslie, thank you but I really need some time alone, I need to come to terms with what happened or at least seemed to happen tonight."

"Of course, I understand, call me will you?"

"Yes, I will, but Leslie, I could have done it you know."

"Done what?"

"Pulled the plug, ended his life, but I failed to do even that for him."

"Oh Brad, its not your fault, you know that he's better off now."

"Do I? Do I really?"

Chapter 38

Harris parked his car in front of the old house, it stood out from the rest largely because of the neglect in the small yard. The 25 foot wide lot didn't allow for much of a garden, this one was high in weeds, he could imagine how the yuppies on either side felt.

Funny he thought, how poor immigrants struggled to get out of here and now it was the place to be, he seemed to remember something about all of the facades having to remain as originally built, a heritage thing he thought.

He looked around carefully, surely the Mounties wouldn't miss this place, and maybe it was just too obvious a place to look for her. However, he needed to be aware; they weren't the only ones looking for her.

He saw nothing, everything was quiet, he decided to walk around to the back of the property, and a narrow sidewalk between the two houses was the only access to the yard.

The kitchen was in back, it was lit, somebody was home, he watched through the window for a few minutes. Seeing nothing he decided to go back to the front door, he knocked no response.

He noticed a hand operated bell right in the middle of the door. He gave the handle a twist and was surprised at the volume level generated by the old mechanism.

He could see someone coming towards him, through the glass window in the upper part of the door.

The door opened by an old lady wearing a kimono tied awkwardly at her middle with some kind of sash. She reached up to her ear, turning up her hearing he assumed.

"Yes? What is it you want?"

The voice was high pitched and reminded him of the sound from an old recording, "Are you Miss McNally?"

"Whaddya say?"

He raised his voice although he was speaking quite loudly in the first instance. He repeated his question.

"Yes, Yes I am, who are you?" She looked expectantly into his face.

He didn't want to stand in the doorway, yelling his questions to her, he held up his badge in response to her question and said, "May I come in?"

When she saw the badge, her eyes grew as big as saucers, she turned and headed for the kitchen, "I'll make some tea then, will I? She said as she walked away.

He called after her to say he didn't want tea, she still kept moving away, he said it even louder still no response.

"The old girl's as deaf as a post, she was reading my lips," he thought.

He had no option but to follow, down the narrow hall, past a staircase to the second level and into the kitchen, he was surprised at how orderly and neat everything was.

She stood at the sink filling the kettle, she couldn't have been five feet tall, nearly bald but for a halo of snow white hair. She wore open backed carpet slippers that slapped the floor when she walked.

He took a chair at the round kitchen table and waited patiently for her to finish putting the kettle on.

When she had, she came to him sat opposite him, smiling, sweetly and asked "OK Copper whaddya want!"

He was astonished, it was totally unexpected, and then she began to laugh.

"I heard that on the telly, did I get it right?"

He couldn't help but laugh, "Yeah, you got it right Aunt Agnes!"

"That was fun, you should have seen your face!"

"To be serious for a moment, I'm looking for your niece Janet, is she here?

The old woman became evasive, she tried to conceal it but she couldn't, "What would the police want with my niece?"

"I would just like to talk to her." At that point, the kettle began to whistle.

I'll make some tea, will I?"

He watched the tea making ritual, heating up the teapot, and bringing the water back to the boil, ""you can't make a good cup of tea with those bags you know, nothing like Darjeeling Tea, right from India don't you know.

Finally the tea was left to steep under the cozy, he hoped now to get to why he was there, if he could just get her attention.

"Tell me Aunt Agnes, is Janet here?"

"I'm not your Aunt Agnes, so don't get impertinent young man!"

"I'm sorry Miss McNally, would you tell me please, is Janet, your niece, is she here?"

"Why would she be here?"

"Please just answer my question."

"My wee Janet doesn't come very often to see her old Auntie anymore, to busy at work, with that father of hers I guess." He thought she was about to cry.

"But, is she here now?" he persisted.

"Oh, I get so confused sometimes, I don't remember things, the price of growing old they say."

He sensed that the old girl was putting him on, she was likely as sharp as any 20-year-old was, and he kept pressing.

"But what do you want of my Janet?"

He decided that shock might be the best approach, "Because I'm trying to save her life!"

The old woman began to tremble, he didn't like to have to rattle her this way, but just as abruptly she said, "Tea's ready." She got up from the table to fetch the cups; "Do you take milk and sugar?"

He was exasperated; his patience was just about exhausted. "NO I TAKE IT BLACK!"

"No need to shout you know, I'm not deaf!"

He reined in his temper and said as soothingly as he could "Look Miss McNally, your niece is in very great danger, if you don't help me she may die!"

She looked into his face, "Can I trust you, can I trust you that you are not one of those that wants to hurt my little Janet.

You seem to have a kind and honest face, but I could be fooled, are you one of these devious people from my past?"

"If you mean, am I from the IRA, then no I am not, does that answer your question?"

"Those bastards destroyed my family and then he came back and took the only thing that ever mattered to me, my wee Janet."

He looked straight into her face so she could not mistake what he was about to say. "I am not one of those people, my only objective here is to save your niece's life."

He could see that she had made a decision, he could only hope it was the right one.

"Come with me!"

They ascended the narrow staircase to a room overlooking the main entrance, it was as though Janet had never left, and it looked like every other 16 year olds room should look.

However, it was empty!

The old woman put a finger to her lips and pointed to the closet door, they had not turned on any lights, Harris decided that was probably a good idea.

He quietly approached the door; he quickly and noiselessly pulled it open.

He was staring down the barrel of a very large revolver, Janet was curled up in a corner of the closet, her eyes looked like those of a doe caught in the glare of oncoming headlights. She held the gun with both hands, she was shaking, and it seemed all she could do was hold the gun up.

"Janet, its OK, I'm here to help you, put the gun down."

"No, No, you've come to kill me, just like you did my father!"

He'd intentionally had left the lights off in the room, it took a while for his eyes to become adjusted to the dim light, but he could see her trembling, the gun could go off by accident.

"Be careful Janet, you don't want to hurt your Aunt Agnes do you?"

"Is she here? I want to see her, I want to see that she's OK!"

He didn't want to put the old lady in the line of fire, so he kept his body in front of the old lady as much as he could, "Your Aunt's OK, see, she's right behind me."

"Oh Jannie! Don't do this, do as he says, he's a nice man, he's come to help you."

"No Auntie, I don't trust any of them, they killed daddy!"

Just at that moment, the front door bell rang; he was remembered just how loud it was. The noise seemed to break the tension at least for a moment

"Who is that?" Janet almost shrieked.

"Quiet, don't make a sound. Harris moved to the window, it overlooked the front entrance, by the street light he could make out two individuals, one was standing by the car, he had parked his own halfway down the block, "Shit! It's Hitchcock!"

He went back to the closet, the girl was shaking even more violently, and she was near hysteria. "Who's there? Someone's trying to kill me!"

"I'm here to prevent that Janet! Give me the gun, NOW!"

She surprised him by meekly handing him the gun, he could feel the relief pass through his body, but it was short lived, the bell rang again.

"Janet, I want you to come with me, will you do that?"

"You aren't going to hurt me are you?"

"No. Just come with me and I will make sure you are safe. No one is going to hurt you.

The old woman suddenly spoke, "Take her out through the back door, in the kitchen, you know."

"The only problem are those two at the front door."

The old lady cackled loudly, "Don't worry pardner, I'll hold them off at the pass while you make a run for it!"

He could hardly suppress a small chuckle, more TV; obviously she likes westerns too.

He took Janet by the arm, the made their way down the narrow staircase, they pressed themselves against the wall where the shadow was the darkest, and Aunt Agnes followed shouting loudly "I'm coming, just hold your horses!"

They reached the main level; Harris pressed Janet to the floor and indicated that they must crawl to the kitchen. That way they would not be outlined by the light coming from the kitchen.

Fortunately, the kitchen door was offset slightly from the line of site from the kitchen door, they were able to squeeze through unobserved and into the kitchen.

He could hear the conversation at the front door, "What did you say? You'll have to speak up, I'm little hard of hearing you know!"

"Who are you? She was speaking through the door; she wouldn't open it.

"Please open the door lady, it's the RCMP! We need to talk to you.

Finally she did open the door a crack, just as Janet and Harris closed the back door behind them. He heard Aunt Agnes say.

"Would you like to come in? I'll make some tea then, will I?"

He laughed to himself; they would be there for hours, "Thank you Aunt Agnes!"

They reached his car, both seemed to sigh with relief simultaneously, as he pulled away, Janet turned to him and asked, What's going to happen to my Auntie, will she be OK, she's very old you know, 87 next birthday, she's very frail?"

Her voice seemed to indicate a regression in her personality, it seemed a like a little girl's voice. He put it down to shock and stress of what had happened to her in the last few hours and days.

"From what I have seen, you needn't worry about Aunt Agnes, she'll have those two so twisted around, they'll be only too happy to leave her in peace, they aren't going to hurt her, so don't worry."

"How do you know that?"

"Because one of the RCMP officers is a friend of mine, he'll make sure she's OK."

"I hate the RCMP, they killed my father!"

Again the little girl voice. Was she regressing? He hoped not, she had information he needed.

"The RCMP didn't kill your father, but I think I know who did, but I'm going to need your help, will you help me?"

"Who are you?"

"I'm Inspector Dave Harris of the Metropolitan Toronto Police Department."

"Are you arresting me?"

"No I'm taking you into protective custody, just as I told you, I'm going to make sure you are safe."

"Where are we going?"

"We're going to police headquarters, we'll get you something to eat, make sure you are comfortable and then we'll talk."

"About who killed my daddy?

"Yes!"

They rode along in silence for some time, he glanced at her periodically to make sure she was OK, she stared straight ahead, unblinking. He wondered if she might be heading for a breakdown, when she suddenly spoke in that little girl voice.

"I know something you don't know." It was said in a sing song way.

"What's that?"

"100

150

13

85"

She kept repeating it "I know something you don't know" and then the number.

She finally stopped when they arrived at Headquarters; he took her gently by the arm and led her into the building. He called out to young policewoman, "Wendy! Could you come up to my office please, I need some help."

The young officer followed with eager anticipation, Harris was something of a legend in the department, at least with the women!"

When they were all inside he closed the door, Wendy, this is Janet Petersen, Janet this is Officer Wendy MacLintock, Janet, Wendy is going to get you something to eat and then help you get cleaned up so you'll feel better, then you and I are going to talk OK?"

She nodded, the young officer made her feel more comfortable and she hadn't eaten in two days, she did feel hungry, she sensed that this man was going to help her and she began to relax.

"I am going to have to leave you two for a little while, I have some work to finish up then I'll be back."

"You promise." Again the little girl voice.

"I promise." He motioned for the officer to follow him outside, "It's OK Janet, she'll be right back."

Once outside, Harris said "Wendy, I want her on around the clock watch, somebody has to be with her at all times is that understood?"

"You mean suicide watch?"

"Yes, I don't think she'll attempt it, but she isn't to stable at this point, so I don't want to take a chance."

"OK, can you tell me why she's in here?"

"She's a Material Witness in the Nelson Homicide, I'm going down to Central Booking to get the paperwork started, I should be back in half an hour. Find somewhere comfortable to hold her and stay with her OK."

"You bet!"

After completing the booking arrangements, Harris contacted Central Dispatch.

"Ralph, it's Dave Harris, I need to have an APB issued."

"Who's it for Dave?

"Nazir Monpetit!"

Chapter 39

"Yes, that's right, Nazir Monpetit." He spelled the name, "Physical description, male, Afro-Belgian, height 6 ft 8 inches, weight, approximately 300 pounds."

"No, he's not known to be violent, likely is not armed." He smiled to himself at the response from Ralph. "No, one car should be enough, he's staying at the Hamden Suites, try there first.

He's wanted for questioning as a Material Witness in the Nelson Homicide.

Thanks Ralph, let me know as soon as you've got him."

He turned to hang up the phone only to see Dwayne Hitchcock; he was not looking very happy.

"Hello Asshole!"

"Good to see you too Dwayne."

"Look, I heard you got the girl, you know this is a federal issue, I want you to turn he over to me right now!"

"That isn't going to happen, I've already had this argument with the Chief and I'll tell you the same thing I told him, she's going nowhere, she's a Material Witness in the Nelson homicide.

"We could get an injunction and force you to turn her over."

"Let's stop the bullshit! If you were going to do that you have already done it, you wouldn't be standing her talking to me about it."

"Have you found the backup yet?"

"Look Dwayne, she's been custody less than four hours, I haven't even interrogated her yet, you've already got enough under C-36 to put all of your suspects away for a long time.

You've got the money trail, the ring is broken up, anything that's on the backup won't likely be admissible in court, illegal wire taps, unauthorized communication intercepts, there isn't a judge in the country that would allow that stuff in at a trial, you know that."

Hitchcock was silent.

"There's more to this isn't there?"

Still he said nothing, then changed tack.

"Why haven't you questioned her yet?"

"I owe you Dwayne, your information helped me so I'll pass this along for what it's worth.

I'm waiting for the department psychologist, I want her present during the questioning, right now she looks like a "head case," I am not really sure that even if we get anything that it will be admissible in court."

"Will you keep me posted?"

"If I come up with anything, Ill contact you?"

Hitchcock turned to leave, Harris couldn't resist, "Did you enjoy your tea?"

"Piss off!"

Harris saw Wendy MacLintock across the office. He called her over.

"How did things go with Janet Petersen?"

"Good, I got her something to eat, I put her in interview room 3, at least there is a sofa there that she can try to get a little sleep.

I can empathize with her, she's been through a lot, she really seems to be in bad shape."

"Yeah, I've got the department shrink coming in to talk to her, maybe she can help, so who's with her now?"

"Audrey Clarke is spelling me off, I have made sure she won't be left alone, that's for sure."

"Good, I assume that you followed the usual procedures with respect to personal effects, removed them from her and inventoried them with properties?"

"Yes and a good thing to, she had the biggest sapphire ring I have ever seen, must be worth a small fortune, we would be in deep doo-doo if that ever went missing while she was in our custody.

Mind you, she screamed like bloody hell when I took it away."

"Strange, I don't remember seeing it."

"You wouldn't have, it was on a chain around her neck, it was a man's ring."

"Hmm, anything else?"

"Yeah kind of strange, it was almost a chant she was doing."

"What was it"

"She kept saying "I know something you don't know" over and over, then she recited 4 numbers and started the whole thing again."

"Did you happen to make a note of those numbers?"

"Yessir, she flipped open her black notebook and thumbed through several pages, here it is, she repeated,

100

150

13

85

What's it mean do you think?

"Frankly I have no idea." He copied the numbers on to his desk pad. "Thanks Wendy."

He picked up his phone and dialled Tim Cassidy's local, "Tim, it's Dave here, can you come up and see me for a couple of minutes?"

The young officer was at his desk in minutes, "What's up sir?"

"You can drop the sir, Dave is OK with me, I wanted to talk to you about the Nelson case, you know that we have taken Janet Petersen into protective custody?"

"Yes, I had heard about it, is she somehow involved with the Nelson homicide?

"I think so and maybe more than that."

Harris gave the Cassidy a complete run down of what he had so far, including his just completed meeting with Hitchcock.

"Do you think there is something in the backup that could help with this case Dave?"

"That and I think much more, just based on CSIS' interest, but frankly I have no idea of where it is or how we might go about accessing it, you're a computer geek, got any ideas?"

"I'm not sure about the geek part, but I can tell you from what you have told me, the file or files would be huge, in the multi-terabyte category. If you did find it, it would take enormous disk capacity to handle it. Then it will likely be encrypted and it may well be that the same virus is present within the backup.

Accessing the backup may well cause it to self-destruct, if we don't have the password."

"Where the hell would they store that much information?"

"Well, there are data warehouse companies on the net that do this kind of thing routinely. Large companies, banks even, utilize these kind of services. It has the added security of off site storage, for example, should there ever be a fire or some other calamity, their data is still protected.

"Can we get a list of these companies?"

"We could do a search on the net, but I'm afraid that wouldn't help much, remember, there is no guarantee that the storage even takes place in this country or continent for that matter."

"Well, I guess the best we can hope for is that Janet Petersen will be forthcoming with this information when I interview her.

Even if she does, where would we download this information to and how would we go about solving the virus and encryption problem."

"Well, if you want my opinion, there is only one place to go, my alma mater, The University of Waterloo Computer Science Department.

This kind of problem would be right up their alley, they have the horsepower and brains to do it."

"Good idea!"

'Has she said anything at all that might be of use?"

"Just gibberish I'm afraid, she keeps saying "I know something you don't know" followed by 4 numbers, doesn't make any sense."

"Four numbers huh?"

"Yeah, here they are here, I wrote them down on my desk pad. Cassidy looked at the column of numbers, he took a pencil from his pocket and rewrote the numbers, but not as a column, he wrote them horizontally and put a decimal point in between each.

"That's it!"

"That's what?"

"I think she has already told you where the backup is!"

"What the hell do you mean?"

"Look at the numbers, the way I wrote them, that's an IP address, 100.150.18.85, if we were to type that address into a browser, it would take you to the site and location of the backup, I'm almost positive!"

"You might be right, but we can't test your theory for fear of setting off the virus."

"Unless you can get her to tell us the password!"

"Thanks Tim, good work! I'll see what I can do."

"OK Dave, let me know if you need anything else."

"Two things, first, maybe you could talk to some of your buddies at Waterloo, give them a "heads-up" and see if the can help us."

"And the other?"

"Are you still seeing that cutie at CFTO?"

The young officer reddened slightly, "Yes why do ask?"

"Maybe you could leak a little news to her about the fact that we have found the Mahoney backup file location and that we are asking the University of Waterloo for help in processing it?"

"Well, I guess it is almost the truth, and she has bugged me about some inside information, but I'm not sure she might be suspicious of the information. Besides, what good can it do?"

"I'm sure that you could just accidentally let it slip, and as for what good it will do, I'm not quite sure, but it could "stir the pot" then we will see what "comes to the top.""

"I'll see what I can do."

"Thanks Tim.

Harris headed down to Interview Room 3, he hoped the psychologist had arrived, as he approached the door he saw a large woman with an outlandish hat approaching from the opposite direction.

"Bella, sorry to get you out this late." He extended his hand, he could already smell the perfume, he hoped he could refrain from sneezing.

She gripped his hand with a many ringed hand almost as big as any man; she shook his with some vigour.

"Hello David, well it's not like I was out on a date or anything! Do give me a rundown on this case won't you please"

He briefed her on everything that he felt was pertinent with respect to Janet Petersen, the death of her father, her fixation that someone was trying to kill her and her apparent regression.

"I see, it sounds like an interesting case, so you want an opinion from me as to her fitness to testify?"

"Well, that and I would like you to attend the interrogation, I'm concerned about her apparent fragile state, yet I need to get information from her to resolve a homicide case I'm working on."

"Do you believe that she committed the homicide?"

"No, rather I see her as an accomplice, either willing or accidental, at this point I don't know which, in fact there is a possibility she has been an accomplice in more than just one homicide."

"OK, let's see the girl, if I think you are pressing to hard or are likely to cause her any damage, I'll will ask you to stop the interview, understood?"

Janet was sitting at a table in the sparsely furnished interrogation room; she looked exhausted. Pale and very nervous, but she smiled when she saw Dave Harris enter.

Wendy MacLintock sat in a chair opposite Janet, she rose and offered the chair to Bella, Harris continued to stand. He dismissed Wendy and walked to the far end of the room, collecting his thoughts on how he would proceed. He returned to the table and switched on the tape recorder, announced the date and time and who was present.

"Are you comfortable Ms. Petersen? Would you like something to drink?"

Why is he acting this way? Why did he send Wendy away? Who is this fat old woman? Why is she here? Is she going to hurt me? I'm frightened, Oh Daddy, why did you have to die?

She looks like she's about to cry I'll try to put her at ease.

"I talked to your Aunt Agnes, she asked me to tell you she is just fine, she enjoyed her cup of tea with the officers, I told her you were safe and being looked after."

"They killed him you know!"

Bella watched the young woman carefully, we must be careful, she seems very fragile, likely been through a lot.

"Killed who Janet?"

"My Daddy, you stupid bitch! Why is she here?"

"Janet, Bella is here to help you, same as me, she can help you, if you'll let her."

"I don't like her, I only want to talk to you!"

"OK, Janet, just calm down, I only have a few questions for you, then we'll see that you get some rest, if you get too tired during this interview, just let me know and we can stop, OK?"

"OK."

Will I be able to get anything useful from her, this could be a ruse, then again she may be mentally disturbed, hard to know with everything she has been through, I'll try.

"Janet, how much did you know about your father's business?"

"Lots."

" What do you mean, "lots"?"

" I knew everything about Soper Research, I knew about how my Daddy fixed the security leak, I know who did it and I know other things too!"

"Are you talking about when your father first got involved with Soper?"

"Yes."

"Do you know who it was that leaked the information?"

Janet tilted her head coyly, like a seven year old would, and in her little girl voice said "Sure, is was Dr. Mytryk, he did it!"

"And you didn't see anything wrong with the fact he was allowed to stay with the firm?"

"No, he paid my Daddy, that made it OK."

"That made it OK?"

"Sure my Daddy deserved it, he was treated very badly."

"And you saw nothing wrong with him taking money from Dr. Mytryk? Even though he might have been a criminal?"

"Not at all!"

"How do you know this to be true?"

The voice changed again, no longer the little girl. This was Janet.

"I did the necessary documentation, the payment agreement, Dr. Mytryk's signed confession, everything."

"His signed confession, what did you do with it?"

"My father kept it in a safe place, in case Mytryk ever reneged on the payments to us."

"And you as an officer of the court, were a party to this?"

"I even witnessed the confession!"

"Do you realize that that makes you culpable in the commission of a felony, you could be disbarred and even go to jail for that?"

" My father reminded me constantly afterwards, but before I did, he told me that it would be a significant sign to him of my commitment and loyalty to him. So I did it!"

Bella sat at the table with her mouth gaping open, she signalled to Harris that she wanted a brief conference with him. They moved to a corner of the room, "Dave, I'm not a lawyer, but shouldn't she have representation, before she incriminates herself further?"

"You tell me, is she legally competent? If I get her to waive her rights to an attorney, we could proceed, what's your opinion?"

"Dave, it's really hard to say, she is after all a licensed attorney herself, that works in your favour. If later she is declared mentally incompetent to stand trial on any of this, then your questioning will be mute anyway. It's really your call."

They returned to the table, Harris opened a drawer on his side and removed a form.

"Janet, do you want an attorney present during this questioning."

"Why would I need one, I'm a perfectly good lawyer myself, why would I want a legal aid turkey looking after my interests?"

"Would you then sign this waiver?'

Without hesitation, she took the pen from him and signed the waiver, Bella witnessed it and they continued.

"Did your father ever pressure you by threatening to release Mytryk's confession? Make you do things you might not have done otherwise?"

"He said that, but I don't think he would've, he was my Daddy you know!"

Back to the seven year old again, she's either extremely clever or she's very sick. I've got to assume the former.

"Did something Dr. Mytryk did make your father angry?"

"Yes, my Daddy said he was going to go to the police and tell them about me, Daddy said he wanted money to keep quiet! My Daddy did all this to protect me!"

"What did he do Janet?"

"Why, he had Dr. Mytryk killed, what else, are you always so stupid?"

"And what about Dr. Nelson, Janet, what do you know about him?"

"My Daddy didn't like him, said he was weak, he didn't like weak people, that's why he told me I had to be strong. He couldn't do anything right, I couldn't be like that, I had to be like my Daddy or he wouldn't like me either!"

"What happened to Dr. Nelson?"

"He died, you really are stupid!"

"How did he die?"

"Daddy had some of his friends get rid of him!"

"He told you that?"

"No, I heard him talking to two of his friends in his office, just after Jim Nelson left, nobody knew I was even there."

"What did they say?"

"My Daddy just told them to follow him and when they had the opportunity, just "do" him, quietly my Daddy said."

"Did your father say why Dr. Nelson was to be killed?"

"'Cause he was upset with Ashley Soper's car accident, he blamed my Daddy, he said he wanted nothing more to do with my Daddy, he was going to tell on him that's why!"

"What was he going to tell?"

"Everything, what's going on at Soper Research, the numbered company in Grand Cayman, all the other programs that we had in place."

The little girl is gone, Janet is back, good, she's more lucid, has more understanding of the events. Let's see what I can get from her.

"Tell me about the numbered company Janet."

"That was my idea, we had selected clients buy shares in this numbered company, the shares they purchased represented special services that we rendered from time to time on behalf of our clients.

In Soper's case, they wanted special treatment from the FDA in the US on the drug certification, as far as Arnie Soper was concerned, this was a payoff to FDA officials for fast tracking the approval process. Payments were made from the numbered company to specific individuals, as dividends in this company. Made the payments harder to track."

"But that is fraud, you know that!"

"Is it? Might have been if the actions taken really happened, there was no FDA official payoffs, it was a scam, take from the greedy and give to the needy, us."

"Still a fraud."

"Only if a charge is laid, who's going to lay a complaint, some corporate crook?"

Clever, now it's time to change tack.

"Janet, tell me about Nazir Monpetit."

"OH he is a very big black man, he is sooo big, you can't believe it! I like him, I like him very much he is my friend, except he wouldn't help me when I needed him same as Brad Soper, he wouldn't help me either."

Shit! The seven-year-old is back; she's starting to cry, crap, I don't need that, is this real? Alternatively, is she playing a game here? I don't know how much more I can get from her, she's really sobbing now.

"Dave, I think that's enough for this session, you don't need a nervous breakdown on your hands, come back to her later if you need to."

He knew that she was right, he was getting tired too, not much sleep lately, he wondered if Ruthie would feed Max.

"Thank you Janet, you've been a big help. We've done enough for now, I'll go and get Wendy, she'll help you get settled in another place so you can get some rest."

He turned to look back as he was leaving, the sobbing had stopped, but there was look on Janet's face, her eyes really, was that a certain slyness he saw for fleeting instant, probably not.

"Bella, I'll get Wendy in to relieve you in a couple of minutes, thanks for your help. Bella nodded and he left the interrogation room.

Chapter 40

Harris and Tim Cassidy entered the interrogation room, unsure of just what Monpetit's attitude might be; he expected anger and resentment. Monpetit seemed even larger than he remembered. He sat on the long side of the table, a looming presence in the room.

Monpetit looked from beneath his broad brow, the whites of his eyes, seemingly accentuated by the blackness of his face. Yes, anger, no doubt, why do I feel so intimidated by this man, it's not just his size, he has a presence like none other I have experienced.

The silence was broken by the man's deep voice.

"Was this really necessary? Wouldn't a simple phone call have sufficed? To be dragged down here in a police car, like a common criminal! I resent it! What right do you have to bring me into this place?"

"Dr. Monpetit, I apologize for any inconvenience this may have caused you, and yes it was necessary. As you are aware, we are investigating the death of Dr. Peter Mytryk, Dr. James Nelson and now Mr. Declan Mahoney.

You are somehow connected to all of them in one way or another, either directly or indirectly, therefore I want to ask you a few questions to further these investigations and bring them to a successful conclusion."

"Am I a suspect in any of this mess?"

"Not necessarily, but you may well be a material witness to events leading up to these crimes, you may be able to shed some light in these areas that could lead us to the solution."

This policeman is no fool, I must be careful, guard what I say, see if I can find out how much he knows. The other one is obviously here as a witness to this, no worry with that one.

"Tell me Inspector, the last time we met, you seemed of the opinion that Dr. Mytryk's death was likely a suicide and that Jim Nelson was mugged, what has happened to changed your mind?"

Clever, he'd like to turn the tables and ask the questions, I better be careful, he isn't your run of the mill perp. I'll feed him just enough and watch his response.

"Additional information has been received that confirms that all three were in fact murdered, as a result, I found it necessary to change course."

"Where or from whom did this information come?"

"I'm sorry, I'm not at liberty to say, but it does seem that Soper Research lays at the root of much that has happened, therefore it seems reasonable to me, that you may have information that would assist us in our investigation."

"I doubt very much that I can be of any help, remember Inspector, I'm a fairly recent arrival to this country."

"Yes, but you are well acquainted with the people involved. Tell me Dr. Monpetit, what is your relationship with Janet Petersen?"

What? Were did that come from, does he really know about Janet and I, or is he just "fishing." Got to be careful here.

Good, that took the wind out of his sails, he wasn't expecting that, keep pressing.

"Dr. Monpetit, did you hear me?"

"Yes, I heard you, what do you mean, "my relationship with Janet"?"

"I think it was a straightforward question."

"I know her as the PR person responsible for the Soper Research account at Mahoney."

"Nothing else? Nothing of a more personal nature?"

The big right hand began to slowly drum on the table, almost imperceptibly. There is more there, dig deeper.

Shit, how did he find out? I can't lie, think! Change direction.

"Where is Janet? How is she? I'm sure this has been a terrible strain on her."

"She's safe, we have her in protective custody, please answer my question. Do you have more than a business relationship with Janet Petersen?"

He interlaced the fingers on both hands making a massive double fist; a bead of sweat was forming on his forehead.

"We went out for dinner together, she drove me to my hotel, she was, is a considerate person, I didn't know my way around the city."

"Is that all, one dinner?"

"No, in fact we began to see each other, more regularly?"

"How much "more regularly.""

"Look, Inspector, she is smart, pretty and single, what's wrong with me taking her out, seeing her socially. Or do you object to mixed race couples?"

He's trying to "get my goat" throw off my pace, well screw you!

"Dr. Monpetit, I have no views one way or the other, and as to your social life, it only interests me when Janet Petersen is involved."

"Why?'

"That doesn't concern you.

Tell me what you and Janet talked about when you were together."

"What are you looking for Inspector, prurient details, all those stories about black men having sex with white women?"

Harris leaned across the table and brought his face within 6 inches of Monpetit's, in a low voice he said.

"Janet Petersen is a suspect in the murders of Mytryk and Nelson, if you do not want to be charged with aiding and abetting her, you'd better lose that chip and answer me truthfully!"

He knows more than I thought he did, must get myself out of this mess.

"Sometimes we talked about business, sometimes we talked about her past, sometimes we just laughed and had a good time.

In some ways I felt sorry for her."

"Why."

"The way she was treated by Declan Mahoney, he was an Asshole! Her childhood, she talked about it a lot, she missed her mother."

Time to poke a little harder.

"Did you know that Declan Mahoney was her father?"

He looked up with surprise, "She told me about it, I had trouble believing it, I never did like that man, but she idolized him. At least she idolized the idea of her father; they are not the same things.

He brainwashed her, there is no other term to use, he made her believe that he had been persecuted and hounded all his life, that she would be too, they had a right to get even, get there share!"

I think he is fighting to keep his head above water now, keep pressing the advantage.

"Tell me the real reason you came to Soper Research."

"I came to be the new Director of Research, I was hired by Arnie Soper, you know that!"

"That's the official story, what I want is the real reason."

OH Christ! This has become such a mess. Can I extricate myself?

"Dr. Monpetit, did you hear me? Tell me what your relationship was with Soper Research, before you came to Canada?"

"I don't understand your question."

"Did you personally have any connection with Soper Research or any of its employees, prior to your being hired to replace Peter Mytryk?"

"Well, I knew Dr. Mytryk of course, we were in the same field, we attended the same conferences, I got to know him, is that what you mean?"

"What about Arnold Soper, did you not know him prior to being hired for your new position?"

"Yes, I had met him once or twice, he had been to our facility in Belgium?"

"At Zaltech?"

"Yes."

"Tell me, exactly what was your role at Zaltech?"

"I've told you, I was their Research Director!"

"And nothing more?"

"What do you mean?"

"I have information that you are in fact the largest single shareholder of Zaltech, that you have a controlling interest, is that true?"

"Yes, it is true, or more correctly was true."

"Why then would you come to Canada to take this post at Soper, surely that is a considerable step downward?"

Harris could sense that he had breached Monpetit's defences, he could see his body sag slightly just before he began to speak.

"Soper Research was very close to being a partner with Zaltech, Zaltech was the exclusive licensee of many of Soper's pharmaceuticals in the European Common Market. It was a very lucrative arrangement for both parties, although there is no question that the arrangement favoured Soper as the principal.

I had once expressed to Peter Mytryk, that a merger between our two companies would be a natural development for both of us, combined resources would have made us one of the most dominant drug companies in the world.

While Mytryk could see the benefit of such a plan, he was convinced that Arnie would never agree, unless of course he owned all of it, and frankly that was of no interest to me.

Therefore, I never pursued the idea of merger, with Arnie Soper. Peter Mytryk called me late last year and told me about Arnie's plan to take the company public coincident with an announcement of a major new drug development. He asked if I would be interested in discussing my original idea. Of course I was delighted.

As it turned out, because of the stock market collapse after 9/11, and the various stock frauds that followed, my own equity position became precarious and I knew that my company could become the victim of a take over.

If this new product that Soper had developed was as good as rumoured and if I could pull off a merger with them, my problems would be solved.

But, if Arnie proceeded with his plans to go public, there would be no way any merger would take place and I had no cash available to obtain a significant position in the new Soper stock issue.

Then I got the expected follow up call from Mytryk, who in turn put Declan Mahoney on the line, after a brief introduction, he proceeded to tell me that he could make the merger happen, for a fee of course.

I asked him what Arnie himself thought of this approach, I was simply told that Arnie would not disagree with what we might be able to achieve, he gave me a story about Arnie wanting to retire, wasn't really happy about going public, he just wanted out. But that it was essential that none of these talks get out to the public, we could run into major obstacles with regulators if anything was to come out prematurely.

I believed him. I guess because I wanted to, and because I needed to, I was in danger of losing all my equity in Zaltech. I had pledged it as security to my bondholders.

From that point on, I dealt only with Mahoney, it appeared that Mytryk was to assume the role of Vice Chairman of the Executive Committee and I would be the new Director of Research, at least that was my understanding of the plan. I would play a low key role, working with Arnie and Mahoney to put the merger together, my job as research Director would also allow me to do "due diligence" on this new product, it seemed ideal.

However, when I got here, Mytryk was dead and Arnie was in the hospital in a coma and I was coupled with Mahoney, handcuffed to him if you like, by some incriminating tape recordings. The rest you know!"

So far so good, now I need to find out his level of involvement with the crimes.

"So, Dr. Monpetit, did this "plan" you made with Mahoney, include all of the murders I have mentioned earlier and did it also include the incapacitation of Dr. Soper and his ultimate death?"

He jumped up from the table; he looked ready to raise his hand, Tim Cassidy moved to restrain him, a rather ludicrous site, given the size of Cassidy.

"NO! I was not a party to any of that, Mytryk was dead before I even came to this country, Arnie was already in the hospital!"

"Well, you don't have to be physically here to be involved in the conspiracy do you?"

"I tell you, I did not do any of this, I regret that I ever got involved even, peripherally in any of this."

"Did Janet ever share with you, any information regarding Mytryk's death or Jim Nelson's?"

"All I can tell you is that she was very upset after each of the events, but as to whether or not she had any prior knowledge, I don't know, she never indicated that to me."

"Did she ever tell you that her father was blackmailing her?"

He knows that too! Did she tell him? What else has she said?

"Yes, she did?"

"Did she tell you what he was blackmailing her with?"

"NO!"

I don't think that's the truth, but let it go for now. Everything he has told me about the state of Zaltech appears to be true, I need corroboration of any direct involvement in the murders, maybe the Mahoney backup can provide it — or not.

"Is that all, may I leave now?"

"I'm afraid nor Dr. Monpetit, I'm holding you as a Material Witness in the murders of Peter Mytryk, Jim Nelson and perhaps Declan Mahoney and Arnold Soper as well."

"But I didn't do anything, I wasn't involved in any murders, I'm innocent!"

"Innocent? Anything but! You're the one that put all of this in motion, if it wasn't for your greed and arrogance, these people might be alive today!

At the very least you have been part of conspiracy to obtain control of Soper Research."

Harris reached over and switched off the recorder and prepared to leave the room.

"Inspector, may I see Janet?"

"No you cannot, she is likely undergoing psychiatric treatment as we speak, thanks in many ways to you, and her father!"

"What's going to happen to her?"

"I don't really know."

Chapter 41

Brad spent a restless night in his hotel, dreaming about his father and mother, crazy dreams, he slept fitfully, twisting the bed sheets with the rotation of his body, and finally he awoke in a sweat.

Shit! What a night, never mind just a night, it's been a nightmare since I came here, murders, deceit, and misplaced trust. Life used to be so simple, I let Janet down, what will I do with Ellis?

Where's Naz? Couldn't reach him last night! Probably out with one of his women! Can I even trust him? Don't know whom to trust. What do I do about Soper Research?

He went to the mini bar, when he saw the Kokanee Gold, he was reminded of Janet again, where is she? What's going to happen to her?

To early for a beer, Pepsi will do, he opened the can and drank almost all of it in one swallow, and he hadn't realized just how thirsty he was.

Need to think can I really run Soper Research? Lester said he'd help me, I owe it to my father, and I'm going to have to try!

As for Ellis, well he's my brother, I don't care who his father really was, at least my father didn't disown him, so neither will I, and nobody else ever has to know!

Can I trust Naz? Can I work with him? At this point does he even want the job?

At least I've resolved two issues, at least in my mind anyway, he finished the Pepsi and flopped back on the bed, the tension seemed to leave him and he dropped off to sleep.

What's that? Must be the phone, where'd I put it, it's under the pillow.

"Hello, who is this?"

"Mr. Soper, its Dave Harris, from Metro Police.

"Oh, yes Inspector, I'm sorry to sound so fuzzy, I was asleep."

"Sorry for waking you, but I wonder if you mind coming into my office this morning, there are some things I would like to discuss with you regarding Janet Petersen and others as they relate to your company."

"Off course, where is Janet do you know?"

"Yes, we have her in custody, could you make it for say, 10:30?"

"In custody?"

"Yes, as a Material Witness, will you be here, we can discuss it all then."

"Of course!" He hung up the phone, bewildered, Janet in jail!

Maybe he should ask Leslie to go with him.

*

Brad and Leslie arrived at police headquarters by 10:30 AM. They were escorted to a small conference room on the second floor, they declined the offer of coffee and were asked to wait for Inspector Harris to arrive.

When finally came in, it was obvious to them both, with the red-rimmed eyes and the beard stubble, he had been up all night, even though his clothes looked might have been slept in, he somehow doubted that.

He sat at the head of the small conference table; they were together to his left. He ran his fingers through his close cropped hair, cleared his throat and began.

"First, I would like to thank you both for coming on such short notice I really appreciate that, and secondly, I wanted extend my personal condolences on the death of your father Brad."

"Thank you Inspector."

"Where to begin? There are several starting points to this sad series of events, but I think we'll start with the one that may explain what caused most of these events.

We'll begin with Mr. Nazir Monpetit, a Belgium national, 42 years of age, arrived in Toronto some 6 weeks ago.

Ostensibly, he claimed that he came to become the new head of research at Soper Research Inc. He claims, and in fact did hold a similar position at Zaltec Inc. in Brussels, but he was not in that position when he left and came to Canada.

We have determined, in fact, that he was the largest single shareholder of Zaltec stock, some 33% of the outstanding shares in fact, making him the controlling shareholder of the corporation."

"What?"

"Brad, if you could just hold your questions until I finish, it would be a great help to me, its been a long night."

"Sorry, of course, please continue."

"You are also likely aware that Zaltec is the largest licensee of your products in the EU, and in fact is substantially larger than Soper, so it is obvious he did not come here for a job.

We need to look at the background of Zaltec to find that out. During the mid and late nineties, Zaltec's sales and profits had soared like many other high tech companies. Like many companies, that wasn't good enough for Zaltec and Monpetit in particular, call it corporate avarice if you like.

"Monpetit replaced himself as Managing Director of the firm and went on the hunt for "hot new properties" to acquire. Just about anything to do with biotechnology became a target, gene-therapy, cloning replacement body parts, new aids therapies.

In fact he purchased 4 such companies in 1997, three were startup companies and one had begun to return a small profit, they cost the company over 400 million Euros!

The was the least of it, he had to pump in almost as much again for continuing research in these diverse fields, Zaltec's reserves were being depleted faster than profits could replenish.

He had to float a bond issue, by this time investors were becoming wary of hi tech stocks, but Zaltec was a strong company with a good track record. So the money was raised, but the lenders wrote a tough deal, a high interest rate, at 2% over prime, and a short term. In fact the expiry date was yesterday, and he had to pledge all of his shares as collateral security.

When the "bubble burst" after 9/11 and the stock market collapsed in the aftermath, he became a desperate man, he knew that it would only be a matter of time before personal disaster struck.

He of course, was well acquainted with your father, and Peter Mytryk for that matter, as a major licensee he had many meetings over the years. We are sure your father didn't let anything slip regarding the Alzheimer's breakthrough, but equally we are sure that Mytryk "spilled the beans," its possible that money changed hands in order to get this information, I have no direct proof of that, but it seems likely.

Monpetit recognized the importance of this break through, the profits on the sale of this new product in Europe would not be enough to save him, but if he could somehow acquire the company, either through merger or acquisition, he could likely renegotiate the bond terms and save his position.

Outright acquisition seemed out of the question, he had no cash to speak of, the only course would be a share swap, a merger of sorts.

Your father of course, rejected any such idea out of hand. He told Monpetit that it was his intention to take Soper Research public. He could buy shares on the open market if he liked.

If Soper is taken public, with its track record and patents on the most revolutionary Alzheimer treatment in history, the bidding war for shares would drive the stock price out of Monpetit's reach.

He needed a plan, he knew just the man to go to with it, Peter Mytryk!

Peter Mytryk was beholden to Declan Mahoney, you will recall that your father brought Mahoney in to solve a security breech earlier, in fact Mytryk was that breech. Mahoney discovered that and held that fact over Mytryk's head until his death.

Mytryk told Mahoney about Zaltec and their interest in acquiring Soper and Mahoney hatched the plan, the idea was to incapacitate your father somehow, put Jim Nelson in as Chairman and sell the idea of merger to the board."

"I'm sorry for interrupting, but why would Nelson agree to becoming involved? He didn't seem the type?"

"He wasn't really, but, and I'm sorry to tell you this Brad, Mahoney had irrefutable DNA proof that Nelson was the biological father of Ellis Soper. He threatened to release this information and Nelson knew it would destroy Ashley Soper and end his relationship with his friend Arnie.

The decision was taken to alter the vaccine specimen they knew your father would administer to himself, you will recall that he always had followed this practice of testing any new medications first.

I do not think that the intention was to murder your father, but of course that has been the eventual outcome, Mytryk blundered somehow, the injection for whatever reason, put your father in the state he was in when you last saw him.

Then things began to unravel for the conspirators, first you came on the scene, Ashley wouldn't cooperate and support Jim Nelson as the new Chairman, nor would Lester Coughlan. Their only hope was to be able manipulate you after having you installed as Chairman.

Mahoney now saw Mytryk as a serious liability, he didn't have the stomach for what was happening, Mahoney feared that he might go to the police and negotiate a deal for himself at the expense of the others.

That's when Mahoney came up with the paedophile scam, he planted all of the evidence, very convincingly too, but he was caught off guard when Mytryk was released on bail almost immediately. It was then that Mahoney staged Mytryk's suicide.

Declan Mahoney tried to pressure Ashley Soper one last time, on the night she died, we know she had met with him in a bar in Scarborough, we can only assume that he told her about the DNA evidence.

While we cannot state categorically that Mahoney was responsible for Ashley Soper's death. We feel comfortable in assuming there was a causal relationship with respect to this meeting and her ultimate death.

Monpetit had been following these events in Brussels, frankly Brad, I have no direct knowledge that Monpetit ever knew of the plan regarding your father, he says not. In fact he said to me, that the reason he came was to try to stop the whole thing, but by the time he got here it was irreversible.

He says that he had intended to tell you all about it just before I arrived to question you both on the FDA matter, after that he decided to keep it to himself."

"But, there was no FDA investigation, Leslie has already found that out."

"That's right, that was part of cute little game played by the RCMP, they dropped that bit information on me to see what might surface at Mahoney Associates or at Soper, they knew I would follow up.

In fact, this is a scam that Mahoney used to extract money from clients, he promised your father a speedy clearance of the new drug by the FDA but he had to pay off an employee to do so.

A month or six weeks improvement in the approval time would have had a tremendous impact on earnings for the company, Greed sometimes makes people do things they might not ordinarily do.

The rest of the scam was to make the payment look like an investment in an offshore research company. From there they could transfer those funds anywhere in the world for whatever purpose they chose.

Brad, that's an investment you will have to write off. That money's gone, either overseas or frozen by the government.

Jim Nelson was outraged at the death of Ashley Soper, there was little doubt that he was in love with her, but it was unrequited, still he apparently felt he had to avenge her death.

He hatched the plan to insert aerosolized ricin into an asthma inhaler, Nelson knew of course that Mahoney used a Soper inhaler, he had initially introduced him to it when the product was first released. He had the opportunity to do this and in fact computer log sheets indicate he was in the lab, alone for about two hours, plenty of time to create the package. He also had the knowledge, as a medical doctor of how to handle it and how big the dosage had to be.

Found near his body was a Soper asthma inhaler, we know he was not asthmatic and his fingerprints were on it.

In addition, I had the Medical Examiner take nail scrapings from under his fingernails and he turned up trace amounts of ricin."

"But I thought, from what I've read, that ricin was untraceable?"

"When it metabolizes in the body, you may remember those terrorist suspects in London, when they examined their apartment, they found traces of ricin too.

This is conclusive evidence that Jim Nelson murdered Declan Mahoney, the irony is that Nelson was murdered before Mahoney was simply because of the time element involved in death by ricin poisoning.

Mahoney had decided that Nelson was too big a risk to have running around loose, so he had arranged to have him murdered, he had no way of knowing what fate awaited him.

This has been a strange case, we have 4 murders but all the murderers are also dead! The only satisfaction I have is that the case is solved, but I have no real perpetrators to arrest.

"What about Janet? What was her role in all of this."

"I'm afraid, at the very least she is guilty of being a part and apparently a willing part of the conspiracy involving your father, and Jim Nelson, she may have also known about Peter Mytryk as well.

I can tell you that she is a very disturbed young woman at this point in her life, it seemed the stress she had been under broke last night during questioning, I think she truly wanted the truth to come out.

It was like a virtual torrent of information that spilled forth.

After a few days rest, she will be undergoing a psychiatric evaluation, it is possible she may never stand trial for any of this."

"But I have known her since law school, how can this kind of thing happen?"

"Declan Mahoney is the simple answer, he filled her head with his accounts of the oppression he suffered in Ireland at the hands of the English. How he was betrayed by his own comrades in the IRA, how even now he continued to be persecuted by CSIS, the RCMP and I guess me for that matter.

He played on her sense of abandonment after the death of her mother; he apparently was not beyond torturing her with the thought of abandoning her again if he had to run. He convinced her to help him.

In so doing he made her complicit in all his acts, she's a lawyer she knew that, but his presence in her life was paramount; there is no way she could have turned him in.

Mahoney perverted her love for him into something sinister; in essence she was "brain-washed"

"How could any father do such a thing?"

"Declan Mahoney was not just any father, he was a beast."

Brad asked "And what about Nazir, what happens to him?"

"That depends entirely on what we find in the Mahoney files, I need corroboration of his active involvement with Mahoney in any or all of the murders. Otherwise, I have no proof to hold him."

"So he goes free?"

"Afraid so, he goes free but broke, I personally find some solace in that, his debtors called the debenture yesterday, he's virtually penniless."

Brad heaved a sigh, "So that's it then, that's the end of it?"

"Well there may be a course for a civil action by you against Monpetit in his admitted conspiracy to participate in the takeover of Soper.

But from what I know, it would likely be a hollow win for you since he is broke anyway."

"What about Janet?"

"Pending what we find out, if she is unfit to stand trial, then, for all practical purposes, this is the end of it."

"I know it sounds like a strange thing to say, but I hope, for her sake that she doesn't have to stand trial, maybe with psychiatric help she can someday return to society."

"We can certainly hope for that, thank you very much for coming in."

"Uh, Inspector Harris, as you likely know, Soper Research has an immediate opening for a Director of Security, you wouldn't by any chance be interested would you?"

"I'm truly flattered by your offer, but I'm afraid I'll have to decline, but I know a well qualified RCMP officer that may be considering a career change right about now."

"I would be happy to talk to him on your recommendation, but would you mind telling me why not?"

"Well its like this you see, I am the victim of a "Faustian Bargain.""

"A Faustian Bargain? With whom?"

"Our esteemed Mayor, by some creative budget shuffling he made it possible for me to get my MBA at York University, but it came at a price."

"Might I ask what that price is?"

"I undertook to work in any capacity the Mayor dictated, without argument, for not less than four years after graduation, if not I must repay the full tuition"

"Do you know what that assignment is yet?"

"Unfortunately yes, its going to be announced later today, I'm to totally reorganize the Criminal Investigation Division of the Metro Toronto Police Force."

"Why unfortunately, that sounds like a hell of an opportunity."

"Frankly, it means that I have to come in off the street, I'll be desk bound for 4 years, you might find it strange but I love what I'm doing."

Leslie interjected, "You could fight this thing and likely win you know."

"That's not the point, the point is I made an undertaking and so did the Mayor, he kept his part of the bargain so I'm going to keep mine. Besides, the job isn't without its perks."

"What do you mean?"

"One of my first tasks is to put my current boss into early retirement!"

He chuckled to himself as he reflected on the prospect, "Maybe he can buy a Tim Horton franchise, naw, on second thought he'd eat all the profits.

They all laughed, Leslie wasn't quite sure why.

Shaking hands all around Brad and Leslie took their leave.

"Well Brad, that's over, it's all behind you now, but I gotta tell you, I'm starving, let's get something to eat, you remember that little place I took you to last, its just around the corner.

They were past the noontime rush and had no trouble getting seated; Leslie picked her seat so she could watch the TV set in the bar.

"You may as well know now, I'm a news junkie and I haven't had my fix yet today" she motioned to the bartender to turn up the volume. It was on the CTV 'all news' channel.

She motioned for him to be quiet when he tried to speak, so he watched as well, he was surprised to hear an announcement that the Mahoney Backup Files had been found and that they had been sent to the University of Waterloo Computer Science Department for processing.

"This late breaking news just in from Ottawa, Ralph Urqhart, Attorney General of Canada has just announced not only his withdrawal as a candidate for the party leadership. He has also resigned his seat in the house effective immediately; he sited health and family matters as the reason for his sudden departure.

He has been considered for some time, to be the front runner for party leader and a virtual shoe-in to be elected Prime Minister in the next election.

This comes as a great shock to those on parliament hill. Those that consider themselves as insiders, it seems everyone has been caught flat-footed on this one.

More to follow at six."

Brad spoke first, "What do you make of that?"

*

Dave Harris called Tim Cassidy and asked him to come by his desk, it was important to see him before he left for Waterloo.

"Yes Dave, what is it."

"Well I wouldn't want you to be able to take all the credit on this backup file thing, so there is something I remembered that might be useful to you in your discussions at Waterloo."

"What's that?"

"There was something niggling away in the back of my brain, and I finally remembered what it was. It was an article about tracking stolen gems.

"What's that got to do with anything?"

"Well apparently, by using crystallography gem stones can be identified by their unique characteristics, you know their structure, the inclusions, that sort of thing."

"I still don't understand."

"Bear with me, its been a long night. I noticed that both at Soper Research and at Mahoney's offices, they used retinal scanners as security devices.

So I got thinking, what if the retinal scanners could also scan a gem stone, then that stone could be used in place of a password."

"Seems like a stretch Boss, besides where do we find the right gem stone."

"If I'm right, its in our property department, Declan Mahoney always wore a large sapphire pinkie ring, he was never without it, when we checked his daughter in last night, she had it hanging around her neck."

"Holy Shit, you might be right!"

"Go down and sign it out of property and take it with you, and don't lose it or you'll be walking a beat at Cherry Beach!"

*

They finished their lunch together and left the restaurant to walk back to their car, it was a beautiful sunny afternoon. They linked arms and strolled past the street vendors, oblivious to everything around them.

Leslie spoke first, "Brad, what day is it?"

"Why its Friday, shit! With everything that's been going on, I completely forgot, I've gotta go get Ellis."

"Can I come, I want to meet your little brother."

"Sure."

"Do you think he'll like me?"

"Of course he is just like his older brother, he loves pretty girls with big…"

"Big what?"

"Never mind."

"You were going to say big breasts, weren't you?"

"Yeah"

She whacked him in the shoulder, "Come on you dork let's get your brother!"

She made him laugh, it was a good day!